the
messy
truth
about
LOVE
cl walters

# cl walters books

OTHER CANTOS BOOKS

Swimming Sideways

The Ugly Truth

The Bones of Who We Are

The Messy Truth About Love

The Stories Stars Tell

In the Echo of this Ghost Town

When the Echo Answers

ADULT TITLE

The Letters She Left Behind

# the
# messy
# truth
# about
# LOVE

## cl walters

Mixed Plate Press
Honolulu, Hawaii
www.mixedplatepress.com

This book is dedicated to women.

Oh. And my high school classmates who thought it would be hilarious to predict I would one day be the president of the National Organization for Women. Who's laughing now, bitches?

(All in good fun, of course.)

Dear Reader,

First, thank you for being here! It's an honor that among all the stories you could choose, you chose this one. I appreciate your willingness to read this story. Speaking of this story, it surprised me. When I started out on the journey with Hannah and Seth, I thought it would be a new adult, second-chance love story set in college. It is that, but the deeper I got into the characters and the narrative, darker things began to emerge I hadn't expected. I think it's only fair to give you a heads up that what you're about to read might be triggering for some. If you aren't interested in knowing ahead of time, feel free to turn the page now to avoid any spoilers.

Those of you who need the warning, here goes.

If you've read *The Ugly Truth*, you already know what has happened to Seth. Both he and his mom have experienced the trauma of domestic violence at the hands of Seth's father. In this story, Seth takes us back in time to some of those moments. These experiences aren't offered in a way to glorify violence but are rather the means of Seth processing his trauma for healing.

In addition to that, at the onset of this story, Hannah and her ex-boyfriend, Sebastian, have broken up. It's been several months, and we learn Hannah is dealing with the grief over the unexpected death of her father and suffering with survivor's guilt. As the story progresses, the relationship Hannah shared with her ex-boyfriend offers anecdotes of the love-bomb, gaslighting, and narcissistic tendencies. While Hannah attempts to draw a line with Sebastian, he refuses to listen to her, and his behavior escalates to an incident of assault.

Please know that my inclusion of these scenes isn't to glorify or romanticize Sebastian's behavior in any way, but rather to offer the portrait of an intelligent young woman who might fall prey to the subversive way an abuser operates.

If you are experiencing violence against your person, please seek help immediately. I have listed a few resources in the back of the book.

With love,

Cami

**Two years ago**

*My Heart Insists Making Wishes Might Help*

Blankets speckled the beach, and stars winked at the crowded beach from the dark, July sky. It was a perfect night for fireworks, still pleasantly warm, despite the Oregon ocean air, and full of anticipation.

Except I wasn't feeling it.

Instead, I was stuck in my head, hands in the sand, pondering the fact that my parents had decided to move and were, at that moment, still going through the garage. We had less than a week until doomsday.

"You're graduated now," Mom had said after I'd complained for the umpteenth time and asked them to hold off until the end of the summer. "Nineteen. Off to college. What's the deal?"

Dad had stopped what he'd been doing with a toolbox to watch the exchange. His engagement was always unsettling for me. I tensed and waited for an explosion, but there hadn't been one for the last year and a half. That was how things worked now. A year and a half from my car wreck, and a year and a half of his sobriety. We mostly talked through Mom. This wasn't a Jack Peter's issue, it was mine. He'd tried, and I'd maintained the distance. I didn't trust him. And I didn't understand how Mom did. How many times had he been on the wagon? Just because he was a year into this stint didn't mean he wasn't going to fuck it up. Her forgiveness pissed me off. It felt like an indictment against me. I was struggling to forgive him, yet I'd been forgiven by Gabe and hadn't deserved it. This awareness slammed me with guilt I didn't want to acknowledge.

"Why can't you just wait until I leave for school?" I'd asked.

"Jobs, Seth," she'd said. She'd put something in a box, then stopped to level a pragmatic look at me, her eyebrows sharp over her eyes. "No one is making you come with us."

I'd wanted to argue with her. They kind of were. How could I afford to live on my own for a month before I moved into the dorms and reported to the soccer team? The whole timing of the move was stupid. But she was right, I was technically an adult. I just didn't really feel like one yet. How did that feel? Did the realization settle on your shoulders and make you feel all-knowing? My parents hadn't acted like adults in all the time I'd known them, so it seemed like the whole idea was a crock of shit.

A while later, I was with my friends on our way to the 4th of July beach bash. Carter was driving. Abby, Gabe, and Hannah were squeezed into the back seat of the car. I'd climbed into the front seat, wishing I could be closer to Hannah but not having a reason to be. I'd been crushing on her the whole year and had been too much of a coward to do anything about it.

I'd listened to her and Abby chatter about remaining summer plans that I wasn't going to get to be a part of. Abby was leaving for Hawaii in less than a month, Hannah for Oregon University. Gabe was leaving for California, and Carter for Washington. I hadn't told them I was moving, but I wasn't exactly sure how to break the news. How did one say, "So, I'm moving to Benson next week. See you on the flipside." What a buzzkill. I was leaving Cantos, and there wouldn't be a reason to return. This could be the last time I spent with my friends, beyond cell phones. While I didn't have a lot of good memories of Cantos, they had been the best thing. And the thought of losing time with them made me angry.

Now, after our picnic of chips and crackers and other kinds of convenience foods (except for the sandwiches Hannah had made). I looked up at the sky and watched for shooting stars before the fireworks began. Maybe the sky held the answer. I could probably ask Gabe to crash at his parents' place for six weeks, but I didn't. He would have said yes, and I didn't really feel like I deserved that. Plus, I didn't have a way to pay my own way. Carter's family was bursting at the seams already. Maybe I could make a wish.

Abby bumped my shoulder with hers. "You okay?"

I looked at her and nodded.

"You seem a million miles away."

I offered her a smile. "Just waiting for the fireworks." It wasn't a lie, exactly.

She looked at me a few beats longer, as if assessing the validity of my claim, seeing through me, then turned back to Gabe. He whispered something in her ear. She smiled one of those kinds of smiles between couples that I wished shared with me and dropped her head onto his shoulder. He kissed her head.

I stood up with the itchy feeling to get away and wove through the tapestry of blankets and people toward an edge, needing to catch my breath and fix my attitude. With my eyes on my feet, concentrating on staying upright in the sand, I ran right into someone else.

We toppled over into the sand.

"Oh. Shit. I'm–"

Hannah.

I was sprawled out on top of her, her hair spread out around her head like a blond halo. She giggled, and I felt the vibration of it in my belly.

"I'm sorry." I extricated myself from the way our limbs had braided together.

"That's okay." She smiled. "You were on a mission."

I stood and helped her up.

Nerves fluttered about inside of me like bouncing and unpredictable dragonflies. I'd been a bundle of nerves all year with her—I liked her, really liked her. Gabe had spent the entire year calling me out on it. "Just ask her out," he'd said repeatedly.

I hadn't, even if I'd wanted to.

Hannah was a good one, and I deserved no part of that. Not given who I was and what I'd done. My insecurities in all the threads weaving me together made me feel like I might unravel, and I didn't want her to see that. I liked her too much.

"I just needed some space to think," I replied. "I really didn't see you. I'm sorry."

Her hand reached out and touched my arm. "Stop."

I froze.

"It's okay. You want to be alone? Or are you okay with some company?"

Just then, the first firework exploded in the sky, a succession of sparking white blooms. A collective gasp moved across the beach.

"I'm okay," I told her. "I mean, I'm sure you want to watch the show with the crew." I'd sort of nodded over my shoulder.

"I'd like to watch them with you."

My heart constricted in my chest. First with awareness, then with hope, and then with anxiety. "You would?" I hated this insecure dude and wanted to take the words back and replace them with something cooler.

She smiled, as if she liked this anxious guy. "Yes. Shall we sit?"

Another firework exploded. I followed Hannah past the last rows of blankets—where people were either watching the show or making out—to a spot up against the dunes behind everyone else on the beach around a little alcove that made it feel private, like our own spot under the sky. Hannah sat down, and I sat next to her, my arms wrapped around my knees. A string of fireworks exploded—red, white, and blue—against the backdrop of a dark velvet sky, and all I could think about was Hannah's shoulder pressed against my arm, creating fireworks under my skin and heating up my chest.

"They're so pretty," she said.

"Yes," I agreed, but I was looking at her. I'd been so stupid, being afraid to tell her how I felt. And now I was leaving.

I'd never have another chance with her.

With my heart pounding a nervous rhythm in my throat, I worked up the bravery to put an arm around her.

She froze.

I retreated, thinking I'd taken it too far.

But Hannah grasped my arm and pulled me back, snuggling in closer. She looked up at me, offered me a smile, then looked back up at the sky, thudding like my heartbeat. When Hannah threaded her fingers with mine, my body melted, aware of the movement of her fingers. Back and forth, a rhythm that had me thinking about more than just our hands touching.

"Is this okay?" she asked.

I could barely hear her and leaned forward, my lips against the skin near her ear. "What was that?"

She turned her face to meet my gaze, and her usually bright eyes were as dark as the sky. "Is this okay? Holding your hand?" Her gaze dipped to my mouth, then back to my eyes.

I nodded, but I was thinking about her looking at my mouth, both surprised and excited that she wanted me to kiss her. My belly tightened with anticipation.

I'd known Hannah since elementary school when we'd played boys-chase-girls during recess and insisted that the other had cooties. I'd never really noticed Hannah. Until I'd been in rehab after the accident, and it had been Hannah who randomly wrote me *You can do it!* cards and delivered homemade cookies. When I'd finally figured out that I had feelings for her, I didn't know how to navigate real ones. So, I'd wasted spring of junior year and all senior year being a coward.

Now, with her wrapped up in my loose embrace and her hand caressing mine, I knew I had a choice: coward or risk-taker? I realized if I didn't take the risk, I'd regret it. Impulsive decision made, I leaned in and pressed my mouth to hers. My heart was outside my body. I waited for her to slap me in case I'd misread her, but she didn't. Instead, she leaned toward me, her mouth soft against mine. When her lips parted, it surprised me, and when her tongue touched my lips, it ignited the fire in my gut. I invited her in, opening my mouth to kiss her like I wanted to. She let go of my hand, turned, and leaned against me, her hands now wrapped up in my t-shirt at my waist. The kiss somehow matched not only the intensity of my heart but the fireworks above us.

My hands framed her face, our mouths exploring one another.

We ended up lying in the sand, me on my back, and Hannah draped on top of me. I submerged my hands in her hair as if she might slip through my fingers or effervesce into the night sky like a firework.

She moved so that she was closer and moaned into my mouth.

I ran my hands over her, stopping at the small of her back and pressing her against me. I was pretty sure that she'd be able to feel my erection.

"Oh my god," she said against my mouth, "Seth," and moved so that she was straddling me.

My eyes opened, hands now on her hips as she pressed herself against me, both alleviating the pressure but building it tenfold. "Oh my god, what? Hannah?" I couldn't speak very clearly, the words sounding like bursts of air as she pressed her body down onto mine.

The fireworks continued above us.

I was about to have exploding fireworks in my pants.

"I can't believe I'm kissing you."

The words tripped me up. I couldn't decipher them and retreated.

"I've wanted to for a long time."

I moved, sitting up and rotating Hannah onto her back, because those words I did understand. "Me too," I said, and kissed her with more fervor, angles, tongue, teeth. I was cognizant that I was afraid to scare her away with my exuberance.

"Me?" She opened her legs wider so I could settle deeper between her hips. "You wanted to kiss me?" Her doubt was said against my lips.

I nodded, surprised by it, and unwilling to end the kiss to tell her yes. I trailed the kiss down her neck, another firework exploding above us vibrating through me. "Hannah–" I started to say, barely able to catch my breath and loathe to stop, but it felt like too much and not enough simultaneously. I wanted so much more, but it felt out of order.

Her hands moved up under my shirt, gripped my back, and she tilted her hips toward me. "Yes? Seth?" She let out a gasped breath as I rocked my hips against her.

Another firework exploded above us, illuminating Hannah's beautiful face.

I stilled. First, because I was going to blow my load in my pants, but also because… this was Hannah. She deserved more than me dry humping her on the beach.

What was I doing?

I was leaving in a week. As much as I wanted this with Hannah, what was it going to mean beyond this moment? We were going to different colleges. She lived in Cantos. I was relocating two hundred miles away in Benson.

I sighed and pressed my forehead against her shoulder.

"What is it?"

"I'm sorry. I got carried away," I said.

"I like getting carried away with you," she said. "I'd like to keep getting carried away."

My resolve almost melted away as another set of fireworks exploded above us. Her touch was fire on my skin, leaving hot trails as she caressed my back with her fingertips. To maintain control over myself and the situation, I moved off her and laid down in the sand by her side, taking her hand in mine as I offered her a smile.

"Is something wrong?"

I could have told her then that I was moving. I opened my mouth to confess. To tell her how angry I was about it. How on the night I'd finally found the bravery to kiss her, show her how I felt, it was too late.

But I didn't say anything, unwilling to ruin the moment. Instead, I shook my head and offered her another smile. Another set of fireworks exploded, resembling shooting stars, and I squeezed her hand and coaxed myself to be content in the now with her even as I made a wish that this didn't have to end.

*My Heart Insists It's a Glob of Viscous Jelly*

My heart thuds when I see who's calling, but I accept the call and press the phone to my ear. "Hello?" Sinking onto the barstool in the kitchen of my apartment, I reach for the counter to steady me. I'm not sure why I've answered, knowing it's him.

"Hannah? Hey. I just wanted to check in on you." Sebastian's voice sounds the same, deep and resonant. Masculine. It's something I've always liked about him.

Nine weeks ago, I'd hoped he'd turn into a troll under the bridge with a voice to match, but that isn't what he sounds like.

Unfair. How can things be so different, yet the threads that make us remain the same? I don't feel the same at all, even if my face appears the same when I look in the mirror.

"That isn't your job anymore," I say.

I picture him sitting at the desk in his bedroom at his own apartment a mile or so away, running his index finger along the edge of the desktop littered with school stuff. His head bent forward—dark, auburn hair perfectly coiffed—and propped up by the other hand. I don't like that my mind slips to picture him so easily in such a casual, attractive image and force myself to remember the last time I saw him: dressed up, standing in the cold, head bent, frowning at the ground with anger-shaped eyes as I waited for my ride. He'd broken up with me that night after admitting he was seeing someone else, then had been angry I'd walked out on him at the restaurant.

Sebastian clears his throat on the other end of his line. "I– yeah. I just–"

I press my finger against the ivory Formica countertop and run my finger along a groove that shouldn't be there. When my roommate walks into the kitchen from the back of our apartment, I look up at her. Jewel tilts her head, her braids framing her face, as she arches her dark brows with the unspoken question: *who is it?*

She gathers her braids and ties them back before mouthing: *Sebastian?* Then she rolls her large, dark eyes and screws up her face, collapsing her features together in a grimace before reaching into the faux oak cupboard for a coffee cup.

"Just what?" I repeat what he's said. I want to know what he wants, but simultaneously don't. Why had I answered his call?

I'd loved him, or so I'd thought. Over the last two months, I've done a lot of reflecting about what I'd thought was being *in love* with him. I'd done all the things to create that perfect picture of it. Spent all my time with him. Exchanged gifts and did things to make him feel special. Took him home to meet my mom and sister in Cantos. Planned a future beyond college. He was the one, or so I'd believed.

When he took me out right before finals and I got the *I'm-seeing-someone-else* talk, I'd been blindsided. Now, I'm questioning if it was really love.

Looking back over my shoulder at our relationship, it was waving yellow flags at me all along. Now, there are sharp edges pressing against the softer skin of me asking that I pay attention, only I'm not sure what I'm supposed to be paying attention to. The ultimate knife—the fact he was cheating—was enough to kill whatever we'd had. What more is there to pay attention to?

"Why are you calling?" I ask.

Jewel leans against the counter near the coffee pot and looks at me over the rim of her mug. She's holding the green one that I got her for her birthday that reads: *I'll bring the sass*. That wary look on her face—her eyes narrowed, her frown—communicates she's less than enthused that Sebastian is on the phone. After we'd broke up, she'd said, "He's the gum that sticks to the bottom of your shoes on a hot summer day."

I'd laughed. It felt good to have her on my side. She was the one holding the tub of cookie dough and spoons after he'd pulled the plug. Then she was the one scooping me from the floor that first week, helping me get through finals. I'm not sure what I would have done without her, and I'm so glad I hadn't moved in with Sebastian when he'd suggested it over the summer.

"Girl," she mutters, shaking her head, turning back to the coffee pot. I watch her add more coffee to her cup. "Tell him to go to hell."

I offer her a wan smile.

"I just–" he repeats and pauses again as though weighing and measuring the impact of his words. "I know the anniversary is coming up, and I just wanted to make sure you're okay."

I have a fleeting impression that maybe he'd been planning on saying something different, but then settled on what I've heard, taking a 90-degree turn. I dismiss my doubt, wanting to be kind even if I'm feeling wary. What he's asked is more endearing than holding onto any negative thoughts about his intentions.

"I'm going home. I'll be okay. Thanks."

Silence stretches between us, creating awkward terrain.

"Was that it?" I say, ready to end this.

"I miss you," he says at the same time.

The silence returns like an earthquake.

My heart stalls at the tremor, waiting for the earth to shift under me, waiting in suspended animation for something visceral to restart it. *He doesn't get to say that.*

"I'm not sure what to make of that," is what I actually say.

Being with Sebastian at one time had been so easy. We'd fallen fast, the instalove I'd heard about and had always thought was bullshit. His attention, at a time when I was hungry for it, felt like a gift. Here was this amazingly handsome, charismatic, talented man giving me attention. But what's the saying? Hindsight is twenty-twenty? The knowledge that I'd been so easy to replace slashes and burns the already damaged parts of me. Hearing him say he misses me drags me back toward what used to be and makes me feel like a hollowed-out version of myself.

"I feel lost," he says. "And you always helped me figure myself out."

My eyes slip shut, because I can't look at Jewel, who's giving me the evil eye. Her gaze isn't directed at me, I know, but at Sebastian, who she loathes.

Everything is about Sebastian, in his world, just like my seventeen-year-old sister had pointed out over the break. "He's selfish," Ruth had said.

Their dislike of Sebastian wasn't always that way. My family and friends had liked him. It wasn't until later, when my relationship with him was the tenuous tension of a series of aftershocks waiting to tremble at a moment's notice, that their acceptance of Sebastian crumbled. Our ending became a relief.

I open my eyes again and look at Jewel. She gives me an encouraging look, her brows arching over her eyes.

As she stands there with a look that says, "You can do this. Stick to your guns," I sigh, draw from her support, and say, "Sebastian. I can't do this."

"Hannah–"

"We're over. Remember?"

His silence is confirmation enough that he remembers those words.

"I can't be your go to, Bash."

"You're right. It's just–"

I lean back, surprised by his acquiescence to my perspective. That's new. The swirls of us had mostly been the opposite. But I'm also worried about sliding into a trap he might be setting, so I say, "I have to go."

"Can I see you later? Or maybe call?"

"I don't know." I inwardly groan at myself.

"Just to talk."

I don't know how to let him down. I don't really want to see him, but he sounds so down, so contrite, and I don't have it in me to just say the words Jewel has suggested.

"Maybe." I lay my head against the counter and listen to Jewel walk from the room. I've disappointed myself. And Jewel will be supportive and helpful and the million other ways she's been in the year we've been friends.

Sometimes, when I look at her, I think, *I don't know why she likes me.* We shouldn't work, but somehow, we do. She'd been looking for a new roommate, and I was transferring schools when I answered her ad. The fact we get along like we do is a testament to some higher power, I think. We're complete opposites. She's an athlete and grew up in Portland, a big city. I'm not athletic and grew up in tiny Cantos. She's blunt. I'm squishy. She hates most people. I'm a people pleaser. She's all business. I'm all emotion. Somewhere along the way, she became my lifeline.

Sebastian continues talking, saying something about later, but I've zoned out, angry with myself for not drawing a tougher line.

When I end the call, I imagine myself in the shape of a gooey heart where everything gets stuck inside the viscous jelly of my inability to set limits. Annoyed, I bump my head a couple of times gently against the counter. Why can't I just be stronger? I'd returned to the term ready to move forward. Returning to rehash Sebastian—even if that isn't what he wanted to talk about though I know that's where it will go—isn't good for me.

It's good for him.

Just like Ruth said.

Why did I answer his call?

I hear Jewel walk back into the room. She stops at the end of the counter. "You're going to see him?"

"No."

"Then what was that 'maybe' for? And why are you mangling your head against that countertop?"

I sit up. "He asked if we could talk."

Jewel sighs for me. "Hannah."

"I know. I know."

"Hon." Jewel sits down next to me at the counter and bumps my shoulder with hers.

"Don't say it," I tell her and tilt my head, laying it onto her firm shoulder. "I know it."

She hums a noise.

"I need to be stronger. Like you."

She leans back and levels a serious look at me, which is uncharacteristic of her usual sarcasm. "You are strong. Stronger than you give yourself credit for." She quirks a brow.

I sit up, take a deep breath, and offer her a quick nod, wishing it were true.

*My Heart Insists on Letting Sleeping Dragons Lie*

ammill Library—the newest building on Western University's campus—has fulfilled the promise of allowing me to disappear among the stacks. I know no one and no one knows me. Granted, it's the first week of a new term, but my master plan is working just like I hoped it would. A clean slate. It wasn't like I was known at my former campus (it was too big), but rather I couldn't shake my own perceptions around my past and its influence on the new start I was attempting to make.

I'm surrounded by people: students, librarians, professors. All of us sit in a field of tables on the main floor, multiple seeded rows, growing crops of bodies bent over their light pine-coated surfaces and harvesting fruits of knowledge from books and computers. All strangers. No one knows Seth, the soccer player. Nobody knows Seth, that guy whose dad used to beat him up. No one knows Seth, the kid who almost died.

A girl at the opposite end of the table where I'm sitting looks up and catches my eye. She offers an inviting smile and tucks a strand of bobbed dark hair behind her ear before looking away. I return to the focus of my laptop and the book I'm perusing for my first history paper due next week. When I look up again, the cute girl catches my eye a second time. I offer her a polite smile, not really into the idea of meeting anyone, and focus on my computer.

There's a couple across the room, heads bent together, working on something. It isn't that I'm adverse to meeting someone. I'm like any guy, I suppose. I want to fall in love, find a partner, and have amazing sex, but historically, I haven't had the greatest track record where relationships are concerned.

In high school, I messed around not thinking about the emotional harvest I was reaping, until Abby. She was my first friend and my first love that ended with her falling for my best friend when we were seventeen. That sucked, but it was exactly what I needed too, weirdly enough. Then there was Hannah senior year, and I'd wasted the year pining instead of acting on my interest in her.

Even if I had though, I was in no emotional place to offer anything to a relationship as an eighteen-year-old recovering from a suicide attempt, which my next relationship taught me. I met Jenny freshman year of college, and I thought I loved her, but she broke up with me because she said she couldn't deal with how closed-off I was. Dr. Bethany and I have spent a lot of time talking through that.

After Jenny, I sampled hookups but always walked away dissatisfied with how temporary and ultimately lonely they were. How easy they were to reinforce being as closed off as Jenny accused me of being.

During my sophomore year, I met Amber and fell for her, but as it turns out, I had more feelings than she did, and she moved on with a guy named Ivan. I heard they are living together now.

I told Dr. Bethany the worst part about the whole Amber thing wasn't that she'd broken things off, it was knowing that I'd gone all in, and I still hadn't been good enough. The next guy had been. A shot to the old self-confidence. Again. It felt a little like revisiting the Abby debacle in high school, dredging up all those insecurities.

Dr. B had asked, *"Do you truly feel you went all in?"* Her question had pissed me off, and she knew it. She followed that up with this gem: *"Why does that question make you upset?"* which she does all the time.

I knew what she was getting at, because anger is a secondary emotion even though it's often my primary setting. I was lying to myself that I'd gone all in with Amber. Typical me. I might have had all the feelings, but I hadn't gone all in with Amber about my past. Instead, I gave her a glossier version, just like I had with Jenny. Dr. B responded to that by saying, *"Perhaps when you find a true partner, you won't feel the need to reserve those parts of yourself? You will go 'all in' as you say by being completely open even about the parts of yourself and your life you try so hard to hide."*

Dr. B is always calling me out like that.

Things ended with Amber over nine months ago, and now I'm starting over in a new place, new faces, new beginning.

This new start is what I want, but then I also wonder if in some ways that clean slate is another way for me to avoid the shit I can't escape. I carry the past in my head and body. The Seth who betrayed his best friend over a girl because of his own ugly insecurity and jealousy. The Seth who faced down his father's dragon each day and usually lost. The Seth who wrecked his car because he'd lost hope and thought death was the better option. My seventeen-year-old-self haunts my twenty-one-year-old, upgraded version. I may have moved towns, transferred schools to shed my old skin, but I can't seem to shed that old shame coating my insides. Sure, I've done a ton of work with Dr. B, and I hear her voice guiding me even now: *Are your historical experiences—good and bad—the only ways to define this current version of you?*

Of course not. I logically know that.

It isn't the rational that clogs up the plumbing of my life. It's the irrational emotions I wrestle with. She knows that too, of course. That emotional part of me who is trying to cleanse himself of the pain, the shame, and his own latent dragon he's working so hard to keep asleep.

I return to my paper resolved to focus on what I can control: the outcome of this assignment.

I've decided that this isn't running away—the shedding of my past for the clean slate of this new start—but it is me looking ahead. It's me redefining Seth Peters without all the baggage. That is what I need to move forward.

My phone vibrates.

I look at it.

My mom's calling.

So much for a new start, I think, and decline the call. I turn the phone over on the tabletop and decide I'll call her later. A part of me is avoiding her and by extension, him, but another part of me says that's okay. Dr. B would say *it's okay to set healthy boundaries and honor what you need. What you need to start this term at a new school without the baggage weighing you down.*

Except it's my mom, and we've always been a team.

I pick up the phone, open a message and text her: *Can't talk. In the library working on a paper. Everything okay?*

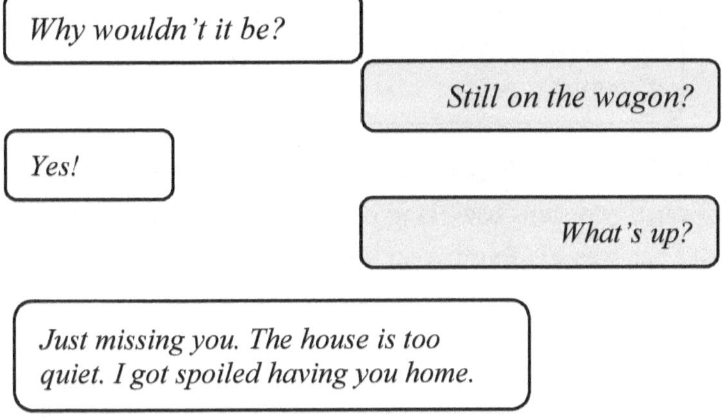


I'd only left home a couple of weeks ago. I text: *Tired of 80's reruns?*

> *☺He even tried an episode of Downton Abbey with me.*

> *And?*

> *He said it was "okay."*

I'm surprised, but I text her back with: *Did he agree to watch another episode?*

> *LOL. No, but at least he tried one. Progress.*

I'd like to say he's a walking antithesis to progress, a one step forward, two steps back kind of guy, but that isn't accurate. This last year was his fourth year sober, so that is progress even if I don't always trust it, or him. I text her: *That's good.*

> *How's your roommate?*

> *He isn't a serial killer.*

The day I'd moved, she'd thrown the 'what if your roommate is a serial killer' at me.

> *Trace is great.*

> *You should bring him home for a visit.*

I don't comment, putting my phone down. I don't want to subject anyone to my parents. I return to the paper I need to write. The phone pings with another message.

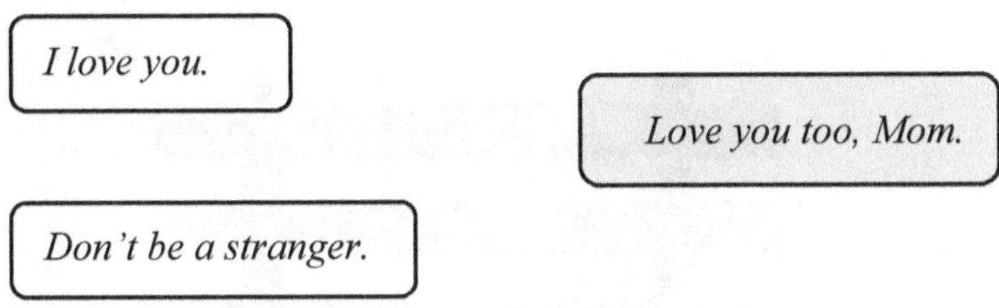


I send her a thumbs up and put the phone down again, then stare at my computer screen with its blinking cursor. I reread the last sentence, but my mind wanders back to my mom.

The day I'd left she'd been different, panicked. It made me wonder if something was going on she wasn't telling me. Dad wasn't drinking. He hadn't been violent and was diligent about attending his meetings and therapy. He seemed to like his new job—he drove a truck for the UPS now. He'd lost weight. While he'd gained weight when he first stopped drinking, which I figure was probably normal for someone who'd been managing his nutrition with alcohol and now wasn't, that had seemed to stabilize when he'd started walking. He and mom walked together. All in all, in the time I'd been home, things had actually seemed… perfect.

But I can't shake the nagging feeling that something is off. That feeling makes it impossible to concentrate any longer on the paper. I close the book, shut the laptop, and prepare to return to my new apartment where I'm sure my new roommate is immersed in a video game tournament of epic proportions. It's good, this newness, everything different and unrecognizable. It's exactly what I wanted.

*My Heart Insists the Flutters it Remembers*
*Are Unreliable*

I didn't need snow today, and it isn't even the good kind. Instead, it's the wet-and-slushy-sinking-razor-cold-teeth-into-everything kind. Fitting really. I was prepared for the rain.

I'm still getting into the swing of things after winter break. The swing of a new term, new classes. The swing of being single again, not that it's much different than when Sebastian and I were together. We'd been going through the motions as a couple far longer than in the rhythm of two people truly in love. I wish I hadn't let it go on as long as I did.

I pull my car into the parking lot and set the brake. A quick look at the clock. I'm running late, having wasted time on that call. With a sigh, I grab my bag and the stack of books I told Jewel I'd return for her and hustle from my car, careful with my steps in case the slush has frozen. Being late is the worst, especially if my supervisor Matilda the Hun is in the vicinity, offering her evil eye and sharp tongue.

I rush through the first set of doors at Hammill, my eyes unfocused, replaying where I went wrong in the conversation with Sebastian, and bump into someone hurrying out. The books in my arms flop out, falling to the ground in a syncopated succession of thuds. "Oh. I'm so sorry," I say and bend down to pick up the books, which I don't want to get wet.

*Shoot. Shoot. I'm so late. Matilda is going to string me up by my nails.*

"So sorry," a deep voice says at the same time. "My fault. I wasn't–" A familiar voice, stalled now on his last word.

I look up into a face I recognize. Warm amber eyes. A dimpled smile. My heart remembers jumping around in my chest with that familiar rhythm before my eyes and mind put that recognition together.

"Hannah?"

"Seth?" A smile spreads across my face and every nagging thought evaporates. "What are you doing here?" My smile won't stop and communicates with the rest of my body that it needs to get involved in the joy. My heart hammers against my ribs. My face heats.

The last time I saw him–

My heart trips over the memory and won't let me visit it out of self-preservation.

He looks like high school Seth, but different. Older. His nose is still slightly crooked. His mouth, with perfectly proportional lips, still cuts adorable dimples into his cheeks when he smiles, which he does, causing his amber eyes to sparkle. His brown hair is darker now, effortlessly styled so that wavy locks stray across his forehead. He's still taller than me. His face is wider, and it makes me wonder about the rest of him hiding underneath the jacket.

My heart adds a hot hum of awareness in my chest.

*He's a friend*—I tell myself—*one I haven't seen in a long time.*

He bends down to help me with the books. "Wow. I'm sorry. I wasn't looking where I was going. And it's you!" We're crouched down together in the entryway of Hammill between the sets of doors.

Someone opens the outer door, and a burst of cold finds its way under the hem of my coat and drifts up my back. I shiver.

"What are you doing here?" I don't know why I glance around, but I do, as if he's materialized from thin air and will disappear again when the spell wears off. "How are you? It's been, what?"

He grabs the last book.

We stand.

He holds the book out to me, and his eyes grasp ahold of mine. "Since that summer after senior year."

July. The beach. I remember.

He remembers?

I tilt my head, surprised.

I know the last time I saw him. The memory played on repeat in my mind, my dreams, my inner-overthinking-monologue far too long after it happened. I try to play it cool. "Yeah! I think it was on the 4th of July get-together at the beach. After graduation." I can't stop smiling, and my cheeks are starting to ache. I wonder what he remembers about that night. We texted some after. Then he moved away, and the chats became fewer and farther between until they stopped altogether.

Someone opens the door from the library on their way out.

I step to the side and grasp the sleeve of Seth's coat to draw him to the side with me. The girl walking past glances at Seth and does a double take. Not surprising. He's always captured the girls' attention. I refocus on his smile. No dimples.

I take the book and add it to the pile in my arms. "What are you doing here? I thought you were at Oregon State. Your parents moved away from Cantos, didn't they?"

He nods. "Yeah. They're over in Benson now. I was at State. I transferred to Western for my major. I thought you were at the U."

My breath catches a moment at the mention. I had been there. Five months before dropping out and moving home. "Was," I finally say when I can work the word through my throat. "What about soccer?"

His warm smile fades, and he looks down at the ground. "I gave it up."

I reach out and lay my hand on his forearm, the fabric of his jacket making a slick noise when I do. "That's got to be difficult. You loved it."

He shakes his head, glancing at my hand, then looks up with a smile. No dimples. "I'm not sorry at all. I thought it would be harder to let it go, but it was a good thing. For me. Besides, now I can play intramurals without all the pressure." His smile deepens and cuts those cute dimples in his cheeks.

There they are.

My heart quickens just like it always did, making me slide back toward a crush I once had. I remind myself he stopped calling and order the rhythm of that rebellious organ to sputter to a stop. It doesn't listen.

"I'm so glad I bumped into you. What are you doing right now?"

I remove my hand from his arm and wrap it around the books I'm holding. "Work."

"Want to grab dinner at that pizza joint off Main—Lindies— after you're done? We can catch up." He's looking down at something rather than at me, adjusting his backpack before allowing that gaze to settle on my face again. He grins. "I don't want to walk out the door and have you disappear again."

My smile hasn't wavered, but the blush intensifies, heating my cheeks and rushing through me like molten gold. "Sure." I look at the top book on the stack, unable to think clearly when I look at his smiling face coupled with the admission he wants to see me. "I can meet you there around 6:30."

"Perfect." He takes the books in my arms. "I'll follow you, because I need your number, you know, just in case." He's smiling. Dimples.

I lead him into the library and glance around for Matilda. No sign.

"So, you transferred for your major?" I glance over my shoulder at him. His tone of voice is more settled and even than the Seth I knew from high school. He'd been playful Seth, who never took much seriously, then. Though, I consider senior year, after his car accident, after he'd nearly lost his life. That Seth had been different.

The thought makes me pause. I'm so different from that girl even if I still look like her. Only then I felt… happier, safer, idealistic. Now, I feel cracked and leaking what used to make me, me.

"Yes." He clears his throat. "Education."

"Really? Me too."

"Secondary?"

"Elementary."

"Perfect," he says. "That's very you."

"What's that supposed to mean?" I ask, turning to look at him.

He continues walking with me, flicks a glance in my direction, and grins. "Whenever I think about Hannah, I think about how kind you were to everyone—even me. You always have been."

His observation makes me heat—which is silly—and I hate it because it's so noticeable against my normally bright, fair skin. Everything heats up making me piggy-pink then splotchy red. It isn't attractive.

"Are you blushing?"

"Stop," I say with a smile I can't seem to temper. Then I grow warmer and shake my head. "Wait here." I duck into the back to drop my stuff in the break room cubby, thankful I haven't come across Matilda yet and grateful for a moment to compose myself. I chastise myself for needing it at all, closing my eyes, and take a deep breath.

I'm not seventeen anymore, and Seth stopped calling.

I press my fingers to my cheeks, wishing the heat of the blush away as I stand in front of the blue lockers. I groan. Logically, I understand that nearly three years have passed. We're both older and more mature, but there's a lot of the past wrapped up in the context of who I was and who he was. Then there was what happened on the 4th of July on that beach, so emotionally I'm unsteady.

"Who is that?"

My eyes fly open, and I grasp my chest with a start. Mason is standing an arm's length away, watching me with his green-eyed gaze, which is far too perceptive.

"An old friend from high school."

Mason makes a humming noise. "I need more of this story. He's–" He stops and raises his eyebrows.

I know. He doesn't need to say it. Seth is gorgeous. "You're assuming there is a story."

"There's always a story." Mason grins. "And I will get it." He scrunches his nose playfully.

I take a deep breath, backing away and smoothing my clothes, then return to the counter where Seth's waiting. I tap the counter. "Put them here."

He slides the books across it toward me. "Your phone?" He holds out his hand.

I pull it from my back pocket, unlock it for him, and place it in his open palm. I notice the width of his hands, the tan color even in winter, the strength, the veins that carve under the skin on the back of them, and the taper of his long fingers wrapped around the phone's pink case. His thumbs moving across the screen.

"This is so we don't ever lose touch again, Hannah Fleming. Got it?" His phone beeps. "I sent myself a text." He smiles again. "Pizza. 6:30."

I'm able to smile at him without added blushing. "I'll see you then."

He nods, hesitates for a brief moment, his amber eyes cataloging my face, taps the counter with the meaty part of one of his fists, then finally turns and walks away. I watch him go, and when he gets to the front door, he turns, and gives me a dimpled grin and a wave before disappearing out the door.

I excuse my racing heart away and press the smile from my cheeks with cold fingertips. I'm in a freefall of surprise. I know better than to allow my adolescent-girl infatuation for a boy that never saw me as anything more than a friend to affect me now. Though that rationalization doesn't explain away that summer-night kiss. But I conveniently ignore it. He stopped calling.

*So did you,* my brain argues.

"There's something sort of… rugged about him."

I jump at the sound of Mason's voice.

"Can you stop sneaking up on me like that?"

"So jumpy." He grins and looks at the door where Seth disappeared. "I wonder why."

I don't respond and take a deep breath. Then I remember I forgot to punch my timecard. "Shoot. My timecard."

I hurry to the back, resolved to remember that high-school Hannah was smart enough not to have flutters for Seth, so grown-up Hannah shouldn't either. Okay. That's a lie I'm telling myself. Everyone had flutters for Seth, but the principle still applies. No flutters. Just friends.

*My Heart Insists It Could Be a Date*

And there it is. My past. I've avoided things that take me back to Cantos, even if it's just my memories. This is because that time in my life casts a pall about my perceptions of things. I was someone different, or I hope that is a truth I tell myself rather than a lie. I have spent most of my life lying, so sometimes, I take a moment to make sure I'm telling myself the truth. Some coping mechanisms linger longer than others. Cantos represents a past I'd rather forget even though that is an impossibility. But since I can't run from the memories, I avoid most things that have to do with that time. That place

And I just ran into Cantos.

Hannah.

What. The. Fuck.

I knew it could be a possibility I might run into someone, but I hadn't considered it might be Hannah.

I hurry through the cold, wet snow and into my car that feels like a cave. After starting it, I wait for the windows to defrost and cup my hands around my mouth, blasting them with warm air. The car faces the brick of Hammill, and I'm dazed, thinking about Hannah. Hannah Fleming. Even though she's exactly what I would have run from to escape memories, seeing her was like a shot of warmth and comfort, not very Cantos at all.

She looked different. Still Hannah. Blond hair, wavy and long. Rosy cheeks. Bright blue eyes. Easy smile. Even more beautiful, if that's possible. A woman now. Seeing her made me feel... joy, but also the poignant sadness of missed opportunities.

I shrug out of my coat.

Dr. Bethany would tell me to sit in the moment, reflect on the feelings to better understand them. *"You don't need to run from your emotions, Seth,"* she repeats each time I avoid them.

I felt happy to see Hannah.

I'd wanted to hold onto that happiness, obviously. I'd asked her to meet for dinner. The nostalgia that wrapped me up didn't feel like I was reopening old wounds, but something different. Sitting in this awareness doesn't reveal what that something is. Instead, I'm surprised I ran toward it. Except there's a giant unresolved memory sitting between her and me. One that fills me with so many emotions.

My heart pounds with both trepidation and possibility.

I lean my head back against the headrest while the car warms up, thinking about that night on the beach. We'd kissed, and it definitely would have led to more. Almost three years removed, and I still feel that heat sitting in the center of my chest.

I press my fingers to my chest now.

I couldn't get over the horrible timing of it, less than a week before I'd left Cantos for good. I'd eventually told her I was moving away. We'd tried to stay in touch, but life moves forward, and standing in one spot is impossible. I'd stopped calling. Such an idiot.

Back then, Hannah had seemed like the summit of a mountain I had no tools to climb.

The windshield is clear of frost, and probably has been for a while, so I drive from the lot to my apartment building, recognizing the unsettled flutters inside me are like the anxiety I felt around her when I'd been eighteen and unable to find the courage to ask her out. And now I've asked her to dinner.

I lock the car and walk the covered walkway to my apartment I share with Trace, or TJ as everyone calls him. Trace Jacoby's last roommate left mid-term, and I'd found his ad online when I decided to transfer.

"Yo!" Trace says from one of the mismatched chairs in the living room when I walk through the front door. He doesn't look at me, his dark eyes focused on the large TV screen where a football player runs down a graphic sideline toward the goal. He leans forward, mouth open. "Imma kick your sorry ass," he says to the screen, but his avatar gets tackled and the reverberation of the suped-up, video gaming setup with surround sound fills the apartment.

"Hey," I reply, closing the door.

Trace glances at me, offers a quick head nod, turns back to the TV, and he selects his next play.

I lucked out on finding him as a roommate, though it's still the honeymoon phase. He's respectful of my space and invites me to be a part of his world. He's tidy—which is great—and he enjoys cooking. He's gone a lot for football—he's a receiver. Workouts. Mandatory study halls. Team meetings. Even though it's the off season, he's always training. He's gone home once since I moved in, and though he says there isn't a significant other, he's spent a few nights out and wandered in the next morning with a smile that says he got action.

There are two other guys spread out in the living room, one I've met, the other I haven't.

"Hey Marco," I say and slap Trace's teammate's offered hand.

"Seth. Dude. Sit. Watch me take out TJ with this next play." Marco's shoulder dips as if he's really in the play.

I walk around the end of the couch.

"This is my boy, DeShawn," Trace introduces the other guy. "He's on the team with us."

DeShawn holds out a hand. "Sup."

We offer one another a bro shake with minimal eye contact, and I sit next to him on the couch. "They keeping it civil?" I ask.

"There is no civility where this game is concerned," Marco says.

Trace laughs. "That's 'cause you're always losing."

Marco swears at Trace, who laughs louder.

The video game whistles, signaling the end of the play.

"Position?" I ask DeShawn.

"Linebacker. Marco!" DeShawn shouts. "What the fuck was that? That was a bitch play."

"Next one."

"You've been saying that for the last five minutes." DeShawn laughs. "Just like your freaking play as a corner."

Marco offers a drawn-out profanity that sounds more like air leaving a tire than someone who cares what's been said, then smiles.

"How was the Ham?" Trace asks me.

"The Ham?"

"The library," Marco clarifies.

Trace twitches with his controller as his football player avatar runs down the sideline again. He stands. "He. Could. Go. All. The. Way!" He raises both arms, signaling a touchdown at the same time the avatar crosses into the video game endzone.

"You fucking cheat," Marco says and hands the controller to DeShawn.

"Don't be butthurt," Trace laughs, reaches over, and pushes Marco, who flops against the back of the couch. "You can't help how shitty you are."

"Kick his ass, D." Marco pouts.

DeShawn sits forward on the edge of the couch. "Oh. That's about to happen, bruh."

"Library was a library," I say and watch Trace and DeShawn set up their teams.

"Any hotties in the stacks today?" Marco asks.

"What the–" Trace stops and looks at Marcos. "Who hunts for honey in the stacks at the Ham?"

"Marco. Obviously," DeShawn snickers.

"Who doesn't?" Marco shrugs. "Better yet, stay out of there, TJ. You don't need to be poaching on my hunting territory."

"Cuz I'd fucking collect all the honey for my own fucking pot." He laughs.

"I was studying," I say, even though I'm smiling. Marco is funny. Since moving in and meeting Marco, I've only ever heard him talk about football, video games, and hooking up.

"Who studies?" Marco asks.

"You're a freaking PE major," Trace says. "Not you."

"Dude. That's messed up. I've got kinesiology this term."

"Whoa. Come to my calculus class with me, then we'll talk." Trace turns to look at me. "Imma show you the Western ropes, Peters. Show you the best places to hunt for honey."

"I'm good," I say. "I can figure that out on my own."

All three of them look at me.

Marco says, "Bro. Who doesn't want to find honey?"

"Not down to hook up," I reply.

Marco is still staring at me. "Really?"

A pillow flies across the room and smacks Marco on the face. "That's cool," Trace says to me, then gives Marco a salty look.

"I ran into a friend," I say. "Thought she was at the U."

"She?" Marco quirks an eyebrow and smiles.

"Friend," I repeat and shake my head. "We went to high school together."

"A hottie?" Marco asks.

"Wasn't looking at her like food."

DeShawn barks a laugh and holds out his knuckles. I tap mine against his.

"What is this? Shit on Marco day?"

"Dude. You walk into it all the time," Trace says.

"What's her name?" Marco turns to me. "Maybe I know her."

"Why would you randomly know someone?" I ask.

"Don't underestimate the power of Marco's knowledge of people. The bro is mayor of Western. He freaking knows everyone." Trace follows it up with a shout. "No!"

DeShawn taunts him about the loss of yards. "That sack was perfection."

"Name?" Marco asks, eyes on the game.

"Hannah."

"Last?"

"Fleming." I draw out the sounds with disbelief that he'd know her.

"Oh, shit. Yeah. That's Sebastian's ex-girl. She's hot."

I'm taken aback. First that someone knows Hannah, though it shouldn't surprise me. She'd always been the friendliest person in school. It would correlate that she'd be friendly here, too, but as someone's ex-girlfriend? The fact he's said it like that makes me feel like there are ants under my skin. "I'm meeting her for dinner tonight."

"Oh shit." Marco gets excited about that. "Wait until I tell Bash."

"Wait," Trace says as if he just heard. "Bash's ex? She's still a free agent? Bash is a dumbass. She's fine."

"He really dumped her for some other girl?" DeShawn asks.

Marco nods. "Yep. Hooked up with this freshman girl after being with Hannah for like, what? A year?" He shakes his head as he watches the game on TV.

"Wait." I feel like I've got whiplash.

"Dude. That other girl was like a ten in looks but a three in personality. Hannah's the whole package," Trace says, his eyes studying possible plays. He selects one.

I'm so lost. "She has a boyfriend?" I ask. I've never known Hannah with a boyfriend. Sure, she dated in high school, but mostly she was… just Hannah. The whole package? My brain feels like it's been pushed through a sieve, shredded, and is now trying to put itself back together.

"Had," Trace says and rolls his arms to the right, controller in his hands, as if they control the football avatar.

An ex-boyfriend. But it's dumb to assume that guys wouldn't find her attractive. She is.

"So is it like a date?" Marco asks. "Dinner?"

I shake my head, but then reimagine the possibility in my mind. A date? "Friends catching up," I clarify and wonder about the ghost of disappointment haunting the house of my body when I say it.

"You staking claim?" Marco asks. "I wouldn't mind trying to hit that up."

"She's a human being, not a tract of land," I say and stand.

DeShawn snickers again, giving me another set of knuckles.

"Got to work on a paper." I head down the hall to my room.

"So you aren't interested?" Marco calls after me.

"Dude. Bash would be pissed if you poached on his ex," Trace says to him. "Bro code."

"He dumped her. What would he care?" Marco asks. "Is there like—an acceptable waiting period?"

"She's a friend," I yell down the hall at them and shut my bedroom door behind me, then drop my backpack and collapse onto my bed.

Hannah had a boyfriend.

And for some reason this news pushes me off a cliff.

Friends is the most accurate description of us, even if what we shared at the beach was anything but. I've never forgotten it, even contemplated it from time to time. But it's weird to hear other guys talk about her like she's hook-up material. I've known her since kindergarten. It makes me feel protective for her.

I want to know more about this Sebastian guy. Did he break her heart?

I ponder her smile. The pink of her cheeks stained with a blush. The heart-shape of her pink lips.

Then I wonder, would a friend recall the shape of her lips today when they'd been picking up books together and how kissable they looked?

Probably not.

*My Heart Insists on Playing Tag with My Brain*

"Time to spill it, Hannah Banana. Who was that gorgeous specimen of a man?" Mason asks as he enters the return cubicle where I'm working on book returns before reshelving them.

I scan a book to put it back into the system and set it on the cart for reshelving. Mason leans against the counter, which I've learned he's very good at, at least until Matilda catches him and threatens him with work-study shifts on Friday nights.

"A friend from high school."

"And…" His eyes seize mine and hold. One. Two. "I can tell by your blush there's more to the story."

My eyes slide back to the stack of returns. "Why do you have to be so hateful? You know not to bring up my single weakness," I say, referencing my unhide-able tell. The book-return beeps as I point the gun at the code on the inner cover of the book.

"Me?" He presses a hand to his heart. "Hateful? Never."

As coworkers for over a year, I've learned Mason's singular flaw: beautiful leaning while watching me work rather than pitching in because "he's too pretty for menial labor."

I offer him a coy smile instead of speaking and check in another book.

Mason lifts himself up onto the counter, plucking at the green and blue plaid wool trousers he's wearing today. He's also got on a green button up and a sweater vest, looking dapper as usual. "So, that's quite a gigantic stack of returns," he says, and his eyes flash to the cart piled with books. "I'd hate for someone to just, oh say, forget to reshelve them tonight. Maybe accidentally misplace the cart for tomorrow's shift? Do you work tomorrow, Hannawnaw?"

"You wouldn't."

He arches a dark blond brow as if to ask, "Want to test me?"

I narrow my eyes at him, then grin. "That's really dirty, Mason Rand. Extortion?"

"Have I ever indicated, Hannah Fleming, that I wouldn't use all the tools at my disposal to get what I want?" He smiles.

I chuckle. "Fine. His name is Seth. We're just friends."

He hums a sonorous note through his nose.

"What?"

"I need more information, Hanzie. Oh. Wait. I don't think I like that one."

"Yeah. Let's pretend you never said that," I reply to his new nickname. So far Mason has named me Hannah Banana, Hannawnaw, Hanz-N-Franz, Hanover, Hannah-it-over.

He slides from the counter. "Give me all the dirty deets."

"There aren't any."

Mason leans against the counter. "Not buying that. Selling and selling it quickly. Those shares are rubbish."

I laugh.

He shushes me and glances around for the Hun. "Your blush alone, Hannah, tells me that there's more there than you're saying. And–" He holds up a hand to hush my protest. "And, I may not be straight, but I'm pretty good at reading guy because I am one— he's interested in you."

I shut my mouth to chew on that bit of information. "You think so?"

He makes a face, most of his features migrating to one side of his face. "Yeah. Couldn't stop looking at you and by looking, I mean looking."

"I'm supposed to meet him for pizza after my shift."

Mason stands up as if someone pulled a string. "Really? Yes! Now, as your love guru–"

"No."

"Please?"

"No."

He pouts. "Please?"

"I don't know if I'm going to go." It's only when I say it that I realize how anxious the idea of meeting Seth makes me. It isn't Seth so much as my own fears. These ideas mixed up in doubting myself, in worrying about what happened last time.

"What?" Mason asks a little too loudly, ducks a smidge, and glances around. "What?" he repeats in a whisper when he turns back to me. "You have to!"

"I just got dumped."

"By a douche!"

I want to argue with Mason about Sebastian being a jerk but know it's pointless. Mason is in the Team Hannah camp—which I'm grateful for—and that makes him, and Jewel, and my sister biased in my favor. I'd like to think that I know the ins and outs of my relationship with Sebastian clearer than they do, but lately, I've started wondering.

"I see you trying to formulate a justification for his behavior, Hannah. There isn't one. So stop. Would you have cheated on him?"

"Fine. You're right."

"Of course, I am. And based on your blush, I'm going to go out on a limb and say you had a crush on this… Seth."

My face heats.

Mason grins.

"I'm only getting out of a relationship."

"Two months ago! Hannah!"

"Nine weeks."

"Exactly. Nine weeks of nine months is twenty-five percent of that original relationship. That calculates to like seventy-five percent over it." He leans a hip against the counter again.

I bark another laugh, then duck, glancing around for the Hun. "That's weird math."

"Regardless. Time to move on."

I sober. "I don't know if I want to put myself out there like that again." Instead of Sebastian, however, I'm thinking about the night at the beach and the fact Seth had stopped calling.

I scan another book.

"I mean, that is an option. There's always the self-pleasure fallback." Mason looks at his nails again, then at me with a gleam in his eyes. "But why go that direction when you could have a nice warm body?" He wiggles his eyebrows.

My face heats.

Mason's grin tempers. "Look, while I'm not disparaging your plan to protect yourself—as you should—I'm not sure closing yourself off from beautiful possibilities is the right course."

I love how Mason, even with all his superficial bluster, isn't. He's deep and reflective, kind and compassionate.

"But we're friends."

"And as some wise obscure person probably said, falling in love with your friend is the greatest treasure."

I scan another book and another, considering his words.

"Don't think of it as starting another relationship, Hanz. You already have a relationship with Seth. This is just a catching up kind of dinner, right? Between friends?"

I look up at Mason, who's watching me with one of his perceptive looks. His mouth curls up on one side.

"Yes."

"So, what's with all the pressure?"

He's right. I'd already decided it wasn't a date, but then slid into remembering all the feels I once had. "It isn't a date." I grin. "You're right."

He grabs my upper arms. "Shit! Here comes the Hun!" he whisper-shouts and pushes me out of the cubicle. "Clock out!"

Then he takes over the job of checking in the books. "Save yourself!"

"Ms. Fleming?" Matilda asks when she reaches the counter. A thin woman with sharp features, I always have this feeling she's about to stab me with one of her body parts. She's so wiry and pointy. "Are you just standing around?" She glances at Mason and narrows her eyes.

He offers her a smile and continues with the job.

"My shift is over," I say and smile at her.

"Then why are you here bothering Mr. Rand? Get gone."

I look at Mason and roll my eyes at him as I back away. "Yes, ma'am."

After gathering my stuff and slipping into my jacket, I check my phone, again, for the gazillionth time to see if Seth has canceled. No cancellation. There is a new text from Sebastian. I ignore it and send Seth a text: *Leaving the Ham now*.

> *I'll get us a table. Drive safe.*

I send a thumbs up emoji and exit the library.

The snow isn't sticking anymore but it's mixed with freezing rain, so I flip up the hood on my jacket and hurry through the parking lot to where I parked my little green car. While waiting for the car to heat, I text Jewel, letting her know where I'll be. When I get to the pizza parlor—five minutes later because Mountain Park and Linden Falls are tiny neighboring towns separated by a narrow two-lane highway running between them—I take another deep breath to settle myself.

It isn't that I still like Seth. It isn't.

While I was infatuated with him in high school, I wasn't the only one. Everyone was. He was just one of those charismatic people that made you feel like the center of the world when he smiled at you, completely unaware of what he did to your insides. The night at the beach was the culmination of two years of infatuation and the presentation of an opportunity. I knew then not to let my infatuation be anything other than that even if my wires got crossed later. I resolve to see this the same. I can enjoy how attractive he is. I can appreciate the fact that we're hanging out as friends sharing pizza. Definitely not a date.

Park the car in the lot.

Deep breath.

Hurry through the sleet.

Push through the door into the pizza parlor.

My eyes adjust to the low light of the interior. It's warm and cozy, the fire blazing in the stove glowing at the center of the room. There are a few kids standing near it, and a mom trying to draw them away. The dining room isn't overly full, not like after a football game, but there are enough tables full of patrons that I have to search for Seth. When I find him, I remind myself: *just friends*. That's safest.

He's sitting in the opposite corner at a table tucked against the wall away from others. His head is tilted forward as he looks at his phone. I notice his hair is a little longer than he wore it in high school, the ends curling a little more prominently. It's also darker, more brown than the honey blond it used to be highlighted with in high school, a little damp. A memory of being in elementary school hits me. We were eight and playing chase at recess. Seth tagged me, laughed, and ran away. His hair had been completely blond then. I smile at the memory as I weave my way around the room toward him.

When he looks up and sees me, he smiles.

Dimples.

My belly warms with a firework's bloom, sprinkling heat that explodes to my extremities. I resolve not to let the attraction become anything more. Last time it led to a dead end. I'm in the process of dealing with the emotional fallout of the last dead end. I can't do any more dead ends.

But Mason's words hit me like a dart into the bullseye of my heart: *he's interested.*

Seth stands. He looks so good dressed in a dark, long-sleeved t-shirt and blue jeans which ride his narrow hips.

When I'm close enough, he draws me into a hug. "I didn't get to do that at the library," he says.

The rumble of his words reverberates through his chest into mine, sitting in the space of my spine that speaks to all my nerves, sending messages of light into spaces in my body that I hadn't realized were empty until that moment.

Muscle memory of our night on the beach kicks in, my heart kicking up sand and nearly choking me. His warmth seeps through my jacket, and instead of fighting it—because I'm tired—I relax, wrapping my arms around him and holding on. My eyes slip shut, and I take a deep breath. He smells clean and refreshing, like soap and citrus. I remember all the ways we were friends, and all the ways I wish we hadn't been.

"I'm still so surprised to see you," I say against his shoulder. He's taller than I am. I notice how strong his arms are, how they flex around me—just a touch more after I've spoken. I notice the way his body has filled in and widened like his face. I want to burrow into him, snuggle, but realize we've been holding onto one another for a more-than-friends length of time. So I step back, because I don't need to be thinking about the strength of his arms or his body.

*Just friends.*

I smile and unzip my jacket. "Hi."

"Hi."

Our eyes catch, and I hold onto his. He does the same, his smile waning, but the intensity of his gaze darkening. He clears his throat, looks away, and sits.

"I hope you don't mind. I ordered."

"What did you get?" I settle in the chair opposite him.

"The hot cheese one with pepperoni and sausage. And ranch."

"Yummy. Thick crust or thin? And yes, this is a test," I tease as I remove the green scarf around my neck.

"Thick."

"Aced it."

He grins and rearranges the napkin holder and the various shakers on the table. "My new roommate. He taught me Lindie's Pizzaria 101 the first week after I moved it."

I adjust my purse and jacket in the chair next to me, taking a moment to center myself. "He did good." Deep breath. *Just friends.* Another deep breath and I turn to him with a smile. "I want to hear all about your life over the last two years."

His eyes search my face as if memorizing it, as if he too is worried I might disappear. "Hold on," he says, his gaze intent and focused. I feel it like a caress.

"What?"

"I'm just…Wow. I can't believe we're here right now."

My skin heats, and I can't keep eye contact, but I also can't contain my smile. "I'm so happy to see you." The moment I admit it, I understand the ephemeral nature of my happiness lately. I can clearly see since my father's death, happiness—the real thing—has been elusive. This feels like the real thing, reminding me how I once felt. It's a scary realization.

Seth nods, his dimples back, then takes a sip of his drink and clears his throat as he sets it back on the table. Then he runs his hands over what I assume are his thighs, hidden from view.

"There's not much to tell. State for two years. Quit soccer. Time spent last term in Benson with my parents. Transferred."

I laugh. "Nope. Not getting away with that. Parents first. Still together?"

His smile fades, and he looks at the clear plastic cup in front of him. "Yes." He grasps hold of it as if needing to ground himself with something.

I know there's a lot I don't know about Seth and his family. There are things I can guess. Everyone knew his dad had been arrested for child abuse when Seth had been in the hospital, but the truth of that is not something Seth has ever shared with me.

"That's a bad thing?" I ask.

His eyes flick up to mine. "No. Not bad. They are still in therapy, and he's still sober."

"You seem–" I search for a word– "doubtful about it."

He takes a sip of his water. "He's been on the wagon before."

"This long?"

He shakes his head.

"Have you forgiven him?"

"A work in progress," he says, then offers a smile. No dimples.

"We all are."

"And you? How are you a work in progress, Hannah? I never thought you had much to fix."

I'm taken aback by his statement. "Why would you think that?"

"You were—are still, I bet—the best of all of us."

I look away, embarrassed, unable to hold his gaze. "What an awful and wonderful thing to say." I don't think he'd say that if he knew the heart of me, of what happened the night my father died, of how selfish I'd been.

"How's that awful?"

"All that pressure." I allow myself another look at him.

He smiles. Dimples. "Nope. No pressure."

A name is announced over the loudspeaker.

"Girlfriend?" I ask. I want to know.

He smiles and tilts his head, studying me. "The abridged version: I dated a girl freshman year. Broke up. Dated a bit. Then I had a girlfriend sophomore year. Lasted about six months and fizzled out." He takes a sip of his water. "You?"

I blush. "Just got out of a relationship, actually."

His eyebrows shift again, and his mouth fades toward seriousness. "How long?"

"We were together for nine months."

"How long have you been broken up?"

"He broke up with me right before finals last term."

"Was it serious?"

"I thought so."

His eyes skitter away like pebbles skipped across water. "He didn't?"

I offer him an easy smile even though it isn't really. I'm embarrassed. "I guess not." It's hard to admit I was dumped, that I wasn't good enough somehow, and when I look in the mirror, I know it's that belief about myself that I reflected to Sebastian. It's probably why we broke up. I hope my reflection is changing, that Seth sees something different. "He was seeing someone new." I press my fingertips to my cheeks. "Sucks to not be wanted."

"He's an idiot."

My eyes flash to Seth and notice the tightened line of his jaw. He looks away as if maybe he's said too much. I decide not to make anything of it. I'd made too much of what happened at the beach way back when. I want to guard my heart. I smile, attempting casual. "I'm going to be a cat lady."

"That is an absolute impossibility, unless that's what you want." He twirls his cup around with both of his hands, the right one pushing and the left drawing it back toward him. It's repetitive and captures my gaze, which is easier than looking at him. His hands are beautiful, which seems like a weird thing to notice, but I can't seem to look away from them. I recall his touch, and I swallow. I didn't realize I had a thing for hands.

He leans forward, drawing my eyes to his. "Why didn't you go to senior prom with me instead of that weird kid from Newport?"

I can't help but laugh. "That's random. You didn't ask me."

"You could have asked me." His light brown eyes, which I notice have flecks of green in them, are bright with mirth.

"Shut up. You name me one girl who asked a boy in high school?"

"Pizza for Seth," reverberates through the room.

Seth stands and swipes his forehead dramatically. "Saved." He grins and walks away.

I scold my heart for bouncing in my chest like a rubber ball as I watch him walk across the room. I notice the way his shirt stretches over his back; it isn't tight, but I can see the definition of his shoulders and the ridge of his blades. I trail the sinew of his body to his hips where his well-worn jeans sit perfectly, hugging his backside and thighs. "Stop," I tell myself, forcing myself to look away and take a sip of my water.

When he returns, Seth slides the silver tray onto the table. "I have decided there is no better pizza in the state." It's oozing cheese and bubbling with pepperoni and spicy Italian sausage. He offers me a plate. "I didn't get you a fork. Want one?"

"Who eats pizza with a fork?"

He grins. Dimples. "My sentiments exactly. You passed your test."

I laugh and pull a slice from the pan to put on my plate. "Okay. Where did we stop? State. Check. No girlfriend. Check. Moved to Benson. Check."

He takes a slice from the pan and bites. "Oh! That's hot!" He puffs air through his mouth to cool the bite.

I look away. The shape of his lips makes me think about kissing and how long it feels since I've kissed anyone. Sebastian doesn't count. It seems like we stopped kissing months before we broke up. I miss kissing. The hungry way kissing explodes. The way it slides through your whole body.

The night on the beach with Seth hits me.

My stomach twirls with the memory, and I squeeze my thighs together to quell the way my body remembers it too. I test the pizza on my plate with a fingertip to reset my thoughts.

"Worried?" Seth asks around the bite.

"Yes." But I'm not talking about pizza.

"Your turn. Parents still in Cantos?"

My heart hooks on an exposed nail.

Just like that, grief dashes any other feeling inside me. I can't bring myself to answer him and refuse to look up. I'm sure he'll notice the way tears fill my eyes. Anytime I think about the loss of my dad, even two years removed, the loss is loose heart tissue. Time has stretched between the then of it and the now, but it feels like I fold the line to return every time I'm forced to look.

"What is it?" Seth asks. His expressive eyebrows are scrunched toward one another over his eyes.

"My mom and sister are still in Cantos. My dad passed away during my freshman year."

"Oh shit–" He reaches out and covers my hand with his.

The warmth is welcome, and it's another contrast to Sebastian, who was usually annoyed that I struggled to *get past it*. That somehow, I just needed to *dig a little deeper and find a way to get over it*. "It's hard to talk about."

He wraps his fingers around my hand, and I'm falling into that touch with too much ease. "I didn't know. I'm so sorry."

My gaze slides up from our joined hands to his face. "Thank you for that."

He offers another reassuring squeeze and releases my hand.

I miss his touch, which is ridiculous. I missed it after having had it that night on the beach, too.

"That was during freshman year?"

I nod. "January."

"Oh." Seth pokes at the crust of his pizza. "Is that why you transferred?"

I clear my throat of the lump and mentally reset myself on steady ground, then offer him a smile. "Yes. I took a year off and then transferred."

"We both took time off."

I'm not sure what to think of the statement, but some part of me grasps for the kismet of it. I wonder if he's thinking the same thing; how if we hadn't taken that time, we wouldn't be sitting across the table from one another right now.

We drop into conversation reminiscing about our shared childhoods, people we knew, and the town where we both grew up, though the night at the beach is avoided. Being with him is easy, and just like I always do, I rotate into the comfort of being aware of him and his movement. He is like the sun, and I'm content to exist in the shadows, except Seth keeps his sun shining on me and forces me to stay out in the light.

"Still talk to Abby and Gabe?" I ask.

"Gabe. Yes. When they broke up–"

I nod, knowing.

"You?"

"Abby."

He takes a deep breath, his chest leaning against the edge of the table on his side. "Do you think it's inevitable that people who date in high school break up?" Then he leans back and takes another slice of pizza, depositing it on his plate.

I shrug. "Some people make it work."

He hums a sound.

"What?"

He shakes his head and offers me a smile without dimples. "Just thinking about circumstances."

I'm not sure what he means, but it makes me return to my crush on him, to relive the moment on the beach. I feel my skin heat and know I need to change the subject. "Are you enjoying Western?" I ask him.

"Definitely is looking up," he replies and grins.

My phone buzzes in my purse against the chair next to me. Unsettled by his statement and the insecurity of allowing the hope of seeing him again to battle with the tempering of my expectations, I grab the phone to allow myself a moment to breathe. Except it's Sebastian. I decline the call and set the phone on the table.

Seth's eyes track my movement. "Any suggestions for my transition?"

This makes me laugh. Western is a fraction the size of State. I shake my head.

"Why are you shaking your head at me, Hannah?"

"I think you'll be okay." My phone buzzes on the table again. Sebastian's face pops up on the screen.

"Do you need to get that?" He nods at the phone.

I shake my head and pick up the phone. "The ex." I wave the phone and slip it into my purse again after declining the call.

"He's still calling?"

"Just today." I take a sip of my soda. "I'm not sure why." I don't mention it's the second time today and that he's texted too.

"You're not?" His eyes haven't left my face, and I feel warm under his focused gaze. During our senior year, I would have considered doing most anything for his attention, even if I hadn't. Or how when we kissed on the beach, I thought I'd finally found what I'd been looking for. It was a story I told myself, wishing it were so but too afraid to do anything about it.

"I'm so glad I ran into you, Hannah." His amber eyes twinkle as he takes another bite of his pizza.

I grab my cup and take another sip, reminding myself this isn't a date. We're just friends.

*My Heart Insists Unresolved Things Need Attention*

My heart hasn't gotten the memo from my head that my infatuation for Hannah is ancient history. Instead, it's grappling in my chest with my logic and reasoning—and winning. The tingly feeling is more like the eighteen-year-old me, tongue-tied, twisted-up, and less like the buttoned-up, more experienced twenty-one-year-old me. Facing these feelings and sitting in them, like Dr. B would advise, I recognize my feelings for Hannah are unresolved. There was a forced end, but never a chance to begin. Like a dash hanging out at the end of a sentence. Waiting.

I drive away from Lindies, the past swirling around in my head. The way we bounced around one another like bumper cars during senior year. The way she reached out, offering kindness, that I realize was an adolescent way of building connection. I'd been too ignorant to recognize it. How perfect she'd felt in my arms at the beach. The fire of our shared kiss.

I replay tonight, rewinding Hannah walking through the pizza parlor toward me and meeting my gaze. Electricity buzzed at the base of my spine, and the elation in my body was a kite riding the wind, swooping, and twisting but tethered to a foundation keeping it secure as she walked across the room. My heart's memory rushed in to hug her. When she finally relaxed in my arms, the full commitment of her choice to hug me back spoke a familiar rhythm. The heat of her hands on my shoulder blades was a reminder of our missed chance. The whole night reminded me of the comfortable way we could slide back into talking like the friends we once were.

By the time I park my car in my assigned spot outside of my apartment complex, I know that I can't wait to see Hannah again. It needs to be soon. I'm smiling like a fool, realizing that while whatever serendipitous convergence of Hannah and me might be unexpected, I feel... fucking happy.

I might have transferred to Western for a clean slate, but life is offering another option. A do-over. A way to reconcile the past of me with the present. Past me hadn't wanted to only be her friend, even if that's where we hung out to protect our young and fragile hearts. Present me isn't going to be content being Hannah's friend either. To make that claim would be a lie, and I made a promise to myself not to be a liar. I want to knock on that door and see if she'll open it.

*Time to be the risk-taker,* I think. *Only this time, I can do it right.*

I pull out my phone and text her: *Thanks for meeting me tonight. I had fun.*

My heart expands, blocking the breath moving through my lungs. I watch the three dots pop up and linger, wondering what she's about to send me, afraid I've overcommitted.

*Me too.*

I take a deep breath and smile as I text her back: *When do I get to see you again?*

I wonder if maybe this is too soon and decide that if I didn't already know Hannah, if I hadn't grown up with her, maybe it would be. But I did.

I remember Hannah wearing pigtails with bows that matched her outfit. She used matching barrettes to keep the shorter curls contained. I sat behind her in third grade—Mrs. Smythe's class—and noticed Hannah's hair escape those clasps. I would pester her with my pencil, teasing the curls on the back of her neck and revel in her annoyance at me. I remember Hannah in eighth grade student council, standing in the front of the student body giving one of the many speeches. I didn't pay much attention because Gabe and I were usually debating something sports related. Hannah is always there in my memories. She's threaded in the fabric of who I am.

So, this isn't too soon. It feels like I'm running a lot late.

*I'm going to Cantos this weekend.*

*It must be before then I guess.*

☺*Coffee?*

Door opened.

*Nope,* I think. This isn't casual, but it can't be too much either. I rip through my brain, trying to think of something that will feel a step up from the noncommittal stance of a casual meet-up for coffee. I recall Trace and Marcos debating the basketball team's merits and the mention of the game.

*How about the basketball game the day after next?*

*You don't want to talk to me?*

*What?*

I second guess the idea, but then am struck by the fact she wants to talk. That's a good sign.

*Basketball games aren't known for places to chat.*

*And dinner?*

It's a risk, sort of, and one I'm fully committed to taking, finally grown up enough to take it.

*I work. Dinner after?*

My smile grows.

*Perfect.*

I'm typing that I'll pick her up, but her text comes through before I can suggest it.

*I will meet you at the game when I get off work.*

*It's a date. I'll be waiting.*

I get out of my car excited about the prospect of getting to spend more time with Hannah. After locking my car, I walk across the sidewalk and start up the concrete stairs to the apartment when my phone rings. It's my mom.

"You missed me so much, you had to text and follow that up with a call?" I ask with a smile. I might be floating up the stairs toward my apartment after time spent with Hannah and the new commitment to correct that regret.

"I do miss you," my mom says. "The house feels extra quiet. I might have gotten used to you being home again."

"With Dad home, the house is never quiet."

She clears her throat. "Be nice."

"I am. I mean the TV."

Mom chuckles. "Right. The volume might be a little loud. What are you doing?"

"I'm just getting home from dinner."

"With your roommate?"

"No. Met a friend from high school for pizza."

"Oh. That's–" she pauses a moment– "nice."

I wonder if she goes back in time when I mention high school. We did some family counseling after the car wreck, so I've heard her share some of her feelings about that time, but then I started my own therapy, and she and Dad have theirs. We haven't talked a lot about it since. Over the last six months that I lived with them, I could see when Mom would drift into her memories. In fact, thinking about it, my dad did too, drawing her back toward him with a touch. When she'd come back, she'd focus on him and smile.

The thought makes me frown.

It's so much easier to think about my dad as a monster.

Makes it easier to justify withholding my forgiveness.

"What's going on, Mom? Is it Dad? Is he drinking?" My worst fear is that she's going to call and say Dad has fallen off the wagon.

It's hard not to go here. I spent the bulk of my lifetime—up until the winter of my junior year—with an alcoholic father who hit me. Hit her. And she stayed. He would jump on the wagon after a particularly bad bender, then fall off. The never-ending peaks and valleys of living with him. This is the longest he's been on the wagon, and I'm still waiting for the slide back into the valley.

Like my thirteenth birthday.

I never had parties, because having one would mean subjecting my friends to the volatility of my father, but my mom tried to make things special. She'd planned my favorite dinner to celebrate me turning into a teenager. Asked Dad to barbeque the burgers. She made me a cake, frosted it green like a soccer field, and decorated it with these special soccer candles she'd found. My dad, on the other hand, spent the day watching hockey finals and drinking. By the time he got to the barbeque, he was angry, throwing things about while he cooked.

I remember being terrified at dinner, the three of us sitting around our little table. Mom and I silent, waiting for Dad's fuse to reach the explosives. And it did. When my mom set that cake on the table, a knife on the platter slipped. It fell into my dad's lap, smearing green frosting across his white shirt and the crotch of his shorts. He lost it. The cake was destroyed, then shoved into my mother's face.

"How do you like it?" he'd screamed, spittle collecting on his lips, his face red with rage.

He'd pushed her, and she'd slipped in the mess, falling hard against the floor where he was bent over her yelling in her face. Then he looked at me sitting at the table, watching him, and froze. I'm not sure what went through his head, but he stomped from the room, then the house.

He came home a few days later sober, having "been to a meeting." With an apology to both Mom and I, he promised to be better. He brought home an old truck a few days later to work on with me, saying it would be mine. It was the truck I drove into oncoming traffic four years later when I thought there was no other way to escape the awful cycle.

"No! Of course not," my mom says emphatically, drawing me back to the present conversation. "It's nothing. I mean, nothing supremely important. I just wanted to let you know that your dad is going to the doctor."

I narrow my eyes and round the platform to the next flight of steps. "Dad's going to the doctor?" My father didn't go to the doctor.

Mom gives a subdued laugh. "Right? I didn't want to text that to you because I thought you might worry."

I'm not sure if it's worry I feel. "How come?" Maybe it is, but that would mean I have more feelings for him than just an acknowledgement that he exists.

"He just hasn't been feeling well."

I recall watching him walk up the porch steps of the house as he helped me pack up my car, thinking he'd seemed old. "Well, Dad agreeing to go to the doctor is concerning."

"Just a checkup," she says, and I don't know if she's telling me or herself. "His stomach has been bothering him, and he's finally agreed to stop being stubborn and get it checked."

I nod, even though she can't see me. "Okay. Thanks for telling me."

"I'll keep you posted. His appointment is next week." She pauses, then asks, "Did you finish your paper?"

I maintain my pace up the steps, rounding the corner for the next flight. "Almost."

"When are you coming home next?"

"Not sure. Why?" I stall, stopping on the final flight and standing at the railing that looks out over the parking lot. The hand holding the phone pressed to my ear is cold, but I can't walk and talk at the same time when it feels like the rug might be pulled out from under me. I wonder if she's more worried than she's letting on.

"Just making plans. I was hoping to see you for your next break. Or a weekend soon?"

"Spring break?" I imagine doing something with Hannah, and my heart picks up a hopeful pace. "I might do something with friends." I look down at my shoes and rest one of them in between the metal bars.

"Right. As you should," she says, but I can hear the disappointment in her tone.

"Maybe one of these weekends," I say.

"I'd like that."

I start back up the last set of stairs and walk down the walkway to my apartment door. "Well, I have homework, Mom. Got a paper to finish."

"Right. Okay. I'm glad I got to talk to you. Don't be a stranger, okay?"

It's a weird statement. The second time she's said it. "I'm your son. Why would I be a stranger?"

With my hand on the doorknob she says, "Promise?" and my hackles go up.

Mom and I ran interference for one another for years. And though we haven't needed it recently, this is reminiscent of that, but I don't know why. There isn't any evidence to suggest my dad is drinking again. She's said he isn't. I don't have the energy to dig for it, however. As Dr. B has repeatedly said, *"You mother is an adult, Seth. She will make her own choices. You are not responsible to fix them for her."*

I take a deep breath. "I won't. Promise."

After we hang up, I wonder if I've meant I won't be a stranger, or I won't promise.

*My Heart Insists It's Time to Move On*

The fluttering tone of my Facetime rings through when I get home. The apartment is dark, and Jewel is at work, so I've got the place to myself. "Pick up. Pick up," I chant at the screen, even though I know it isn't going to change whether Abby is available to talk or not. I just want to process this with her. She knew how bad my crush was on Seth during our senior year, so of everyone in my life, she's the perfect one to talk to about this. The glowing light from the phone helps me pick my way through the dark apartment to my room, where I flip on the light.

It connects, beeping, and suddenly Abby is smiling at me on the other side of it. "Hannah!"

"How warm is it?" I ask and sit on my bed to remove my boots, comforted by the sight of my friend, the one who has known me through the most difficult points of my life and is still present.

"Super cold," she grins. "Only got up to 75 degrees today."

I scoot back on my bed until I'm leaning against the headboard. "I'm so jealous. It snowed here today."

Abby laughs and adjusts herself wherever she's sitting twenty-five hundred miles away. "What's up?"

"I had to call. Guess who I ran into today. Literally ran into." I'm a little nervous to share seeing Seth with her; I know how important he is to her, even if they haven't kept in touch.

Her eyebrows shift over her dark eyes with a question, then her image pixelates, freezing. "Who?" The question warbles with the connection.

"Abby? Can you hear me?"

The image reconnects to the sound. "Yes. I can. Who?"

"Seth."

"Peters?" The circumference of her eyes widens. "Really?"

"He transferred. To Western."

"I haven't seen him since the summer after graduation."

"Me either. Until today."

"Wow." She looks away, and her smile fades with the weight of the complicated history they share.

Junior year had been tumultuous. She and Seth had been childhood friends flirting with more, but Abby's heart leaned toward Gabe, Seth's one-time best friend and long-time rival. It was an awful bunch of wrinkles that eventually got ironed out, but not without some painful struggle. They seemed to find their way through senior year. Then Seth moved away, Gabe and Abby broke up, and lines of communication were severed between them.

"I need to hear this story."

I fill her in about our chance encounter at the library, our pizza meet-up, and his recent texts. "He asked me to go to a basketball game with him."

A smile grows on Abby's face. "What?"

"Don't be weird," I tell her and look down at my comforter; my cheeks are hot. "We're friends."

"Okay."

But when I look back at her face, she's grinning, though, the closed-mouth grin that I tells me she's trying to temper the look. "So, is this a mutually agreed upon meeting or is he picking you up?"

"I'm meeting him after work. Dinner after."

"Intriguing." She wiggles her eyebrows. "Why are you freaking out?"

"After I agreed to go, he texted, 'it's a date.'" I make air quotes for her with one hand. "Now I'm stressing because I don't know if that's what he meant."

She squeals with excitement and bounces on the screen. "Of course you're stressing out. That's what you do—overthink and stress. I think you should just go and have a good time. Don't overthink."

"As friends."

"As whatever the night decides." She smiles. "Hannah, you're always putting rules on yourself..." She pauses and readjusts again, dropping out of the screen for a moment. "Look, you had a mad crush on him, and you have the chance to see if what you felt then is something now. Why would you waste the opportunity by putting rules on it?"

My face heats. She knows me. And Mason had said essentially the same thing.

I'd be lying if I said I wasn't attracted to Seth, that I wasn't curious to see if what I'd felt then translated to now. I'd always been attracted to Seth, but then I was Hannah from high school, and now I'm older Hannah, who can't seem to get past my screw-ups. "I don't know if I have the emotional capacity to just see where the feels take me," I tell her.

"Is this about Sebastian?" she asks, her smile gone and the frown pulling at the corners of her eyes.

I try to say no, but the word doesn't flow from my mouth like it should. It catches there and grabs hold, making me think about her question, forcing me to be honest. "Yes, but not because of Sebastian, but because of me."

"What? You? He was the dick in the scenario."

"Not in that way–" I say. "In the way I was with him." I look away from the screen. Abby's incredulous look—her dark eyebrows raised with her angry set mouth—is keeping me from thinking clearly. I see the lamp from my room reflected in the dark window next to my bed. "I've been thinking about it a lot lately, how throughout us being together, I felt like I didn't deserve him."

Abby makes a disgusted sound. "That pisses me off, Hannah."

"If that sound was any indication–"

"It was always the other way around–"

"You're partial."

"Fuck yeah, I'm partial." She takes a deep breath. "So?"

"I've been missing something in myself, and what worries me is dragging that into a relationship with someone else. And if that person was Seth–" I pause, then shake my head. "He just walked back into my life. If I complicate it with all these feelings–"

"So there are feelings?" She smiles.

"Of course there are feelings. The moment I saw him, it was like all those unresolved *what-ifs* rushed back in to plague me. What if I follow that trail and–"

"Wait. Wait. You're sounding like Hannah from senior year. I hear what you're saying. And…" she says, drawing out the word, "what if those fears keep you from what you need? What if you take the risk and it's exactly what you need to figure out what it is you're missing?"

"I hate that."

"What? Getting what you need?"

"No! That you're right."

She grins, and her eyebrows arch up higher. "Well…"

"Don't let it go to your head."

"Already did." She laughs and mimics her head expanding with one of her hands, stops, then sobers. "I just want my dearest friend to be happy. And I don't want you to miss a possible opportunity of figuring out what you need to be happy because you're afraid."

"I'll think about it. It could just have been an expression–"

She dips her chin. "Hannah? I specifically remember you telling me one time, many, many years ago that Seth asking for a date didn't read as 'just friends.'" She gives me the sly, I-just-ruined-every-argument-against-this grin.

I change the subject instead. "Are you coming home for spring break?" I ask her, hoping I might get to see her.

"Nicely done." She laughs. "I'm not sure. I'm thinking of staying here. Maybe you could come to Hawai'i. Chill with me."

"As amazing as that would be, I'm not sure I've got the funds."

"What funds? Once you're here, there's nothing to worry about. I've got you. If you can just get a flight."

"Maybe."

"Don't maybe me. I need more from you."

"I'll look into it." But I'm thinking about those possibilities she's mentioned. Possibilities that might include Seth.

She smiles, and there's a noise off the screen, which make her glance beyond the camera, then back at me. "I think my roommate is locked out. She's always forgetting her house keys." She moves. "You must call me after the game. I want to hear about this non-date date with Seth." She winks.

I laugh as we say goodbye and disconnect.

After a shower, I set up in my room and work on a paper for my philosophy of education class, but I'm struggling to keep Seth in the part of my brain where he belongs. I reimagine his arms around me, then recall them around me that night on the beach. I see his mouth in my mind's eye, talking, smiling, eating his pizza, then remember kissing him. The strong rhythm of my heart and the way my extremities tingle remind me of that, and how I'm lying to myself by thinking I don't want that again. Chills race across my skin and considering it makes me ache with want, a foreign feeling that needs a translator.

My eyes cross with exhaustion as I lose focus on the paper I'm writing, so I give up the fight. I flip off the light at my desk and crawl into my bed. Just as I'm about to fall asleep, my phone pings. My seventeen-year-old sister's name is in the notification. I swipe the screen open.

*Nanna, are you coming home this weekend?*

Hi Rue. Yes, I'll be home.

Okay. Bring me some of those gummies from the school store? Pretty pleeeeaaaasssssseeee.

I got you.

I put the phone on my nightstand and roll over toward the wall, conflicted about going home. It isn't going home that I don't want. It isn't seeing my mom and my sister, but rather the gaping hole left by my father. I close my eyes, willing the awful memories away, only the memories have nowhere else to go and haunt me instead, reminding me how badly I'd messed up.

I'd been at a party with my roommate freshman year, the first party back after the holiday season, a new term, and a good time to let loose because we weren't slammed with papers or tests yet. I'd gotten drunk, probably a little too drunk, but I'd needed the liquid bravery to do what I intended, which was to let go of my virginity with a guy named Hunter I'd flirted with in writing class the previous term. I trusted him. We had fun together. I didn't carry any preconceived notions that the experience was going to be anything more than what it was, and though I'd been told my whole life not to have sex until I was married, I didn't figure I was going to hell because I wanted to make an empowered choice for myself.

We'd stumbled back to his dorm room, had mediocre sex, then fell asleep together. I'd woken up in his bed, hungover, but we'd walked over to the cafeteria together, chatted over breakfast, and joked about the walk of shame. When I made it back to my dorm room, I hunted up my dead phone which I'd accidentally left behind and plugged it in to charge while I took a hot shower. When I checked my phone, the screen was stacked with missed notifications and messages from my family.

My heart in my throat, I'd listened to one message after another of Rue or my mom, "Hannah. Call. Right away." "Hannah? Where are you?" "Hannah. It's Dad."

I'd immediately dialed Rue, who had picked up, her voice raw and hoarse. "Hannah? Where are you?"

"I didn't have my phone." Guilt for being without it, for being at a party getting drunk, for having sex with Hunter had hit like a succession of punches. I'd been having sex with Hunter while my family was trying to find me. "What's wrong?"

Recalling that moment has a surreal quality to it, as if I'd disconnected from my body to survive it. I think I thought she was calling to tell me Dad had a terrible bout of food poisoning, or maybe broke something because he'd taken a fall trying to take down the Christmas lights by himself. My dad—Gregory Hammish Fleming, III—was invincible, after all. While my mind had made up plausible stories, my heart was in my throat, as if it knew this was something else. My sister's tearful voice, and the insistence of the message were clues to something so much bigger. I'd denied the intuition. Dad was fine.

"They took him to the hospital last night." Her voice cracked open.

I'd swallowed and shook my head. "Okay. And?"

"He just collapsed." She was sobbing. It was difficult to understand her, the words mired in the swamp of her sobs.

My hand had covered my mouth and tears sprang to my eyes. "Is he okay? I'll come home now." I'd twirled in the spot where I stood, unsure and unsteady, nothing making sense. *My dad collapsed.*

Ruth had continued her tearful replay, "The firemen and the ambulance people. They were working on him."

"Oh my god," I'd said, even though I knew not to use the Lord's name like a swear word. I hadn't meant it like that, but out it came. "I'll go straight to the hospital." I'd fallen to my knees and looked for an unused duffle under my bed. I hadn't been thinking; I didn't have a duffle under my bed. "Or did they rush him to a different hospital?"

"Nanna."

I'd frozen at Ruth's lament in my nickname. My throat constricted while my insides tightened into slick glass.

Her tearful explanation continued. "He didn't make it, Nanna. Daddy. He's gone."

Still folded over on my knees, I'd look at the blue-gray carpet, at the loops and the variations of color. "Gone where? Did they transfer him to Salem?" The words had slid from me through my slick-glass body, nothing able to hang on and find purchase.

"No. Nanna. Daddy died."

I'd cut the call, trying to find the breath that wouldn't hold, sliding around the slippery surface of my insides. I'd panted the word "no," over and over while staring at the loops of the blue carpet, wondering why someone had chosen this shade of blue. A terrible color. Dingy. No. No. No. No. Depressing. Then I'd unrolled from the ball onto my back, looked up at that ceiling so high above me and wailed.

Caroline, my freshman roommate, found me sometime later, tear-soaked and numb. I could barely string together words, but she'd helped me pack and drove me home. I'd walked into the house that used to feel like a refuge and found the arms of my sister as if there was a magnetic pull of familial grief guiding my way, like birds flying south for the winter. By the time I'd walked up the stairwell to my mom, she'd been buried in her bed.

The vast emptiness of his loss was visceral, a gaping nothing that seemed to suck everything familiar, and happy, and known, and comfortable into that void.

I'd walked into the bathroom and was sick.

Now, I roll on my bed to stare at the ceiling again, wondering where my tired went.

This weekend marks two years. I'd messed up that night, forgotten the truth of who I was supposed to be, the good girl who could always be counted on to do the right thing. I hadn't been there for my dad and if I had, maybe I could have said goodbye. I would have been there for my mom and my sister, at least. Instead, I'd been selfish, and it had reaped an awful, heavy, guilt-ridden fruit.

Mom has said repeatedly that I can't blame myself. That even if they could have gotten ahold of me, I wouldn't have made it home in time. But she doesn't know where I'd been, what I'd been doing. I deserve this shame.

Not blaming myself had been a part of Mom's argument to get me to go back to school. To appease her, I agreed just after the first-year anniversary of my dad's death. Then I'd met Sebastian a few weeks later, unbound and broken. Hating myself. In many ways, Sebastian had saved me. Made me feel whole when the gaping hole left by the loss of my dad was so large. He'd made me feel protected. He'd made me feel safe. I know there were things wrong with my relationship with Sebastian, but it wasn't all him.

Silent tears slip from my eyes, and I roll back to my side and try to alleviate the grief and regret with sleep, slipping into that darkness to find peace.

A noise down the hall jolts me awake.

The darkness is stark and whole.

I reach for the light next to my bed and twist the knob on. It clicks and cuts the darkness. "Jewel?" I call out from my bed.

There isn't an answer from the hallway.

I check the time on my phone and know she should be home. She hasn't texted that she's staying at Joy's. After waiting a moment, I get up and walk to my bedroom door, open it, and peek out into the dark hallway. "Jewel?"

A loud crash makes me jump.

My heart thuds in my ears like bass drums.

"What the fuck was that?" Jewel asks from her bedroom doorway at the other end of the hallway.

"I don't know," I whisper.

"We better check," she says and disappears into her room. I hear the low sound of her words to Joy. When she reappears, she's shrugging into a hoodie and walks down the hallway toward me.

I follow her, knowing that I might be backup, even if I'm useless.

"What was it?"

I look over my shoulder at Joy, Jewel's girlfriend, standing in the hallway. She rubs her eyes and yawns.

I shrug.

By now, Jewel is at the door. She flips on the light, peeks out the peephole, walks to the window in the living room and looks out. "No one's there," she says, looking through the window again, rocking back and forth for a full view.

"No one? I wonder what that noise was." I take a relieved breath and look over my shoulder at Joy, shaking my head. When I look back at Jewel, she's looking through the peephole again.

"I'm going back to bed." Joy disappears back into Jewel's room.

"Should we open the door?"

"Now why the fuck would we do that?" Jewel asks me, incredulous that I've even suggested it.

I nod. "You're right."

We retreat to our own rooms. Once I'm back in bed, it takes me too long to fall asleep. When I finally do, it's restless, and I toss and turn to dreams of a shadowy creature banging on the door, snarling at the windows, trying to get in.

The following morning, after moving through a sleepy haze, Jewel opens the door, saying something to Joy about her coat collar and reaching to help her fix it.

"What's that?" I ask, stepping toward the door.

A scrap of paper is taped to its surface. Chills race across my skin, and a tremor rocks my muscles.

Jewel plucks the note from the door and looks at it, then turns and holds it out. "It's for you."

"What?"

"It's got your name on it."

I take it and retreat with it to the kitchen counter.

She meets me at the end of the bar. "Who's it from?"

I recognize the handwriting: all caps, only it's messier than usual. "Sebastian."

"Are you telling me, he was the one making all that racket last night?" Joy rolls her eyes. "Figures. Such a selfish jerk."

Jewel makes a frustrated noise that whooshes through her nose and mouth, then rubs a hand over her face. "That fucker. Leave it to him to scare the shit out of us."

Now that I know that last night's sound was Sebastian, the tension in my muscles ease. "I'm sure he didn't mean to scare us."

"Maybe not, Hannah, but you're too nice about it, regardless." She pats my arm. "We're going to go." She looks at Joy. "Ready?"

"You're deserve better than that, Hannah," Joy says as she follows Jewel out of the apartment.

"See you later," I call after them as they disappear, then look back at the note Sebastian has left, confused. He's called, he's texted, and now he's come to my place in the middle of the night to leave a note.

Maybe he thought it would make me remember how attentive he could be, but irritation takes a grater to my insides. I consider throwing out the note without reading it, but curiosity wins out, so I pull it across the countertop and remove it from the envelope to read:

HANNAH,

I WANTED TO TALK TO YOU. YOU DIDN'T ANSWER YOUR PHONE. I FUCKED UP, AND I THOUGHT WRITING A LETTER WOULD BE COOL. ROMANTIC. IT COULD SHOW YOU THAT I NEED TO TALK TO YOU. MORE EFFORT THAN TEXTING, RIGHT? I MISS YOU.

AND I WANT TO FIX THIS. FIX US.

PLEASE

CALL ME.

YOURS, SEBASTIAN

I read the letter again, and a third time, trying to make sense of what I'm seeing. I can tell his handwriting isn't confined to his normal neat and controlled print. It's slanted, the letters uneven, and I have the sense he wrote it drunk. Sebastian drunk-noted me. The thought makes me snicker. Then I smile, but not because I'm moved by the gesture, but rather because of the wonderful way it makes me feel… nothing.

That, in and of itself, is progress.

I wonder if I would have felt that way if Seth hadn't somehow miraculously walked into my world yesterday. I recall how difficult listening to Sebastian yesterday morning had been. I'd known it was over but hadn't put that into practice yet. Perhaps Seth's reappearance is a fortuitous gift from God to reinforce my need to walk away from whatever had been with Sebastian rather than allowing it back into my life. Of course, I feel bad for Sebastian's hurt, but I also know that nine weeks ago he was the one who asked for this.

I fold the letter, return it to the envelope, and throw it away before leaving for class.

*My Heart Insists This is Just Right*

Waiting outside the gym freezing my balls off, I wish I'd just gone to pick up Hannah instead of meeting here. I bounce, trying to keep warm as Timberwolves fans pass me. The door to the building opens, releasing puffs of warm air and the sound of sneakers on a gym floor. My hands are shoved deep in the pockets of my blue jacket and my gray beanie cap is pulled low, but it doesn't seem to matter. Billows of steam from my mouth escape into the crystallized darkness of an Oregon January night. The snowy slush has frozen, making things slick. As each person passes, I glance at faces, sure that Hannah will see me, just like she had at the pizza parlor, rather than miss me standing out here covered from head to toe.

It's been two days since our dinner, and I haven't stopped thinking about it. About her. Hannah's smile and the sound of her laugh. The feel of my arms around her when I hugged her, then hers around me, a pleasant weight that made my heart tumble. The way she tucked her hair behind her ear when she was thinking about what she wanted to say. The way she blushed when she was embarrassed, or maybe secretly pleased. The way her eyes sparkled as we reminisced. Her mouth curled with a smile—lower lip fuller than the curved heart of the top—full and kissable. I knew, tossing in my bed, zoning out during class, dreaming about the beach, replaying our kiss, that the attraction I'd had for Hannah senior year was alive and well.

My heart has done a complete face plant.

I chickened out so many times during our senior year, like failing to ask her to prom. I'd wanted to but hadn't, even with Gabe nagging me. Next thing I knew some kid from Newport was her date. I went stag with some of my soccer friends. I remember she looked so pretty. Her dress, a dark color—a deep red, maybe—her hair long and sleek over her bare shoulders. I'd asked her to dance once, stealing her away from her date who'd seemed content to sit at the table, staring at his phone instead of dancing with her.

It was a slow song.

Holding her had been torturous, in a good way. She'd smelled like summer—peaches and cream. With my hands on her waist, I'd wanted to talk to her, like we usually did, because that was something we could do. I just couldn't find words, my tongue tied up in knots. Her body pressed against mine made me worried my body might do something embarrassing. I felt stupid, which wasn't a normal feeling for me, then I'd slipped into being stupid, which was normal for me. Instead of talking to her, I'd talked to my friends dancing near us. Then the dance was over, and I was walking her back to her lump of a date.

Now, I remove my hands from my pockets and blow warm air into them, still bouncing on my toes, wishing I'd been braver back then, too worried about rejection.

Graduation came and went, along with the 4th of July at the beach when we'd kissed, then Cantos was in the rear-view mirror. There'd only ever been one other girl that made me feel upended and insecure in my own skin: Abby. In retrospect, I can see now it was because I cared about her. I cared—care—about Hannah.

All the rest of my flirtations and hook ups hadn't been because I cared. Even Amber. I'd lied to myself to insist my heart was all in. I never have been. I can see now what Dr. B meant by not completely committing to those relationships. Those interactions were going through the physical motions confused with emotional connections.

"Seth!" Hannah walks toward me down the sidewalk, coming into view under the streetlights. When she gets closer, I see her coat is dark green, and her hat and scarf and gloves are matching hot pink. Her blond hair peeks out from under the hat, waving around her jaw.

I descend the entry steps of the gym to meet her. "Hey." I offer my arm. "It's kind of slippery," I say. It isn't, because the sidewalks and steps have been cleared, and the concrete sprinkled, but it gives me an opportunity to be closer to her.

She accepts my offer, slipping her gloved hand around my elbow to link her arm with mine. She smiles. "Thanks."

I have a fleeting thought that I wish it was summer, so we didn't have all these layers between us. "I already got us tickets."

"Let me know how much I owe you."

"Nothing."

She turns her head to look at me. "Thank you."

I give her arm a squeeze with mine.

Once inside the gym, the warmth dictates the removal of outer wear, which means I don't get to touch her anymore. I pull the cap from my head, shove it into my jacket pocket, and run a hand through my hair to temper the disarray. Then I unzip the coat to take it off. Hannah does the same, only she's unbuttoning her jacket and drawing it off. I help her, holding it for her as she adjusts her scarf. Her smile and sparkling eyes offer a thank you.

The moment gives me the time to admire her. She's wearing black jeans that hug all her curves and a pink top that has slipped over a shoulder. A black bra strap catches my attention. My throat constricts. I imagine tracing the slick fabric with a fingertip, following where it disappears, and look away, swallowing to right myself.

She looks down at herself and blushes.

"You look great."

Her blush deepens, which heats my insides. "I had a little time to run home and change."

I think about that fact. Hannah went home to change. To get ready to see me. The thought fills my insides with added heat.

"This way." She leads us through the gym.

The players move through their warmup on the court. People are speckled throughout the bleachers, but my eyes keep coming back to Hannah as I follow her, admiring the view. She's got this gorgeous heart-shaped ass, the curves moving as she walks. I remember grabbing that at the beach and will my mind to remain in the gym. The attraction I felt for her two years ago definitely hasn't gone away. I'm also braver now and not planning on moving away anytime soon.

Hannah climbs the bleachers to an available spot. "How's this?"

"Perfect."

We settle side by side, our jackets stacked on the seat between us.

"How was work?" I ask, trying to find a topic that feels safe.

"Good. I enjoy working at the Ham."

"My roommate's friend says it's the pick-up spot on campus." *Dammit, Seth,* I think and wish I could retract it. I don't want her thinking I'm only thinking about hooking up with someone.

Thankfully, she smiles. "There's some of that." She blushes, and I wonder what she's thinking about. I wonder if someone tried to pick her up in the Ham stacks.

"You must have all of the guys flirting with you."

"What?" She looks shocked that I've said it, as if it would be an impossibility, and I have the sense that Hannah doesn't understand how amazing she is. "Not at all."

"Fools," I tell her with a smile, though the smile is because I'm glad. I'm hopeful that she might want to be more than friends. There is a slight hesitation of possibly ruining a good and easy thing between us, which I wouldn't like to happen. "What do you like about working there?" I mentally give myself a pat on the back for keeping a sane and grown-up conversation moving forward.

"Books, of course."

"Of course."

"I thought about library science as a degree at one point but changed my mind."

"How come?"

"A list of reasons." She uses her fingers to name them. "Available positions. Pay. Job security." She looks at me, her face serious and contemplative. "You'd think that in a democratic society we'd do a better job taking care of people and jobs that provide access to knowledge."

"No shit." I watch the players doing a drill and look at her again. "Like paying teachers." Her eyes skim my face, and I smile, my insides heating.

"Do you enjoy reading?" she asks.

"Most stuff."

I'm feeling a tension building between us that I don't think is one sided, and I'm wondering how I can broach this topic. Maybe after the game.

"Hannah?"

Her eyes flick from my face over my shoulder to see who's spoken her name, and she frowns. I turn to look at a stranger standing on the steps of the bleachers. He's tall—taller than me—and built like a linebacker with muscles on muscles. He's good looking.

"Seth!" Marco walks up the stairs a few steps behind the guy, who has stalled on the steps near us.

I stretch out my hand to greet him.

He gives me a hand slap. "You met Sebastian?" Marco asks. "Hey Hannah."

This is the guy? The guy who was an idiot to break up with Hannah, but fuck am I glad he did. I glance at Hannah, who looks like she's withdrawn somewhere else. When I turn back to Marco and the guy—clearly a football player—is frowning. His blue eyes are boring holes into Hannah, begging for her to meet his gaze.

"Just now," I say, standing and holding my hand out, drawing his attention away from Hannah.

He glances at my outstretched hand with what seems like condescension. I mean, I *am* sitting with an incredible person he used to date, but his beliefs about social etiquette seem to insist that he greet me. "Sebastian Mossman. You guys on a date?"

Unsure what to say, I stall. I don't want to do anything Hannah wouldn't want. A *no* leaves the door open for their possible reconciliation. That makes my skin crawl. It would also mean that we're just here as friends, and I want this to be more than that. A *yes* would signify she's moved on, but it isn't my call to make. It's Hannah's.

And then, I don't have to say anything because she says, "Yes."

I grin. Surprised and happy.

Sebastian doesn't like it and shoves his hands into his pockets. "Did you get my note?" His handsome features harden, and his lips thin into a frown.

I drop my eyes to Marco, who's still a step behind the ex-boyfriend, and consider this information. He's still pursuing her? I picture his face popping up on her phone a few nights ago while we were at pizza. Her ignoring the call.

"The one you taped to my door in the middle of the night? Yeah."

I glance at Hannah. She looks annoyed, her lips a tight line. I turn toward Sebastian again, working his jaw as if chewing on her response and he doesn't like the taste.

"Great," he says, though the tone of his voice would suggest anything but that. He mutters something I don't really catch and continues up the bleachers.

Marco shrugs and taps the top of my shoulder with a fist, then follows Sebastian up the steps.

I have a feeling this isn't the last Hannah has heard from her ex-boyfriend. He doesn't seem like the kind of guy who backs down from something he wants, and clearly, he seems to still want Hannah. A sobering and worrying thought.

Hannah leans toward me after I've sat back down, her shoulder bumping mine.

"I'm so sorry," she whispers.

I turn my head to her. She's staring at the gym floor where the team captains are meeting with the officials at center court.

"Why?"

She looks down at her lap where her hands are tightly knitted together, her knuckles white. "For him. For insinuating this is a date, that we're more than friends. I don't know what's gotten into him. He was the one who ended it." She sort of rambles it out on a breath, reminding me of the Hannah I knew before.

Taking a risk, I reach over and untangle her hands, taking one of them in mine. "I'm not sorry," I tell her and feel grateful when her eyes meet mine. I offer her an easy grin which belies the racing of my heart. "We'll make this whatever you want it to be."

She squeezes my hand with hers. "Thank you."

"That's the infamous ex, then?"

A buzzer sounds as the teams assemble around the center court circle for the opening jump.

"Yes."

"Would he be the Sebastian Mossman that everyone says is getting drafted this April?"

"The same."

I don't say anything, just hum an affirmation.

There was a time years ago when I'd been a complete ass because I'd been jealous about a girl and my best friend. I'd like to think I've grown up and am more mature about stuff like that, but I'd be lying to myself if I didn't say that I wasn't nervous sitting next to Hannah with her hand in mine, worried she's mulling over what just happened with her specimen of an ex.

"How do you know Marco?" she asks.

"My roommate, Trace."

"Jacoby?"

"Yeah. How–" But I shouldn't be surprised. She dated his teammate, and as Marco proved just the other day, everyone seems to know someone.

"Small school," she says with a smile, squeezes my hand, then lets it go.

I miss her skin connected with mine but am okay with whatever she needs.

The game begins, and the pressures of the external world slip away for a while. It's just me standing next to Hannah, our arms grazing every so often and laughter and joy shared between us, which, I think, is exactly how it should be.

*My Heart Insists He's a Good Guy.*
*The Alternative Means I Misread Everything*

The acoustic guitar and gentle voice of the folk singer set up in the corner of the coffee bar creates a comfortable atmosphere that makes me feel more like my old self. She's been absent for a while. Either that or it's Seth drawing her out, which is more likely.

He walks toward the table where I'm waiting, carrying two giant cups filled with coffee. When he notices me watching, he smiles, revealing those dimples that make him so charming and endearing. It's no wonder everyone loved him in high school.

He sets the white ceramic cups that look a lot like soup bowls on the wooden table. "You were right. These are huge." He sets our order number which he'd stashed under his arm on the table.

"And delicious. What did you get?" I eye his cup piled high with whip cream and sprinkles

"A mocha."

"A chocolate guy huh?"

"Is there any other flavor?"

I smile, raise my eyebrows, and take a sip of my honey latte.

Seth watches me, his gaze lingering on my mouth.

After holding my hand, the sizzling of our arms brushing for the last two hours at the game, and the eye volleys, I don't think I'm imagining the tension straining between us. "Do I have something on my face?" I ask.

His eyes flick back to mine, and he offers me a smile with a point. "Some foam."

I dab it with a napkin, my stomach twirling in my belly.

He tastes his mocha and runs his tongue over his lips.

My heart picks up speed, thinking about his tongue and the things he might do with it. I imagine Seth leaning over me, devouring me with his mouth. I press my knees together and blink, reaching across the table with my napkin.

Seth leans forward. "That's really good."

I nod and dab the whip cream from the tip of his nose, reorienting my short-circuiting thoughts with the movement. It's been a while since I've felt the hunger of physical attraction. I'm touch starved, I decide, and craving physical connection.

"The food is good too," I finally say.

"I believe you."

With the sexual tension searing my nerve endings, I'm tongue-tied. I know I keep telling myself I wanted to focus on friendship, but I'm beginning to recognize the futility in it. I just don't know if I'm imagining the way our bodies seem to be speaking to one another. Maybe it's a lie I'm telling myself because I want it that way. A sexual confirmation bias.

Seth clears his throat, glances at me, and takes another sip of his mocha.

I reach out and straighten the number, making sure it's on the edge of the table so that the server will see it. I don't really care about the number, but it's something to do with my hands. After taking a deep breath, I readjust my cup so the handle is on the opposite side. Then I twirl it back around.

"There's something, right?" Seth asks.

I look up at him.

He's smiling as if he's amused.

"Something?" I ask, but I know what he's alluding to.

He runs a hand through his hair. It flops back into place except for the stray waves that seem to have a mind of their own as he rests an elbow on the table, his head still in his hand, and gazes at me. Then he straightens, returning his hands to his lap, and shakes his head.

My filter stops working momentarily, and because it's on my mind, I bring up the broken bridge between us. "Do you remember the beach? 4th of July?" I keep my eyes on the surface of what's in my cup.

"I have a BLT with fries here. And a grilled cheese with tomato bisque," the server interrupts.

I lean back, a mirror of Seth, who has done the same.

"BLT," Seth says with a hand up, and thanks the server when he sets it down.

The server places my grilled cheese in front of me, and I thank him before he walks away. I put my napkin into my lap and watch as Seth does the same.

"That looks delicious," Seth says, leaning forward and eyeing my soup and sandwich.

"Want some?"

He shakes his head. "To answer your question, yes, I remember. Hard to forget."

His admission unlocks a piece of my heart. "You do?"

He leans back and checks under the top piece of bread before putting it back and tapping it. "Fuck, Hannah. It was hot."

I'd thought of it as romantic—kissing on the beach with fireworks blasting overhead—but he's right. I hadn't had many sexual experiences by then, some make-out sessions with a couple of guys, some touching and exploration, but no penetrative sex. I remember wanting to that night—with Seth. I've since been intimate with two partners. It has been enjoyable, but that isn't how I remember the beach that night. I remember the way his touch had made me feel like I was burning from the inside out. How his kiss had been lighter fluid. The way every part of me wanted to combust. Hot is a good description, and it makes me blush remembering.

Seth's grin broadens, lighting up his amber eyes with flashing fireworks. "You're blushing, Fleming."

"Stop." I press my fingers to my cheeks, but I can't stop smiling.

"I regret that I waited so long to tell you how I felt."

"And how did you do that?" I ask. "There wasn't a lot of talking, if I recall correctly."

He grins but ducks his head and picks up half of his sandwich. "I don't recall the exact turn of phrase, but I think I remember something like, 'I wanted to do that for a long time.'" He takes a bite.

"Fair enough." I take a nibble of my sandwich, suddenly too keyed up with the conversation to focus on the food even if it looks delicious. Now, I'm thinking about that kiss, and knowing what I know now, picturing how it could be. I picture wrapping my legs around his hips as he enters me. My body clenches, imagining it.

My eyes slide from my food to Seth, who's watching me.

I blush harder.

He covers his mouth with his napkin, but I see his eyes curl, and I know he's grinning. I'm pretty sure he knows exactly where my mind went, and if mine went there, is that where his is too?

"You stopped talking to me." I swirl the spoon through my soup.

He hums a noise. "I did."

"I did too," I admit.

"Would you have stopped if I hadn't?" he asks.

It's a fair question. The truth is I would never have stopped talking to him. I valued him as my friend as much as I had a crush on him, so I shake my head.

"It's not a great excuse, but I just wasn't in a good place back then. Me dropping off the face of the earth never had anything to do with you, Han. Just my own shit."

I nod, offer him a smile of understanding. "I get it." And I do; that's where I've been since losing my dad. "And now?" I ask.

"Am I planning to drop off the face of the earth?"

I smile at my grilled cheese, picking at a piece of charred cheese stuck to the bread, then look up at him as I put the morsel in my mouth.

He watches my fingers, adjusts in his seat as he glances down at his plate before looking back at me. "I think I've come back into the atmosphere and I'm coming in for a landing."

"Me too," I say with a grin.

He picks up the sandwich he's smashed together and takes another bite, chews.

I watch his throat move as he swallows.

"I've actually been thinking about that night a lot," he admits.

"What night?" I ask, lost in watching him.

"The beach."

My eyes dart back to his face, then to my food. "You have?" I take a spoonful of my soup.

"Why are you surprised?"

I sit with his question for a few seconds, mulling it over. "It has been a tough couple of years," I finally say.

He nods with understanding. "Think it will be a smooth landing?"

I grin. "Started out a little bumpy, but it's looking better."

He grins back at me, then chuckles.

We finish our dinner trying to keep our conversation more focused on less personal topics. The game and school. It feels like an easier place to reside. By the time I return home, I float through the front door of my apartment with a smile. Jewel and Joy are cuddled up on the couch like blanketed caterpillars in cocoons, watching something on the computer in front of them. Jewel smiles at me. "You look all hot and bothered. So, was it a date?"

My cheeks heat, and I curse my bright tell. "I think so."

"Not with the beast, right?" Joy asks, frowning, her dark eyes expressions of annoyance at the thought.

"Am I the only one who liked him?" I ask with an incredulous sound that comes through my nose.

"We just don't like how he hurt you. He was shit about it," Jewel says.

"Not Sebastian," I say. "I met up with an old friend from high school."

Jewel presses pause on the computer, cutting the sound. "Oh." Her deep brown eyes are big and bright with possibility. "You didn't mention that earlier. Talk!"

I don't want to get into all the intricacies about Seth, but share an abbreviated version, finishing with, "Sebastian was there."

Joy rolls her eyes, deep and thorough. "Don't tell me. He went all alphahole on you?"

I chuckle. "No. Besides saying 'hi', asking if I'd read his note, and the 'is this a date' question, he left me alone."

Joy's dark eyebrows slash over her dark eyes, and she huffs a sound through her button nose.

"Why? You think he's an alphahole?"

Joy nods. "Under the right circumstances, yes."

This isn't ever how I've seen him.

My phone pings with a new message. I fish it from my purse and smile when I see it's from Seth.

*Did you make it home safe?*

*Just did. You?*

*All safe and buttoned up.*

> *Good. Thank you again for the game and dinner.*

"Look at her cheesy smile," Jewel says to Joy.

"Stop," I tell her and giggle, my face so hot.

Jewel and Joy laugh.

> *When do I get to spend time with you again?*

"He wants to know when he can see me again." I look up at my friends and wiggle the phone back and forth.

Jewel unfolds herself from the cocoon, trips out of the blanket, and jumps up like a kernel of hot corn. "Let me see!" She snags the phone from my hand.

"Don't text anything!" I grasp her hand and draw her back to me, taking the phone from her. "What should I say?"

There's a knock at the door.

Jewel walks across the room to open it. "You should tell him you're in need of some good dick," she says and laughs with her nose scrunched up as she opens the door.

My smile fades.

Sebastian is standing on the other side, his hands shoved into his pockets. His frame takes up most of the doorway. When I see him, I recall how easy it was to feel attracted to him; he is very attractive. His handsome face is etched with perfect symmetry and proportion, his mouth framed by a strong and defined jaw covered with facial hair. His auburn hair is styled into that coif that rises over his forehead and his thick eyebrows shift over his light eyes with a question mark. Strength moves through his body even when he isn't moving. He's a beautiful person on the outside, and he isn't so bad on the inside either, even if he's hurt me.

"Speaking of dicks," Jewel says, walking away from the open door.

"Hi to you too, Jewel." Sebastian's eyes jump from her back to me with a scowl on his face. There's never been much love lost between them. "I was wondering if we could talk?" he asks me.

"We'll watch this in my room," Jewel announces as she and Joy shuffle down the hallway rewrapped in blankets, carting the laptop with them. When the door to her room clicks shut, it's as loud as if she'd slammed it.

"What are you doing here?" I ask. "I think we've already had this conversation."

"May I come in?"

I step back, and he steps over the threshold. I have a fleeting thought that I just invited a vampire into my home, allowed him to cross into my space to suck me dry. I take a deep breath to center and focus myself, turning to walk into the kitchen where I can put the counter between me and my ex.

After closing the door, Sebastian follows but doesn't say anything.

I face him, leaning against the counter on the opposite side of the kitchen. My hands holding onto the counter on either side of my hips, I wait.

His gaze runs the length of me.

Six months ago, that look would have initiated a glowing warmth of want. Now, I just feel impatient, which is strange considering I'd thought myself in love with this man only three months ago. I'd thought he was the one I'd marry.

"You look good."

"That's what you came to say?"

He runs a hand through his hair, swipes it back and forth, rearranging the locks until they are in the right place, and sighs. "You didn't text me back."

"Right. I didn't."

He looks at me, waiting for a more detailed response.

"Wait. Did you think you were owed one?"

He makes a noise through his nose. "Yeah. I mean, isn't it only polite to reply? And I wrote you a note. The least you could do–"

"The least I could do?" I lean against the counter, its edge sharp against the small of my back, and cross my arms over my chest. "The least I could do," I repeat, shocked, shaking my head.

"I would always text you back, Hannah."

"Really? Because I'm pretty sure there were a lot of times you didn't."

"You're always so sensitive." He shakes his head with a slight grin. "I always told you why at least."

"You think I should tell you why?"

His lips press together in that characteristic line of annoyance. He doesn't answer, and in the past, I would have noticed and jumped in to placate him, keep things even and easy. But that need doesn't feel as strong. I'm settled in not being with him.

"I'm not going to tell you why. I don't have to anymore."

With a frustrated sound like an engine attempting to turn over, Sebastian leans over the counter toward me, elbows on the countertop. He waits several seconds, takes several breaths, as if waiting for me to fill the silence, which I would have done at one time. When I don't, he says, "I wanted to say I'm sorry."

I want to narrow my eyes but keep them impassive. I tilt my head. "Okay."

"I miss you. I messed up, and I just want to know if we could start over."

Had he asked me before I left for winter vacation, I probably would have said "yes." I was hurt, but I would have rationalized that people make mistakes—I had, after all. I would have convinced myself that Sebastian had seen the error of his ways. That I'd never find another person like him, someone so attentive, so caring; someone who needed me.

All the reasons we failed rear their ugly heads. We'd stopped talking, really talking. We'd started existing in motions of coupledom, in the comfort of just having someone. We'd stopped kissing, and touching, and having sex. We'd started fighting. A lot. He'd insinuated that night we broke up that I wasn't enough, and I'd believed him—still sort of did, on an emotional level even if my rational side is beginning to offer me a new narrative. He was seeing someone else before ending it with me.

Now, I shake my head.

"Don't say no, Hannah. Not yet. Not before you've heard me out."

We have nine months of history between us. There's the first time we spoke in the stacks at the Ham, when he asked for my number. Those excited flutters in my chest told me I was special because I'd somehow captured his attention. There was our second date at a tiny little rib joint in Old Town when he offered a little vulnerability about his last girlfriend and my heart reached toward him. That's where we shared our first kiss that same night when I'd swiped barbeque sauce from the corner of his mouth. The list of a nine-month life together stacking experiences upon experiences: meeting one another's families, sex, planning a future—our future—beyond college, hanging out with friends, doing the things couples do. When the essence of what once made us leaked away, all that was left was a hollow version of the couple we'd become. In hindsight, I see why he'd cheated, and despite all that history, I know I can't go forward by going backward.

"Here's the thing, Sebastian. I don't have to hear you out. You said what you needed to say weeks ago. You communicated all you needed to. You're with someone new. And now, you've asked forgiveness. Great. I've heard you. Forgiven." I hold my hands out as if letting it go.

He groans and moves around the counter, leans against it opposite me, his hands on the countertop framing his hips.

I consider putting more distance between us by walking past him into the living room, but I hold my position.

"I'm not with Chelsey. I mean, we went out a couple of times, but I promise, Hannah, over the break all I thought about was you. She isn't you."

"And you didn't call? No text. No Merry Christmas. No Happy New Year. You waited until two weeks after we returned to school."

He looks down at his feet. "I was trying to figure some stuff out."

"Did you?"

He looks up and pins me with that disconcerting stare of his. A stare I once found difficult to extricate from the dendrites of my brain firing on Sebastian cylinders. "Yes. I did. I realized I'd made a gigantic mistake ending things with you. I want you back. What we had–"

Only those Sebastian cylinders have weakened in my head and aren't in my heart anymore. "You were right to do it," I admit. "And an *us* isn't going to happen."

He shakes his head and straightens. "No. No." He closes the distance between us.

I straighten, backed against the counter, tense and trapped. He's so close, and large, and encompasses the space around me, sucking up all the oxygen. I'm not afraid of him; Sebastian hasn't ever been anything but respectful of me physically, but now, he's invaded my space, and I'm not liking it. The good, nice girl in me—who justifies that we've been closer than this before—wars with the one who would like to shove him away. He isn't touching me, but I'm caught between his arms, his hands on either side of me, hemming me in between him and the counter. I suddenly feel very small.

"That's not how this is supposed to go," he says.

"It was over long before you ended it," I say, staring at his chest, somehow finding the bravery to express the truth, but my voice has a thready quality to it. "It just took you walking away to make me see it."

He shakes his head and presses his forehead to mine. "Hannah. Please. We were good together. I miss you."

I smell the spearmint of his breath, a scent that at one time I found pleasing. I press a hand to his chest and push him away. He capitulates, stepping back.

"I need you to go."

He looks shocked, as if this wasn't the outcome he expected, and I can probably imagine the outcome he did. Twelve-weeks-ago Hannah would have taken him back. I'd have acquiesced, found a way to accommodate his needs and silence my own. There's even a fraction of me who wants to do it now, so I don't upset the balance of things, to return to what's easy, comfortable, the path of least resistance. Except there's been a shift inside me.

It's not a seismic earthquake upending me, but cracks shifting my perspective from what it was, to expose the truth and the pain from which I've been trying to rebuild. I'm noticing.

When I sat with Seth, and we laughed like we used to. When he took my hand, offering me comfort rather than the other way around. When the underside of my skin burned with just the reminder of our shared kiss. I was more alive than I have been in a long time, like the version of Hannah I once liked, long before my dad died.

"But–" Sebastian stops, his brows shifting over his eyes with confusion. He's reeling and confused because he's not getting what he wants.

My phone, still in one of my hands, pings, but I don't move.

Sebastian takes a fraction of another step away. "Is that him?"

Tiny kindling of an angry fire ignites in my gut. "I'm not sure what business it is of yours."

His frown deepens. "Marco says you knew him from high school. Is he the one? That crush you had?"

I don't respond because I'm annoyed, and it's suddenly clear why Sebastian is here. This isn't about me at all, and I think that hurts even worse. To know that the only reason he's here is because there might be someone else in my life. That he didn't want me nine weeks ago, but now he doesn't want to let me go so I can find my own happiness. It makes me feel sick.

"I need you to go."

"I'm going to win you back," he says. "He's not right for you."

"That's not for you to decide. Please go," I say again.

"Hannah!" I hear Jewel before I see her. She rounds the corner from the hallway into the kitchen. "I wondered if–" She pauses, coming to an abrupt stop at the edge of the linoleum. Her eyes narrow as she crosses her arms over her chest. "Oh. I thought you'd gone."

Sebastian takes another look at me, his face a strange mixture of crestfallen and determined. His eyes are large and pleading, while his mouth is shaped with a frown. Shaking his head, then looks at Jewel and says, "I was just leaving." He turns and disappears through the front door.

"Are you okay?" Jewel asks after he's gone.

"You were listening."

"Fuck yeah, I was. He wasn't going to go. You asked him like a thousand times."

"Two."

"One too many."

"Thanks, Jewels."

"That's why I'm here, sis." She backs out of the kitchen. "Got a movie to finish and a girl to take care of." She wiggles her eyebrows. As she backs away, she says, "See." She points at me. "Strong." She smiles.

I smile to reassure her, because I love her, and when I'm alone, I take several deep breaths to calm the way my heart bounces around erratically inside my chest, not wanting to consider any more sinister possibilities had Sebastian been less than a good guy.

*My Heart Insists that it's Time for a New Pattern*

Although I've told myself not to make a big deal about the fact Hannah has left me *on read*, my heart and body haven't gotten the memo. While the logical side of me is trying to tell the rest of me to remain calm, my insides are bouncing around with anticipation and worry, like balls from one of those lottery ball machines. I'm lying on my bed, showered, and thinking, replaying all the moments we shared that night.

Her ex-boyfriend showing up at the game could have derailed our time together. It hadn't.

The risk of taking her hand in mine hadn't felt like too much of a risk. I'd been responding to her on an emotional level, which could have been an overstep, but she'd seemed to need comfort. It was accepted, reciprocated even.

Our history rooted in friendship took us back to the beginning when laughing and enjoying one another's company was as natural and easy as breathing.

And then dinner. There had been a shift between us.

Talking about the beach. Her blush.

She's still into the idea of us, and I think I probably floated through the rest of the meal.

I look at my phone and wonder if maybe I should have waited to text, but that feels like a younger Seth choice. A game, or rather, a lie. This new and improved Seth is really working hard to stay present in his feelings. To be honest with himself, and now her.

She texted back right away, but now she's gone quiet.

I'm in my head, freaking out and wondering if I've done something that was too much, came on too strong. When my phone alerts a new text, I jump from my skin—lunging for it—and push the device off my nightstand where it thuds on the floor. I dive for it, hanging off the side of my bed, and slide the screen open. When I see Hannah's name, I take a breath of relief.

> *Sorry. Got caught up with something.*
> *Yes. I'd like to hang out more.*

I right myself on the bed and text her back: *Everything okay?*

> *Yes. Sebastian showed up at my apartment.*
> *Thank goodness for my roommate.*

My body tenses. It's the last words that freak me out: *Thank goodness for my roommate.* Thoughts swirl filling gaps of what isn't said. Why would she be glad her roommate was there? Was she threatened? I text her back:

> *Whoa. Did you need your roommate there because he was out of line?*

> *No. No. Sorry. He was trying to beat a dead horse, and I had to ask him to leave a couple of times.*

He'd gone over to get her back, and I suspected he would do as much at the game when I saw him. I'm not sure how I knew, but there's something about him that feels familiar even if I can't identify why, yet. *A couple of times?* I wonder if she's being flippant about his appearance and his disrespect of her wishes for my benefit or telling herself it isn't an issue. I wonder what she wants and ask her:

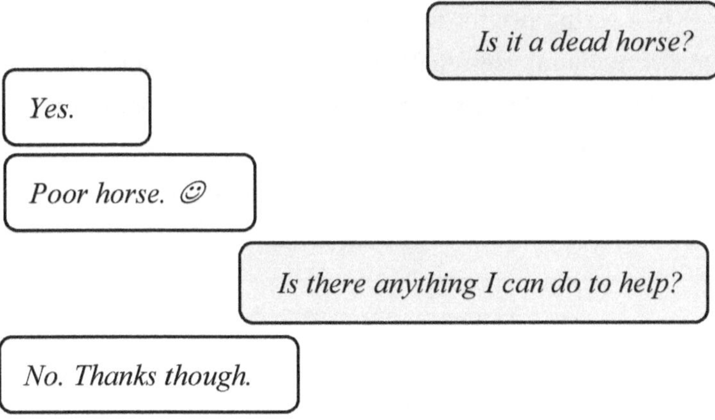

I decide it's probably best to change the subject and get to the reason we're texting in the first place.

> *So if you're open to hanging out some more, what are you doing this weekend?*

> *I'm going home. To Cantos.*

> *Right. When do you get back?*

> *Sunday. Maybe we can hang out when I get back?*

> *I'd like that.*

Not seeing her for two days sounds like a horrible stretch of time. I remind myself that I've been without Hannah for two and a half years before reestablishing this connection, but it doesn't bring me comfort.

> *I'll text you when I get back to town.*

> *Great. And you don't have to wait until then. ;)*

> *☺ Good to know.*

I'm not sure how to keep the thread going since it seems like we've come to a stopping point, but I don't want to stop talking to her. I just don't know what to say to build a new bridge. I don't want to say the wrong thing or be too forward. I know we're friends, but I also know that the reality is we're getting to know one another again. She's had experiences I don't know about, and the same for me. As I'm overthinking it, my phone alerts me.

*What are you doing right now?*

*Lying in bed, texting with you.*

*Want to talk? Instead of text.*

Fuck, yes! I sit up.

*Sure.*

*Let me get a quick shower. I'll facetime you after.*

I can't stop the smile that spreads across my face.

*Okay.*

While I wait, I clean up my space. Not that it's super messy. I tend to be neat. There was a time when I believed I did it because I grew up with a drunk tyrant who beat the crap out of me if things weren't in their place. So, to avoid conflict, I did everything to appease my father's mercurial moods. Some things stuck. I once told Dr. Bethany that I tried to be a mess after I left home, during that first year of college, and hadn't been able to do it.

"Why do you think that was difficult?" she'd asked.

"I think maybe I'm still afraid," I'd said. "Like if I step out of the line he set, then the world will collapse into what it once was."

"Could you predict the line of his that you might cross to make it collapse?"

"No. I mean, I knew what had set him off before and did everything I could to make sure not to repeat those mistakes."

"And by not repeating the mistakes, did it keep him from hurting you? From getting angry again?"

"No."

"So, what if your need to clean up has nothing to do with him, but instead, something *you* like?"

Dr. Bethany's question had been the first time I'd considered that my opinions were my own in and of themselves and not some way to stick it to my dad or keep him from lashing out. That moment had felt like a mental turning point.

My phone rings.

I situate myself on my bed, leaning against the wall with a pillow behind me and answer it.

Hannah's face comes into focus on my screen. She looks so pretty in the low light of her room that has those strings of tiny, white lights, and she's leaning against a wall. Her blond hair is wet, slightly waving around her smiling face. She's got on a teal sweatshirt. "Hey." She smiles. "Every time I see you now, I freak out for a split second."

Her admission makes me grin. "Why?"

"I went so long without seeing you. And now, when I do, it's like my heart does a little double take to remind myself you're real."

Her words hit me like a gut punch, and it's a good thing I'm sitting down; they'd take my feet out from under me. I don't know how to interpret them, but I can interpret the feelings rushing through me that have me trying to catch my breath. Happiness and hope, and I don't know if maybe I'm feeling them too soon. I remind myself that maybe she doesn't mean them like I've interpreted them. "I'm real last I checked."

"I'm glad. I mean, glad that you're here."

I notice her blush, which warms my insides. She can't hide them at all, which I think is really cute. "Me too." I grin at my screen. "Why are you going to Cantos?"

Her smile slides and while her lips remain curled, it's the smile in her eyes that tempers. "It's the anniversary of my dad's…"

"Oh." My heart twists for her. "Do you have a plan to honor him?"

She shrugs. "He had some favorite things he liked to do. That's what we did last year." She clears her throat and offers me a smile. "What will you do? Here?"

"Really important stuff. You know, homework and working out."

Her smile brightens. "No parties with Trace?"

I shake my head, my smile slipping this time. "I don't really party anymore."

Her head tilts, taking that in. "Oh. Really?"

I offer a self-conscious affirmation with a slight movement of my head. This is the past catching up with me. Those from Cantos are aware of part of the truth, and my difficulty facing it. My heart speeds up in my chest. I've always thought these truths make me unlovable. I mostly know that isn't true, but there are days when that lie rears its ugly head. Having to confront it with Hannah makes it terrifying. "Better if I don't. I don't really drink anymore. After the accident–"

She takes in what I've said and ponders it. I can see her thinking, a sliver of her bottom lip disappearing between her teeth. Her head tilts a touch further, and her eyes jump around until they reconnect with me. "Is that what you meant when you said you were going through stuff? Back then?"

"Yes. That and some."

She nods, empathetic to my explanation. I can see she wants to ask about my dad, but for whatever reason, doesn't.

"My dad is an alcoholic," I share, which I hope lets her know I trust her. "In high school, I think I was right in line of finding a way to step into his shoes. But–"

She waits for me to continue speaking.

I'm self-conscious. Other than Dr. B, Gabe and, Abby, I haven't really talked to anyone else about it. My ex-girlfriends knew a glossy, abridged version. It isn't easy to face.

"You don't have to–"

"I want to, Hannah." With her, I do. I think. But my insecurities wreak havoc on my rational thoughts, however. "It's just … ugly."

She takes a deep breath and closes her eyes, making me wonder if she has her own uncomfortable layers I don't know. And why wouldn't she? Why wouldn't any one of us? Life is like that.

Like Dr. B says, *"Life has a way of moving us around in similar patterns until we face the discomfort and make the change."* I wonder what Hannah's patterns are. I can see mine. Shutting down, like with my exes. Being afraid of opening up. Which makes me realize I can keep doing the same thing with Hannah or make a different choice. That Einstein quote about insanity and doing the same thing but expecting a different result. I'd lived that and am trying to change it.

"I'm here to listen, you know, whenever."

"I appreciate that," I tell her and smile. "I knew that then, too."

"You didn't talk to me."

I shake my head. "I didn't really confide in anyone. Just Abby and Gabe."

A bit of her lip disappears again, and I try to focus on what we're talking about rather than the image of drawing that lower lip into my mouth with my teeth, which grabs ahold of my gut and spins it. I feel the thought deep and take a breath.

"We were friends. I would have listened."

I nod. "There's a big difference," I say, and regret it because the follow up is going to reveal a lot about my feelings.

"And what is that?"

I realize I have a choice to tell the truth or to play it with a glossy version. I hear Dr. Bethany's question: *What do you gain by playing your life safe?* So, I take a deep breath and commit. "I didn't have a crush on Abby or Gabe," I admit and offer her a smile. "That's what's different."

She fumbles the phone. "Sorry," she says when her face reappears. She's beet red, and I can't help but smile. "You did?"

"Are you telling me you didn't know?"

"I didn't."

I laugh. "And here I thought I was super obvious."

She smiles. "How? You never said a thing. There was only one time, maybe two that I wondered about, then fantasized with hope."

"Fantasized?" I can feel my surprised expression on my face slide toward my belly with heat.

She grins, still blushing furiously. "This particular teenage girl fantasies probably aren't the same as what I think you might be imagining."

I laugh. "Okay, then. I'm curious. What were these infamous moments you wondered about?"

She adjusts, and I can see she's shy about it, her eyes somewhere else. "Well." She stretches out the word and situates herself into what I assume must be a more comfortable position. "There was this one time when we were working on the homecoming float. It was just you and me stuffing the chicken wire with tissue paper on our own side of the float." She stops talking.

"And?" I prod. I don't remember it but wish I did.

She's blushing. "That's it."

"That's it? Goodness, I must have really given myself away." She giggles.

"You're going to have to jog my memory with more specifics, Hannah."

She groans and covers her face with a hand. "I don't know. There was just this moment...  when our eyes met...  and I couldn't–"

"Couldn't what?"

"Couldn't stop analyzing it." She shakes her head with a sheepish grin.

"And then?"

"That's it. You got up and walked away." She says it sort of strung together so I have to decipher it.

I can't help but grin. "Most of the time I was around you during senior year, I wanted to kiss you. I bet I just got nervous and moved."

She peeks through her fingers, then takes her hand away from her face. "You're teasing me."

"No. I'm not. I wanted to ask you to prom and chickened out."

"Why didn't you?" She leans forward with the vehemence in her question.

"Because that kid from Newport beat me to it."

"He didn't ask me."

"What?"

"I asked him because I was afraid no one was going to ask me, and I needed a date because I was on the committee."

"Had I known that, Hannah, I would have asked you to dance more than once."

"I remember that dance."

It's my turn for a blush to warm my face, the heat suffusing my head and neck. "I'm sorry for that."

"Why? It was my best dance of the night."

I'm taken aback by her admission. "How can that be? I didn't even talk to you."

"Because it had been with you."

My palms heat, and I remember her hand in mine earlier. My heart is a thousand marathon runners pounding against the inside of my chest. I don't want to play this safe. She's my friend, yes, but I'm feeling so much more than friendship. I want to know if

I'm interpreting her honestly or through colored lenses of want. "Hannah?"

"Yes?" Her voice is quiet.

"I wanted to kiss you all the time. I probably did want to kiss you when we were working on that float. I wanted to kiss you at prom when we'd danced, and I'd been too nervous to even talk to you. I wanted to kiss you after graduation. When we finally did during the 4th of July party, I didn't want to stop." I swallow. "And to be completely honest, I wanted to kiss you tonight. And I'd like to kiss you now."

She covers her face, again, and makes a strangled sound.

I freak out, a little worried I've revealed too much, given too much of myself away too soon, but I remind myself I'd played it safe with her before. I'm facing a pattern—my pattern—and trying to change it.

When she takes away her hand, she's smiling, bright and bold, and so Hannah from high school. "I would have kissed you back all of those times," she says, "tonight, too." Her eyes look glossy and bright, and I wonder if she's tearing up.

"Did I say too much?" I ask. "It is too soon?"

She shakes her head, and sure enough a tear slips from her eye. She swipes it away. "Sorry. I thought it was just me."

"You're crying?" I adjust myself, sitting up straighter, and wish we were sitting next to one another instead of talking over Facetime. "Shit, Hannah. And right after I admit that I'd like to kiss you. That's a confidence killer." I smile, hoping to disarm her.

She giggles. "No! It's just that, I feel–" she cuts off what she would have said and adds– "it feels a little surreal. And now I don't want to go home, but it's the anniversary, and my mom needs me, so I have to. But I'd rather stay. Rather see you." She strings the words and thoughts together. A very Hannah thing to do.

"Are you going to be okay going home by yourself?" And I wonder why I've asked. Am I willing to go with her, back to Cantos? And I realize I would.

She nods. "Yes. Now I'll be looking forward to coming back." She smiles and scoots down into her bed, laying down. Her hair spreads around her face like a halo, and my belly tightens thinking of the possibility of seeing her in real life like that under me. My body sheltered in hers. I look away to stop the train of my thoughts.

We continue to reminisce, laugh about being adolescents.

Eventually her eyes flick to something off screen as she says, "You know about my last relationship. Came face to face with him. What about yours?"

Amber. I take a deep breath. "That ended a while ago. April of last year."

"May I ask about it."

I adjust myself on my bed, laying back, preparing. "Sure. Go."

Hannah looks up, her eyes and face scrunching to one side as she thinks about what she wants to ask, and I wish I was with her again. Wish I was lying next to her, so I could press a finger against her pretty mouth, then run it down the curve of her chin, trace her neck. My heart slams against the inside of my chest cavity with force.

"Did you love her?"

"We were together for five months. I think I thought I did, but there were lots of things that contributed to us breaking up."

"Like?"

"Me, mostly."

Her eyebrows arch over her eyes as if I've surprised her. I suppose it might be a surprise to someone who knew me way back when. Taking responsibility for the part I played in things hadn't been my strong suit. I didn't start that journey until after I woke up from the car wreck. She doesn't say anything, though, waiting for me to elaborate.

It's only fair, I figure, but I also hear Dr. B's words in my head. *A new pattern.*

"I'm not the greatest at opening up."

"What? No!" Hannah grins at me.

I chuckled. "Shut up."

"Tell me more," she says and pulls her blanket up to her shoulders.

So, I do, and as the story emerges from inside of me and out into the space between us, I realize how much better I feel having taken the risk to be honest with her, to be vulnerable. I'm still alive, still smiling, and full of feelings of victory, somehow.

We fall asleep with the app open, because when I wake up, my phone is dead.

*My Heart Insists that Home has Changed*

Walking into my childhood home is a messy mix of emotions: poignancy, relief, grief, and impatience. Most of which are in competition with one another and make me feel stripped of my protective covering. I'm a kaleidoscope of feelings, all of which are working to make me feel unsettled and uprooted. A torn and scattered mosaic trying to be put back together into a cohesive pattern. I wonder if I can call this home anymore when a percentage of me is being tugged back over the mountain from where I've just driven, where there's something new blooming in my heart. A reawakening. What's new is the insecurity in it. Over the last year the only place I wanted to be was home. I wonder if my desire to return to the reconnection with Seth is my allegiance being tested, and I'm failing. But my allegiance to what?

The house where I've spent most of my life is quiet when I walk inside. "I'm home," I call as I stomp my boots on the rug in the mudroom between the backyard and kitchen, then toe off my boots to stash next to the others: my mom's, my sister's. My eyes linger on my dad's boots still sitting there.

"Hello?"

I catch sight of a box filled with items set on the bench seat. Inside is a cup that my dad had in the garage workshop. Other items include stuff he used around the house but aren't necessarily useful to anyone else. I wonder why they're sitting there, knowing my mom hates things out of place.

I traipse into the kitchen. "Hello? Mom? Rue?" I call, thinking they must be upstairs. With my overnight bag in my hand, I lug it up the stairs and dump it in my room on the end of my bed. The space looks the same as the last time I was home over winter break. My double bed is covered with a quilt my grandma made, a rainbow of colors. My walls are still buttercream yellow. They still have a mixture of posters and framed pictures with inspirational sayings on them. Still dominating the wall next to my bed, situated just above a desk, is a tack board with mementos pinned there I thought were important at the time.

I walk closer and skim the saved items. Pictures of my family, a ticket to a movie, a flier I'd made announcing the trick-or-treat community service project, several pictures of my friends and me. I look for Seth and find him, the essence of him the same, but younger; my body feels the smile on my face as I study them.

There are several articles I'd printed, pinned to the board. My heart flutters at Seth's face prominently displayed on one. He's at the center of his team, being held up among them, a giant smile on his face. It was taken from the state soccer tournament. They'd won the semi-final game, even though our team had gone in as the underdog.

We'd followed the bus into the valley to watch and cheer. I remember sitting with Abby and Gabe in the stands surrounded by our schoolmates and parents, then driving an hour home to Cantos, to wait for the bus's return.

There are flashes in my mind of it. The bus pulling into the parking lot. The feeling of excitement rushing through me knowing Seth was there. Seth's smile and his eyes meeting mine as he descended from the bus. His animated gushing about the game winning goal. He'd hugged me, and I remember wondering if he held on just a little longer than usual.

One of those moments I'd replayed over and over in my mind.

I'd been happy then, but it wasn't just happy, it was secure. When my father died, I think besides the grief and the guilt, perhaps that security had been stripped from me. I thought I'd found it in Sebastian and see now that belief had been misguided. My father would have been the first to tell me that my security must be wrapped up in myself. I'd lost sight of that when it felt like my choice tore my world apart. But when I look at these pictures of me and my friends, I see it in my face. I remember that feeling, and it wasn't just about my dad being alive. I'd lived it, as if I understood it was in the foundation of what made me, me.

I glance in the mirror as awareness races across my skin. A deep inner voice—a quiet one—tells me to grasp hold of that thought and cling to it.

With a sigh, I leave my room. "Mom? Rue?" I peek into my mom's room. Empty. No Answer. "Where are you?" Ruth's room. No answer.

I skim the surface of the main floor. No one.

I go down the stairs and peek into the finished basement. Also empty.

When I'm standing back in the kitchen, I send Ruth a text: *Hey? I'm home. Where are you?*

She doesn't answer, which is odd, because Rue can't seem to function without her phone in her hand.

My heart picks up speed, but I remind myself that someone would have called me. Right? If there was an emergency? Unless both—

No.

I force my thoughts to remain in the present.

I text Mom: *I'm home. Where are you?*

Mom answers immediately, and my heartbeat finds a normal pace.

> *Hi hon! At the high school with your sister.*
> *She has a cheerleading competition today.*

Irrationally put out by not knowing where they would be turns from worry to irritation. I drove home to be with them, made the journey to collectively grieve Dad together, and they aren't here. Then I feel the slam of guilt. I hadn't been there when he died. They had been.

> *Come join me. Ruthie would love it.*

> *I'll be there soon.*

I don't want to go to a cheerleading event, but I love my sister, so I'll go to offer her my support. Besides, I came home to be with them.

I'm not sure how I feel about returning to my high school where I'll be faced with memories, even if they are good ones. I'll be surrounded with memories of Seth, reminding me I'd rather be back in Linden Falls, closer to an opportunity to spend more time with him. Maybe get to kiss him. My body warms from the inside out considering it, his admission almost 12 hours later still making my heart flutter. Only, I'm supposed to be concentrating on my time here, honoring my dad.

If I thought walking into my house was strange, returning to Cantos High School is even stranger. The single-story building with multiple wings stretches out across the campus like a brick, metal, and glass mid-century nod to Frank Lloyd Wright. I haven't been back since I graduated, so driving into the parking lot, selecting a spot away from the one I'd gravitated toward while I was a student feels unnatural. I do it anyway.

With a green umbrella dotted with black umbrellas that look like raindrops, I walk from my car around the campus to the gym entrance. Once up the steps, I stop at the sign outside the gym, juggle my umbrella, and somehow snap a selfie. I send it to Seth, then to Abby.

I glance at the steps. We used to sit out here on warm spring days. I remember junior year, sitting here watching a bunch of the guys throw a frisbee. Seth had sat with me and Abby then, watching, because he'd still been in physical therapy to get his body functioning again after the accident. I don't remember what we talked about, but I remember the contentment.

I pay my admission fee at the door and walk into the public lobby of the gym. Nothing has changed, as if I was just there, walking the campus as a student, telling secrets with Abby. And yet everything has. The swirl of cadenced voices, the throngs of matching teams moving as herds, the smell of popcorn at the concession is controlled chaos. I remember sitting in the space, watching people walk by, waiting for class to start, hoping to catch glimpses of my crush, senior year, Seth. I remember the aftermath of a win, emerging from the gym on the way to a dance, or someone's house, the joy, the unencumbered vibrancy of those emotions.

"Nanna!"

I twirl, hearing my little sister's voice call the nickname she coined at age three. She nearly knocks me over, rushing at me full throttle.

"You're here!"

"Of course."

She steps back, all smiles, and I'm struck with the fact she looks older even though I just saw her a few weeks ago. Her blond hair, a touch darker than mine and not as curly, is tucked into her tight ponytail. It's secured with an overly large red bow. She's grinning, her blue eyes dancing as she looks at me.

"I didn't know you had a competition, or I would have been here earlier. I'm sorry." Now that I'm standing here and looking at that bright smile on her face, I'm glad I'm here supporting her.

"I forgot to tell you. It's okay." She tugs at her black and red uniform skirt. "Did you bring the gummies."

I nod. "Did you perform yet?"

"The first round." She glances over her shoulder at her team sitting at the tables near the wall, then back at me. "We're waiting for the results to announce the second round."

"Think you made it?"

"Yes."

"How many rounds?"

"Three."

It will be a long day, I realize. "I'll go find Mom, then."

Rue points out where Mom's sitting through the doors, then gives me another heavy-handed hug. "I'm so glad you're here."

With my sister's arms around me, I am too.

When I finally find Mom, she's sitting in the bleachers talking with a man I don't recognize. I get an uneasy feeling noticing their smiles. They look like flirty smiles, not polite ones, eyes glittering, leaning forward, bodies turned toward one another. I notice the familiarity in their countenance, in the way I've been feeling this week with Seth but ignore the hypocrisy in feeling bitter about it. Instead, I narrow my eyes. "Hi."

My mom turns her head and takes a split-second too long to recognize me. Her head is somewhere else. "Hey sweetie." She adjusts so I can sit next to her, patting the red bench seat next to her as she looks up at me, her blue eyes twinkling with happiness.

I lean and give her a hug.

She hugs me back. "It's good to have you home."

I glance at the man a few feet away, who's now staring at the floor where a team performs. He looks like a handsome guy, salt-n-pepper hair, physically fit, and a strong profile. Mom isn't looking at me, staring at the cheerleading team with a smile on her face.

Her gaze shifts to me when I take a seat next to her. "How was the drive?"

"Easy. Clear roads." I lean toward her and drop my voice, "Who's your friend?"

She leans back to look at me, confused. "Who?"

I tell her with my eyes.

She glances at the man, then back at me. "Oh. That's one of Ruthie's teammate's dads."

I wait for more details, but she doesn't add any, which seems louder and more telling than if she had. "Does he have a name?"

"Oh. Right. Kit."

"Married?"

"What's with the twenty questions?" she asks with a defensive edge in her tone as she smooths her hands over her jean-clad thighs.

She's flustered and glances at the mysterious Kit again. He's now staring at his phone; I wonder if he's trying to listen to our conversation.

My first reaction is annoyance, though it's irrational. I'm feeling protective of my dad's memory. It makes me feel prickly, and I wonder if Mom is attracted to that stranger. Even rationalizing that dad's been gone two years, I can't seem to disengage the daughter part of my brain.

A selfie of Seth vibrates my phone. He's in the student athletic center, dressed in workout apparel, the indoor climbing wall behind him, the colorful feet and handholds looking like stray, colorful chewed bubblegum stuck to the surface. My stomach flutters at his smile, dimples pronounced in his cheeks, his amber eyes curled up and sparking with light. He's used a band to push the hair off his face, and I notice the way the fitted black athletic shirt leaves very little to imagine about his body, the slope and ridges of his shoulders and arms. He might not be competitively playing soccer anymore, but he's fit. Fit. Fit. Fit. Fit. He's giving me a single thumbs up.

> *Please don't hurt yourself.*

> *Pfft. ;)*

"What's so funny?" Mom asks.

I click the screen closed in a tiny rebellion not inclined to share if she isn't either. "Nothing."

"Third place is a great finish," my mom tells Ruth later as we sit at The Diner after the competition.

Rue slumps over the ivory table looking at her phone, still dressed in her red and black uniform, blending in with the red booth seat and the black and white checkered floor. The jukebox plays an Elvis song. One of her arms stretches out across the table, her head in her hand, the other one scrolling through her phone with a repetitious flick of her thumb.

"I know that," she says, without glancing up, and takes a sip of her soda, barely moving when she does.

I see my mom press her teeth together with strained patience.

I'm not sure why it makes me want to laugh, but I opt for diplomacy. "I enjoyed it." It's a partial lie. I enjoyed being supportive of my sister, but I didn't like spending the day at the gym watching multiple cheer routines that all looked the same after a while. I'd have rather been hanging out with Seth.

We're still waiting for our food.

"Oh my god," Rue says, her eyeballs bulging out of her eye sockets as she ducks her face. "Hide me."

"Ruth Fleming! Don't use the Lord's name in vain," Mom scolds her.

Rue shushes our mom at the same moment I catch sight of two young men walking toward us. Twins.

Abby's brothers, Nate and Matt. They look so grown up. The last time I saw them was that summer just after graduation. Their dark, wavy hair is naturally streaked with honey highlights, light brown skin sprinkled with freckles on their cheeks and noses. Dark brown eyes and heavy eyebrows to frame them. They're taller—at least six feet now, I figure—taller than Abby. Both are athletically fit—Nate plays football, Matt, soccer. Both play basketball. There's a promise in the way they will eventually grow into their bodies in the coming years.

I glance at Ruth, who's blushing furiously—cursed with the same tell as me—and using a death ray stare on her phone.

"Nate? Matt?"

"Nanna," Ruth angry-whispers at me, mortified that I've tried to get their attention.

Both look at me in unison, which is disconcerting when you aren't used to watching two people move as a unit.

Nate smiles. "Hannah!" He closes the distance to the table. Matt follows.

I stand up and hug Nate, who hugs me back. "How are you?" I ask.

Matt leans forward. "Hey, Hannah." He gives me one of those awkward side hugs. It makes me smile, the way these two boys are so different from one another and yet the same.

"Good. Really good," Nate says.

"Seniors now, right?" I ask. "The countdown is on."

"Ready to graduate," Nate answers with his kind smile. I suddenly miss Abby so much seeing them. I didn't get to see her over winter break, since the family spent it in Hawaii.

"Get your acceptances yet?" I ask.

"I got early admission to NYU," Nate says. "But it's expensive. I'll probably stay here in Oregon."

Of course he did. And of course he'd think about what's most responsible. "That would be cheaper." I look at Matt.

"No acceptance yet," the other twin says.

"Got a first choice?"

"There's this art school in Georgia, I'm interested in, but I applied to some other schools too."

"Art?" I'm not sure why this surprises me.

"Animation," he says. "Computers."

I nod as if this clarifies. "Not following Abby, then?"

Matt makes an incredulous noise that moves through his nose, but he also smiles. "No way." Even with Matt's contrast to Nate's friendliness and ease, I know how much he loves his sister.

"What are you doing here?" Nate asks.

"Just came for a visit with my family. You know Ruth, right?" I glance at my sister, whose face has suddenly morphed into the most apathetic expression with a twinge of bored indifference—except for that blush.

"Hey," she says with a slight wave.

Matt offers her a head nod.

Nate, a smile. "How did the competition go today?" he asks her.

Rue's blush deepens, and she sputters before finding her tongue. "We came in third place."

"That's good, right?" he asks.

"See," Mom says. "That's what I said."

I notice my sister push my mom's foot with her own under the table, though I'm not sure anyone else would pick up on her subtle movement. Mom glances at my sister and resumes smiling. I'm suddenly thinking about Seth and our senior year, how I never knew he was interested in me, and how hard I worked to hide my own interest. I glance at Ruth a second longer before looking back at the twins.

"Well, I won't keep you. It was good to see you both," I say.

"Abby will be jealous we got to see you," Nate says and glances at Matt, who's already walking away. "See you, Hannah. See you at school, Ruth." He gives me another hug and follows his brother.

I sit back down and glance at my sister, who's staring at her phone. "What the heck, Rue? What was that all about?"

"Stop," she snaps. "So embarrassing."

I look at Mom with a question on my face; she shrugs. Ruth has got a crush on one of the twins, obviously, though it's anyone's guess which one.

Later, once we're home, showered and settling in for the night, I'm in my bed staring at the picture of Seth when there's a knock on my door. Self-conscious, as if I've been looking at porn, I stash the phone under my hip.

Rue peeks inside. "May I come in?"

"Sure." I put my phone down on the nightstand and make room for her as she climbs into the bed with me. She bounces around getting comfortable and pulls my quilt up to her chin. "You planning on a sleepover?"

"Yep."

"Okay. Entrance requires you answer a question."

She turns her head and tilts her head to look up at me. "Go."

"Which one of the twins are you crushing on?"

She sighs and pulls the quilt over her head. "Was it that obvious?" she asks, her voice muffled under the multi-colored quilt.

"Probably just to me, because I know you," I say.

"Nate," she says, still under the blanket.

I smile, and my mind jumps to Seth, and all the ways I crushed on him when I was Ruth's age. All the ways I couldn't admit I felt the way I felt.

The blanket flops open, and Ruth looks at me, sitting up with her hair full of static electricity. "He's just so nice, Nanna. To everyone. How would anyone ever be able to tell if he likes them?"

"Maybe you should try being nice back to him."

Her eyes grow. "What? I am nice."

"You weren't very nice, today. You were more like Matt."

She frowns. "I was not."

I laugh. "Yes. You were."

"He's such a jerk."

I laugh again. "He isn't. He's just–" her description seems right, but I know him, and his off-putting behavior is just– "He's just more reserved," I finally say, settling on the right description.

"So, you're saying I was being a bitch?"

"No. But maybe someone who doesn't know you as well might misinterpret you."

She flops backward against the pillow and raises the blanket over her head. Then she wiggles around under the cover as if she's been electrocuted. "He's just so hot."

I laugh, scoot down in the bed, and draw the cover over my head so I can see her. "Technically they both are, since they are identical."

She shakes her head and rolls to face me. "No! I can totally tell them apart."

"How?" I ask.

After she gives me her analysis of how Nate is different from Matt, we talk in the darkness dissecting every interaction she's had with him over the last month. As she talks, I feel the familiarity of her teen world, but realize how removed I am from it. Different. Grown, I suppose, even though it doesn't seem like that much time has passed since I was her age. It makes me think about how little I knew then and how much I thought I knew, and how my experiences since then have made me more aware.

But I can see how little I still know.

I picture mom sitting with Kit earlier. Standing in her shoes, I understand she's two years removed from the death of Dad. She's fifty, young really, with another lifetime to live. Last year, there was a gigantic hole in my chest. Tears and guilt consumed me like a black hole drawing everything into its mass. I don't feel like that same girl anymore. I know Mom isn't the same. Ruth isn't the same. Though I'm not exactly sure what those changes mean facing an unclear future.

When I wake up the next morning, the light of day shines above the haze of a gray, winter sky. It might be nice to stay in bed, but today is the anniversary of my dad passing. It's why I've come home. I get up, leaving Rue to sleep a bit longer, and go downstairs to find Mom.

"Morning." She glances over her shoulder at me. Her blond hair is pulled back in a short ponytail, and she's dressed like she's going to work out.

"Morning." I drop my head onto her shoulder and wrap an arm around her. "That smells good," I say, already aware of what she's made.

"Dad's favorite," she says, flipping a silver dollar-sized pancake. Sausage links are sizzling on a griddle.

I go for a cup of coffee.

"Pigs-in-a-blanket?" Rue asks as she walks into the kitchen. She's already combed out her hair and shrugged into one of Dad's old USF Law sweatshirts.

After we're situated around the breakfast bar with our plates of food and have said our prayer, we dig into breakfast. Ruth and I recall the first time we each remember pigs-in-a-blanket with Dad. As I take a sip of coffee, I notice Mom isn't eating.

"You okay, Mom?"

She offers a wan smile and takes a sip of her coffee. Then she sets down her cup, crosses her arms, and swipes her hands up and down with a sigh. "I want to go through your father's things. Donate them. I'm ready."

My heart freeze-dries, the blood cracking with the ice until it's just suspended sludge inside of me. When it restarts, I think of the box in the mudroom and suck in a breath.

My mom's eyes jump to mine. "Hannah–"

"I'm okay," I say, nodding, informing myself of this as much as I'm informing her. "I am."

"I'm freaking out about it, and I could use some help, but I can call Rita to come and help me too, if you girls can't…" she says, as if the words are water in a stream finding a way through a rough patch of rocks.

"I don't mind helping," Ruth says, but her voice has lost the brightness.

Though I have tears in my eyes, I nod, because I know it's the right thing to do. It's time—if not for me, then for Mom.

Dad isn't his old clothing, or in the plastic mug that was on his workbench. He isn't the mud boots he wore to work in the yard still sitting in the mudroom. These things were just a way to remember that he was once here walking the world with me. A concrete reminder of his presence in the everyday. The security they represent in the way I could slide into his shirt and remember his hug or step into his dress shoes and remember him as a foundation.

Only we don't need these things to remember.

I glance at my mom as a tear slides down my cheek. She doesn't need to hang onto the ghost of him; none of us do when what we have are the memories.

So I nod again. "I'll help."

After breakfast, we face the task together, and as we do, we talk.

"Remember this tie?" my mom asks and smiles. "It was his favorite." She rubs the lavender silk. "Every time he put it on, he'd stand here." She moves across the room she shared with my dad to stand in front of the full-length mirror. Then she mimics him tying the tie. "He'd talk about the time he wore it to your ballet recital and how much he missed when you both were little."

And so it goes, each of us offering stories as we work through the items. I keep a t-shirt with holes in it that reads *Father of the Year*. I remember Ruth and I gave it to him for a Father's Day; he wore it proudly whenever he worked in the garage.

We cry together.

We laugh.

We remember.

Once everything is bagged, we carry it down, shove it into Mom's hatchback with every intention of taking it to donate. We get into our places, Mom behind the wheel. She starts the car, and then she sits there for a long time, the car running.

"Mom?" Rue asks from the back seat.

She starts and offers both of us a teary smile. "It feels like I'm having to let him go all over again."

We share tears, and after swiping them away, Mom drives to the Goodwill. We help her donate Dad's things. On the way home, Mom stops at a grocery store for some flowers, then drives us to Dad's grave where we clean it and place the fresh flowers.

When the afternoon begins to wane toward evening, it's time for me to drive back to campus. It's been an emotional day, but where I was worried about leaving my mom and my sister last year, this year I can tell we are different. Our bones are sturdier, somehow.

Now, I'm looking forward to getting back over the mountain, to seeing where this journey with Seth takes me. Suddenly I understand my desire to begin something new with Seth isn't a test at all. It isn't about having to choose between one thing or the other. It's about me moving forward more whole.

And if I deserve that—because I know I do—so does my mom. With my blessing.

"Mom?"

"Yes?"

We're standing in the kitchen waiting for Rue to come down for a final hug before I head out. "Are you interested in that Kit guy?"

She blushes. Clearly, Rue and I come by it naturally.

I smile. "I just want you to know, I understand. I think it's good you want to put yourself out there."

Tears fill her eyes as she looks down at her feet and wraps her arms around herself. "I'm not sure I'll ever be ready. Can you be ready for something like that?" She sort of laughs, the sound a little nervous and awkward. She pauses and looks at me. "I loved your dad."

"Yes."

She pauses and studies me. "Thank you, Hannah." She reaches out and tucks a strand of my hair behind my ear, then presses her palm to my cheek. "I hope you extend the same grace to yourself."

"What do you mean?"

"I know you blame yourself for not being here. That night."

My mouth opens to protest, but no words come out.

She shakes her head. "I know you." She gives me a wan smile and reaches out to touch the tip of my nose with her finger. "You should never feel guilty for living your life." She takes a deep breath and searches my eyes, then adds, "Self-blame. Guilt. Shame. Fear. These feelings can't be driving emotions. They are prisons. We couldn't have known what would happen. We couldn't control it. You couldn't control it."

It's my turn to feel the sting of tears.

She wraps me in a hug. "Dad would never want us to climb into the grave with him."

By the time I leave Cantos behind, I feel so much clearer, and realize coming home was exactly what I needed.

*My Heart Insists that I'm Good Enough*

"Do you think you're good enough for her?"

I hear the voice before I see where it's coming from. I'm halfway up the climbing wall, focused on my next move rather than the random voices in the student recreation center, so I ignore it at first. It probably has nothing to do with me anyway, since I don't know many people. I contemplate the blue jug-hold higher than where I am that will require me to push off from the wall, using my leg strength to leap up to it. I know I could pick a closer hold, but I want the challenge.

"Hey. I'm talking to you."

I glance down at the insistent voice and the tone which carries the sharp edges of animosity, wondering who's about to get into a fight. Then I realize, the words were directed at me. It's Sebastian. He's standing on the ground, hands holding the strap of his duffle, looking up in my direction. I refrain from rolling my eyes.

"Me?" I ask anyway, just to be sure.

"Yeah."

I turn my head, focusing once more on my climb, dismissing him. "I'm kind of busy." I bend my knees and push, knowing the harness and rope will catch me if I miss. But I don't miss, my hand catching the blue handhold just like I pictured. I'm relieved I didn't fall in front of the guy braying at me like a jackass down below.

"Do you think you're good enough for her?"

I know he's referencing Hannah, and I know for sure I'm not. I don't think anyone is. Not me, any more than this caricature throwing shade in a very public way. I also don't think I need to walk into his noxious exchange to reinforce his dumbassery or my own. I don't need to add fuel to any of my own errant emotions that might make me meet his stupidity with my own idiocy. It's an unwinnable poker game. So I don't respond.

"Hannah's mine."

With a sigh, I close my eyes to center myself. Dr. Bethany is fond of saying *"you choose how to respond when faced with your emotions."* This guy is pushing my buttons with the same energy as my father way-back-when. Hannah telling me he'd come over to her house uninvited, trying to get her back, was worrisome enough. Knowing she'd sent him on his way compounded by the fact he's claiming her like she's a piece of property, I can feel the dragon inside me, the one that's never far, huffing an angry breath in my chest. Now that I also know she's interested in me—which has kept me smiling the last twelve or so hours—I know it would be easy to rise to his bait. The better response is to determine how I want to approach it.

I'm not a stranger to anger.

My body is a walking testament to it. Though my father's a recovering alcoholic, and I'm a recovering victim of his abuse, I wrestle with demons constantly. Managing my emotions and insecurities are always on the center of the mat.

"You're nobody to her."

This guy isn't going to stop. I know the kind. I lived with someone just like him. His words hit my bullseye.

I push off the wall, and the ropes lower me gently until my feet connect with the mat. I unclip the harness from the rope and walk toward the other guy with as much calm as I can muster. "Is this your usual MO?"

His thick brows bunch together on his face. "What?"

I tip my chin up a touch to look him in the face. "Bully people to get what you want?"

"Fuck you." He takes a step toward me, arms now at his sides, and looks me up and down with derision. I see my father in his action—the father I grew up with, because he's different now—except Sebastian doesn't have the same power position as my father had over me. If this were happening in the past, I would have already been on the ground with a foot in my gut. Now, I don't have to attack or cower or prove anything to this person.

"Is that what you've done with Hannah?"

He's pissed and jerks toward me, but someone—a teammate, I guess—grabs him and keeps him from closing the distance. The teammate mutters something like, "the draft, dude."

I continue to hold my ground. This guy has no idea what I've been through. "Look, Sebastian, right? Right." I nod before he can say anything. "Hannah's a grown woman with a mind of her own. She's not yours any more than she's mine. She's hers, so let's cut the bullshit."

"The bullshit, bro, is that you're encroaching."

"On what?"

"You've climbed over my fence."

I turn and look around as if I might find common sense sitting somewhere nearby so I can hand it to this dude. People float past, watching the interaction, pretending to be engrossed in their phones. "Am I really having this conversation?" I ask no one in particular, then look back at Sebastian.

"You don't want to fuck with me."

I narrow my eyes at this cartoon character. "How am I doing that exactly?"

"By talking to Hannah."

"You know who's missing from this conversation?"

"Who?"

"Hannah."

He swipes a hand over his face with frustration and takes a step back. His teammates retreat with him, two guys, tall and built like him. I get the sense they're there to make sure Sebastian doesn't do something to mess up his draft stock, but this is something they couldn't keep him from trying. Sebastian is all emotion, and none of them harnessed in viable ways. Rather, he's trying to hold himself together by some standard he thinks he's supposed to be exuding to the rest of us.

I watch him deflate, sort of, and he crosses his arms. When he looks up, the set of his features isn't as hostile, but there's still a knife in his gaze. "I just want a chance to fix things with her. I'm asking you, from one guy to another, to back off so I can."

I see Abby in my mind's eye when I thought I was in love with her. While I did love and respect her friendship, what I'd been in love with was the idea of her, all the ways she represented truth, kindness, love. All the things I wanted and didn't have. My ideas about what it meant to love someone else were stitched together with the volatile world I grew up in that had been tightened into an ugly, mismatched tapestry. The last four years, I've been unraveling those threads. When I look at Sebastian, I'm reminded of the scraps of past me. I hear his entitlement, his fear, his insecurity, but it doesn't keep me from being real.

"Again, Hannah's decision." I loosen the harness.

"You're saying 'no'?" He seems surprised.

I step from the harness. "I'm saying that as long as Hannah wants me in her life, I'll be there, but that's her choice. My choice is to work to deserve her attention. Maybe that's what you should be thinking about instead of threatening me."

I can see he wants to come at me. He's breathing a little like a bull. I'm sort of waiting for him to paw the ground with his foot, but he doesn't. Instead, he narrows his eyes and stares at me, then he says, "Watch your back, bro." He says *bro* like it's a disgusting thing.

I refuse to respond and dismiss him by turning away to hang the harness, offering him my back. It's a risk, but if he tries anything, he'll have instigated it. I don't think he wants to put his football career in jeopardy. When I turn back around, he's pushing through the entry doors, and I'm wondering when I signed up to star in an 80's movie.

Rap music blasts on the speakers when I get home to the apartment. "Hey," I shout over the cadence and bass as I close the door behind me.

The music volume lowers, and Trace appears in the doorway to the kitchen. He's got on an apron that reads *kiss the cook* and holds a spatula. "Dude, what the fuck did you say to Sebastian?"

I roll my eyes. "You heard already? What is this? Middle school?"

"We're on a team, dude. If someone farts across town, we all smell it." He disappears into the kitchen.

"What's with that guy? Are his roid rages constant?" I toe my feet out of my shoes and tuck them neatly by the door.

Trace laughs and calls out, "Dude isn't on roids. He's a badass defensive end though. Led the league in sacks. What did you say to him?"

"Jack shit, bro. He's the one who came at me." I walk a path into the kitchen where I get a glass of water, then lean against the counter while Trace cooks. "I was just getting in a workout. He showed up at the rec center throwing words instead of hands."

"Why?"

"Hannah."

Trace hums a note and continues to stir whatever he's frying. "The dude doesn't like losing. You should see him on the field. He's an animal."

"What does that have to do with Hannah? She's a person, not a contest. His words–" I lower my voice into a Sebastian growl– "'she's mine.' Like I'm all for going after what you want and shit, but he's taking it to an extra caveman level."

Trace looks at me over his shoulder. "He's in the wrong here. I mean he dumped her. At least that's what he told everyone."

I take another sip of water. It matches what Hannah told me. "Well, whatever. I just told him it was up to Hannah."

"You not wrong." Trace's eyebrow quirks along with the tilt of his head to the side. "What's up with you and her, anyway?"

"Told you. We're friends."

"For real? Marco said Sebastian was all butthurt at the game because she was with you. And by with you, I mean, into you. All cozy and shit."

I try to keep my face noncommittal, but then can't because I'm so happy. I glance at Trace over the rim of my glass; his back is to me so he hasn't seen my response, but I decide that I think I can trust him. He hasn't given me a reason not to. Besides, trust is one of my struggles, and as Dr. Bethany has said, *If you withhold trust, you will withhold yourself from living. It's a requirement.*

"I do like her," I admit.

He turns and looks at me, his brown eyes wide and his lips quirked again in one of those *I knew it* shapes. Then he grins. "She's into you?"

I avoid his question and say, "I liked her when we were seniors in high school."

"Did you two hook up back then?"

I shake my head. "Not really. Kissed once. She didn't know how into her I was."

"And now, you think you've got the game to make that play?"

I can't keep the smile from my face.

Trace laughs and does a little dance in the kitchen to whatever he's cooking. "You got this. You got this," he chants, then holds out his hand for a couple of palm taps. He straightens and removes his meal from the stove top. "That's what's got Bash's panties in a wad then."

I wash my cup and set it in the strainer. "His problem. Time for some homework." I leave the kitchen, shower, and sit down on my bed, my mind drifting to Hannah. I don't reach out. I know she's spending time with her family celebrating her father's life.

The next day, however, I'm impatient because all I want is to see her.

I study and then study some more. I play a video game tournament with Trace, Marco, and a couple of other guys from the football team. I work out. Then, because I've got nostalgia on my mind, I Facetime Gabe. I doubt he'll answer, because he's in season, but am surprised when he does.

"Yo! Scrub," he says, his face too close to the screen so all I see is his forehead and curly black hair. When he leans back, he's smiling. "What's up?"

"Just checking in. Game today?"

"Practice. Game on Thursday."

"How's the season so far?"

"Are you admitting you haven't been watching?"

I smile. "You know we don't get all the games. But I've been keeping track. You can give me the inside scoop."

He glances around and leans in. "Not sure. We'll be lucky to make the tournament." He leans back. "You know I'mma give it my all though?"

"You always do."

"So, you don't usually call. You got an emergency?"

He's right. I don't. Usually, he reaches out. "No emergency. Just checking in. Guess who goes to school with me here. I ran into her."

"Western?" His blue eyes look up as he thinks. "No guess."

"Hannah."

"What? Shit!" He smiles. "Bro. Remember that crush you had on her senior year, and you freaking wouldn't ask her to the prom?" He shakes his head and makes an airy noise with his mouth. "I told you."

I grin. "You did, and yes, I remember."

"How is she?"

"Good. She called me out."

One of his eyebrows draws up over an eye. "Better and better. I love when people call you out, Peters. On what this time?"

"Not keeping in contact."

"Why didn't you?"

"Avoiding the past." I realize I avoid everyone, because it reminds me of how much I hated me then, and that's a me I don't like to remember.

"And now Hannah's in your face." He smiles.

"Yeah."

"But? Sounds like there's a but in there."

"She's got this ex, and he's been badgering her. He showed up to warn me away."

Gabe's lips curl in distaste. "Bad news. What did you say?"

"That I'd be in Hannah's life as long as she wanted me there."

His grin spreads, and he nods. "My boy. You going to pursue it?"

"Yeah." I nod. "Fuck yeah. It feels like a second chance."

"Nice." He high fives the screen. "Oh shit. Is that the time? Hey, I want to hear this, but I gotta jet to practice. Coach is a tyrant when we're late. I'mma holler back."

"Talk then."

The call disconnects. I move from my desk to my bed and flop onto my back. I study the ceiling though I'm not really looking at it. There's a lot of crap between Gabe and me, and yet somehow, we found our way through it, even if it's still a lot of thick underbrush we hack away at sometimes. He forgave me. Lots of my insecurities are wrapped up in my relationship with him, though I know he was just the scapegoat for my fucked-up relationship with my dad and my jealousy of Gabe's amazing adoptive dad. Most of the time, I don't know why he forgave me, but he did. We made it through senior year and through the last few years still checking in.

Guilt climbs around between my skin and muscles picking at weakness, knowing I received forgiveness from Gabe for what I'd done but haven't been able to extend it to my father. Some, maybe, but not completely. How does one extend complete forgiveness to someone who treated me like a punching bag?

Irritated now, with myself, with my father, I flip open my laptop with a little more force than necessary and find the document I need for the paper due next week for my Sociology class. Mentally resetting myself with schoolwork helps most of the time, providing distance between my emotion and my body, but as I attempt to focus, my eyes grow heavy. Maybe I just need a second to rest my eyes, so I lean forward, my head on my arm draped over my desk, shut my eyes, and drift to sleep.

*There's a white door washed in blue light. It's the door to my childhood bedroom in Cantos, and I'm sitting on my bed staring at the bright outline seeping through the spaces between it and the floor, the frame, and the ceiling. Fear sits inside me, slithering through and around me my gaze fixed on that door. It is as if it's breathing, a monster on the other side waiting for me to step through. I don't need to open it to know it.*

*Though I haven't moved, it unlatches with a loud click.*

*My heart jolts with terror, then sprints as if looking for the nearest exit. The air wheezing in and out of my constricted lungs isn't enough to keep me alive.*

*The door creaks open, a slow and deliberate swing of the wood, a great penetrative darkness beyond it rather than the light that seemed to be there before.*

*I look for a monster's hand pushing it open, but instead, in that maw of darkness, I find glowing red eyes piercing my fear and pumping it fuller so that it might rip me apart.*

*I want to jump from my bed and run, but I'm frozen with fright, a helpless hare, weak and insignificant. Only I can't look away. Afraid that if I do move, do look for an escape, whatever is waiting in that darkness will consume me whole.*

*Except the clock is ticking. I can hear it. Only it isn't a clock; it's a jack-in-the-box toy, the warbled music of* Pop Goes the Weasel *clicking down to the end. Dah dum dah dum dah dum dum dum dum…*

*There's a rush of movement, a growl, and the creature pops from the darkness, only it's my father's face, then Sebastian's, and then mine.*

My eyes fly open as my phone blurts out an alert.

I sit up with a start, realizing I've fallen asleep, my heart pounding a staccato in my ears with the lingering dream. Disoriented, I blink my eyes open, staring at the ceiling above me, and feel around for my phone, nagging me again. I look at the notification.

Hannah.

I smile, my heart regulating with a more pleasant rhythm as I take a deep, settling breath. I click the messaging app open.

> *I'm home. Come over?*

I smile and text her back: *Send me the address.*

*My Heart Insists This is Home*

"I won't be back tonight," Jewel calls as she rushes back down the hall to grab something. "I'm sorry, I know you're just getting home. Joy's family is doing this thing for her grandparents' anniversary, and we're staying in Portland, so I won't be back until tomorrow."

"Don't worry."

Jewel returns and shoves something into the bag on the stool, then stops and runs a hand over her braids, her lips moving as she goes through whatever list is on her mind. "You sure?" she asks, her dark eyes cutting to me.

"I'm good."

"You don't think Sebastian will stop by? I'm a little worried about that."

"No. I don't think so." I can't help my grin. "Besides, Seth is coming over to watch a movie."

A smile erupts on her face, and she gets a cheeky look, her right eyebrow arching. "Oh really?"

I giggle, wishing I could make that look. "Yes. So don't worry."

"I won't then." She zips the duffle and swings it onto her shoulder. "I think I've got everything."

"You're only going to Portland, not the Arctic."

Her phone beeps. "Shit. That's Joy. She's going to be irritated that I'm late." She gives me a side hug, then answers her phone. "Hey babe, I'm walking out the door." Then she waves at me and closes the door behind her.

I lock it once it's closed, and I'm alone. The apartment is quiet. Seth is on his way over. My heart twists in my chest. I hurry to take a shower and put on something presentable. I don't want to try too hard, and now is when I need Jewel. I dial Facetime, my nerves dialing up my tension, and thankfully Abby answers. "How are you doing?"

"I'm okay. I need your help. Do I look okay?" I turn the screen so she can see my reflection in the mirror.

"For what?"

"Seth's coming over."

"What?!?" She screeches, but I can't see her. "Okay. Okay." She releases a breath. "What is this for?"

"Watching a movie. At home."

"Are those jeans? Maybe leggings instead? Dress comfortably, but cute. Casual."

I turn the screen back to face me. "Is it dumb that I'm nervous."

"No. That isn't dumb at all."

I sink to my bed.

"What is it, Hannah?"

"What if, like, dating Seth changes being friends? What if he realizes he doesn't like me? What if being together is terrible?"

"Would you say you've been friends the last couple of years?"

"You're right."

"You aren't going to have any answers to those questions until you take the risk, Han."

I nod.

"Go get changed and call me back when you're done."

"Thanks, Ab."

I settle on black leggings with an oversized sweatshirt. My hair is still a little wet, so I leave it down, but before I can dial Abby, there's a knock at the door. I text her that I'll call her later and take a deep breath. When I open the door, Seth is standing outside the door, holding a Lindie's Pizza box.

He smiles. "Hi." Dimples. He holds up the box. "I thought we might get hungry."

I'm surprised my bones are still there since I feel like I've melted in my spot now that he's here. Stepping back so he can come inside, my heart thrums in my chest as I close the door behind him. "Yum. You can take it into the kitchen."

He sets the white box on the counter, and I slide past him over the linoleum in my thick socks to get some plates.

"There's some drinks in the fridge," I tell him.

When I turn with the plates, he's removing his jacket. He's wearing a heather gray t-shirt that shows off the slope of his shoulders to the swell of his arms, and I feel a jolt in the base of my spine. The fabric drapes around his body in a way that allows me to admire the way he looks, and there's a beautiful sinew in the muscle visible as he moves. He lays the jacket over one of the barstools. When he walks around the counter, I notice the way his black sweatpants ride his hips.

I swallow, and my face heats (curses!) as I move across the space to the counter bar while he opens the fridge.

"What would you like?"

"A soda."

He retrieves two and returns to the counter.

"Thank you."

He sets them down and looks at me.

That spark sizzling at the base of my spine spirals up my back when our gazes connect.

I look away to hide my blush. "Napkins." I turn and slide across the room.

"Are you in training for an ice show?" he asks, his tone light and fun.

I smile. "Yes. Actually."

"Need a partner?" He joins me in the kitchen, sliding in his socks over the linoleum with me.

He holds out his hands. "Esteemed audience, I'd like to introduce you to the linoleum stylings of Seth and Hannah."

I revel in the feel of my hands in his strong ones.

With smiles on our faces, we slide around like we're dancing though there isn't any music except our laughter. Seth spins me out, away from him, then draws me back in, his arm wrapping around me, holding me close, our fronts aligning. "They just executed a perfect double-sock, circular maneuver. Did you notice that skill, Frank?" He mimics an announcer-style voice, his body slightly bent over mine as we move together.

I let my head drop back, laughing, heart racing with a different beat.

Seth straightens, grasps my hips, and twirls me around. "It looks like Seth is doing most of the work. His partner needs to go to training more frequently."

"Oh, my stomach!" I grasp my belly aching with mirth now, bent at the waist.

"What? Are you okay?" Seth seems concerned, his body pressed to mine, my back to his front.

I straighten and turn, Seth's hands still on my waist. "I'm fine." Only fine isn't the right word at all. I'm overheating. I'm anticipating… more.

"I'm all about fun, Hannah." His eyes dip to my mouth, and he steps away from me. "I used to do that when I was a kid," he says and launches himself across the linoleum. "I forgot. I used to pretend I was a hockey player." He looks over his shoulder and offers me an unguarded grin. I'm not sure I've ever seen one so authentic on him. Dimples for days. "I think we've discovered the next Olympic sport."

I giggle and return to the pizza.

He joins me, his shoulder bumping against mine when he comes to a stop.

"Thanks for dinner," I say.

"Of course. I hope it becomes a thing."

We each take a slice.

"How was home?" he asks and moves around the other side of the counter.

"Strange."

He brings a stool around for me, then returns to a seat across from me before he takes a bite. "And?" he prods and waits for me to keep going, which shakes me a moment. With Sebastian, I was always listening to his woes and triumphs, his thoughts and opinions. I realize how rare it was to have his undivided attention unless I was offering my thoughts about him. When I did talk about my stuff, it never felt like he was listening, but rather baiting me with his teasing until I was frustrated. Then I'd shut down.

"It feels like we're moving forward."

He nods, encouraging me to continue.

"A year ago, it was like we needed to be together, a support system to walk through each day. This time, we were able to smile and laugh. It's still painful, but like a dull ache rather than a sharp one. I'm not making any sense, am I?"

"You're making perfect sense."

I pick at a slice of pepperoni. "I think my mom might have met someone."

His eyebrows rise over his eyes. "Really? Why do you think that?"

"A feeling. She didn't say, but I don't know. There was this man at my sister's cheerleading competition." I fill him in on the rest of the weekend. The competition, the mysterious man named Kit, seeing Nate and Matt, wanting to come back.

He tells me about his weekend, which was mostly video games and homework.

"Did you enjoy the rec center?"

He tilts his head, and the shape of his eyes asks the question, *how did I know?*

"You sent me a picture in front of the climbing wall."

"Oh. Right." He pokes at the crust before he picks it up and takes a bite. There's something in his tone that suggests he's holding back. I'm not sure how I know this, but I think about Seth sliding around in his socks versus what he's just said, and those are incongruent when juxtaposed with one another.

"Everything okay?" I ask.

He pinches his earlobe and tugs on it, then frowns, and I miss his smile. I note his mouth in any shape is alluring, but now he's gone serious. "I don't know if I should mention it."

"Mention what?"

"It feels kind of self-serving, and that isn't what I want."

"Well, now you have to tell me." I offer him a smile.

"I saw Sebastian."

My smile fades as I imagine how that played out. "I'm sorry." I drop my face into my hands.

He grabs my wrists and pulls my hands away from my face. "Please don't apologize for him. Whatever he does isn't yours to apologize for."

"I'm imagining the worst."

"Why?"

I hesitate. It isn't because I'm afraid of how Seth might react, but rather more concerned about how crappy, how used my last interaction with Sebastian made me feel. "He asked me to give him another chance the other night, and he wasn't very happy with the outcome."

"Because he didn't get what he wanted?"

I offer Seth a short smile. "Yeah. And he isn't used to not getting his way, you know?"

"Yeah. I do."

I drop my chin to my chest and stare at the uneaten crust of my pizza, then sigh and shake my head. "What happened?"

Seth moves around the counter and stops next to me. When I straighten my shoulders, he grasps them and makes me turn to face him. "Look," he says and lifts my chin. I comply, and he searches my face, paying most attention to my eyes. "Maybe instead of worrying about him, what he does or doesn't do, let's focus on us?"

I smile, a more complete one.

He's right.

I nod.

He wraps his arms around me, drawing me into his embrace, and I rest there, enjoying the strength in his back I feel under my hands.

"What would you like to do," I ask, changing the subject and moving away before I start feeling him up, very conscious of the feel of his shape against mine.

His eyes widen, then narrow. "Are you sure you want to ask me that, Hannah?" He grins. "Because there's a lot I'd like to do." Dimples.

I smack his arm playfully. "I thought maybe we could watch a movie?"

"Sure."

We clean up, linoleum skating as we do, laughing until our stomachs hurt. Then we set up on the couch, side-by-side, with my laptop on the coffee table in front of us. We scroll through a streaming service until we find something to watch.

I sit, folding my legs under me, my knee resting on Seth's thigh, and pull my hair up into a loose bun. When I turn to look at

Seth, he's watching me, his mouth neutral, his eyes cataloging my movement.

"Do I have something on me?" I ask and swipe at my face.

The movie's opening song plays.

Seth grabs my hand. "No. I was just thinking about how beautiful you are." He doesn't release my hand.

My heart swells to the size of a balloon but grows heavy in my chest as it works to keep beating and drips warmth into my belly. My cheeks heat, and I give him a self-conscious smile. "I don't know what to say."

"Nothing. It wasn't a question." He smiles.

I turn to watch the movie, the credits flashing, but I'm not thinking about it at all; it's background noise to what's happening inside of me. I've tucked myself closer to him, my hand in his. His thumb moves over my skin. I'm thinking about Seth and the way I am both feather light and rock heavy simultaneously. I'm thinking about his other arm stretched out behind me. I'm thinking about how I haven't felt like this in a long time. I'm thinking about what I want and realizing that what I want, and have wanted for a very long time, is him.

His fingers caress my neck, a repetitive graze that kindle sparks under my skin.

I turn to look at him.

He's still watching me and smiles. "Is this okay?" he asks, touching the skin near my collar.

I nod, a current racing trough my body. I say his name.

"Yes?"

My heart picks up speed, my nerves sharpening into points that might break me apart, but I think about what my mom said about fear driving my emotions, being a prison. "Remember what we talked about before I left?"

"We talked about a lot." His finger continues to blaze trails over my skin.

My face heats, and I look at the computer. "About how we felt."

"I'm teasing you, Hannah. Of course, I remember."

I look at him then, my eyes drifting over his features, his smile, memorizing them. Drawing from that foundation I rebuilt during my visit home, I say, "I would really like to kiss you."

He releases my hand and leans toward me. His eyes search my face, survey it, mapping if what I've said is written there. When he reads the truth, he exerts a gentle pressure with his hand in my hair, cupping the back of my head, and draws me toward him, but he doesn't kiss me. "I thought maybe you'd changed your mind," he says, his eyes dropping to my mouth.

I shake my head, leaning against his touch, longing for more weight, more pressure, more. "No. Why would you think that?" I search his face and am struck by the fact I'm here with Seth, who occupied many of my girlhood fantasies. My heart pounds with ferocity, as if it knows this is what I've been waiting for.

He shrugs, and for a moment I see a flash of insecurity.

I move so I'm facing him, his hand still in my hair, his caress drawing power from inside me. I press a hand to his jaw. "I can't stop thinking about the night on the beach. And maybe I've been dreaming about this my whole life, if the beating of my heart is any indication." I lean forward to press my mouth to one of his dimples.

After that initial touch, Seth sighs and turns his face so that his mouth finally meets mine.

It's perfect and wraps my heart in a warm, protective embrace.

I slide one hand up over his chest, meeting the other around the back of his shoulders, and pull him closer.

Maybe it's a strange thing to think, considering that Seth and I are only reorienting our spheres, but kissing him feels like coming home.

*My Heart Insists It's Finally Home*

Kissing Hannah is like finding True North, and I've suddenly found the direction I was always meant to travel. My hands in her hair. Her mouth against mine. Her hands around my shoulders. I tilt my head to grant her access and my own route. While it might be more prudent to slow down, I touch her lips with my tongue. She moans and lets me in. My heart dissolves in my chest, until all I feel is the hunger in my belly. The kiss finds an addictive direction and spreads out a complete map to guide me home.

Images of Hannah are flashpoints in my mind:

Hannah joking with me as we passed in the hallway.

Hannah sitting at lunch and laughing with Abby.

Dancing with Hannah at prom.

Hannah waiting for me after soccer games.

Hannah lighting me on fire at the beach.

She's in my memories, everywhere, always, even when she wasn't standing in the center.

I craved her, even then, and had been too afraid.

I'm not afraid anymore.

I grasp her hips and draw her into my lap. She straddles me, and I squeeze her hips with my hands. "Hannah." I say her name against her lips, and my chest tightens. I need to be closer. I want to tell her what the rhythm of my heart is reminding me, but I don't want to stop kissing her. I don't want to stop feeling her hands in my hair. But she wraps her arms around my shoulders, tugging me as if she is feeling the same.

"Closer," she says against my mouth and sinks down against me.

She is.

I miss her fingertips at my nape, but I like the feel of her chest pressed against mine, the friction of her body pressed against my erection. The sound of her moan when we each move just right. I run my hands up her back and back down to her hips to ease the pressure, but it only adds to the ache of wanting her.

She gasps, "Oh. Seth."

Then I need to see her face, to see if she's feeling what I'm feeling, because suddenly, that matters more than anything else. I pull away and open my eyes to look at her.

Her lashes flutter open and her usually bright, blue eyes are mostly black. With her mouth slightly open, her lips swollen from kissing, she's breathing erratically just like my own breath pulsing through my body in bursts. She looks like I feel.

I stroke her hair and her cheeks, then her shoulders and back to her hair. "I knew. My heart did."

"Knew what?" she asks, and her eyes drop to my mouth.

"That you were always living in it."

A smile curls her mouth, and a deepening blush suffuses her cheeks with pink. "I thought maybe I was making more of it than I should."

I float with her words and bury my face in the space between her shoulder and her neck. She smells so good, like peaches and linen dried in sunshine. She feels so good in my arms. I squeeze her tighter. I don't want to lose her again. Ever.

"Me either," she says, and I realize I've given my thoughts a voice. Her fingers trace my eyebrows, then the outline of my face.

The movie has moved on without us, the witty dialogue and musical underscore offering an underscore to my beating heart, but before I can kiss her again, a knock at the door draws us apart.

Both of us look at the door.

Her eyes return to mine.

"Expecting someone?" I ask.

The angle of her brows and the width of her eyes indicate she wasn't. "No."

"Maybe don't answer it," I say with a smile, though my heart has compressed. I have a terrible feeling I know who's on the other side of that door.

"I'll get rid of whoever it is." She disengages from my arms and climbs from my lap. I watch her adjust and smooth the oversized pink sweatshirt; it dips so that I see her collarbone and shoulder.

"Who would come over this late?" I stand, thinking about pressing my lips against that space between her neck and spine she reveals as she lifts and twists her hair into a bun. I adjust myself so my hard on isn't as noticeable.

She stops halfway to the door and glances at me. "I don't think it's him." She's said this quietly, as if reciting a spell to make it so.

"Who?"

"Sebastian." Her eyes cling to mine, and it's the first time I've seen the doubt that she might not believe her words. "Last time— I was clear. I told Jewel, my roommate, he wouldn't come."

The rap of the knock against the door reminds us someone is still there.

"I'm here," I tell her. "If it is." I pause. "What do you want me to do?"

"Wait here?"

I nod, even though I'd like to throw the door open and throw a punch.

I can see her and the door from where I'm standing. She looks through the peephole and sighs, then leans her forehead against the surface of the door, which tells me I was right. When she opens it, it's just enough that whoever is on the other side can only see her head and shoulders, a clear indication whoever's there isn't welcome. Though I can see her, the door blocks whoever it is from my view and me from theirs.

"Hey," Sebastian's disembodied voice says, verifying my initial assumption.

"What are you doing here?"

"I wanted to bring these."

"Go give them to someone else."

"I got them for you."

"It's almost ten. You can't just stop by like this."

"You didn't mind. Before."

She sighs.

"I'm trying here, Hannah. I'm trying to fix it. I fucked up."

I want to kick myself. I'd told him to try and now he is.

"Except there isn't anything to fix. How many times do I have to say this?" Hannah asks.

"Can I just come in?"

"No. I'm busy."

There's a stretch of silence, and I know that Sebastian has just become aware that I'm on the other side of the door, just like I knew it was him outside. "He's here?"

"I need you to leave."

Sebastian pushes the door open at the same time Hannah says to stop. He doesn't cross the threshold, just stands there holding a bouquet of roses upside down at his side. His eyes find mine, and I can't help myself, I smirk at him, but it isn't because I'm trying to be a prick or to instigate anything; it's a mechanism to keep the dragon I wrestle from coming alive inside me. That monster is in there, waiting on the edge for permission to engage. I imagine going for Sebastian, launching through the doorway to pummel him with my fists. He might be bigger than I am, but I wonder if his body is held together with stitching that has made it a necessity to control the dragon?

*"How do you know when anger is healthy?"* I'd asked Dr. Bethany. *"Because I feel anger a lot, have experienced it, and it never feels healthy."*

*"Anger is perfectly normal, Seth. The key is to recognize that anger is a secondary emotion. There's a different feeling informing it. That's what you're trying to identify."*

Right now, anger is a secondary emotion to… but I can't settle myself enough to identify it.

I'm pissed he's ignored Hannah's wishes.

I'm pissed he's interrupted us.

I'm pissed he's standing there like he deserves to be heard.

"I see," he says, and his eyes slide back to Hannah with accusation.

"You can't do this, Sebastian. You can't just keep showing up."

He drops his chin toward his chest. "Can I talk to you privately?"

"No."

"You owe me that."

I start forward, but Hannah's angry words make me freeze. "I don't owe you anything." She's fighting this battle, but when I see Sebastian's face, he's seething, his own dragon coming to life inside of him.

My eyes bounce between them. Concerned. I can't staunch the thought that he could have hurt her, picturing my mother. The bruises. The broken bones. The sadness. And that's when I understand what the emotion is behind the anger: fear.

Because I'm afraid he'll hurt Hannah.

I'm afraid because of their history, she might not choose me.

My mother didn't, not until I was lying in a hospital bed.

I can't be second. Not again. I can't doubt her intentions. I take a deep breath and run my hand through my hair. "I can go," I offer, though the sound of my voice is only for her.

"No." Hannah's gaze pins me where I am, and for a moment, Sebastian blurs from my vision and all I see is her. I'm thinking about how sexy bossy Hannah is. Then she looks at Sebastian. "You need to go. And I don't want you doing this again. We're over," she says.

"Hannah–"

"No. I'm sorry, but I'm done." She shuts the door, locks it, turns, and leans against it.

"Fuck!" Sebastian yells on the other side of the door, then hits the wood.

Hannah jumps at the sound, then drops her face into her hands.

"What the fuck, Hannah," Sebastian says, the door between them. She doesn't answer. "Nine fucking months for this shit." A thunk sounds from the outside, followed by silence.

I want to go to her, but I'm not sure what she wants. It feels like the security of a few moments ago has been shredded, and I don't know what to do to fix it. I'm also not feeling as steady, my fear pulsing with angry frustration. "What can I do? Would you like me to go?"

Hannah raises her head, tears in her eyes. "I'm so sorry," she says through them.

I cross the room to her and gather her in my arms. "You have nothing to be sorry for. This isn't your fault," I tell her. I hear my mother in her words and realize I've said this same phrase to Hannah a bunch of times in the last week. It makes me wonder about the kind of relationship she really had with Sebastian. "His shit isn't yours."

"I feel bad."

"For what? If you feel bad about anything it should because he's being a dick to you," I say.

"For him."

I'm taken aback by her statement, though this is Hannah, so maybe I shouldn't be. "Whatever for?"

"I don't like hurting someone."

"But it's okay if you're hurt?"

Her silence says everything.

"Hannah?" I lean away from her so she can't hide her face.

She lifts her head, her misery in her tears.

And it makes me hold the words I want to say. I want to tell her to forget him, but I don't know that she'll hear it. So instead, I ask, "Do you want me to go?"

She shakes her head. "No."

I settle her back into my hug.

She finally wraps her arms around me, her hands flat against my shoulder blades, the pressure welcome. "Would you stay?" she mutters into my shoulder.

"What?" I'm not sure I heard her right. "Stay?"

She nods, then leans back against the door, wiping her eyes. "Yes." She sniffs. "Would you stay? I mean, Jewel won't be coming home, and he probably won't be back, but then I didn't think he'd show up tonight either, and I just don't know if I want to be alone." She rambles the words like they're all connected.

"Yes."

She gives me a smile. "I'm so sorry."

"Hannah. Stop." I hold out my hand, wanting to comment on her constant apologies, but I don't. Instead, I draw her out of the moment. "I think we need to practice our linoleum skating. With the trials coming up, we need to be ready."

She smiles and takes my offered hand.

I lead her into the kitchen. As our socks slip and slide over the linoleum, this time to real music because Hannah has put some on to inspire us, we laugh. Each of her touches distracts me, and I want to kiss her again, but I don't. While I've known Hannah for a lifetime, I've been without her for the last two years. I've decided this isn't a day trip, it's an odyssey.

*My Heart Insists It Isn't a Glass Jar*

"You're sure you're okay to stay?" I ask. There's an awkwardness settling in around me like an errant spirit, as if I've overstepped for asking, and my encroachment will change things by being the specter that plagues everything else from here on out. I'm afraid to look at Seth—to showcase how not-put-together I really am—so I busy myself and pull a clean toothbrush from a package of extras in a drawer. But I can't avoid meeting his gaze forever and look up, holding the toothbrush out toward him.

He doesn't look upset. At all.

He leans a shoulder against the door frame in my room and watches me, patience on his face with a gentle upturn of his mouth and relaxed eyes. I'm a little unnerved by his focus, mostly because that kiss is still on my mind. I'm standing in the center of my room, after our linoleum dancing, my nerve endings sizzling from his touch and angling for more connection. If I just reached out and pulled him to me, I could reconnect. I don't, however, too worried that the link between us may have been damaged and shorted out by Sebastian showing up. The tension between us is still there, but I can't be sure if it's the kind of tension that needs a bit of air let out or the kind that needs time and distance. I'm curious to see what would happen at his end of the string if I tugged on my end.

Seth pushes away from the door and steps into the room to take the offered toothbrush. He fills the space. "I said so. Do you doubt me so easily?" He grins. Dimples.

My face heats. "I'm sorry."

He tosses the toothbrush; it bounces on the bed as he grasps my wrists. "Hannah!" Pulling me toward him, he wraps me in a hug, my body flush against his, my wrists still captured by his hands. "Why are you always saying 'sorry'?"

I'm caught, but I don't hate it at all. I open my mouth to apologize for apologizing and realize what I'm about to say. He's right. I close my mouth, but now Seth's watching it. His look sears me with heat, and I contemplate the intense warmth his body offers mine in every place we touch. Connection. The rigid stress in my center melts, changing into desire that pools lower.

He waits, his eyes moving over my features. When I don't respond—not because I don't want to, but because I can't seem to find a conscious thought—he releases my wrists and presses his hands to the small of my back to keep me close. "I'm happy to be here for you. With you." He leans forward, drops a quick kiss against my cheek before letting me go, and grabs the toothbrush.

I lead him from my room to the bathroom and collect my own toothbrush from the jar on the counter. "Are you angry?"

His brows bunch together. "Why would you think that?"

I hesitate and ponder his question. Sebastian. "You probably don't want to hear it." I offer him a placating smile. "History."

"I do want to hear it." He turns to face me and leans his hip against the bathroom counter between me and the open door behind him. "It's the history of Hannah Fleming. It's important. I want to know all the stuff I've missed." He reaches out and tucks a strand of my hair behind my ear, his touch lingering even if his fingers haven't.

I could tell him the whole Sebastian story and even further back to the night my dad died, but right now, these stories feel like seeping wounds, and I just don't know how to face how inadequate and unworthy they make me feel. "I'm going to go brush my teeth."

"You're not getting out of sharing, Hannah." His arms relax to his sides, and he grins at me. He holds out his toothbrush, dimples in his cheeks.

I ice the brush for him, using that to keep my hands to myself. "Okay." I maneuver around him to get out of the bathroom, careful not to touch him.

"I'm going to get it out of you one way or another," he says after me with a laugh.

My belly disintegrates inside me, and the bits float around, as if he's promised he's going to—I blink in a hard reset while standing at Jewel's sink in her bathroom. "Brush your teeth,

Hannah," I mutter at my reflection, then rush through my bedtime routine. By the time I close Jewel's bedroom door and return to the hallway, Seth is leaning against the wall between my door and the bathroom door, waiting. He turns his head to look at me. My body heats as he watches me walk past him to return my toothbrush to its place.

"Do you have a blanket or a sheet I can use?" he asks when I return to the hall. "For the couch?"

I look over my shoulder toward the living room, which is dark now, and I know I'm about to make a very important choice for myself, for whatever is happening between us. But it isn't really a decision, now is it? It's been something I've wanted since I was eighteen. I cross my arms over my chest, recognize it for the insecurity that it is, and uncross my arms again. "Would it be okay to sleep with me? In my bed?" I force myself to meet his eyes, my cheeks hot.

He steps closer and gives me that grin that chases away my doubts and insecurities. "I didn't want to presume anything."

I smile and swipe a lock of my hair off my face, then take his hand and lead him into my room. When we're both in my bed, the lights off, we face one another, and I can't help but giggle.

"What?" he asks.

It's dark enough that I can grab ahold of the bravery to share, and he won't witness my blushes. "If I'd have told my seventeen-year-old self that I'd have a sleepover with Seth Peters when I was twenty, she would have laughed in my face."

He makes a noise that expresses his own amusement. "If I'd told seventeen-year-old Seth that I'd be lying in a bed with Hannah Fleming, he would have–" The words stall, and he goes silent.

I grin, thinking about seventeen-year-old Seth, then realize he was seventeen when he'd been in his car accident. My smile fades. I reach out and touch him to reassure myself he's really here.

"Hannah?" he asks in the dark.

"I was just thinking about being in the hospital, after your accident." I recall his dad walking into the waiting room and breaking down to tell whoever was still there between sobs that it was time to say goodbye because they were going to take him off life support. I'd cried. When it was my turn to visit him, I'd sat with unconscious Seth and begged him not to go. The memory is so vivid: his pale face and hair dark against the whiteness of everything else. His injuries. The ventilator breathing for him. The click and beeping of machines working to keep him alive. Just recalling it closes my throat.

"That time is–" He stops.

I run my hand across the skin of his arm from elbow to wrist. I don't know what to say, but at his bedside then, I'd begged him to stay. It had been the first time I'd been faced with the truth of loss, and what it would be like to lose him. I'd looked at the truth of what I felt and couldn't ignore it anymore; I had feelings for him I'd never admitted to myself until I'd been faced with him not being there. "I remember being afraid."

"Of?"

"Losing a very important person in my life." I squeeze his wrist.

Then I lost my father two years later.

I take a deep breath. I need something else to think about and find his hand to thread my fingers with his. "It feels strange to be able to do this," I say. "To reach out and touch you."

"This was only in eighteen-year-old Seth's fantasies."

Silence moves around us, between us, but the shadows of it are full of things not being said. The words I want to tell him, which seem ridiculous and presumptuous. Words that would express how I've missed his presence in my life, even though I hadn't been aware until I'd run into him at Hammill, and how big of a void the loss of him has been. Words to express the way I'm looking over my shoulder at my relationship with Sebastian, ashamed it took so long to see I'd lost myself, that I'd been lying to myself it had been something worth saving.

Seth squeezes my hand and pulls me closer. He's so warm. "Why do you apologize, Hannah?" His voice is quiet.

"I don't know why," I whisper, but I don't think those words are true even if they are when I say them. They drift from my lips like flashing fireflies; I see my mother and sister, broken and waiting for me to come home after my father's death like cracked glass jars, and the realization I'd thought I'd been made of something different—I was always glass too. I see the weight of Sebastian's disappointment each and every time I couldn't get whatever it was he'd wanted right, adding cracks to the glass of me and leaking my essence like shards flaking away into slivers at my feet. I am a cracked jar, fragmented and littering the space around me, a version of a girl who believed she wasn't good enough and had to apologize for existing.

There isn't much of me left.

Tears fill my eyes when I recognize it, but I don't know how to articulate that to Seth because it feels pathetic.

"Is it because of all that history?" he asks. His reticence presses in around us, keeping us guarded and safe to share our secrets.

"I think so."

He takes my answer, and I expect him to ask for more, but he doesn't. Instead, he whispers, "I don't want you to apologize to me anymore." He lets go of my hand, and his fingertips trace the skin of my arm up to my shoulder.

I shiver, and his hand gets caught between my neck and my jaw.

"Are you cold?"

"No."

"Is this okay, Hannah?"

"Yes," I whisper and move closer, tucking my arm around his back and pressing my length against his.

His hand caresses my hair. "May I kiss you?"

"Please."

His mouth meets mine, and my heart climbs up my chest into my throat, swollen with longing. The kiss begins sweet but changes into a different kind of kiss. Last time it was new and exploratory. Now, it's lips, teeth, and tongues, hungry, greedy, and pursuant. I clutch his back, pressing him as close as I can, then roll to my back, bringing him with me. His weight shifts to cover me, a sublime gravity that has me moaning for more. I find the hem of his t-shirt and slip my hands underneath so I can feel his hot skin.

He shudders, then makes a sound in the back of his throat as if he's unzipping himself.

I take hold of his shoulders, and my touch, skin-to-skin, flips a switch. He moves, adjusts himself, leaning up on his hands, as if to unburden me of his pressure, but his mouth is still connected to mine. I wrap my legs around the back of his thighs and pull him back. I want this. I want him. But I don't say it, the words trapped in the glass where I protect myself.

"Hannah?" he asks, trailing kisses from my jaw down my neck. His hand burns a trail from my neck to my ribs, to my waist at the waistband of my leggings. "Is this okay? May I touch you?"

"Yes," I say, running after my breath. "Yes."

I've never felt like this. It's as if I've been dipped in oil and every part of me is burning. I've enjoyed kissing and sex, but in retrospect, my two partners were lackluster in comparison to this moment. It didn't help I heaped guilt on myself, which then impacted the intimacy I shared with Sebastian.

It had been a while since Sebastian and I had been intimate. It's dismal to consider I hadn't noticed. If it had been like this, however, I would have. I would have chased it. I'm chasing the fire now, needing a way to feed it with more.

"Hannah," Seth says, his voice raw. "I don't want to move too fast, but–" He swears and finds my mouth again with his, and we kiss each other until we're panting, our hands finding purchase in exploring one another. Suddenly he's gone, up on his knees, sitting on his heels before me. The cold of the winter night finds my skin. His hands grip the outside of my thighs as if he's at war with himself.

I come up onto my elbows. "What is it?

I'm remembering the beach. The night we kissed like we were on fire, and this is like that, only better. He'd stopped then, too, and laid next to me. We'd held hands and watched the firework show, reorienting toward one another with newfound awareness. We'd oohed and ahhed at the explosions in the sky, and I'd thought about how much I wanted to kiss him again but was too scared to try. Then we'd found our friends, and he'd disappeared from my life.

"I don't know if sleeping next to you is a good idea."

My heart cracks open, and a few fireflies escape. "What?" I touch my lips with my fingertips. They're exquisitely swollen, expertly kissed. I understand what he's saying, but not why. We're both consenting adults. "You don't want to have sex with me?" I miss the pressure of his body, the feel of his mouth and tongue, the caress of his hands.

"What? Fuck yes, I do." The lid to the jar slams back on as he slides up my body, his erection pressed between my legs. "Feel that?" The lid tightens.

I nod.

His head is nestled in my neck, and the sensations he's creating with his mouth and his hips make me arch my back toward him. I can't keep the whimper from slipping from my mouth.

He grabs my knee and draws it up over one of his hips so he can settle even deeper. "I want you so fucking bad, Hannah." He lifts his head, and his eyes are shiny in the dark. "Nineteen-year-old Seth would have been done already." He laughs quietly at himself. "And twenty-one-year-old Seth is fucking close."

"Then what is it?" I ask. Even with the evidence of his desire, my insecurities seem to be working harder than his words.

He sighs and moves so that he's lying next to me, taking my hand in his, and turning his head so that he can see me. "Full disclosure?"

I turn so I can look at him. "No. Partial is adequate."

He turns his head to look at me and grins. "Okay. Smart ass." He rolls to his shoulder so he's facing me. Though my eyes have adjusted to the darkness, I can only see his outline clearly. "I've been in therapy since the accident."

I roll onto my shoulder, facing him. "That's good."

His gaze, glittering in the darkness of my room, slides up to mine. "Sure. Yes. It's good, but you don't know everything."

"About your dad?"

"Yeah." He takes a deep breath. "It's a lot."

It makes me realize I'm not the only one who's walking around with a glass jar for a heart.

*My Heart Insists It's a Runaway Freight Train*

I could tell her it wasn't an accident. But those words in my mouth feel like a freight train crushing my innards with its velocity, and the moment I release them, they'll run over everything good outside of me too. I'm not sure I've done the right thing, bringing up my dad. At all. The extended cut of my life is ready for viewing, but the ugly truth of how that story plays out feels like an over-the-top black and white melodrama with the train tracks, the villain, and a rope to tie me down while we await the train that's going to kill me. Except I'm not a hero. My dad and I are both villains in this tale, and I wonder which one of us the train is going to take out first?

Dr. B would ask me, *"Why are you holding back?"*

If I say those words to Hannah, and the way she looks at me changes, I know it will be me.

I've only admitted the truth—that the accident wasn't an accident—to a handful of people: my parents, my therapists, Abby and Gabe. I've never committed to telling any of my girlfriends this; even the shit about my dad has been told in short vignettes without sound and fury. Detached. A quick acknowledgement of what was so that—should questions arise—I'd have an escape hatch: "Remember. I mentioned it."

I used to tell myself that was all that was necessary. Offering up those painful truths serves no purpose but to highlight pain. Except I see now what those same girlfriends meant when they accused me of holding back. I wouldn't drop the wall low enough to let them understand the vulnerable me hidden behind it.

Hannah isn't my girlfriend, but fuck, I think I'd like her to be. Only jumping right in to sleeping with her feels like more of my same methods of operation: connect to the physical but leave the rest out because it's too difficult. Stick with what's easy. Except I don't want to lose her. Already did that. And I don't want to be watching her move in with the next guy six months from now, telling me I wasn't enough, that I didn't give her enough.

But admitting this horrific truth to Hannah—my dad, the car crash, who I was before therapy—makes me feel like I'm standing on the edge of a one-inch precipice, back to a raging blizzard, clinging to a cliff face with bloody fingernails, and I'm about to lose my grip.

"What is it?" She breathes the question more than asks it.

I sift through all the explanations in my head trying to find the words around the shame of it but hear Dr. B say in my head: *"Seth, you must own this story. Use it as a point of empowerment. There is no shame in being your authentic self, and as difficult as that time of your life was, rewriting your story to hide those scars dishonors the boy in you who needed help."*

I take another deep breath.

The sudden warmth of Hannah's hand on my arm offers me comfort. "You're cold," she says and draws the comforter up and over us. "Tell me," she says from under the cocoon we're suddenly inside.

It's as if she knew exactly what I needed—a way to block out the rest of the world and exist in suspended animation with just her. But I can't tell her everything. As much as I want to, I can't. I can give her the truth about my dad. A starting point.

"My dad used to hit me and my mom."

Hannah lays a hand on my arm and offers a reassuring touch. "I remember when he was arrested."

I don't say anything else because the memories are awful, and I've only been able to put them together after a ton of time and a ton of therapy. The night of the car crash, before he was arrested, unfurls in my mind like an antique movie on 8mm film. Our turning point. I'd already been hurt after a fight with Gabe. My dad had fallen off the wagon—again—and he'd tossed me across the room for fucking up his feel good, for standing up to him, for refusing to do what he said. There was screaming, breaking new ribs on top of those that were already broken. I'd landed on a table that broke under me. Unable to catch my breath. Mom screamed for him to stop. I stumbled from the house, got into my truck, and drove away. The last thing I remembered was turning the wheel and allowing myself to drift into oncoming traffic, which makes me even worse. I'd been willing to take someone out with me. Unforgivable really.

But that victim visited me while I was in the hospital and extended his forgiveness, just like Gabe had. I seem to be the only one who's fucked up trying to forgive.

Hannah is silent, waiting, and I imagine it's because she's afraid to break the spell and keep me from talking, because where I'm taking her is so horrific. Her fingertips move lightly across my skin, offering a nurturing touch. "I'm here."

"He was just a mean drunk. One time, when I was little, I was skating through the kitchen in my socks–"

Her hand squeezes my arm, and I know she's thinking about us earlier.

"I'd been imagining I was a hockey player, moving the puck for a score. I'd been yelling, pretending to be the announcer and the crowd all at the same time–" the words die away, but then I take a deep breath and continue– "He didn't like it when his television time was interrupted sober, but when he was drunk, he wanted blood for it."

Hannah doesn't say anything at first, instead pulling me close. "Oh, Seth."

I adjust and wrap my arms around her, swallowing.

"I didn't know."

"I hid it, and he hit me in places it was easy to hide. No one knew." Which is a partial truth. Abby and Gabe knew, but I'd kept it from everyone else and punished both of them for trying to help. I'd gotten so good at avoiding being seen. Hiding in my clothes, eventually in lies, in my humor. There are lots of ways to misdirect and offer people a more palatable version of ourselves.

Her arms tighten around me. Vibrations from her body move through mine. I grasp her face, and my thumbs discover the tears on her cheeks.

"Why the tears?"

She leans forward and kisses me, but this is a different kiss. It isn't wrapped up with desire, but rather empathy, a desperation to impart her emotions, her support. Her hands are on my cheeks, her fingers in my hair. Then she pulls away. "How did you do it?"

"Not well. I drank, partied, and acted like a jerk. I was on my way to becoming him."

Her fingers remain in my hair, moving through the locks. She's working through what I've told her, and I'm tense, worried, and afraid that sharing this part of the truth might have been enough to end things before they've even begun.

"When I was let into your room at the hospital to say goodbye," she says, "I begged you to stay."

I draw away so I can look at her, the familiarity of her words hitting my heart with melodic notes I remember. Except I was in a coma. How could I? It's hard to see her in the darkness of our cocoon, so I focus on the feel of her hand in my hair, the sound of her voice, the sensation of her legs entwined with mine in this world we've created for the time being.

"I remember I told you that you made a difference in my world, or something like that…" Her voice drifts a moment. "But it wasn't until I told you that, that I understood how true it was." She takes a deep breath. "Maybe you made mistakes then, but you did what you could with what you knew. And–" the word catches in her throat a moment, as if it's trying to move through her emotion. She adds– "and we all make mistakes." A sob breaks through. "We all have them–"

I pull her tighter and understand her meaning, but emotionally can't reconcile if she understood the darker mistake, she'd still recuse me from my own culpability. I don't. But her words make me see how my life might have impacted someone I thought so peripheral to me then. That I didn't know I was important to someone else because I didn't feel important to anyone.

"The night my dad died," she starts but stops.

I touch her hair, allow my palm to drift over the silk and wait for her to talk, wondering if she's going to open the door for me.

"I was out partying with my friends. I'd forgotten my phone. The next morning—when I got back to my dorm room—there were all these messages."

"You couldn't have known," I tell her and pull her closer.

She snuggles in, her arms around me. "Even so." She sniffs. "It doesn't take away how easy it is to blame myself for not being there."

It feels good to be allowed inside her world, and I'm struck with how sharing my vulnerability has allowed me to glimpse hers. My heart expands in my chest with the awareness, and I shift, drawing closer to her and pressing a kiss to her head.

She sniffs, and her fingers leave my hair. I feel her move, and I think she's looking at me. "When I was seventeen, I had a gigantic crush on you, Seth Peters." Her fingers skim my skin. "Everyone else did, too, so I refused to admit it to myself. Besides, I couldn't imagine that you would ever notice me. But that day— in the hospital—when I thought I was going to lose you, I stopped lying to myself."

I run a finger from her cheek down her jaw. "I didn't know."

"I still have a massive crush on you, Seth Peters," she whispers.

I lean forward and press a kiss to her cheek and kiss toward her mouth. "I'm glad, because it's probably nothing compared to the crush I have on you."

"Thank you for trusting me."

I squeeze her with a hug, unsure what to say to that. Sharing this with her has quieted the freight train, releasing a few of the cars it's dragging, but the rest of the truth is still there, a heavy load on that track. "I don't want to mess this up," I tell her.

"You think sex will mess it up?"

I laugh quietly. "No. I've been the leap-before-you-look kind of guy, and just jump into the physical part of the relationship. It's easier to ignore these heavier things. My last two girlfriends told me that I was too closed off. I don't want… I don't want to risk messing this up."

She makes a humming noise. "So what are we going to do then?" She moves in the darkness of our cocoon, and I feel her lips near my ear. "Because I really, really want to have sex with you. I've wanted to since the night at the beach."

I inhale quickly, the breath catching in my chest, expanding my crystallized lungs so that it hurts letting go of it. I grip her hips, as her leg rubs mine with sweet friction, then squeeze her tightly and press our hips together. "Hannah. Fuck."

"Fifteen dates?" she asks. I feel her smile against my skin, and her hands work their way under my shirt, sliding up my abdomen and around to my back.

"Ten?" That sounds like so many, and I start calculating. "What's a date? Coffee? Technically we could work in two or three in a single day."

She laughs, her mouth against my neck.

I really like that sound. The sweet and slightly husky notes send chills racing across my skin. "Five?" My voice, on the other hand, sounds strangled and needy.

"A minimum of five dates. Okay." Her hands spread across my shoulder blades.

Her boobs are pressed against my chest, and I resist the impulse to tilt my hips further to meet the resistance between her legs. Instead, I draw a ragged breath and disengage, moving away from her. "I'm drawing a line between us." I swipe a hand along the sheets. I sound ridiculous. What am I doing?

She laughs again.

"Never mind. Fuck that." I move back across my self-imposed barrier and draw her back into my arms. "Am I being ridiculous?"

She shakes her head which I feel against my shoulder. "No. I think you should listen to what you need. Spoons instead?" she asks.

"I'd rather be a fork, but okay. Spoons it is. Are you little or big?"

"Little." I hear the comforter rustle as she turns over.

"I apologize if this spoon is sharp."

She laughs again, wiggling her hips as she settles into me.

I groan but wrap my arms around her and smile. "Perfect." I nestle my nose in the space between her neck and shoulder, inhaling her clean, peachy scent. "Thank you, Hannah."

She presses in closer and makes a noise acknowledging what I've said.

I don't remember falling asleep, but when I start awake in an unfamiliar place, it takes me a moment to remember where I am, who I'm with. Hannah's body heat warms me, removes me from the haze of a bad dream I can't remember. I don't sleep well, and never have, too cognizant of the need for self-preservation and survival living with a father who liked to throw punches when he was drinking. Old habits die hard.

It's still dark—early-morning dark when the world is waking, stretching its arms, and finding the will to leave a warm bed.

I lift my head and check on Hannah. She faces me, curled like a pill bug. Her head is pressed against my chest, and her knees drawn up, pressed against my thighs. I wonder about this position that appears like she's protecting herself from something, even in her sleep. I move a lock of her golden waves from her face, in awe that I'm lying beside her now.

When I was eighteen and Hannah became someone I saw—which is weird to consider I hadn't always noticed her—she became a lighthouse. I think that began in earnest my junior year. I'd been so caught up in my own self-centered drama, I hadn't been clear about a lot of things, but I remember coaching myself with the mantra *What Would Hannah Do?* I'd admired her strength, her kindness and compassion for others, her integrity to stand up for what she believed in, and her comfort in her own skin. Things I'd wanted for myself and had little ability to emulate before the wreck. After the car crash, as I'd focused on the act of healing my physical body, I'd made a conscious effort to work on my emotional and mental body too.

She's different now.

But so am I.

I wrap an arm around her, and she sighs, relaxes, and shifts against me in her sleep. I move my hips so I don't startle her awake with a stab of my morning wood. I need to pee, but I don't want to let this moment go. It's the fruition of what feels like a lifetime of dreaming. I'm suddenly so grateful that Jenny and Amber broke up with me, so grateful I've transferred, so grateful that all the steps I've taken have led me here.

I lie there with my hand drawing from the heat of her back and try to remember when I finally understood that I felt more than friendship for her. I don't allow myself to return there often. I don't like the person I was then, but for me, Hannah was always a sun.

It had to have been before prom, because I'd wanted to ask her.

It had to have been before Abby's birthday, because I'd remembered watching for Hannah to arrive at the party.

It had to have been before the annual Basin bonfire.

Hannah remembered the homecoming float.

There was this moment at the onset of senior year, after one of my soccer games, I remember walking from the field with Carter to the bleachers. Abby, Gabe, Hannah, and Darnell, and a bunch of our other friends, had been waiting for us. We'd won, so the energy was high and their voices loud and exuberant. The group cheered us as we walked from the field. I remembered studying the group, but the face I searched for had been Hannah's. When my eyes had met hers, and she'd smiled and waved, it felt like I could draw an even breath. Just like seeing her again in Hammill, or when she'd walked across the pizza parlor toward me. Understanding I had feelings for her wasn't like the flash of lightning, but rather the gradual awareness that she was who I was always looking for.

It makes me consider Dr. B's statement again about finding the right partner: *"You will go 'all in' being completely open even about the parts of yourself you try so hard to hide."*

My bladder insists it's time to get up, so I do my best to extricate myself without waking her. As I sit up and climb from the bed, she moans, "Where are you going?"

"Bathroom." I press a kiss to her cheek.

After addressing my morning needs, I slide across the floor through the kitchen with a smile, thinking about sock skating, a new memory to replace the old one. I can't remember having as much fun with someone else for a very long time. It isn't so much a surprise as a reinforcement of how I've always connected to Hannah.

I look for all the stuff to make coffee and get a pot going, then retrieve my phone while it brews, leaning against the counter to reconnect with the world beyond this apartment. My mom has reached out with a phone message. Gabe and Trace have texted.

I open my friends' texts first.

Gabe *So? The scoop?*

He'd been answering my text about going to spend time with Hannah.

I wait to answer him and check Trace's message.

Trace *You good? Thought you'd be home.*

I text Trace back first: *All good. I'm alive. Be home soon.*
Then I text Gabe: *Bro!*

Next, I listen to the message from my mom: "Hey. I need you to call me as soon as you get this message. Love you."

There's something about her message that puts me on edge. I call her immediately.

"Hey," she answers. "Good morning. It's early."

I ignore the small talk and walk around the end of the counter to sit on one of the stools. "I got your message. Everything okay? You sounded a little off."

"What? No."

That response in and of itself feels off.

"How are you?"

"Good," I say. I'm not one to drag out conversations with either of my parents. Because of the baggage between us, I'd be lying to say I trust either of them. But like Dr. Bethany suggested: *"Forgiveness doesn't mean the hurts magically disappear. Forgiveness means not allowing those hurts to claim space in your future."* I just need to figure out how.

"Hold on," Mom says, and there's a stretch of seconds when she doesn't talk. I can hear her moving and what sounds like the click of a door. "I just needed to duck into the laundry room for a moment."

"Is he drinking?"

It's hard not to ask this question.

"No. No. He isn't, but he didn't want me to call you about this."

"So, he went then? To the doctor?"

"Yes. His doctor is ordering some tests for him."

"Tests for what?"

"Bloodwork and such. The usual. He hasn't been in so long."

"Can I do anything?" I hear the way that sounds even if that wasn't my intention and add, "I mean—do you need anything?"

"No, Seth. I just wanted to check in. And maybe see you sooner rather than later."

The guilt.

I don't know that this is how she's meant for me to interpret it, but I do.

"How's everything there?" she asks, changing the subject.

I turn when I hear footsteps. Hannah walks into the kitchen. Her hair is pulled up into a messy bun, and even though she's wearing oversized pink flannel pants and a fitted pink tank that shows off her boobs—which I'd like to get my hands on—I'm equally attracted to her regardless of what she's wearing. Every time I see her, she looks good. I think I like this Hannah best, unguarded. "Good. I like it. I've got to go, Mom. I'll call you later."

I disconnect the call after Mom says "bye" and turn in the stool to face Hannah.

She stops an arm's length from me, tentative.

I reach out, grab her hand, and pull her toward me until she's standing in between my legs. My hands find her hips, the flannel soft against my palms. "Good morning."

She moves her hands through my hair, which awakens all my nerve endings. I imagine laying her down on the floor, kissing my way down in between her legs to feast, but keep it in my fantasies. Five dates. I lean back to look at her face, but then close my eyes, relaxing with her touch as I hum with pleasure.

"That feels really good." Dismissing any lingering worry, I tune into this moment, to Hannah's touch, to the joy of rekindling something we both want.

She leans down and places her lips against my temple. "When I smelled the coffee, I realized I hadn't dreamed you were here."

I draw her down onto one of my thighs. "I loved having a sleepover with you." I kiss her cheek and leave my mouth there.

"Thank you for staying."

I lean back and catch her gaze. "I want to be here for you."

She smiles, blushes, and stands. "Thanks for the coffee."

Five dates.

"Tell me this counts as a date?"

Hannah walks through the room and retrieves two cups, which she fills. "Cream? Sugar?"

I shake my head. "Black."

She sets a cup of steaming coffee in front of me. "No. It doesn't count." She smiles. "We'll have to work a little harder." She picks up her cup and smiles over the rim of the yellow mug, before taking a sip.

*You brought this on yourself*, I think. "Do you have plans tonight?"

"I work tonight. And Jewel will be back tonight." Her eyes meet mine. "I can therefore release you from your chivalrous knightly duty."

I lean toward her. "What if I don't want to be released?"

She grins and leans toward me.

I kiss her, no hands, just mouths. She tastes like minty coffee. Irish Cream.

I withdraw a fraction so I can still feel her mouth graze my lips as I say, "Can I take you out after?"

"At ten?"

I shrug. "Or make sure you get home safe?"

She grins. "I'd love to see you." Pressing a hand against my cheek, she gives me one of her beautiful Hannah smiles that hits me like an arrow in the bullseye of my heart, causing it to sputter. "And now I don't want to get ready for class. I just want to stay here with you."

I give her another smile and offer her my raised eyebrows. "I could help you get ready." I wiggle my eyebrows.

She giggles. "We'll never make it to class."

I laugh quietly as she disappears down the hall. After a sip of my coffee, I return to my phone while I wait. Gabe has texted back.

*WTF? It's the freaking butt crack of dawn. Why are you up so early and sending me texts that wake me up?*

*Why isn't your phone set to* do not disturb?

*And the butt-crack of dawn is when all the early birds catch the worms.*

*Who the fuck wants worms?*

*If it means winning, me.*

*What did you win?*

*Hopefully the girl of my dreams.*

*I want all the deets.*

No kissing and telling.

So there was kissing and something to tell.

No comment.

I'll call you later.

When Hannah and I finally leave the apartment, I open the door, laughing at something Hannah said, then notice her freeze, her smile sliding from her pretty face as she looks down at something. I follow her gaze. On the mat outside the door is the bouquet of roses Sebastian brought over, though it looks as though he smashed them. Some of the blossoms have been decapitated, petals littering the ground around it.

My insides tighten with familiarity as the freight train picks up speed once more, and I wonder again just how similar Sebastian and my dad really are?

*My Heart Insists It's Really Over*

I'm not afraid of Sebastian, but I can't get what Seth said out of my mind either. *You can't know, Hannah, as much as you'd like to be sure you know someone.* He'd walked me to my car and leaned in to say it, after I'd insisted that there wasn't anything to worry about. I'm not sure who I was really trying to convince. Seth's right. He's speaking from experience. He'd been hiding a huge secret behind the smile he wore to school every day.

Thinking of Seth makes me tuck my chin into the collar of my jacket and smile a secret smile as I walk across campus from my car to class. Walking into the kitchen with him there, coffee brewing, made my insides liquify. He'd sat on the stool, his gray t-shirt stretched across his shoulders, his phone pressed to his ear, his eyes brightening when he saw me. I think about his hands against my skin, about kissing him, wanting him.

I climb the stairs into the building, go directly to my class, and sit through a lecture about the Philosophies of Education with a focus on Piaget's Theory of Cognitive Development. I'm in and out, my mind traipsing back to the night before with Seth, and each time it does, it's as if little fairies are running through my body leaving footprints under my skin.

Five dates.

I glance at the clock on my phone counting down to when I can see him again, as if it will make the five dates pass faster. There's a text notification.

It's from Sebastian: *I'm sorry about last night. I overstepped.*

I flip the phone over my desk face down, feeling as if I have whiplash. *Yes, you fucking did*, I think.

My first impulse is to text Seth, but I check it. It isn't because I want to keep it from him, but there's a line between Seth as my friend, and Seth as someone I want more with, which is very clearly the case. Sebastian looms like one of the inflatable marketing tubes, whipping back and forth at car lots between Seth and me, and I don't want him to be there.

I ignore Sebastian's text—it's easier—and text Jewel instead: *Sebastian showed up last night.*

I set the phone back on my little desk, face up, knowing Jewel went straight to work from Portland. She'll text me when she can, so I'm surprised when I see the three dots.

*WTF?!?*

About what I figured her response would be and type: *Are you on a break? Don't worry. Seth was there.*

*Did they throw hands?*

*LOL. No hands thrown. I told Bash to leave. Seth stayed.*

 *Oh. He did. The night? Hmmmm. I don't want any of the nasty straight-ass deets.*

*No deets. Just kissed.*

*What? Such restraint. Good at least?*

*You said you don't want deets. Yes.*

*You home tonight?*

*Why? You going to invite your bootie-call over?*

*Jewels.* 

*LOL*

*Sebastian texted me again today.*

*I'll be home. With Joy too, probs. And WTF? I don't like this guy's obvious inability to listen to you. WTFX2*

*Maybe he's just lonely?*

*You tell yourself that Hannah, and then get mind-fucked because you give his entitled ass the benefit of the doubt. There's a fine line between being nice and being foolish. Don't be a fool.*

*Yes, ma'am*

*I'm being fucking serious.*

*I KNOW! I'm listening. Seth said something similar.*

*Humph. I'll look forward to meeting him. Tonight?*

*No. I work. Another time.*

*K. G2G. Frankie is giving me the evil eye because my break is over. <3*

When class finishes, I walk across campus to the student center for a coffee. There's a line, but I don't have anywhere else I need to be immediately, so I get into it. While I wait, I check social media, stepping forward as the line moves.

"I thought I might find you here."

I know it's Sebastian before I turn, but when I do, I give him a cursory glance. "Are you stalking me?" I ask, before facing forward and offering him my back. I focus on the red jacket of the girl in front of me, the slick sheen of it anchoring my mind there instead of on who's behind me. The espresso machine hisses, and I tense.

"You didn't answer my text," he says from behind me.

"I don't have to, and what you did was fucked up."

"I apologized."

I don't respond. So like Sebastian to think that he's owed something for his actions. I take a step forward as the line queue moves, my frustration climbing.

"I meant it. I really am sorry, Hannah."

"Great. Thanks. You can go." I give him a look over my shoulder.

"Can we grab a coffee? Like old times?" He holds up his hands. "I don't have any ulterior motives or anything. I was just hoping to clear the air."

Part of me wants to tell him to go to hell, but another part of me knows that isn't nice. I suppose in his shoes, I would hope someone would give me the opportunity to find closure. Except that stronger voice inside me, the one I quiet so often because the last time I let her rule I lost the most important person in my life, says that he didn't offer you the same kind of consideration. The nicer side of me rationalizes that I need this to be done. That I don't need to act like him. I glance around. It's a public place, and I'll have a guaranteed out with my next class. I nod.

When I'm situated at a table with my honey latte and waiting for Sebastian to join me, I grab my phone to send Seth a text. I know he's in class, but I'm hopeful he's got it set to silent. Earlier, I'd refrained from texting him about Sebastian, but now it feels like it's important to openly communicate. I don't want Sebastian between us, but I also don't want Seth hearing secondhand that I'm hanging out with my ex for coffee. I don't want Seth to feel like he ever has to question my intentions. Staring at the blank message box, I type, then erase it and try again. I'm not sure what to say. I try again: *Having coffee with Sebastian. Talking.*

"Figure out what you wanted to say?" Sebastian asks as he sits.

I hit send and put my phone away. I don't want Sebastian anywhere near what's going with Seth and me.

"That looked serious."

I sigh. "Look, Sebastian, I can't do the small talk stuff with you. Just say what you wanted to say?" I pull my coffee cup toward me.

He frowns at his coffee cup. "Bash" is written in thick, black ink with a heart on the white cardboard of the cup. The additional attention from other women—jersey chasers—because of his status as a football player, and a very talented one at that, was a norm of our relationship. I tried not to let it bother me when we'd been together, attempting to rise above jealousy. Now I just find it annoying, wondering if Chelsey—the woman he cheated with—was one of those.

I look at Sebastian across from me and wonder if there's a part of me that still cares. Watching him take off his jacket, I note he still looks like the Sebastian I met. He's as handsome as always. He glances at me, flashing one of those grins I used to find so charming. It hits me that I don't find it charming anymore. I don't find anything about him remotely enticing. And I don't feel sad about it, I feel… relief. As if I somehow won something because I got away, which is weird to think. But we'd been broken long before we broke up, and I see that now. I'm done. Ready to move on.

"This isn't going to be a rehashing, right?"

His blue eyes look up before he rubs at his ear. Then he leans on his hand, elbow on the tabletop, before sitting up and putting his hands in his lap. This isn't the cool, confident Sebastian I have come to know. He's nervous.

Seth's warning reverberates in my brain: *you can't know someone. You know what they want you to know.*

I have the fleeting thought to wonder if Sebastian would pretend to influence me. I can't think so ill of him, because if I do, what does that say about me? But Jewel's warning lingers: *don't be a fool.*

Sebastian opens his mouth to say something, then closes it and looks back at his coffee cup. He plucks at the lip of the plastic lid.

"What is it?"

I spent nine months with this man. If someone had asked me to describe him, I would have said confident and collected. I would have said he might appear arrogant, until you get to know him and realize he's just very self-reliant and assured in his skills. I would have said he was charismatic and funny, but this isn't the man that's sitting across the table from me.

"I ended things with Chelsey." He seems to brace himself for my outburst, as if this is characteristic of me. It's not.

"I know. You told me. Doesn't change anything."

He nods. "It's just… my parents–"

My heart constricts. It's the one place I know I'll struggle separating from Sebastian, because my need to help will tug on my heart. There's this strange dynamic between him and his parents. His mom is his enabler. In her eyes he can do no wrong, but she makes up for what little relationship he has with his dad, who's around but impossible to please. When he isn't emotionally absent, he offers harsh criticism and disapproval. It's this uncomfortable dichotomy between indulgence and abandonment. Maybe a different kind of abuse. It messes with Sebastian's head.

I don't respond. I can't. I know it in the deepest parts of myself, even if the squishy parts of me want to swoop in and make him feel better. My footing is stronger now, since going home, since talking with my mom, since Jewel's support, since reconnecting with Seth. My vision is clearer, as if a cloudy film was washed away. I know I can't—don't want to—go backward.

"My mom really likes you. She helped me see I wasn't thinking clearly when I ended things."

—I think he's meant to tell me this to showcase my importance in his life, only it feels wrong. The information sits like a tree that's crashed through a house, misplaced and damaging, only I'm not sure how, unable to put the thoughts and feelings together—

"That I owe you an apology for that."

I keep my face passive though I want to say, *so you're apologizing because your mother told you to?* Instead, I look at my own coffee cup and shrug. I need this over. "Okay. You already have."

"That's it?"

"Does it change anything?" I ask. "You ended things. It doesn't change the circumstances regarding what's already happened and where we are now. What do you want from me?"

"When I ended things, I thought it was the right thing to do."

"It was," I say. "Still is."

"But it doesn't feel like the right thing anymore."

"And what's that? What's the right thing?"

"Us together." Sebastian reaches out and grasps my hand.

I pull it from his grasp. "You'll find someone new, Bash," I tell him.

He shakes his head. "Hannah—" But he stops and watches a pack of students walk by and sighs.

I'm not sure what to say to him. "I'm moving on," I tell him.

His head snaps to me. His eyes study me, and I think he's about to argue it, but then a veil falls over his eyes, separating the Sebastian I know with a version I don't.

I lean back in my chair.

"It's that guy? From last night?"

"I'm not discussing it with you. But it's time to let whatever it is you're holding onto go."

He doesn't respond to that, staring at his cup, which I find unsettling for some reason.

"We were always good friends."

"Sebastian–" I look away and shake my head.

"Don't do this, Hannah."

I shrug into my coat. "You have friends. A team worth." I shake my head. "I don't need any more friends." I gather my things and stand.

Sebastian grabs my hand. "Hannah. We are good."

I extract my hand from his again, needing a little more force to do so than I should. "We're through."

He must accept it this time; he drops my hand as if I've burned him. "So, you're choosing him?"

"I'm choosing me," I say and walk away, leaving Sebastian behind. But I can't get his look out of my mind.

He looked despondent, the tethers to that weight pulling his features down, threatening to turn him inside out. And even though I've said "no," worry festers in my gut, though I'm not exactly sure what I'm worried about.

*My Heart Insists I Take a Deep Breath*

I'd like to think I'm above sinking into the mire of my insecurity, but the moment I read Hannah's text, I nosedive like I'm free-falling without a parachute. It makes me want to jump up in the middle of my European Renaissance history class and go call Dr. Bethany.

The professor is at the front of the auditorium, small and dim under the lowlights, the slide show illuminating his face every so often. He talks about the history of the period using art and artifacts to explore themes, and here I am focused on the phone in my hand.

A student two seats away glances at me. From the annoyed look on her face, I'm guessing my phone is distracting her, though I'm not sure how with the tiers of laptop lights lining the room. I flick the phone off anyway, which seems to placate her. She looks away, returning to her pencil and paper.

Which I should be doing too.

I look at the blinking cursor on my laptop document.

Deep breath in.

Dr. B would ask me, *"What do you know?"*

Gabe said that to me once, too. Asked me what I actually knew and what I'd assumed. *You never asked me,* he'd pointed out. When I'd double-crossed him at fourteen because of my insecurities about Brook. My memories slide into my past self at seventeen when I'd constructed narratives around my assumptions and jealousy. There was never an excuse for my assumptions, but like Dr. B has offered: *sometimes we respond with the only tools we have*. My assumptions fucked our friendship, and even if both Gabe and Abby have forgiven me, it is a huge source of my shame.

I have better tools now.

Deep breath.

What do I know?

Hannah is having coffee with Sebastian. She took the time to text me about it.

Deep breath. Another.

She owes me nothing. We haven't established anything but the desire to see one another again. Deep breath.

She might change her mind, but why text me?

I attempt to focus on the lecture, and type notes into the document, but it devolves into what's on my mind: *Hannah. Hannah. Hannah. What do I know? Worried. Worried. Worried.*

I decide that what worries me the most is Sebastian. He seems volatile. That isn't something to be insecure about. That's something to worry about with respect to Hannah's safety.

What can I do though? Not a whole lot.

Deep breath.

That's not exactly true. I can be there for Hannah.

Deep Breath.

I unlock my phone. My neighbor glances at me, rolls her eyes, and sighs. I have no idea what her problem with me is. I ignore her and text Hannah back: *I'm here if you need me. To talk or whatever.*

Three dots pop up right away.

> ...

> *He apologized for overstepping.*

I'd like to tell her Sebastian is manipulating her, but I don't know that. It would be a lie. I'm thinking about my father, and how many times I heard "I'm sorry" from him over my lifetime. How many bruises and broken bones my mom and I suffered after an apology. I remind myself that my experience isn't hers and text:

> *That's positive.*

Fuck. I hate typing that. About as much as the girl in the next seat hates that I'm texting instead of taking notes. She turns in her seat as much as she can so her back is to me. Sort of. I want to lean over and tell her she can move—there are other seats—but I don't.

> *He asked to remain friends.*

Fuck! I want to yell it, but I shout it in my head instead and adjust my body in my chair with as much force as if I'd actually stood and moved places. I'm tense. I don't know how to respond to that without sounding like a jerk. My mind goes back to constructing narratives like I once did with Abby and Gabe, filling gaps with assumptions, but I take another deep breath, reminding myself that won't serve me. Hearing Dr. B's voice asking me again, *"What do you know? What's real?"*

Hannah texts again, saving me from myself:

> *I told him no.*

Deep breath. A grin blooms on my face like spring flowers as I reread her words.

> *Do you feel good about that?*

Deep breath. Because I sure do.

> *I know it's the right thing. For me.*

> *I'll talk to you later?*

> *Yes.*

I press the button to sleep the phone and return my focus to the lecture and my notes, feeling much better. Then I think about seeing Hannah today, because I'm not sure I can wait until tomorrow. Perhaps I can see what this whole flirting in the Ham is all about.

*My Heart Insists Chemical Reactions*
*that Combust are Fun*

The term is still young enough that Hammill isn't packed, and it's late enough in my shift that students have social engagements to draw them out and beyond the doors of the library. The regulars—those who function better among books or use the stacks to insulate themselves from the struggle of the collegiate social life—are about; a few students interested in getting ahead of their syllabi, along with the staff are scattered in carrells or behind tables. The library, then, is sparsely populated as we near closing.

Mason is off tonight, so I've been left to my own devices and thoughts. I push a partially emptied cart of books that need reshelving into the elevator and select the button for the top floor. When the door opens, I move the cart out and down the walkway between carrells, stacks, and dark study rooms to the dead end of the building where the stacks end abruptly. I'm not usually creeped out on my late shifts, but the interactions I've had recently with Sebastian have me on edge. I wish Seth was going to meet me after work, but we've decided to meet up tomorrow.

Thinking about Seth makes me smile. I realize I must look like an idiot grinning to myself as I reshelve books, but I can't remember feeling so happy. Not in recent memory anyway. Not before my dad—I clear my throat to chase the tightening that happens anytime I think of my dad being gone and shelve another book.

Movement catches my attention, and I look over the top of the books on the shelf in front of me through the rows to track it, watching a blue sweatshirt move through the stacks.

I return to reshelving.

Before Dad passed away, my life felt secure enough to challenge my place in it. It wasn't like I wanted to upend everything, but I figured freshman year was the perfect time to examine those parts of myself I wasn't sure fit. But if I hadn't, I would have been there when he needed me; I would have been able to say goodbye. This is what I tell myself, anyway, even if Mom has given me an out.

I've realized being with Sebastian had been comfortable. Easy. He'd had that easy smile, and we seemed to connect on, well, everything. We slid right into dating, talking daily, until we were staying at one another's houses. The ease of it still surprises me, but now, with distance, I'm noticing the red flags everyone else had tried to tell me were there. My acquiescence. His need for attention. My excuses for him. His demands for my time. In retrospect, the relationship had allowed me to remain in my bubble of grief. Sebastian hadn't asked for anything more than my attention for him, which I gave willingly. It didn't require me to look at my own grief, but to focus on taking care of him, feeling purposeful. I'd been able to hold onto him to avoid slipping into the black hole spinning beneath me.

Sebastian ending things had forced me back into the black hole, only it wasn't a black hole anymore. It was a shallow divot where I could stand on my own two feet. I couldn't avoid facing the truth of my grief anymore, but it wasn't as intense. I could see beyond my pain, then climb out of it. Today, sitting across from Sebastian and the lack of feeling for him helped me see it.

Now, there's a sparkling new star shining in my center every time I think about Seth. Happiness again. Happiness like I remember before.

I check the next book and walk the few feet necessary to shelve it, crouching down to return the book to its place. As I do, I notice the white canvas shoes on the other side of the shelf facing me. I stand, keeping the figure in my line of vision. Dark blue jeans, a book tucked under an arm. Royal blue sweatshirt with a white t-shirt underneath. A smile. Dimples. Amber eyes.

The muscle of my heart thickens and begins pulsing wildly to find its shape again. I smile. "Hi," I tell the gorgeous man on the other side of the shelf.

"I didn't know you wore glasses," Seth says, grinning.

I blush and push my glasses up over my forehead, and they catch my hair under them. "Just to read. I was just thinking about you."

"You were? I hope they were good thoughts."

"Very good thoughts." I smile but can't look at him, returning my glasses to their place as I continue pushing the cart toward the end of the shelf, stopping to reshelve the remaining books as I go.

Seth moves at the same pace on the other side. I can see him between the books and love knowing he's here.

"I like the sound of that," he says, "because I was thinking about you, too."

"You were?"

"Yes."

We reach the end of the shelf and Seth faces me, leaning against the end of it, a book in one hand as the other finds a pocket. I study his hands a moment before my gaze meets his again. He's noticed, and his grin widens.

"I hope they were good thoughts," I tell him and move to tuck a strand of hair behind my ear.

"I'll tell you mine, if you tell me yours."

"A lady never reveals her secrets."

"Oh, but I think a lady should."

"Why's that?"

"Because her secrets are the only ones worth knowing."

A little flustered by him, and my insane desire to reach out and touch him, I fiddle with the remaining books on the cart instead. "You're here," I say. "I thought–"

"I had some stuff to work on." He waves the book he's holding. "Besides, my roommate—well, not my roommate, but one of his friends—told me that the Ham is a hot spot for meeting hot girls. I thought maybe I should check it out." He looks around.

I follow his gaze.

The third floor is mostly deserted.

"Oh. Really?" I cross my arms. "As you can see, a veritable nightclub."

He smiles and reaches out to touch the book cart. "So they say, and since I know someone who works here, I thought I might get the inside scoop."

"About what?"

He gently moves the cart, clearing the way to me, and steps closer. We might not be touching, but I can feel his heat. I can smell the clean scent of him, like salt water and soap. My heartbeat hitches and shifts, making room for my lungs, which are suddenly struggling to grab enough air to fill them.

Seth leans forward and whispers near my ear, "Like maybe the best places in the stacks to say, kiss someone?" The warmth of his cinnamon breath and the intermittent caress of his mouth on my cheek send chills across my skin. "That seems like good insider intel."

I don't move away, but instead turn my head, just enough so I can look into his eyes. I notice he has a dark copper ring around the outside of his iris. There's a firework of dark brown in his right eye I've never noticed before. "I might know of some places," I whisper, "but that kind of insider information will cost you."

His eyebrows rise over his eyes, and I feel the smirk rather than see it. "Oh? Really?"

I nod. He's so close I can't seem to formulate coherent thoughts. I grasp onto his sweatshirt at his stomach, not that I need to—I want to.

"How much?"

"Too much."

"I might be willing to pay a lot for that information." He reaches out and touches my collarbone, moving my black cardigan slightly so that he can press his finger to my skin just above the collar of my black t-shirt. His remaining fingers curl around the back of my neck, his eyes following his touch.

"How much?" That spot he's touching is on fire.

His eyes return to mine, serious, the pupils more prominent. "Right now? Maybe my soul." Then his eyes curve with his smile.

I laugh, a low sound in my chest and gently push him, walking him back into the row where he came from. "I think I might be able to negotiate. I'll be expecting a down payment." I continue to walk him backward until his back is against the bookshelf.

His eyes widen, and his breathing is erratic, suddenly matching mine. He swallows. "Anything. I'll pay anything."

"You sure?"

"Oh, god, yes." He licks his lips, his gaze dropping to my mouth.

I can't play anymore, because I want this connection more than anything I've ever wanted in my life. I press my mouth to his. There's the thud of a book hitting the floor, and I revel when his hands grasp my hips, tugging me against him. It's needy. Our tongues dance the tango around one another, with suggestive promises as he tilts his head for better access, deeper connection, and submerges his hands in my hair.

My glasses get caught between us.

Then I remember I'm at work.

I step back, my back smacking into the shelf behind me, the books thumping at the force. "Oh." I feel wild.

"Fuck," he says at the same time. He looks as wild as I feel, his eyes so dark, his chest pulsing with each breath.

In all my years and all my kisses and all my experiences, I have never felt that. I want that again. And again. And again. I reach up and touch my mouth.

Seth looks shocked too, like we mixed a chemical concoction and it exploded. I can imagine the chemical reaction changing my appearance, as though I look askew. That's how I feel, in the most addictive way.

Then, because reason and chemistry don't seem to work in conjunction, I move at the same time Seth does, closing the distance, and we connect every way we can in the middle of the library stacks. With abrupt head angles, gripping and sliding hands, we find ways to kiss and touch that make me even more restless, not less.

"Fuck, Hannah," Seth says against my mouth.

Somehow, my reason establishes a reconnection to my brain. I pull away, breathing like I just ran a marathon. "Five dates?" I ask because I don't want five more dates. I want it right now. I want to grab his hand, take him out to my car or into one of the dark study rooms, and go where we both want to go.

He swallows, nods slowly, and fists his hands at his sides as if to keep from touching me. "Five dates."

I can see he's wondering what he was even thinking. I sidestep away from him, my hands touching the shelf as I go to keep myself tethered to reality. "I better get back to work." I shake my head and take another step away. "I have to finish reshelving, or I'll never be done."

He nods, similarly tongue-tied, or so it would seem. "I'll meet you downstairs. Walk you to your car?"

I nod and duck around the shelf to hurry through the rest of my work, unsure I'll even be able to focus. I wish Mason were at work to push the clock faster, but he isn't, and the time moves at a snail's pace.

When I slip through the doorway from the back, Seth's waiting by the front door, leaning against the wall. He looks up at me from his phone and straightens. "Hi," he says when I get close enough.

"Hi." I feel the heat of my blush.

He grins, holding out a hand.

I take it, and he pulls me toward him, drawing both of us out the doors into the cold night.

"How was your day?"

"Better now," I tell him, my eyes on my feet. "Yours?"

Our steps crunch over the frozen snow turned to slush.

"Let's see. I woke up next to Hannah Fleming. Awesome. I freaked out a little bit when she met with her ex for coffee. Not awesome. I made out with a hot girl at the Ham. Awesome. Holding hands and walking her to her car. All in all, a solid day." He squeezes my hand and turns to look at me with a grin that makes his eyes twinkle and my legs weak.

"Sor–"

"Don't even do it, Hannah."

I smile, shiver, and look away from his gorgeous face. "I didn't want you to hear it from someone else."

He nods. "I appreciate that, which is why I think it's okay to admit I freaked out, not to make you feel bad or anything. I know it isn't cool to admit shit like that, but I just want to be real with you."

We make it to my car.

I lean against the driver's side door and face him, taking both of his hands in mine. "That's what I want. To be open."

Seth takes a step closer. "Full disclosure then." He smiles and leans in, his mouth near mine. "What happened in the library was so fucking hot, I've been a walking hard on since."

I giggle.

He presses his lips to my cheek. "It's time to get these official dates started, Hannah."

I nod. "Tomorrow night?"

"Yes. Right." He groans it.

I grasp his jacket and turn my mouth to meet his, nipping at his lower lip. He makes a frustrated noise, grasps the back of my head, and angles his head for deeper access to the kiss—and it explodes. His body is pressed against mine, pinning me in between the car and him. I love it but hate all the layers between us.

"Is everything off the table?" I ask under his lips.

He hums a question.

"Sex is. But everything else?" I'm thinking of touching him, about going down on him. "If I get you in the car…"

His body still pinning me, Seth leans back to take in my face in the cold parking lot illuminated by evenly spaced light posts. He smiles and straightens. A rush of cold fills the space between us, and I long to fill it back up with our warmth.

"Better not," he says. "If I get you in that car, Hannah, I'm going to town."

I laugh.

He tucks a strand of my hair behind an ear under my cap, leans forward, and plants a sweet kiss on my mouth. "Call me when you get home? So I know you're safe."

I nod, my heart warmed by his thoughtfulness, then get into the car, and start it so the heater warms the space. Seth walks across the parking lot to wherever he's parked his car, disappearing into the darkness. When the car is warm enough, I drive the few minutes it takes to cross town to my apartment building and park, gathering my things before starting across the complex.

Headlights slash the driveway in front of me, and I pause to let the car pass.

But it doesn't. Instead, it veers onto the curb, blocking the path to the stairs. I retreat several steps, confused.

Then I realize it's Sebastian. My heart constricts, then freefalls through my body toward my feet.

He jumps out. "What the fuck, Hannah!"

I scuttle away from him, drawing my phone out of my pocket simultaneously, placing a call to Jewel, who's on my emergency contacts. "You need to leave, Bash."

He walks around the still running car, his body cutting the flare of the headlamps and casting a shadow as he passes. "You moved on really easily. I went out of my way to see you after work, and you're nearly fucking him in parking lot."

"I told you it's over between us," I say. "I've said it repeatedly."

He points at me. "It's over when I fucking say it's over. And it isn't."

"Don't be ridiculous, Sebastian. You broke up with me, remember. You moved on. You needed something else. You need to stop this."

"Fuck!" He yells it at the top of his lungs, and my breath catches. His anger turns him from the Sebastian I knew into a scary stranger.

I wrap my arms around myself and start toward the stairs, giving him a wide berth. "You need to leave me alone."

He turns in his spot, watching me go, but doesn't come after me. "You're mine, Hannah."

"Hannah?" Jewel yells from three floors up. I hear her footfalls on the stairwell.

"Here," I call out to Jewel, now around the car and moving up the walkway toward the stairwell. "This stops now, Bash. Or I'm calling campus security."

"For what?"

"To report you. This isn't okay."

"And who do you think they'd believe?" He sneers at me.

It feels like a threat even if the words aren't, but my belly clenches, and a sour taste works its way up my throat. I shake my head, but words feel disconnected and unavailable. He's a football star. He's the golden child going in the draft. He's the hometown prince. Who am I? I swallow and wonder what's happening.

What has just happened?

He hasn't touched me.

My feelings are careening inside of me like pinballs: fear, rationalization, anger, frustration, logic.

Then Jewel is next to me, taking my hand in hers. She points it at Sebastian. "Get the fuck out of here and stay away from her."

"What are you going to do?"

"What are you going to do, Sebastian?" Jewel asks, throwing his words back at him.

"Are you threatening me?" he asks her.

"Were you threatening her?" Jewel asks.

I tug on her to get her moving with me up the steps. If security wouldn't believe me when it comes to Sebastian, they won't believe her. It might be worse for her. I grab her arm. "Let's go."

Jewel and I retreat up the steps. "I'm so sorry," I tell her over and over.

"Hush now," she says. "This isn't your fault."

"Mine, Hannah! I'll fuck everything up," Sebastian yells, his voice still loud and invasive. "I will."

I know he's talking about Seth, and I can't, for the life of me, fathom why Sebastian even cares.

*My Heart Insists I Might Be a Supernova*

The door to Hannah's apartment isn't opened by Hannah, but instead by a tall, muscular woman, with a head covered in braids tied at the back of her neck. She's lean and sharp, angular in a way that communicates the agility of her body. She's scowling, then offers a polite smile when she realizes that I'm not whoever she thought I was on the other side of the door, which makes me look around to check even if I don't know who I'm looking for. This must be Jewel, and I admit I'm slightly terrified of her badassness. She takes her hand off the bat next to the door, and I'm curious why she'd think she needed it.

I'm afraid I already know.

"You must be Seth." She steps back to let me in and glances at the wrapped gift I'm holding, then back to my face.

I'm not sure I've ever felt more judged, but if this is Hannah's gatekeeper, I'm all for it.

"And you must be Jewel."

"The one and the only. That gorgeous woman on the couch is my girlfriend, Joy." She points, and I turn around.

A cute woman, cocooned in a hoodie with the hood up and a blanket, offers me a quick wave. "Hi."

"Where are you taking our girl?"

"Well, there's this puppy bakery and cafe in town. I thought we'd go there."

"You're taking Hannah to Puppy Paws and Cupcakes?" Jewel's eyes are wide, and I can't discern if this is because it's a terrible idea or not.

I nod.

She shakes her head but smiles. "She's going to want to adopt them all."

I smile because that's exactly why I chose it. Hannah is going to love the place. "I promise not to bring home a dog."

"Oh but–" Joy says, unfurling herself from her blanket with excitement.

Jewel points at her. "Three years, Joy. Three. We've discussed this."

Joy deflates back onto the couch with a pout.

"You're here!" Hannah says, walking into the main room from the hallway, and my heart palpitates seeing her. She's dressed in fitted jeans and a cute, fuzzy pink sweater, her long, naturally curly blonde hair waving around her face. She has these gentle, round features that make me feel awake: pretty blue eyes framed by dark lashes, a smallish nose, these soft pink lips with a slightly fuller lower lip. I remember thinking she was pretty in high school, but now her level of hotness is otherworldly, as if I'm floating through space caught in her gravitational pull.

"You look great."

She stops, and I can see she'd like to touch me but doesn't. I don't reach for her. Jewel snickers like she knows and retreats back to the couch.

"I got this for you," I say and hold out the gift.

"What is it?" She turns and sets it on the counter.

I stand next to her, our backs to the living room. Our arms brush, and the sensation races across my skin, lighting up all my nerves like the opening sparks to a brush fire.

"Open it."

She grins, looking pleased, and a blush creeps across her cheeks. When she unwraps the fuzzy socks decorated with hearts, she looks up at me. "Socks?"

"You have some serious practice to do if we're going to make the Olympic team."

Her grin widens, and she giggles, and pressing the socks to her heart. "I love them." She gives me an awkward cheek kiss, which I completely understand. Five dates. After what happened in the library, I think any amount of touching might cause us to combust, and with Jewel and Joy a few feet away, that might be even more awkward.

She sets the package in a basket near the door, retrieves her gray coat from the rack, and slips into black ankle boots. "Ready?"

"Yes."

"Don't wait up," she tells Jewel and Joy.

"Didn't intend to, but text me anyway."

I follow Hannah from the apartment and as soon as I close the door, she turns to me, reaching up to frame my face with her hands. "Thank you," she says, then she presses her mouth to mine with a sigh.

I grasp her hips, then wrap my arms around her, and pull her closer. The kiss is as bright as the sun. Hot and illuminating all the space I didn't know existed inside of me, sending light to those hard-to-reach spaces I've tried to hide. I can't help the noise I make, a sigh mixed with a note of frustrated need, my hands squeezing her as I do.

"Same," she says into my mouth and pulls away, grinning. "I needed that." She shrugs into her jacket.

I did too, but I don't say it. Instead, I take her hand in mine and lead her to my car. When I park in front of Puppy Paws and Cupcakes a few minutes later, she looks at me with wide eyes and a huge grin.

"Puppies?" She claps. "I need this!"

I don't have time to ask what she means, but another red flag is raised in my head. Jewel and her bat. The scowl. Why does Hannah need this? But I let it go. For now. I concentrate on Hannah in the present.

Hannah with puppies is perfect. *Way to go, Seth.* I'm proud of myself for thinking of it. Being with bundles of furry energy makes her look so happy. We hang out, playing with the puppies, then grab some cupcakes for Jewel and Joy, before I take her to dinner at a local microbrew spot where Trace said the food is dope. I might not drink, but I'm down for good food. The light is low, the music loud but not overpowering, and it's full of people.

"That was so much fun," she says, scooting into the high-backed booth across from me. After taking off her jacket, she uses her hands to flip her hair.

Watching her is satisfying, like with the puppies. Her smile. Her laughter. The way she bites the inside of her lip sometimes when she's thinking. "The puppies were cute," I say, even if I was more enamored with observing her. She'd sparked to life, which made me realize that the Hannah I've been reconnecting with hasn't been sparkling like she used to. I saw through a window in the wall that didn't used to be there.

"I wanted to take them all home." She grins and leans forward.

I try not to notice her boobs, but it's fucking hard. She looks good enough to eat, a confection in that pink V-neck sweater. I imagine tasting her, my tongue sliding along that seam, then blink, chastising myself for my inability to think straight. What had she said? The puppies. Right. "Jewel said as much."

Hannah straightens, both saving me from my baser thoughts and torturing me because my curiosity is deactivating my brain and reducing me to instinct. Why did I sit on the other side of the table from her? If I were closer, I could kiss her. Oh. Wait. That's why.

The waiter returns with water and takes our drink order.

"She knows me," Hannah says about Jewel.

I look at my glass of water and take a drink, hoping to reset my brain. "She answered the door with a bat. Is that the norm?"

Hannah blushes. It's noticeable even in the dim lighting of the pub. Her eyes slide away to look at one of the TVs hanging in the room, and I know she's not telling me something. I'm not sure how, but I've spent a lifetime spinning tales in the name of self-preservation. Maybe it's because I know myself. I'm not entitled to whatever is in her head, but it adds another red flag to the others I've been collecting.

The waiter returns, sets down our sodas, and glances at Hannah, his eyes lingering, though I don't think she notices. We order. *Move along, buddy,* I think and realize I'm being ridiculous. I just can't seem to help the response. Sitting across from Hannah like this was years in the making, and now I'm possessive of it.

I take a breath to focus myself on what's important—Hannah. Right now.

"What is the normal door-answering protocol at your place?" I ask, curious. "I don't remember seeing the bat the other night." I grin at her.

Hannah's mouth screws up to the side, and she bites her bottom lip, a nervous movement. I have a feeling I know what her answer is going to be.

"That's a new thing." She takes a sip of her soda and glances at me. When she says, "Sebastian showed up to our place," I understand.

I knew it. "Again?"

"Can we not talk about it?" She leans forward and sips her soda again, then leans back, and moves things around in front of her, reorganizing them. It's a tick I recognize, having done it my whole life. Putting things in their place, perfecting the space, trying to get it just right. It's a control thing, when everything else feels like it's chaos. I know why I do it, and it makes me wonder why Hannah is doing it.

"I don't want him here," she says, "on our date."

"Sure," I say, "but now my mind is going to spin on it anyway. So… may I ask some questions to get rid of that?"

She gives me a short smile. "Okay. Go."

I move through our timeline, aligning opportunities. "When?"

"When I got home from work. The other night."

My heart seizes up thinking about the possibilities of what could have been. I should have made sure she got home safe. There's something about that guy that's cracked. "So, Jewel thinks she needs to answer the door with a bat now? Did he hurt you?"

She shakes her head and looks at the TV again, the smile gone from her face. I wonder what she's leaving out. I know that technique too, but I don't press her. It won't work. Instead, I reach across the table and touch her arm lightly to get her attention. "Are you okay?"

Her eyes bounce from where I've touched her to my eyes. She nods. "Now." She smiles again. A real one. "He didn't touch me. His words were enough."

I want to rant at her about that guy. I want to tell her she shouldn't go anywhere without pepper spray, or that she should get campus police to escort her home after work, or to call me and I'll be there waiting. I want to tell her not to talk to him, to ignore him when he tries, but I'm not in a position to do those things. It doesn't take away the desire to, however, to protect her from what appears to have been an abusive relationship. I would know that too.

I want to confront the prick.

My dragon wants to burn him to ash.

"Are you safe Hannah? Because–"

"It's fine," she says, cutting me off. "Let's talk about something else."

I don't want to move on, but I want to respect her agency. It's probably a good idea. I'm heated, and not in a good way.

Deep breath.

"Favorite puppy earlier?" she asks.

"The yellow-lab mix."

"A yellow lab." She picks up her phone.

"What are you doing?" I lean forward.

She holds her phone out of my line of sight, typing and smiling. "What your dog choice says about you," she reads. "Since a lab is a sporting dog, it says you are agreeable and conscientious." She grins at me. "I concur."

Good thing she doesn't know what's on my mind. "Yours. And no peeking." I grab her phone.

"The dachshund."

I scroll through her phone for it. "Tenacious, bossy, and want your own way." I laugh.

"I take it you agree?"

I slide the phone back over the table toward her. "That's the Hannah I've always known. A person who knows what she wants and makes it happen."

The waiter returns with the food and sets it on the table.

After he's gone, I refocus on Hannah, seeing she's lost some of her sparkle. "Did I say something wrong?"

She shakes her head. "I feel different now."

"I don't think you're alone in that. We all change."

She nods and moves her silverware, rearranging the pieces again. I reach out and lay a hand over hers. "Since my dad died." She looks up at me and turns her hand so she can hold mine. I like that she does this, connects.

I wish I could give her smart words, and I think about what Dr. B might say, but my brain flatlines with nothing. It's the anger about Sebastian. It's being so close to her. It's my fear for her, because I can't seem to not put her in the same category as my mom. I'm somehow reduced to my lowest common denominator. I squeeze her hand.

"I've carried a lot of guilt for not being there." She's looking at our joined hands, but she's somewhere else in the memory of it. Then she pulls her hand from mine and puts it in her lap, disconnecting. "I sort of fell apart."

It makes me wonder if I could tell her what I'd done. The truth about the accident. But I can't get the admission past my lips. I'm ashamed of it, and even though Dr. B says that I don't need to feel ashamed, I do. It hasn't ever felt safe to share that with anyone, which is why I haven't, aside from those that already know. I know that Hannah is a safe person to talk to, but that's not the reason I don't say anything. It's about self-preservation.

That thought suddenly makes me wonder if I'm sliding into my old pattern of behavior, but I dismiss it. That's not it.

Instead, I say, "I think you're entitled to fall apart, Hannah."

"Except my mom did. My sister did. Who was left to hold our world together?"

And it makes me wonder when she allowed herself to fall apart. If she ever has.

After the server has delivered our diner, I say, "So," and cut my hamburger in half, "even though you're the dachshund between us, would it be okay if I plan our next date? I mean, if you're willing to go on another date with me?"

She smiles. "I'd love that," she says and takes a bite of a French fry.

"You sure now?"

She nods, sparkling again. "Yes, but then I get to plan the one after."

"Will that be date number three?" I glance at her.

She's staring at me, her eyes sliding to my mouth. My stomach clenches and shoots energy around to the base of my spine, lingering there, before climbing up my back. What was I thinking, sitting across from her instead of next to her?

"Yes. You'll plan date two, and I've got date number three," she says, and I'm pretty sure her thoughts are in the same place as mine.

*My Heart insists It's Time to Get Angry*

Seth drives his car through the parking lot at my apartment complex, and I glance at him, taking in the glasses he's wearing as he drives. The moment I saw them, my belly tightened. He's got this gorgeous, nerdy jock thing going, and I'm all for it. It makes me want to jump on him, mess up his hair with my hands while riding him in this car. Glasses on. It's worse because he's humming to the radio—a song that reminds me of high school—with a lovely melodic voice. My blood is at a rolling boil, my heart bubbling in my chest. How am I so lucky to be sitting next to him right now? How is it even fair that I would have a second chance? I suppose there wasn't ever a first one, but this feels like another opportunity, considering we missed out on the first one.

After parking and setting the brake, he turns his head to look at me and smiles. I want to jump on him. His dimples make my heart turn in twirls of sock skating in the kitchen.

"I had fun tonight, Hannah."

"Me too." I don't want the night to end. I don't want to watch him drive away.

My feelings for Seth have exploded exponentially, reminding me of those little gifts I used to get from a vending machine as a kid. I'd take the coin treasure home and remove the tiny, dehydrated blob from the plastic bubble, plop it in a glass of water, and watch it expand into a giraffe or something recognizable.

I didn't feel this way with Sebastian.

Taking things slow is a wise idea. Especially now, because of Sebastian. When Seth asked, I'd considered sharing everything, but held back. Afraid. Not of Seth. No. More afraid of what it would do between us. I don't want Sebastian between us, but I can't get his threat out of my head. And despite my best efforts to be clear about that relationship being over, I can't seem to get him exorcized. And frankly, I'm embarrassed. Embarrassed I didn't see the truth of who he was, who I was while I was with him.

Despite all that, I find myself asking Seth, "Would you like to come up?"

Seth taps the steering wheel with his hand. "May I walk you to your door?"

This makes me smile. "I would like that."

He gets out of the car and meets me around the passenger side as I climb from the vehicle. I take his offered hand, and he pulls me closer than he needs to. With my hand in his, we walk side by side through the lot to my building, discussing the finer highlights of the evening, joking about puppies up the three flights of stairs and into the alcove where my apartment door is located. My heart continues its beat, stuck relaying the morse code of all the physical sensations of each second.

Jewel has left the outside light on for me.

"What kind of puppy are Jewel and her girlfriend talking about getting?" Seth asks.

"Joy? They argue about it. Joy wants a little fluffy thing. Jewels wants a pit bull."

Seth chuckles. "What kind of puppy would we get? I mean–"

I step up to him and press my fingers to his mouth to silence him. "We'd have two dogs. A yellow lab and a dachshund."

He smiles under my touch, his dimples deep, and my belly tightens while the rest of me melts.

"Thank you so much for tonight," I say, releasing his mouth. I glance at the door. "Would you like to come in?"

"I don't trust myself to be smart." He leans forward and presses his lips to my cheek, a smidge to the right of my lips. After another kiss even closer to my mouth, he adds very quietly, as if he meant for it to stay inside his head, "I'm imagining all the things I'd like to do to you."

My breath catches, and I grasp ahold of his jacket as I take part in imagining it. His mouth and hands. His body between my legs, filling me with his heat. Desire pools between my legs, and I take another step toward him so all that's left between us is a breath. "I'd like you to show me."

Seth grabs my hips and pulls me so all I feel is him, his thighs, his solidness against me. The knowledge he's as needy as I am makes me want to drag him into the apartment like a cavewoman.

"One good night kiss for our first date," he says with a smile and cradles the back of my head in one of his hands. When he gets close enough to kiss me, he stops and waits, his breath erratic. "Or is this the second one? Maybe the basketball game and dinner after counts?"

My breath catches. "It counts. It so counts." I pull him to close the distance between our mouths.

We greet one another, lip to lip, and then tongue to tongue, and hands to bodies, as if reminding ourselves that we're both really there. The kiss is a summer thunderstorm. The strong grip of his hands. The warm slick of my body, needing more friction. The depth of the rumble in my head, lost in the moment, warning me lightning is a breath away. But Seth ends the kiss. With his forehead against mine, he groans, squeezes my hips again as if conflicted, then steps back.

He takes another fortifying breath and nods. "I'll see you tomorrow?"

I'm wrestling with need and desire and when I can formulate a thought, I say, "Text me when you're home?"

"You got it."

He waits until I'm inside the apartment. I lean to look out the peephole as I lock the door, and after he hears the click, he walks away. With a smile, I turn and lean against the door, and release a contented sigh.

Best date ever.

After dropping my stuff inside my room, I shower. When I open the bathroom door after I'm done, my phone in hand because Seth has texted, I'm smiling.

"Took you long enough."

My heart jolts, and I grasp my towel at my heart, startled. "Shit! Don't do that."

Jewel leans against the wall opposite the bathroom door. "A little jumpy, aren't you?" She grins and looks around me into the bathroom. "No Prince Charming inside there with you?"

"No. If he were, you would have heard it." I stick my tongue out at her and flip the light off, casting us both in shadow.

She barks a laugh and follows me down the hall into my room, then flops on my bed.

"Where's Joy?" I slip into the pajamas under the light of my bedside lamp casting us both in its warm glow.

"Sleeping. I heard you moving around and wanted to hear about the date. See if you brought a puppy home. Joy and I had a bet. I thought I heard claws tapping the linoleum."

I towel dry my hair. "Who won?"

"She did."

I press my hands to my heart. "I'm touched that she knows me." I slip into a hoodie. "How did–"

"Seth told me."

"I had a good time. Really good." I smile a smile I feel inside my body.

My phone pings. It's Seth.

*Home. I'm looking forward to tomorrow.*

*Me too.*

*Good night.*

I grin and glance at Jewel, who's watching me with one of those shrewd looks she's often assessing me with.

She sits up and scoots across the bed to the edge. "Good. I'm glad." She stands and glances at my phone. "That Prince Charming?"

I wag the phone at her. "Yes. Look."

She reads his message and smiles. Then she walks to the door and turns to look at me. "Sebastian's over then? Right?"

I scrunch up my face and sit on the edge of the bed. "Yes! What—why would–"

Jewel shakes her head. "Good. Seth seems like a great guy. Sebastian–"

"That's over."

She leans against the door frame and crosses her arms. "I was thinking about my Aunt Tally."

I nod, unsure where she's going with her thought process but frowning at my recollection of that awful story. I consider moving closer to her, to offer her support should she need it.

She pushes away from the door. "Sebastian has ugly vibes like the dude that killed Aunty T. I'm not saying Bash is like him or anything but I'm pretty sure, because you're you, you don't want to think bad of him."

"Things are over with him."

"For you, but it's clear he's not getting that message."

I hate that what she's saying rings true. I didn't want to think of Sebastian in that light. Our relationship hadn't been perfect, but Sebastian had been there for me as I wallowed in my grief. I don't deny what Jewel is saying, but I don't reinforce it either. It's hard to argue against it after what happened the other night.

"I think you should file a report. With campus security, or the police."

"And say what, exactly?" I ask. "'My ex-boyfriend showed up outside my apartment because he wanted to talk.'"

"That wasn't talking, Han."

I press my teeth together, look away, and stare at the lamp. "But what was it, exactly?"

"Did you feel afraid?"

My eyes flash to hers. I nod.

"That's why. That's what you say. Because you shouldn't have to be afraid of someone in your life."

My mind goes to Seth. To his dad. To what his dad did to him. I swallow and nod.

She gives me a hug. "I love you. I don't want anything bad to happen."

I hug her back. "I love you, too." I squeeze her tighter. "Thank you for being here."

"I'll go with you to report it, if you want to me to."

"Okay."

She squeezes me once more before she leaves.

I crawl into bed and close my eyes, my thoughts weaving through all the variables of my life. Seth, mostly, but then there's Sebastian and the incongruence of the way he once was with how he was the other night. I don't think I can fix him, even if that might have been my belief system at one point in my life. There's a part of me struggling to see Sebastian clearly, wanting to give him the benefit of the doubt. I suppose that part is trying to keep him in a neat and concise box, since it's easier than contemplating a different alternative.

Eventually I find sleep. I dream of a field of wildflowers that stretches around my subconscious. I'm lying on my back looking up at the flowers overhead, outlined by gray sky, rather than standing up with them tickling the palms of my hands.

I wake, feeling unsettled by the dream, and reach for my phone. It has blown up with dozens of texts. When I open my messages, I see that most of them are from Sebastian. I only read the first line of the notification to know how those are going to go:

> *You're a fucking slut!*

My heart slams against my ribs with a punishing rhythm.

I don't want to open those.

I open the message from my sister instead.

> *Guess who texted me last night.*

> *Good morning, Ruthie Rue. Nate?*

The three dots pop up, so I scroll through some of my other apps until I'm notified she's finished typing.

> *I wish. No. Bash.*

I sit up, my heart tucking into itself, frozen. I Facetime her instead of texting. Her cute face pops up when she connects, and she smiles. "Hi!"

I want to dodge around in safe sister territory for a bit, but I can't. "Why would Sebastian text you? Has he done that before? Isn't that weird?"

Her smile fades, and her nose scrunches up. "I thought so. Maybe once before—needing advice for your birthday or something. But not since."

"What did he say?"

"Get this—'checking in with his favorite little sister,'" she says as one of her hands uses air quotes. Her nose scrunches with disgust.

"I don't understand." I frown. It's true he doesn't have little siblings. And he was always nice to Rue when we visited, but this is off.

"He asked me questions about you. It seemed like he was fishing."

"What kinds of questions?" Now my heart unfurls with anger. The audacity of him to use my family, my sister.

"Like how you're doing since the breakup. And I was thinking, way better now that you're not in her life. I didn't say that, of course. But I thought about it. Then—get this—he asked me if you were seeing anyone." She pauses, her eyes studying me, then smiles. "Are you?"

I blush but chills race across my skin, considering what Jewel said last night.

"You are! Who is it?"

Stupid tell.

"Did you tell him anything?"

"Of course not. Who are you seeing?"

"Early days, little sister. I don't want to jinx it." I smile at her. She narrows her eyes. "I'm going to text Jewel."

I smile. "Fine. His name is Seth."

"That name sounds familiar. Didn't you have a classmate with that name?" She pauses, drawing from what she knows, then her eyebrows arch over her eyes as she tilts her head. "As in Seth from our high school Seth? Hottie Seth? The one who all the girls crushed on for infinity and beyond Seth? Like a fifteen on a scale of ten. The one who's in the trophy case at school, part of the soccer team Seth? The one who's plastered all over the bulletin board in your room? This wouldn't be the same Seth, right?"

"Stop! Yes. Seth Peters."

"How?!" She screeches with excitement, the camera bouncing around with her.

"He transferred to Western."

Her eyes grow. "Fuck off, Sebastian."

I laugh. "I've got to go. I have a date with Seth later." I wiggle my eyebrows at her. "Don't answer any more of Sebastian's texts okay. He shouldn't have done that."

She salutes. "Aye, Aye, captain."

"And if you want to talk to Nate. You text him."

Her smile fades. "I don't know. That sounds terrifying."

"If there's anything between you, he might be just as unsure as you." I think about all the time I wasted in high school wondering about Seth. Learning he'd liked me makes me add, "If you want to know, then just do it. Then you'll know one way or the other, right?"

"True."

"Love you, Rue."

"Love you too, Nanna."

I disconnect the call and frown at the phone. What the fuck is Sebastian doing? As much as I want to discount Jewel and Seth's warnings, now I can't. Sebastian reaching out to my sister changes things, but I'm not sure how to measure it. How much it weighs in the how strange things have gotten.

I'm so angry, angry enough to look at the messages he's sent and see them through an outraged lens.

> *What the fuck?*

> *I told you how I felt.*

> *You've thrown it in my face over and over.*

> *You will never get anyone better than me.*
> *I have everything, Hannah.*

> *I heard you were with him at Tonks Brewery last night. Fuck!*

> *What does he have?*

> *I love you.*

*I told you how I felt.*
*Why don't you care, Hannah?*

*You're going to fuck us up like you*
*did with that Hunter guy.*

*What if I died while you were*
*fucking him? Like you did to your*
*father.*

*Why do you have to be a fucking whore?*

*A fucking cunt!!! With the first dog that*
*sniffs around.*

*With some guy who doesn't care*
*two shits about you.*
*I fucking care!*

*You're mine.*

*I care!!!!*

*WTF!*

*Hannah. Answer me!*

*Where the fuck are you? You're probably fucking him.*

*You're a fucking slut!*

*My Heart Insists It's Time to Stop Muscling It*

Leaning against the wall outside the student center staring at my phone, I wait for Hannah, who's said she'd meet me after her last class. Date number three because the basketball game and dinner counted. The thought makes me smile.

While I wait, I scroll through Instagram with one hand, the other shoved into the pocket of my jacket. I visit Gabe's posts on his feed first. He's got a series of on-the-road basketball stuff. He looks happy, and based on what we've chatted about, I think that's probably true.

Next, I search for Abby. She's posted a picture of her and some friends at the beach. The weather in Hawaii beats this Oregon steel sky. She seems happy too, and I figure that's probably true, but we lost touch after she and Gabe broke up. It makes me sad sometimes because of how important she was to me. Though, truthfully, if she were walking up the sidewalk toward me, I imagine she and I could slide right back into being friends just because of how easy our friendship has always been, even when it was at its worst.

Finally, I look up Hannah's feed. Her last post was a picture of a stack of books at the library. It was months ago, before she and Sebastian broke up. When I scroll backward, all her pictures are innocuous and devoid of… well… Hannah.

I don't think she's happy. There are moments when I see her and recognize her for the girl I used to know, but then it's like she slams the door. I know it has to do with losing her dad, but I don't think that's the only thing. There's stuff she's not saying, and I'm not sure what to do for her other than just be there. There's an essence in it I recognize, as if she's releasing a pheromone that people who've suffered from trauma or abuse recognize, and it makes me wonder, especially about Sebastian. She insisted that things weren't like that. That Sebastian isn't violent. But there are other kinds of abuse. My dad wasn't always throwing his fists. I mean, he did, but the shit I went through was mental and emotional too.

And I can't judge Hannah for slamming the door. I get it. I hold the tough stuff tight to my chest, afraid. Maybe it's weak, but letting someone in to see into the dark side of who I am is like walking nude through a snowstorm and knowing hypothermia is the guaranteed outcome and doing it anyway. To know what I did to myself. To Gabe.

And Gabe is still my friend, for some inexplicable reason. I text him: *Yo! Good game.*

He'd dominated on the court with twenty-three points, six rebounds, and four assists.

*Thanks. How you?*

*Good. 2 dates down onto the 3rd.*

*Oh. So now you're kissing and telling?*

*No K&T here. Just checking in. How are things?*

*Busy. Game tomorrow. Practice every day. Mandatory team study hall. That's where I am now.*

*Happy?*

*Yup. Content. You?*

*Relatively. Mom called. Said Dad is getting tests done. Kind of weirding out about it.*

> *Whoa. Need to talk?*

> *Not yet. Maybe not at all.*

> *I'll be in Cantos in June for my mom and dad's 35th anniversary. They're renewing their vows or something. Come stay with me?*

I adore Gabe's adoptive parents and if anything could get me back to Cantos it would be them, so I answer:

> *Sounds good. Keep me posted.*

> *Can I ask you a question?*

> *Shoot.*

> *I see what you did there. Bad.*

> *LOL.*

> *Do you and Abby still talk?*

He takes a little while to respond, the three dots appearing and then disappearing.

> *...*

*We don't. I mean, not like we once did. Comments on one another's IG and shit. But we don't call one another or anything.*

*Why?*

*Just worried about crossing boundaries with H and losing her as a friend.*

*Think you can handle just being her friend? I mean, hanging back and watching her date some other guy without shooting your shot?*

*I'd hate that.*

*Or the flipside, if it implodes, could you handle not having her in your life?*

*That's what I've been asking myself. I feel like I'm in purgatory.*

*That kind of seems like your answer then. You'll know one way or another if it's hell or heaven once you take the risk, right?*

*Would you take it back? Being with Abby knowing you wouldn't be talking now?*

*...*

*No. I wouldn't.*

*That wait made me feel like you had a lot more to say.*

*None of which really matters now other than being with her while it lasted was great. And breaking up because of college and distance—while shitty—was probably the right call. Follow your heart. And whatever you do, don't go silent. Communicate.*

*Thanks.*

*Got to go. Stupid term paper. Keep me posted on H and your dad. I'll keep you posted on Mom and Dad's anniversary.*

I send him the thumbs up and go to pocket my phone, grateful for Gabe's friendship. All those years, he'd been the one who reached out, the one who'd visited me in the hospital, the one who'd apologized to me for falling in love with Abby knowing how I'd felt about her, when it had always been me who owed him the apology. Of course I'd apologized, and over the last two-and-a-half years, we've chosen friendship. It's humbling, really, because God knows I don't deserve it.

As my thoughts drift toward my father, my phone rings. Afraid it's Hannah and she's calling to say she can't make it; I pull it from my pocket. It's my mom, as if my thoughts have conjured her. I press the phone to my ear. "Hey, Mom. Still on the wagon?"

"Does every time I call mean your father has fallen off the wagon?"

I roll my eyes, the bitterness seizing everything up inside of me. "Yes. Four years seems a short exchange for seventeen. How many times in those seventeen years did he fall off?"

She sighs. "Seth."

"Mom," I say. "Look. He can get the attaboy from you. You decided to stay married to him. If that's working for you, great. And I can admit he's made a change in his life, but it doesn't take away all the shit we went through."

"He's got something."

I hear her sniff.

"Are you crying?"

"No."

But I can hear she's lying. "What is it?"

"He had that blood work done. The doctor called and wants him to come back in for a scan because some of his numbers are high."

"Okay. When is that?"

"Setting up an appointment for next week."

"Will you call me after?"

"Do you want me to?"

I stand and push a pebble with the toe of my shoe, then kick it into the old snow pushed into melted and refrozen piles along the walk. It sticks, and I think: *goal*.

"Yes. I want you to call. You okay?" I ask.

"I don't know."

I shake my head even though she can't see me, because I know exactly what she's feeling. "Well, it isn't anything yet. Don't make it something until it is," I tell her.

"You're right." She sniffs again. "When are you coming home?"

I turn and look up at the winter sky and think *never*, but that isn't true. I've always gone home, even when it was at its worst. "I'm not sure yet. Maybe spring break." I return to looking at the parking lot and see Hannah coming toward me. "Soon enough?" I ask Mom and watch Hannah. She's wearing leggings again, a sweatshirt underneath her jacket. Her blond hair is pulled back into a ponytail that swings with her steps. Her cheeks are rosy, and her eyes brighten when she sees me. I love that.

"I got to go, Mom. I have something."

Mom sniffs and makes a noise of affirmation. "I'll call you after the meeting with the doctor."

Hannah stops in front of me, smiling.

I hold a hand out to Hannah. She takes it. "Call me as soon as you know."

"Okay. Thank you, Sethie."

The sound of her voice slams me with the realization that she called because she needs me, needs my support. I grit my teeth in frustration at myself for being too selfish to not realize it. "Thanks for calling, Mom."

"Everything okay?" Hannah asks as I slide the phone into my jacket pocket.

I'm not sure there's anything to tell yet, so I nod. I don't want to bring this date down. "Ready?"

"What are we doing?"

"You'll see." I lead her into the student athletic center, and we stash our shit in cubbies near the climbing wall. "Ta da!" I tell her, holding my hands out to present it.

Hannah looks up the wall, her eyes the size of full moons. She blanches. "We're going to climb this."

"You'll be harnessed in," I tell her. "And I'll be right there with you."

"I haven't done this."

"Scared of heights?"

"A little."

"We'll only do as much as you want, okay?"

Her eyes find mine. "What if I don't want to do any of it?"

I study her face to formulate a response.

I'd picked this because at dinner I'd had the sense she needed to tackle something and overcome it.

I started indoor climbing during my freshman year during the off season, when some of my soccer teammates invited me. I was hooked. There's something about the precision of it, combined with the infinite possibilities that makes it interesting to me. Dr. B suggested that it's a mashup of my desire for control while fulfilling the discomfort of being out of control at the same time. I got what she was saying. When I'm climbing, I'm not thinking. Instead, I'm focused on the wall, on the way my muscles sing as I move through the motion from one foot and handhold to another, in the rest with my arms straight as I plan my assent, in the way my brain goes quiet. It's about me and the wall, overcoming what feels like something insurmountable and taking it down. Dr. B asked me one time, *"Might it help you process the trauma?"* I've thought about that a lot since, and figure there's probably symbolism in it, but mostly, I just really feel at home in the climb, like I used to on the wave.

Rather than push Hannah—because I know what it feels like to be pushed—I say, "Then we'll go do something else."

She looks from me back at the wall, then nods. "Okay. I'll try."

I smile, leaning forward to kiss her cheek. "Awesome."

She blushes and grins, then shrugs out of her sweatshirt.

I admire the way her athletic clothes fit her curves, wondering if this was such a good idea for my sanity. *Date number three*, I think.

We start on the practice wall to help Hannah get a sense of the handholds and laugh at jokes we make about the way it looks like chewed bubble gum, which goes on way too long. When Hannah's ready, we get into all the safety equipment—harness and headgear—and once we're at the bottom of the wall, I tell her, "The best thing you can do is think ahead before you even move. So let's look at the wall and consider possible ways up."

"Okay," she says, stepping closer to me, and leaning against my side.

I smile at the wall, enjoying that she wants to be close to me but keeping my hands to myself, because I know the moment I touch her, I'm a goner.

"I think I'll start there," she says.

"Great. When you climb, you want to remember to use your legs, over your arms."

"But my arms have to hold me up."

"Yes, sort of. Your legs should be doing the bulk of the work. They have way more muscle, so rely on them."

"Okay."

"I'll be right next to you."

It's different climbing with someone else. I find that I'm worried about Hannah rather than my own journey up the wall, and while under different circumstances that would bother me, it doesn't. It's Hannah. I want to support her to face this obstacle, to make her feel as accomplished as it makes me feel. To share this with her. I've been on this wall enough since moving here to have a strong sense of it from any starting spot. "Toes," I remind her as she tries to use the middle of her foot.

She looks at me and drops to the floor.

I drop down next to her.

"You okay?" I ask.

"Frustrated," she says and shakes out her arms.

"At me? Am I being too much?" I smile at her and bump her shoulder with mine. "Sorry. I love doing this."

"It shows," she says. "No. At myself."

"How come?"

"I feel like I should be able to do it."

"Why? It's your first time."

She looks down at her feet, and I see her—high school Hannah who excelled at everything—juxtaposed with Hannah now, who seems to be struggling with herself. She looks up and shrugs.

"When I first started, I used too much arm and tried to muscle everything. Really, I did everything wrong, until someone helped me. I started watching videos and practicing things I learned, and slowly, I just got better at it. It took time though."

"Are you saying I'm trying to muscle it?" She smiles.

"Maybe–" The words catch in my throat as the thought hits me. That's exactly what I've been doing. With being afraid to share about the crash, with carrying that shame, with forgiving my father. I've been trying to do it alone. I swallow down the emotion that suddenly hits. "We all do that, you know, muscle it and get tired, instead of using what's around us to help us out."

She smiles at the floor, then looks up at me, eyes twinkling. "Life lessons with Seth Peters. I think we have a kids show in there somewhere."

I grin at her. "Want to go again?"

She nods.

*My Heart Insists It's Time to Let Go*

"I'm not sure I can hold on any longer," I say. My muscles are screaming at me, and though I've tried to remember to keep my arms straight and use my legs, I've barely made it halfway up the wall. On the other hand, I've had so much fun with Seth. We've had to start over so many times just for laughing. Regardless of winning the wall, or what I would have previously perceived as completing the task, Seth's earlier words wrapped me up in a cocoon of safety.

"Can you wait for me to come to you?" he asks, looking down at me.

I'm enjoying the view. His strong legs in his navy shorts, and the way the sinew of muscle flexes under his dark gray athletic shirt when he reaches and moves. If I had it in me to do so, I could reach up and touch his foot—he's not that far away.

He's already started back down the wall.

"Sure," I say.

It isn't long, a few seconds and he's next to me, grinning so deeply that his dimples are on prominent display. I have the urge to lean toward him and kiss him. I don't. I'm not sure I could concentrate on what I'm supposed to do if I did.

"You did it." He beams at me.

"Did what?"

"Hung out on the wall for–" he glances across the room at a clock– "over an hour." He leans forward and presses a kiss to my lips as if reading my mind. "You're going to feel it later."

I smile at him. "I'm already feeling it. I'm expecting a massage later."

"Are you trying to kill me, woman?" Seth asks. He leans closer and says in my ear, "If I get these hands on you–"

I laugh. "I'm not sure I can make it down."

"Let go."

I look down at the padded floor, which looks inordinately far away. "Jump?"

"You've got the harness." He reaches out and taps the cord tethered to the harness I'm wearing. "You don't have to hold on when you're tired, Hannah."

I always feel like he's trying to tell me something in the layer of his words. "Just let go?"

"Yep. Here. I'll show you. I'll be waiting at the bottom to catch you."

When he lets go, the harness lowers him to the floor. "See," he calls, now below me. "Now I'm here to catch you."

The idea of letting go of the wall is slightly terrifying, but the harness digging into my groin reminds me I'm covered. I take a deep breath. "Okay. Here goes."

"I got you."

I let go.

The harness catches my weight and lowers me steadily to the ground. Seth folds me in his arms the moment I touch down, my back flush against his front.

"See. You did it," he says in my ear.

Turning in his arms, I grasp his face between my hands, then press my lips to his, suddenly needing more than the flirting we've been doing for the last few days. I need this connection with him. I want this connection with him. His arms tighten, his hands clasping behind me, resting at the small of my back. When I end the kiss, Seth smiles, and I'm basking in a warm glow of beach sunshine.

"Hannah?"

I close my eyes at the intrusive voice. Sebastian. The glow sputters around me, and anger sparks to life to take its place.

Though Seth and I both straighten as I turn my head toward the voice, Seth doesn't let me go all the way, one hand resting at the small of my back. Sebastian is standing on the other side of the pad, a bag slung over his shoulder, glaring at me.

"Sebastian," I say.

"It's Sebastian now?"

I feel Seth tense next to me.

After unhooking my safety rope from my harness and handing it to Seth, I walk across the pad to a place where I can remove the harness. My heart races like a wildfire across a meadow, and I'm suddenly that raging fire wanting to consume everything in my path.

From the corner of my eye, Sebastian walks around the perimeter of the space toward me.

I recall sitting at coffee with him and his meek demeanor then, the apology, the acceptance that I was moving on. Then him that night outside my apartment after work, saying ugly things and throwing around threats. How Jewel had to run interference. Learning he texted my little sister to get information. Barraging me with emotional and hateful texts. And now, interrupting me with Seth, with a look on his face like I'm the one who cheated on him!

For the last several months, I've tried to be understanding, tried to respect the time we spent together, tried to honor the human that is Sebastian instead of being resentful that he lied to me, that he cheated. And yet now, instead of feeling like I owe him something after all we've been through, I just feel angry.

By the time he reaches me, I'm shrugging out of the harness, letting it drop from my legs to the floor. I reach down and snatch it off the ground, my movements like punches.

"What are you doing here with him?" Sebastian asks, though the words sound more like a hissing snake speaking through clenched teeth. "You're making me look bad."

"With Seth?" I ask at normal volume and meet Sebastian's gaze. "We're on a date." I tilt my head in challenge, hating myself for all the time I wasted feeling weak. Today, I feel justified. "You're making yourself look bad."

His brows collapse over his eyes, and he scowls. "I told you how I felt about that."

"You lost any right to tell me how you felt about that when you cheated on me. Now, I need you to leave me alone. I need you to stop texting Ruth—I went to campus security today."

His eyebrows arch over his eyes.

"You need to fucking stop."

Sebastian rolls his eyes, and offers me one of those placating smiles, as if that's all he needs to do to get me back in line. The horrible realization is that's all he'd had to do for a long time. "So like you, Hannah. You're getting worked up about nothing. Like usual."

"Excuse me? Nothing?" For a split second, I doubt myself. I check my feelings, second guessing that maybe I've been disrespectful, then imagine Jewel shaking me and telling me to wise up. Imaginary Jewel is right. I straighten my spine and face him. "I'm not worked up. I'm fucking pissed."

"You're always making more of shit than it needs to be. Like that shit in December. And I texted Ruth to check on her. You don't need to be unhinged about it."

"Unhinged?" His words hit me like a smack in the face. All the ways we didn't fight during our relationship because I cowered in the belief that perhaps I was being too overly emotional. He'd said it enough. *Too sensitive.* I'd just thought it was my grief, but right now, the anger has burned away the haze. I take a deep breath. "First, that shit in December was you fucking cheating, Sebastian. Second, you showing up outside my apartment to yell at me isn't appropriate. And third, texting my little sister to get shit on me isn't checking on her, it's using her. And I don't appreciate your slew of rude text messages. You need to stop. This," I move my hand between us, "is over."

He leans forward as if to say something, then freezes.

I feel Seth's presence behind me before I feel the comfort of his hands on my shoulders. "You okay, Hannah?"

I look over my shoulder at him. "Can we just go?"

"Sure." His hands squeeze me gently, but his eyes—shaped with rage—are digging mines into Sebastian. The energy radiating off Seth is dynamite ready to unleash and take down the mountain.

Sebastian shoots me a glare, backing away—he must recognize it—then turns and disappears deeper into the athletic center.

I walk to my cubby and yank out my bag, then shrug into my hoodie with clipped, angry movements. I'm shaking.

Seth's at my side, eyes on me, shrugging into his own sweatshirt.

"I'm sorry," I tell him.

"Remember what I said about apologizing to me, Hannah?" He sounds angry—but it isn't directed at me.

I nod, sling my bag onto my shoulder, and walk from the athletic center out into the cold, where light and quiet snowflakes have begun to fall. Tears brighten my eyes, and I blow out a breath, the steam making me feel like there's a sleeping dragon inside of me.

For some reason, I think about my dad. It didn't snow very often in Cantos, since we were near the ocean, but when I was little, I remember trying to make a snowman one of the few times it did. Of course, that isn't the kind of snow that falls near the beach on the Oregon Coast. It's slushy, and if it sticks, it's temporary because it always turns to rain. But Dad had followed me out into the yard anyway.

When I'd cried because I couldn't get a proper snowman, he'd pulled me into his arms. "It's okay, Hannah Banana," he'd said.

"You tried. And from where I'm at, you tried your best. That's all anyone can ask for."

I miss him.

Suddenly, my hand is in Seth's. He pulls me against his chest, his front against my back. With an arm draped just under my collarbone, he presses his cheek to my temple. "Feel like going home?"

I shake my head.

"Want to come to my place?"

I nod.

"Okay if I drive?"

He leads me to his car, opens the door for me, waits until I've gotten into the passenger seat before shutting the door. Then he joins me and drives us across town to his apartment.

It's quiet when we walk into the main room.

"Trace went home and won't be back until later tonight," Seth tells me. "Mind if I shower? I'm sure I smell awful."

I give him a smile. "You don't." I like the way he smells even after working out, like a mixture of iron and salt.

"Would you like to shower? I can use Trace's." He seems nervous, moving about without purpose. "I should check to make sure the bathroom is presentable." He disappears down the hall and reappears a few moments later. "All clear." He smiles. "Come on. I'll show you."

I follow him down a narrow hallway to a door, the light reaching out into the hallway. When I walk into the narrow bathroom, I see one of those tubs with the frosty glass sliders. It's older, the tub and sink a muted blue gray. A large mirror stretches across the length of the wall with one of those movie star light bar fixtures across the top. He points out all the features, soap, shampoo, then disappears and reappears with a burgundy bundle of fluff. "Towel." He puts it on the counter.

"Thank you." I press a hand against the towel and resist the urge to draw it up to my face to hide. I'm deflating from the adrenaline and anger. Though I still feel justified, now I just feel…

"Hannah?"

I look up at him from the towel, registering the concern in his voice.

"You okay?"

I want to smile. I want to say, 'yes.' I want to reassure him and make him comfortable. But I've been doing that a long time, I realize, making sure everyone around me is comfortable. My mom and Ruth. Sebastian. And I'm suddenly so tired. I recall Seth standing at the bottom of the rock wall telling me to "let go," and I can't hold on anymore, and I know there's no harness.

I shake my head. I can't stop the tears that start.

Seth's arms are around me in the same instant. "I've got you."

In his arms, I let go.

*My Heart Insists It's Time to Let Go*

'm not sure what to do. Hannah's in my arms, sobbing, and while I think I know why, it feels bigger than that. So I just hold her and wish that I had Sebastian's face on the other side of my fists. It's clear she doesn't need my frustration toward Sebastian, or my frustration at learning what he's done. I'm pissed. I knew it was more than what she was saying.

Now, I know why there's a bat at the door.

What had Hannah said? *It's not appropriate to show up outside my apartment. To text my sister for information. To send me texts.* I wonder what they were. Damn. There's so much wrong with this situation, including the fact that Sebastian just gas-lit the fuck out of Hannah at the gym. And if that was what their relationship was for nine months, no wonder she's always saying, "I'm sorry."

I squeeze Hannah tighter, and she holds on, as if I might slip away.

Eventually, her sobs subside to just sniffles. "I'm a mess," she says into my shirt. She takes a breath to say something, but I interrupt her.

"Don't say I'm sorry, Hannah."

She closes her mouth and giggles against my chest.

I lean back to look at her.

She lifts her chin, her eyes red and swollen, her nose running, and she offers a tentative smile, as if unsure.

I hand her a tissue. "Better?"

She laughs again and swipes her eyes with her fingers, her nose with the tissue. "No. Not really, but sort of at the same time." She gives me another teary grin as she throws away the tissue. "I feel clearer. For the first time in a long time. Thank you for that. I think it was the rock wall."

I grin and lean forward, pressing a kiss to her cheek. "Ready for a shower?"

She glances at the tub. "I–" She stops and looks down at her feet.

"I'll get it started for you. The temperature gauge is a little tricky." It isn't, but it seems like Hannah is working something out. I reach around her and slide the door open to turn on the water, one hand still holding onto her. When I pull the stopper so the shower starts, I straighten. "There."

"Seth?"

I make a noise to tell her I'm listening.

"I know this might seem weird, but would you stay?"

*Not the time,* I remind myself. *Not the time.*

"Sure. You want me to sit outside the door?" I glance at the toilet on the other side of the partition wall and turn my head to look at the hallway. I have no idea where I am, and it's probably because my brain isn't fully functioning because it's stuck like a scratched record, thinking about Hannah in the shower. Naked. I turn to leave, but Hannah stops me with a hand on my arm.

"Or–" Her voice catches my attention, and I look back. Her blue eyes map my face.

"Or?" I ask, terrified.

"We could shower–"

My heart stops for a moment, then bounces with a jolt of electricity. "We?"

She nods, then grabs the hem of my shirt and slides her hands up my torso, lifting my shirt over my head. "You need to get clean too."

I duck out of it, stunned. "What about the dates?" I ask and swallow.

She draws her hoodie over her head and follows it with her shirt, so she's standing in front of me in a hot pink bra. Boobs. I've had my hands on them. But damn. My mouth dries out. God.

"What about them?" she asks.

My breathing increases. "You were just crying."

She pushes her leggings down over her hips and pulls her legs from them, her lace panties a different shade of pink from her bra, then pulls her blond hair from the ponytail and runs her hands through the curls that fall just below her shoulders.

She looks amazing, and I'm already hard. I can't hide it. Shit. Not smooth.

"Are you hesitating because you don't want to shower with me?"

I shake my head. I can't formulate words.

"Are you hesitating because I was crying?"

I nod.

"Are you adverse to showering?"

I shake my head.

"With me?"

I shake my head.

She pushes the bra straps down her arms and draws her arms through the loops so all that's left is the clasp, the lace still cupped around her breasts. "But?"

All the words I'd say to tell her why this isn't a good idea leave my brain. They don't exist anymore because this is the best idea that's taken root in my mind.

"If you're worried that I'm vulnerable. Don't. I'm not doing this because of what happened earlier. If you're worried you're taking advantage of me. Don't. I'm going to step into that shower wanting to be in there with you, Seth, for no other reason than I like you. And I trust you. And I realized today, I've wasted a lot of time apologizing for stuff to make everyone else comfortable instead of thinking about what I want. So I am unapologetically asking you to get into the shower with me because I want it. I've wasted a lot of time holding onto a wall when it was time to let go."

I clench my teeth together with frustration. Frustration because I want her so bad. But also, frustration because I felt left out of the loop when it comes to what's been happening with Sebastian. It's like going back to high school and being a third party to Abby and Gabe, feeling like the last to know, and feeling like a fool.

But then, I also know that I'm not Hannah's boyfriend. She doesn't owe me anything.

We like one another.

We have a shit-ton of chemistry.

I want something long-term with her.

*But you haven't shared either.*

The truth of that thought stops up my lungs. How can I be upset to be the last to know if I haven't been willing to be completely honest?

I swallow. "I can't." I choke it out because it isn't about wanting it. Closing my eyes, I shove a hand through my hair, and take a deep breath. "Fuck, Hannah."

And just like I thought she might do, her arms come up, crossing her torso to hide.

I grab her wrists. "Hannah. No. Please. It isn't you," I say and unfold her arms. "It isn't you." I prove that point with a flick of my eyes to my hard dick at full salute between us.

Her eyes drop down, then jump back to me, her cheeks stained with a deepening blush.

I pull her into my arms and press my nose into the space where her neck meets her shoulder, drawing a deep breath. "There's just stuff I need to say–" I draw in another breath, feeling how tense she is in my arms.

My heart unhooks itself from it's space suit and floats around in my chest untethered. I'm afraid I've just fucked this up.

I walk backwards, keeping Hannah with me until I bump into the door, then pull her down with me to the floor, until I'm sitting. I'm still holding her hand. "There's something I need to tell you."

"This feels bad–" she says but straddles my lap, a knee on either side of my hips, which doesn't help my raging boner.

I let go of her hand and push my fingers into my hair, knowing I've committed to being truthful and terrified that I've done it. This is right. I know it is, but I just want her so much. The emotional part of me is afraid that she won't want me anymore once she knows the truth.

A crease forms between her eyes.

"I want you so fucking bad, Hannah. So bad. And I don't want to lose you–" I know she needs to know the full truth. I look up at the ceiling. "I'm just afraid–"

I chance a glance at her eyes. It's time to stop muscling it.

Her blue gaze maps my face, her look swirling around my features, then connecting with my eyes. She reaches up and plays with my hair. "You have me."

The tension in my body releases, like a wave folding over and losing its shape as it rushes the shore. I drop my hands to her hips and squeeze her, the lace of her panties soft against my palm, then wrap my arms around her. I commit to finally telling the truth. "It's about the accident."

She doesn't say anything, just waits.

"That night, the night it happened—my dad had fallen off the wagon, again." I take a deep breath. "We'd gotten into a fight. I'd lost all hope." I drop my forehead against her shoulder.

Hannah lifts my head with her hands, her palms pressed against either side of my jaw, holding me in place as she tilts her head to meet my eyes. "Tell me."

I search her eyes for a trap even though I know there isn't one, a technique in self-preservation that seems to lurk even when I've worked so hard to overcome those defense mechanisms. But this is Hannah. In all my interactions with her from elementary school to the present, not once has Hannah ever hurt me. Now I understand why I held back from sharing with Jenny and Amber. I didn't trust them with the truth. I trust Hannah.

"I did it to myself," I say, ripping off the Band-Aid.

Her mouth falls open, and I hear her quick intake of a breath. Then she holds it.

My eyes fill with tears, burning like razor blades. It's hard to see her through them. "I drove that truck into oncoming traffic. I thought it was the only way to escape the pain of–"

A tear spills down my cheek, followed by another.

I drop my gaze, unable to look at her. "And I'm ashamed of it," I admit. "You see—you should know the truth."

She lifts my head by my chin and meets my gaze. Her eyes are filled with tears. "Thank you for... for trusting me with it."

"God, Hannah." I breathe her name and reach up to frame her face with my hands. "Trusting you wasn't the hard part. It's admitting what I did. To know you'll think... differently about me."

"There is no shame in your struggle."

"Other people were hurt because of what I did."

She nods. "That is your regret?"

I nod. "I don't remember thinking about that. I don't remember anything but the pain, the hopelessness–"

She leans in, wraps her arms around my shoulders, and presses her lips into the nook between my neck and shoulder. "I'm so sorry, and so, so fucking grateful." She sits back up. "So grateful you're here now."

I take a deep breath, feeling somehow lighter, freer, and I get what she's saying, so grateful. I'm sitting here with Hannah in my arms, and she's looking at me like I'm still me. I straighten, leaning to press a quick kiss to her lips.

The hot shower, still running, humidifies the room, but I don't want to let her go. I run my hands up her back until I'm cupping the back of her head. She leans into my touch, giving me control, and her lace-covered boobs graze my bare chest. Air moves quicker through my body, suddenly floating with the freedom, with the knowledge that this woman accepts me and my truth. My breath locks up in my lungs, and all the blood rushes from my brain to my groin. I just need her. I need her. I need her. I–

"Hannah," I say. "I want you."

"Yes. Yes," she chants, her hands caressing my skin.

I run my thumb against the edge of her bra, over the swell of her breast, and push the edge to reveal the treasure underneath. "I don't want to wait for more dates."

She draws in a quick breath. "Me either."

"You are so beautiful," I say, running a thumb over that sensitive place, then lean forward to kiss her, to claim her mouth as I press my palms against her soft flesh.

She moans into my mouth and sinks against my erection pressed between her legs. "Oh," she whimpers. "Seth." She rocks her hips. "I want you. I've wanted you–"

The sensation works its way up through me, and out as a groan. I trail my mouth from her lips, down her neck, until I have a nipple in my mouth. She's holding the back of my head, gasping with sweet sounds that push me forward, that make me take her in my arms and move us so she's on her back, and I'm seated between her legs.

The kiss rocks me, the feel of her around me, like the warmth of a perfect day. I love her. I love her. I understand this now. That's why this means so fucking much. Shocked with the understanding, I pull away from the kiss and look at her. Her lips are swollen with my kiss. Her blue eyes flutter open, dark with her own pleasure and desire. My heart dips with new awareness, tightening and thudding heavily in my chest. It wasn't just about trust, was it. It was about love.

I could let go.

But the blue of the tub is in the corner of my eyes, the weird pattern of the linoleum behind beautiful Hannah. "I want this with you, Hannah. But not here on the bathroom floor."

"Take me to your room."

We disengage and our movement becomes a collection of hands and mouths, teeth, tongues, mixed with needy sounds. After shutting off the water, I kiss her, walk her through the hallway still kissing, and kick the door to my room shut behind us. She pulls me onto the bed with her.

"You're sure about this Hannah?" I ask. "I'm clean. I've been tested."

"Me too. After Sebastian. And yes, I've never been surer about something in my entire life," she breathes, her hands on the waistband of my boxer briefs. "You?"

"Oh, fuck, yes, Hannah."

She pushes the elastic over my hips, and I shimmy out of them while simultaneously drawing Hannah's panties down her legs. She helps me until all we are is heaving bodies, excited and full of need. I stop, staring at her, taking in this beautiful woman, feeling like perhaps I've been given a gift I don't deserve. "You're so amazing."

She comes up onto her elbows and looks at me on my knees in front of her. Her skin is warm with a blush. "I imagined this, you know," she admits. "Fantasized about us."

I climb up her body, my weight on my arms. "I did too," I admit. "Jerked it quite a bit imagining being with you, Hannah Fleming." I offer her a grin.

Her eyes bounce from my lips to my eyes. "What if–"

"Don't say it."

"–it doesn't…" She shivers under me.

"Do you want to stop?" I ask. "It's okay if you do."

She shakes her head. "No. I want this. I'm just sort of afraid."

"Of what?" I hold my breath, waiting for her answer.

*My Heart Insists I Understand What's True*

I scan Seth's face. His beautiful face. The angles of his jaw. The fullness of his mouth, kissed by me but frowning. The worried shape of his amber eyes etched with dark brown flecks. The way his hair hangs around his face since he's looking down at me.

"Afraid of what, Hannah?"

I trace the shape of his neck and his shoulders with my gaze, the planes and ridges of his chest and abdomen, the sinew of his arms holding himself up.

My breath catches at the way this feels surreal. The pleasure of it, but also the pressure. And it isn't the pressure; it's the possible consequences of losing something—someone—I'm realizing is so important to me.

"Hannah?"

I meet his gaze, unsure how to explain what's going on inside me if I don't even understand myself. "I'm not afraid of you. I'm not even afraid of sex."

Seth moves so that he's no longer above me, no longer poised to move forward with the act. "Talk to me," he says and waits.

I have this horrible feeling he might think it's because of what he's shared, but that couldn't be further from the truth. His willingness to be vulnerable with me makes me understand his struggle, to feel even closer to him.

Seth reaches out and smooths a lock of my hair off my face, and I turn my head to look at him. "I think I'm afraid that I'm not good enough, for this, for us. And as much as I want this—and I want it so much—I'll ruin it somehow."

"How could you possibly ruin it?" he asks.

I can't find the thread, but Sebastian sitting across from me in a crowded restaurant just after Thanksgiving and saying he'd met someone else is a series of images in my mind. "Maybe you're right."

"About?"

"Waiting. I don't want to lose you."

Seth rises onto an elbow. "You're not going to lose me, Hannah. And we don't have to do this yet to prove that. We still have another two dates. And I can wait for you even longer than that. Five more dates. 10. A year. Whatever you need, because–" He stops, and his eyes fall away with the weight of whatever he's left unsaid. His eyes find mine again. "I will wait for you, Hannah."

I shiver.

"Cold?" Seth gathers me in his arms.

"No," I say even as I shiver again.

"Shower?"

I hear the smile in his voice and nod.

Seth has left clothing for me when I climb from the shower. His clothes. I slip into them, noticing how intimate it feels, enjoying the idea of Seth's things as if it were as concrete as a hug. I listen for him when I open the door. There's sound coming from the kitchen, so I pad down the hallway in socks, and when I reach the living room, I follow the noise to the kitchen.

My heart is racing, more nervous now than before

Seth, his hair curly and damp, reaches for a pepper mill over a clear dish on the countertop. When he hears me, he glances up, his eyes crinkle with his smile, which broadens as he looks at me in his clothing. Those dimples. "Hey, gorgeous."

"I look silly." I look down at his clothes. The sweats are long, because he's tall, but my body fills them out.

He shakes his head. "No. You look amazing." He meets me for a kiss. "Feel better?"

"Yes. You?"

He nods, returns to the dinner, and finishes seasoning what looks like chicken slick with olive oil and sprinkled with capers, lemon, and rosemary. He picks it up and slides it into the oven, setting the timer.

"How can I help?" I ask.

"Help me with the salad?"

I sit at the bar counter, and Seth slides a cutting board, a knife, and tomatoes toward me.

"Can I ask you about something?"

"What about?"

"Something you said to Sebastian."

"He's taken too much room in my life." But even as I say it, I hear the wall I'm putting up, and maybe by closing the door on it, it will continue to be a wall between us. I don't want that.

Seth pauses, leaning toward me across the counter, his elbows holding him up, then says, "I'm hanging up on feeling like you're facing some serious shit. That I'm powerless to help you, and I worry." His eyes measure me for a moment. "The question isn't about him so much, as it is about the situation."

I set down the knife, take a sip from the cup of water he gave me, and commit to opening the door so there isn't anything between us to ruin a possible future. "Okay. Ask."

"I heard what you told him—at the gym. And I just wondered if you trust me to know about what's happening in your life? You hadn't said anything. I know that you don't owe me anything, I just want you to know you can trust me."

My eyes fly up to his, shocked. "I do trust you," I say. "Completely."

"Then why didn't you tell me?"

I look away from him back to the tomato under my hand and press a knife into the fruit. The red flesh splits under the knife, and the juice drains across the cutting board. When I'm able to formulate the why, I say, "I feel like if I talk about it, he becomes this mountain between us. And I don't want him there." I set down the knife, and add the tomato to the bowl, sprinkling it over lettuce. When I look at Seth, and his gaze jumps from the tomato to mine.

"That if I keep him in my thoughts, in my mouth, he won't ever go away. I want what's happening here about us, and to leave that time of my life in the past."

Seth moves around the counter, sliding the bowl and the cutting board away, then turning me on the stool to face him. "Except he isn't in the past."

I look down at my empty hands. "I want him to be."

"Take it from me, Hannah, the past has influence on the present."

I look up at him, understanding the risk he took to share what he did and grateful for it. His relationship with his father, the abuse, the car crash, all of it has shaped who he is now. Despite all that negativity he's experienced, I'm staring at an amazing man.

He reaches up to move a lock of my hair from my forehead, his eyes tracking the movement. "Your experiences shape you. And I want to be here for you and help you through the shit stuff and to celebrate the good stuff."

My heart fills, the beat slowing with the added weight, and the pleasure of, well, him. I stand and wrap my arm around his neck, pressing a quick kiss to his mouth. "I want that."

He smiles. Leans forward to kiss me again, slow and savoring.

Later, sitting next to him at the bar top with the remnants of a wonderful meal littering the surface, the conversation between us has flowed. We've talked about our families, about school, about our future hopes, about silly memories from school days, nothing awkward between us even after almost sex.

"Thank you for dinner. That was amazing." I reach for Seth's dish and stand. "Done?"

He grabs his dish. "You're not doing the dishes." He twists, blocking the dish from my hand, and grins over it.

"You cooked. I clean. That's the rule."

"We're making rules?" He grins. "I like it, but no." He stands, carrying his dish around the end of the countertop to the sink. "You're my guest, and I don't make guests clean."

I wrinkle my nose and chase him into the kitchen. "Seth."

He laughs when I crash into him from behind. He turns, wrapping his arms around me, pinning me against him. "Stubborn much? Fine! We can do them together."

I smile as he releases me and think about how sweet he is. He's a guy my dad would have called "a good egg." Realizing this makes me feel like the earth has started spinning in the proper direction again, only I hadn't realized it had ever changed. I mean, sure, the grief about my dad put me in stasis, but when I met Sebastian, I think I'd thought I was finally waking up. Only, I'm realizing, maybe it was only the Shadow Hannah who had, and the real one is breaking out of her chrysalis, finally realizing how hidden she made herself.

Because of this man.

Seth scrapes the leftovers on the dishes into a bin, and I notice the way his yellow shirt shifts around his body as he moves. I imagine laying my hands against his shoulder blades so I can feel the strength of him but step up to the sink next to him instead, fitting the stopper into the drain and turning on the water.

"Where did you learn to be such an amazing person?" I ask, moving so he can get under the sink.

He grins as he puts the bin back and closes the cupboard, then offers me a side-eye. "You mean, being respectful isn't the norm?" He picks up the soap and squeezes some into the running water.

"I think you might be an exception to the rule." I look for the sponge in the soapy water.

"How did you learn? To be incredible," he asks.

"I'm not an incredible person."

"I think you are."

His words make me feel warm in both a good way and an embarrassed way. I realize how hard it is for me to take compliments. I think there was a time in my past when it wasn't so difficult and I wonder when that shifted—but even as I wonder it, I already know the answer. The night my dad died, and the guilt and regret I still feel about where I was when my mom and sister were trying so hard to get ahold of me. "My parents. I guess. Good friends."

"Both are good places."

"You dodged my question." I smile at him and realize he does this a lot, when the questions swing around to focus on him. He deflects. I'm not sure I noticed it until now.

"I've had some good friends. A good therapist. Definitely not my parents," he says.

"Feel like talking about it?"

He adds what's leftover into a container and slips the dish into the filling sink. "Not really."

I try not to feel hurt by this, but it pinches a little. Here he's asked me to trust him with Sebastian but is reticent about sharing this very important part of his experience. But I don't say anything, even if I think it. I shut off the water.

He looks at me, as if maybe he knows he has hurt me, and shakes his head. "I'm sorry. Old habits die hard sometimes." He takes a deep breath. "I suppose I watched my dad and how he lived and warned myself not to ever be like that fucking guy. And I watched how my mom was treated and told myself to do better. To want more."

I submerge my hands in the bubbles and scrub the first dish with a sponge. "With them as models, though, I suppose you've got an excuse?"

"What? To be an asshole? I don't think anyone has an excuse to be an asshole."

He steps behind me and reaches around me into the water. With the front of his body pressed to the back of mine, I notice three things. First, we fit together, the shape of us somehow perfect. Second, the feel of his warmth ignites a fire under my skin that makes my heart expand, heating in my chest. Third, I feel so safe. His quiet strength covers me like a cozy sweater.

Seth fits his head over my shoulder, runs his hands down my arms to my hands under water, takes both the dish and the sponge from me, and begins washing.

"And I didn't escape being the asshole. I had my day, faced the consequences of it, and had to decide who I wanted to be." He presses a kiss to my neck, then nudges me out of the way. "Dry?" He indicates the hand towel he set on the other side of the sink.

I pick up the towel. "The wreck?" I ask.

I see him swallow, thinking about it, and understand how difficult it must be to talk about. I know that facing the death of someone I love has been upending. Losing my father—someone so integral to the safety of my world, to the understanding of myself in relation to how I fit into it—has been like receding into deep space and floating in that vacuum of grief alone. I can't imagine what it would feel like to face my own death, the reality of that. He nods but goes quiet, his thoughts slipping into the water with the dirty dishes.

"What is it?" I ask when he hands me a dish and finally meets my eyes again, as if he's come back to the moment.

He shakes his head and offers me a smile.

No dimples.

"It was hard to share?" I guess.

He nods.

Without overthinking, which is a very non-present-day-Hannah thing to do, but something I suddenly realize was very me before my dad died, I commit to sharing with him. Trusting him. "So, about Sebastian–" I glance at him to see if he still wants to hear it. I figure changing the subject is what he needs, but I also have to be willing to demonstrate my trust.

He leans against the sink with his hip, facing me, washing the dish in his hand, and waiting with his head tilted.

I take it as a signal he wants to hear it. "I met him right after I transferred here—a year ago. I'd been working at the library, and we bumped into one another in the stacks."

"Like us the other day?" he asks, frowning, and turns to resume washing the last of the dishes.

My skin heats remembering. "No. Not like that." I smile and dry, stacking the dish with the others when I'm done. "It was pretty innocuous, but he asked me out. We hit it off. It kind of felt like a too-good-to-be-true kind of thing. Everything between us seemed so perfect." I stop and look at him. "You sure you want to hear this stuff?"

"Yes." He pulls the stopper from the sink, draining it. "I want to understand Hannah, and that means learning about everything I've missed."

"I wasn't in a very good place when I met him. With the death of my dad, and the year off school, I think I was at the lowest point in my life. I hadn't even planned to return to school, but my mom sort of sent me a lengthy guilt trip about me being a martyr and that wasn't what my dad would have wanted."

"She was probably right." He grins and wipes the counter. "And hey, we're here right now."

I dry the last dish, and Seth moves around me to put them away. "I'm wondering if the perfection of Sebastian was me trying to fill in the emotional gaps I had without my dad. Like if I met him now, I'm not sure I would feel the same."

"Because you feel different."

I nod and fold the dish towel, laying it on the counter and smoothing it with my hand. "I knew when we broke up, it was the right thing, and maybe I'd made excuses for him doing it, but I was clear enough then to know we hadn't been well for a while."

"Why?"

I turn to lean against the counter and cross my arms, suddenly a little cold. With a shiver, I wonder if it's more because of the emotion of looking at this reflectively and honestly, or because of the temperature.

Seth steps in front of me and rubs my arms with his hands. "Would you like to stay here tonight?"

I smile and nod.

He takes my hand and leads me to his bedroom, and this time, I take it in. It's neat. The bed made with a blue comforter, his laptop closed and centered on his desk, all the clothes put away. "Want a sweatshirt?" When he opens the closet, and it's just as neat in there, and he retrieves a blue sweatshirt from the shelf on the top. I shrug into it as he sits on the bed.

After I text Jewel to let her know where I'll be, I crawl past him and get under the covers.

He follows me in, facing me. "So, why wasn't your relationship well?"

I roll to my back and sigh. "So many things, really. Let's see. The laundry list–" I pause a moment, then say, "Sebastian needed my attention constantly. If I didn't go to his games or do something he wanted to do, he'd pout. So I just relented rather than fight. Which was easier. When we fought, I found myself shutting down. And I think it's because he'd twist things around on me and make them seem like my fault somehow, or that I was the unreasonable one. It was easier to stay quiet, instead. To keep the peace." I stop a moment.

Seth takes a deep breath and pulls me closer.

"Then we were spending a lot more time apart, and instead of feeling upset by that and missing him, I just felt relief. We'd stopped having sex. I just couldn't find it me to be intimate. I think that's why when I found out he'd cheated, I wasn't surprised, and I also wasn't as mad as I think I should have been. It was almost like I'd expected it. I felt hurt, but it was more like I was delivered from the deep hole I'd dug to bury myself. Like I could finally climb out and walk away."

I stop, and though I'm nervous about seeing the look on his face, I turn my head to look at Seth. A tear leaks from my eye. "Do you think I'm pathetic?"

Seth reaches out, cradles my cheek in his palm, and swipes the tear with his thumb. "Not all, Hannah. Not in the slightest." He leans forward and presses his lips to the place he's wiped the tear away, then gathers me in his arms. "I'm so glad you're here now. With me. Thank you, for trusting me."

I tighten my arms around him, so grateful this is the present.

When I open my eyes to the twilight of morning, I don't remember falling asleep. I remember talking. I remember the eventual brushing of teeth, of turning out the light, of making out, the heavy want sitting in my body, but the way waiting to have sex now seems more like an important act of getting it emotionally right. The sounds of Trace coming home and his crew coming over to play video games. I wasn't sure I'd be able to sleep, but somehow fell into its abyss.

Seth reaches for me, mumbles something, and pulls me against him. "Good morning."

"Morning."

"I like waking up with you." His arms tighten around me.

I smile, warm and glowing, and cuddle in closer. "I like this too. Maybe too much."

"Why too much?" he asks, his voice filled with sleep, and it's sexy.

I think about it. "Because it's addicting and I'm going to want it all the time, until it's something I need to survive rather than just want."

He moans and pulls me tighter, fitting his head into the space where my neck meets my shoulder. We lay together like that for a while, and I think I might even drift back into a morning nap, until Seth gets up, and I feel the cold of the loss.

"Coffee?"

I roll and look at him. His shorts are askew, and he covers his groin with his hands, which makes me smile. His brown hair sticks up around his head, and I don't think he's ever looked sexier. Okay, maybe naked with me, our bodies sliding against one another. I press my thighs together. "Yes, please."

He smiles as if he can read my mind and leans forward to kiss my cheek. "I'll bring you some." Then he disappears out the door, shutting it behind him.

Instead of lying there, I get up and put on Seth's sweatpants and the sweatshirt over the t-shirt I slept in the night before. After making the bed, I pad down the hallway through the living room past a smattering of sleeping men on the couches like blankets thrown haphazardly across its surface.

Seth is waiting for the coffee, which has already started brewing. When I walk into the kitchen, he turns and smiles, his eyes drifting over me, then returning to my face. "I love seeing you like this," he whispers.

"How's this?"

He opens his arms, and I step into them. "In the morning. Here. In my clothes. Is it weird it turns me on?"

I giggle. "I will never be giving them back."

His arms tighten around me.

"Oh. Shit. Morning."

I turn my head and see Trace standing at the end of the counter. He rubs his eyes.

Seth tightens his hold as if anticipating me pulling away. I relax against him, smiling at his territorial declaration.

"I wasn't expecting that. Sorry." Trace grins. "S'up, Hannah."

"Good morning."

"Coffee?" he asks, flicking his hair with a shake of his head, and it bounces back into place.

"Brewing," Seth says. "You guys were up late."

"Yeah. Played a quick tourney."

"Who won?" Seth asks.

Trace grins. "Do you even doubt it?"

Seth chuckles, and the vibration of his laugh inside his chest moves through me.

"Did we keep you up?" Trace lifts an eyebrow, and I know what he's thinking.

"Nope. All good," Seth says at the same time the coffee pot sputters and beeps. He turns and withdraws three cups, fills them all, then pulls some creamer from the fridge, which he presents to me.

I add a dollop to mine and hold it out to Trace.

"Thanks."

There's an awkwardness that drifts around us, and I know it isn't between Trace and Seth. It's because of me. Because I'm Sebastian's ex-girlfriend, and Trace is a football player. He's probably wondering where his allegiances lie: with his roommate or with his teammate? I don't like that, but I also know this isn't something I can control. This will get back to Sebastian. We go to a tiny school, where everyone knows everyone else. The thought would have made me anxious a few weeks ago, but now, I'm over it.

Marco sits up on the couch, his black hair exploding around his head, and walks into the kitchen. He takes a second look at me. "Hey Hannah." I hear the surprise in his voice, but he recovers. "I thought I smelled coffee."

I look over the rim of my coffee cup at Seth, who's chatting with Trace and Marco about Trace's trip home, then the video game tournament. He glances at me and smiles. Dimples. The amber of his eyes glow, making my heart flutter. I know without a doubt these feelings pulsing through me like electricity are so much larger than just infatuation or attraction. This is deeper, layered in the fact that I'm infatuated with someone who is a friend, someone I have known most of my life, and who has suddenly become so very important in my day-to-day that the thought of him not being in it makes my heart constrict with fear.

That's not how I ever felt about Sebastian, and it hits me—I never loved Sebastian.

What's moving through my body for Seth is most definitely love.

*My Heart Insists the Truth is Messy*

The new beat of my heart is disconcerting. It's leaning so hard toward Hannah I'm afraid I might topple into her and knock us off course. Except I think she's revolving around me too. How we crash together is still to be determined. As I watch her press the button for the giant sphere floating in the center of the Oregon Science Museum, changing it to a projection of Earth, I can't help but feel that gravity tug on my heart toward her. What makes the sensation more terrifying is that I haven't felt this way before, and I'm not sure how to navigate it.

"Look at this one!" Hannah says with a gigantic smile on her face. She presses the button for the floating planet, changing it to Mars. "Could you imagine all the things we could do here with elementary students?"

"I can imagine." I reach out and touch her, needing to ground myself by pressing my hand against her lower back, testing if she's real. If this is real. She straightens and leans into me, proving I haven't made this up.

"Did you still want to watch the Hubble Telescope film?" I ask. I glance at our tickets. "It starts in ten minutes."

She takes one of my hands in hers. "Lead the way."

I pull her away from the rotating projection of the planet, and we move through the dark exhibition hall, out into the bright lobby toward the escalator. A wall of windows framed with metal supports rises several stories, offering us views of the Portland skyline beyond. The museum sits on the east side of the Willamette River, the city on the other side. I can imagine settling in this city and picture what that might be like, only Hannah is in every version of my vision.

She steps onto the escalator first. I follow her onto the next step, and she leans back against me as we travel down to the main floor. I wrap my arms around her, drawing her closer, and press a kiss to her temple. It hits me then. I can't picture life without Hannah because she's it. I'm done. There isn't anyone else I want besides her. My heart has always known it, and my mind is catching up.

The fact that she knows about all the messy stuff in my life and still wants to hold my hand, still wants to kiss me, still leans against me as if I'm a support system, is reinforcement of how right this is. And *that* is what's so terrifying about the prospect. I could mess this up somehow. She could meet my family and decide we're too much. There could be all kinds of reasons this could go wrong. My heart skitters in my chest as if looking for a shelter from all those fears, but I'm completely exposed.

Once we're seated in the IMAX theater, Hannah leans against my shoulder, and I wrap my arm around her, kissing her temple again. The theater gets dark, and a Technicolor image of space fills the screened wall ahead of us, a dizzying array of the cosmos. It makes me feel as if I'm floating through space. A floating heart.

Hannah squeezes my hand and tilts her head to look up at me. My tether.

I lean and kiss her, the Orion nebula moving around us in a gorgeous rainbow of color, though I've close my eyes to focus on the woman who's become my universe. I want to tell her how I feel, but fear holds the words hostage.

By the time we return to Linden Falls, it's dark, and it has been a perfect day. I drive us through town toward Hannah's apartment, her hand in mine, listening to her chatter about the museum. After I park, I look over at her and smile. "Date four. Check."

She's staring at me.

"What?"

"I had so much fun with you," she says, echoing my sentiments, but her face is so serious I'm afraid there's a *but* in the rest of her statement.

"Why don't you look like you had fun right now?"

She gives me a self-conscious smile, and unbuckles her seatbelt. "Make room for me," she says, then slides over the center console and situates herself in my lap.

I like the feel of her there, her rounded ass pressed against my thighs. I lay a hand just above her knee and give her a squeeze. "I'm thinking all kinds of thoughts, Hannah."

"Me too," she says and slides a hand up my arm over my shoulders, burning a trail up my neck, a touch without purpose, really, just physical connection, but I love it and squeeze her again, pulling her a touch closer.

"What is it?" I ask. I might have felt afraid had she remained in her seat, but she wanted to be closer, so my heart jumps in my chest with excited anticipation.

She swallows but doesn't say anything. Instead, she leans forward and presses her lips to mine, her hands framing my face. It's not a kiss filled with physical need, but I can feel the emotional longing. When she leans back, disconnecting the kiss, she says, "I don't want to be without you."

Her words hit me like a punch, a calibration of my feelings with hers. It makes me groan, and with my hand wrapped around the back of her neck, I pull her back to me to communicate all my feelings with physical connection.

But she presses a hand against my chest, and with an understanding smile, says, "Wait. Let me finish."

I tilt my head, pressing my forehead to hers. "Hurry up, Hannah."

She giggles. "I need time to think, and your kisses steal my thoughts."

I hum and press my mouth to her collarbone. "Patience isn't my virtue. But okay." I press more small kisses against her skin, loving that she tilts her head so I can access more, letting my fingers drift across the skin of her thigh.

"I was a little worried we were moving too fast," she says. "Not physically or anything, but emotionally. It was a little like that with Sebastian."

I stop kissing her and sit up, trying to meet her gaze in the dark. "I don't want what we have to resemble what it was like with him at all. That's—"

She shakes her head and presses fingertips to my mouth. "No. Let me finish. With him it was like this explosion of feeling all at once, like an emotion overload. He was always saying we were soulmates, and I remember doubting it, but never forcing myself to look too closely at the doubt."

"Where are you going with this, Han?" Her words have my heart pulsing with heavy beats of concern.

Her fingertips smooth pieces of hair from my skin, and her eyes following the movement. "At first, when we reconnected, my feelings felt so big—like that. It worried me. I thought maybe I was making more of what I feel for you than it was."

"Please let there be a 'but' in there."

She makes a soft, mirthful noise. "*But* I realized something today."

"What was that?"

"You were never a stranger." She leans forward and kisses my cheek. "You've been in my life since kindergarten. And maybe we lost contact for a little while—"

"Like the telescope in space?" I kiss her again and linger there.

She smiles against my mouth. "Yes. But we've traveled back into range."

I wrap my arms around her and rest my face in the space of her neck. "Hannah—"

She pulls my face away so she can look at me. I wonder what she sees in the dark of my car. I'm seeing her bright eyes, shiny and dark in the light beyond the car. "I love your dimples," she says, then kisses one side of my mouth.

"And?"

She kisses the other side. "I don't know what I'm saying," she says and smiles. I know she's blushing. "It's just that, I need you to know how happy I am. Right now. How these last weeks feel like rediscovering myself and who I once was, only now also who I'm meant to be."

I grasp her face. "I know exactly what you mean. Exactly," I whisper and press a kiss to her mouth. Then another. And another, until we're both struggling to get closer in my car. I slide my hand up her thigh, under the hem of her short dress to her hip, the lace of her panties imprinting my palm. I want them gone.

She squirms against me, a gasp of breath when my fingers trail the skin over her stomach at the edge of her panties.

"I want you, Hannah." I slip my fingers under the lace waistband, sliding over her hot skin until I'm touching the core of her, the soft spot that makes her grab hold of my shoulders and moan, "yes."

"You feel so good," I tell her. She's hot and wet. "So good," I murmur and use my hand to make her gasp my name. She wiggles against me, and I use my mouth to swallow the sounds, taking them into my soul.

"Seth," she says against my lips, gasping, mewling, her fingertips digging into the skin under my shirt. "That feels—"

But I know how it feels. Good. She draws in a breath, tilts her hips against my hand, and tells me she's coming, which I can feel as her body tightens around my fingers. I kiss her harder, needing her, needing this. Then she wilts, curling in against me, depleted but smiling. "Oh my god," she says, her forehead against my shoulder. After she catches her breath, she kisses my neck, and between each kiss says, "Come up. Stay with me."

"I'm not sure I can walk yet," I smile. "I'm fucking hard as a rock.

She giggles as lights from a car outside illuminate the darkness around us. A loud rumble, indicative of a muscle car, accompanies the light. Hannah's smile freezes as she breaks apart from me and tracks the slow-moving vehicle moving through the lot.

She sinks against me like she's hiding. "Sebastian," she whispers.

I look out my rearview, expecting to see Sebastian standing there, but I can't see anything but the illuminated landscape in the mirror. "What? Are you serious?"

She nods. "That's his car." Then, as if we're sixteen and caught by our parents, she adjusts her clothing and slides back into the passenger side of the car. It stabs my heart and fills me with annoyance.

The car stops right behind my car. Then it sits, rumbling.

My annoyance blooms into anger.

I'm not sure if Sebastian knows Hannah and I are sitting in the car, or if he's just waiting there, looking up at Hannah's apartment.

But I'm angry. Angry at the whole situation. Angry that this guy is stalking her. Angry at Hannah acting like what we have is something to feel guilty about. Angry about Sebastian fucking up what's happening between us.

I snap. "This is fucking stupid and needs to stop." I reach for the handle to my door, but Hannah lurches over the center console and grabs my arm.

"No. Please, don't."

I'm not sure why this adds to my anger, but it does. I can't decide if it's Hannah afraid for me or afraid for Sebastian. Maybe the fragile part of me thinks she doesn't believe in me. Or maybe it's the Cro-Magnon man feeling territorial. Or maybe it's a seed of doubt that whatever Hannah has with Sebastian isn't over, and I'm caught in a triangle again. Before I can respond, the car backs away, leaving the lot in darkness once again.

*What do you know?*

I try to grab ahold of the lessons, only my heart has been squeezed and isn't pumping properly. Rational thoughts aren't reaching my brain, and that makes me afraid.

*You aren't your father.*

"Are you upset?"

I look at her, but I don't answer her question, retreating. "I'll walk you up," I say instead.

Hannah grabs my arm. "Talk to me."

I've slipped into my normal way of being, throwing up a wall. Here I'd thought I was so much further along than resorting to my usual way of dealing. But I'm hurt, and I slide back into silence. "Not now," I say and extricate my arm from her touch. "I need–" I need her, but I feel wrong, and I need to figure that out before I pull her into my darkness.

Hannah gets out of the car, following me. "Don't shut me out."

"Come on. I want to make sure you're safe."

"Seth."

I whirl and snap, "I'm pissed!" my voice raised just to the underside of a yell.

She leans away from me, and I hate it.

The movement, the feelings on her face just add to my anger, but at myself. I turn away from her, shove a hand into my hair then turn back to her. With a lower voice, I say, "I don't want to fuck this up when I feel like this. Just give me–"

But she doesn't let me finish, moving past me up the stairs.

I follow her up, every step I take feeling heavier. I don't understand the feelings, but I know I don't want to do or say anything more to mess up what was good just a moment ago. I don't want to be my father.

When we get to her door, she uses the key to open it and walks inside. She leaves it open for me to follow her in, but my anger is burning away to regret, shame, and embarrassment. I don't cross the threshold. Dr. B's words drift through me: *it's how you respond in the face of your emotion*. I don't know if I've failed the test or passed it.

Hannah puts her stuff on the counter and turns. "Well?"

I don't want what was otherwise a great night to end this way, but I don't know how to get back to it with all these other feelings swirling through me. I take a step away from her. "I'm going to go," I say. I see her swallow, and I'm afraid she's holding back tears, which makes me feel terrible. I want to say something to fix it, but what comes out of my mouth is, "Why did you stop me?"

"I don't want anything to happen to you–"

"You don't believe in me?"

"Of course I do!" she says, her arms coming out to her sides. "That's ridiculous." Her arms drop back to her sides. She sighs. "When he showed up the other night, after seeing us together at the library, he threatened you."

"So you don't think I can't take care of myself?"

"That's what you get from this? I don't want him between us. I just want him gone."

"But don't you see, Hannah, he is!"

"And? What are you trying to say? You don't want this?"

"That's not what I'm saying at all." But I don't know what I'm trying to say because my feelings are making it difficult to sift through my thoughts. I'm just mad that assholes like Sebastian get to act the way they do without consequences. And I suppose that goes back to my father, to my mother taking him back. All that bitterness and anger stored up. "I'm just angry. I don't like that he's doing shit like this, and I want it to stop. And maybe that's what an asshole like Sebastian needs—someone he sees as a threat."

"But at what cost?"

"Exactly. At what cost? You? I'm not willing to put you on the line with someone like him, Hannah."

She crosses her arms over her chest, but it doesn't look like she's blocking me out, rather it looks like she's trying to hold herself together.

"I'm going to go," I say and take a step away from the door. "I need space to think."

She just nods.

I pull the door shut between us, press my forehead against it, and wait to hear the lock. It takes a while for the tell-tale click of the lock, but when it does happen, I take a step back and look at the door.

With a heavy sigh I return to my car. I sit afraid to drive away. Afraid that I may have just ruined the best thing that's ever happened to me and wondering how I'm ever going to be able to fix it?

*My Heart Insists It Knows What It Wants*

"So?" Mason says, quirking one of his eyebrows higher than the other and irritating me because I can't do it. He leans over his desk to look at the paperwork a little closer before turning to look at me.

"So what?" I look away at my own paperwork. Though I know what Mason is asking, I play dumb. I'm still smarting at how things ended the night before with Seth—our first fight I suppose—unclear about what it was actually about. Sebastian? My fear over a confrontation? I don't think it's something I've done, and while this understanding is progress for me, it doesn't make it any easier. The outcome is out of my control, and I don't know how to fix it. Then again, repairing it isn't up to me. It's the chaos I feel about whether Seth wants to fix it that has me unsettled.

It does make me realize, however, how different fighting with Sebastian was in contrast. How I would bend over backwards to placate him. How I would avoid conflict out of fear of being emotionally dismantled. How I couldn't bring up the way I felt without being disassembled as oversensitive or unhinged. How I was always apologizing. This fight with Seth is illuminating in a way that makes me understand whatever happened with Sebastian in many ways wasn't about me, but about him and the way he would derail me. Seth, even in a fight, was reassuring. He'd said, "I need space," without accusation, responsible for his own feelings.

It's very clear that whatever I had with Sebastian wasn't right, and I hate that it's taken me so long to acknowledge it. That it took Sebastian ending things to wake me up. I'm understanding now that what I just thought was us falling apart was an unhealthy relationship rooted in control and manipulation. And I let myself fall into that pit. I hate that, but I'm also understanding now that I hadn't known what I hadn't known.

I do now.

I know that I deserve someone to listen to my concerns and validate my feelings.

I know I should never have to hide either of those things to make my partner feel secure.

I know that my hopes and dreams are equally important to my partner's.

I know that I should never make myself smaller.

I know that my partner should respect my wants and wishes.

I know that I shouldn't have to say 'I'm sorry' for being me.

Mason turns in his seat to fully face me, and it creaks under his weight. "Hannah! You better spill it."

I look at the list of research topics I'm supposed to search for a professor, ignore him, and type some keywords into a search-engine database.

Mason leans forward and pokes my arm. He's supposed to be doing the same thing, but he's being Mason.

"You're distracting me." I offer him a smile.

"Please. You totally love being distracted by me. I want to know what happened with Hottie."

"We went to OSM." I don't want to share that we've had a spat, but realizing that we've had a weird, somehow very civilized fight, it feels very on-brand for Seth and Hannah, which does make me smile a little bit.

His eyes narrow. "You're withholding. I can tell by that sly smile on your face. There's no way that you date a guy that looks like that and not let your freak flag fly."

"Freak flag." I snicker and mark a few possibilities in a database to examine as pertinent sources.

Mason grins. "I'm happy for you. You seem–" he stops and looks at his computer, as though doing a search in a database for the right keyword– "at peace." His sparkling eyes return to mine. "That's a good thing. You take more of that for yourself."

"That's the plan." I offer him a smile, typing in another search term. "Whose article are you doing the grunt work for?" I ask, changing the subject to something else so I don't have to think about missing Seth, hoping to occupy my thoughts with research monotony rather than replaying the fight.

"Dr. Hadley. He's writing an article on critical race theory as it relates to Oregon and indigenous First Nation People."

"Sounds more interesting than Dr. Whistler's examination of biodiversity on the bacteria derived in Eastern Oregon plant life, and its correlation to medical breakthroughs for skin ailments."

Mason rolls his eyes. "I couldn't do this."

"What?"

"Be an academic. All the rush to write the next big thing. All the research." He makes a disgusted sound.

"Probably why you're studying business management."

He nods. "Seriously. I'd rather look at spreadsheets and explore target markets any day of the week as opposed to this." He makes a face and a sound to match.

"You mean you don't want to study bacteria?"

"No. I like things clean and tidy."

I laugh and note another article. "I agree. Give me my elementary lesson plans any day. I can explore photosynthesis on the most basic level and come up with art projects for second graders to learn it."

"Could I get some help here?" someone asks.

I turn toward Seth, standing on the other side of the counter, and temper my smile. He offers a smile as subdued as mine, clearly nervous as he shifts on his feet.

"You're here?" I ask. It doesn't sound quite right, and I see Mason give me a double take.

"I have a research paper to do for my history class. Thought I'd come in and work on it since I was going to come and get you anyway."

I check my impulse to jump over the counter and attack him with a hug, to tell him to stop being mad, and instead introduce him to Mason, who is polite, but I notice the awareness on his face. He leans forward, and I can see from the corner of my eye that he's assessing the awkward tension between Seth and me.

"It's nice to meet you," Mason says. "Do you need any help finding sources?"

"You know. I might." Seth looks at me.

"Hannah is really good at research. We were just talking about how much she loves it." Mason winks at me and mouths, *you can thank me later.*

I smile, amused by Mason, but calm the excitement at the prospect of being with Seth out in the wilds of stacks. We need to talk. I don't know if it will happen and what the outcome will be. There's every possibility that Seth might not want the drama that comes along with me trying to navigate out from behind my ex.

"I can help." I walk around the counter.

Seth falls in step with me, his fingers brushing mine, sending sparks up my arms that explode like fireworks at the base of my spine. I quell the urge to take his hand and lead him to the elevator.

"I wanted to see if I could take you out to eat after your shift?"

"Date five?" I ask and walk onto the elevator. "Or for something else?"

Seth follows me in. The doors slide shut behind him, but neither of us move to press the button for our destination. Instead, I'm staring at him.

He looks down for a fraction of a second, then back up, meeting my gaze. "Hannah. I'm sorry." He takes a step closer.

"About what?"

He takes a deep breath. "I got angry, and it scares me when I do."

"Why?"

He doesn't answer, but his eyes fall away from mine, as if he can't hold them up, weighted with something else he doesn't want me to see. And I recognize it. I've felt it. Shame.

"Your dad?" I ask.

He nods, still averting his eyes. "That shit Sebastian pulls… he just–" He pauses a second, then finally meets my gaze. "He reminds me of my dad. When you didn't want me to confront him, even if it was from a good place… I just felt weak."

I step toward him. "You are the farthest thing from weak, Seth Peters."

"I shouldn't have shut you out."

"Except you're here now, letting me in. And what did you do except be honest about what you needed? I can respect that." I reach up and smooth a lock of hair from his forehead. "I was afraid you might not want–"

"What?" He grabs my hand.

"Maybe it was all just too much."

He shakes his head. "No, Han. No." Then he presses his lips to my palm, walking me backward until my back is pinned between him and the elevator wall. "Are we okay?"

I grab his head, my fingers in the silk of his waves. "We better be," I say and draw him down to kiss me, smiling against his lips. "Because the alternative doesn't work for me."

Seth wraps his arms around me, and the kiss he offers is filled with promise.

Because I'm at work and run the risk of the Hun opening the elevator, I break the kiss and reach around Seth to press the button for the sub-basement. The elevator moves.

Seth leans against the wall across from me. My breath rushes through my lungs, wanting another kiss, wanting his hands, his body pressed against mine.

He grins, sheepish—dimples—which is even more charming, if that's possible.

"How about the Sandwich Spot on Main?" I ask.

Seth pushes away from the elevator wall, and the anticipation in the air crushes my lungs as he takes the two steps to me. "I can't wait."

I grasp ahold of his belt loops and pull his hips against mine. "The next two hours are going to be torture knowing you're here, waiting for me."

He leans forward and presses his lips to the sensitive spot between my ear and my neck. "You smell good." His tongue tests the skin. "And taste good too. I want to wake up with you again. I want my head between your thighs."

I whimper at the thought.

With a tilt of my head, Seth settles in against me and tests a spot on my neck gently with his teeth. My nerves spark with energy that radiates outward, and I can't help but make a little noise.

"Hannah," Seth says and moves his hips. I can feel his excitement pressed against my belly. "I missed you last night. I hated walking away."

"I hated it, too."

The elevator bell announces we've arrived, but it takes an extra beat for Seth to step away. Truthfully, I don't want him to, but there's time.

The fluorescent lighting in the hallway is garish and makes the green linoleum appear sickly and institutional. The sub-basement is not my favorite spot in the library. It's a mix of the old library with the updated one that was renovated several years prior.

"Where are you taking me?" Seth asks from behind me. "This looks shady. I feel like I'm in a 1930's mental hospital or something." A few steps later he says, "Are you bringing me down here to have your way with me?"

I laugh quietly. "You see my sinister plan so clearly." I look over my shoulder at him and smile. When we reach one of the study rooms, I turn on the light. Inside is a round table with several chairs placed around it, and a computer linked to the library's database system against one wall. "It's very quiet, and not many people like to come down here. The new part of the library is sexier." I lean against the wall next to the light switch.

"This is very… private," he says and drops his backpack on the table with a thunk. He turns and takes a few steps to reach me. "How often do you think people come down here and get it on?" He lifts his eyebrows with amusement, then reaches out, grabs my waist, and pulls me closer.

"Probably more than I'd like to think about."

With a hand, Seth reaches out and closes the door, cutting off the outside world. "Let's see what it's like," he says, his voice deep and raspy. Then he kisses me.

I grab ahold of his face, then wrap my arms around him. Desire courses through me feels like a flood, the dam having broken. Tongues, hands, quiet inhales of breath mixed with needy want.

Seth reaches down and picks me up.

I wrap my legs around his hips.

Our mouths remain connected.

He walks forward and presses my back up against the wall, the pressure of his body a sweet antithesis to mine. I strain toward him, needing and seeking relief. I'm not sure where I end, and he begins.

"Hannah," he says, drawing his mouth away from mine, dragging his lips and tongue across my skin.

"Yes?"

"I want this. Just you. Always."

"Yes."

He shakes his head and stops, leaning back, his hands still squeezing my hips as he looks at me. "I want to be yours. I want you to be mine. Exclusively. You and me. Your boyfriend. My girlfriend."

I search his face, and my heart expands in my chest, sort of floats up toward my throat with elation. It's as if everything in my life is suddenly in harmony. My skin erupts with a chill, the synchronicity of things coming into place even though our paths diverged, and my body communicating it physically. I frame his face with my hands and swallow the tears that want to fill my eyes with joy. "I want that too. I want to be yours and you to be mine. Your girlfriend. My boyfriend."

He kisses me again with even more fervor. Words like 'happy', and 'lucky', and 'fuck' peppered between kisses. His hands skim my thighs, grab my ass, squeezing and holding me hostage against him. I moan into his mouth, do my best to sink into him. I want to crawl inside him and set up my home in his heart.

"Hannah... If we don't stop–" He pulls away and offers another of those cute, sheepish smiles, then presses his forehead to mine.

"True," I say with broken breaths.

"How long?"

"Two hours."

He leans back so he can look at me, and his gaze flicks back to my lips before returning to my eyes. He nods. "Back to work."

I don't want to go back upstairs, but I don't say this. I just offer him a smile and press a kiss to his dimple. "I am working."

He laughs. "This is part of your job description? Kissing me?"

I smile. "I want to kiss you all the time, and now, kissing you is a perk of my job."

He makes a growly noise but lets me go, stepping away. "You're going to be the death of me, woman." He puts the table between us. "History paper. History paper. History paper," he chants and adjusts his pants.

I smile and smooth all my clothes back into place. "What's your topic?" I ask and walk around to the computer. After a quick explanation and several keyword searches, we have a list of materials to hunt for and head out to scavenge for them in the stacks. By the time we collect what we can find, spending as much time as we can touching one another in small but meaningful ways, and sneak in another several kisses in the stacks, I'm down to the end of my shift.

I collect my things and meet Seth at the front door.

He takes my hand in his and walks me to my car. "How about I follow you home, so you can park your car, then we can go to the Sandwich Spot together?"

"That sounds like a good plan," I tell him and give him a quick kiss before getting into my car. When I drive into the apartment complex and park my car, I remember that Jewel isn't home because she texted she's at Joy's. Suddenly, I'm not hungry for a sandwich. I want Seth, and with an empty apartment, that's exactly what I'm going to get.

*My Heart Insists I Want Forever*

I follow Hannah into her dark apartment, glad I'm there with her, worried about if I hadn't been, Sebastian and his shark eyes would be waiting for her. I'd realized as soon as she shut the door the night before, and when I walked into my empty apartment, that my anger was secondary to my fear. If I'd been thinking clearly, I could have owned that and moved forward. If I had, I would have been sleeping with Hannah instead of by myself, but sometimes distance and time is the right calibrator for clearer perspective.

Showing up at the library was less about writing the paper and more trying to find a clear opportunity to apologize. I'd been lucky she'd been able to talk rather than having to wait to take her to dinner.

Now, I shut the door behind me with my thoughts on what's ahead: taking her out, reminding myself that being alone doesn't mean sex. But I'd be lying if that wasn't on my mind. It's so fucking on my mind. What happened in the study room at the library, the way I wanted to bang her against the wall or thought about the top of the table. The night before in the car.

I take a deep breath to clear my mind. "Where's Jewel?" The apartment is quiet. I glance at Hannah.

She looks over at me, sets her backpack into the seat of the stool at the counter, then retraces her steps back to me. Without taking her eyes from mine, she reaches around me and locks the door.

"Not here. And I don't want to go to the Sandwich Spot," she says and pulls the scarf from her neck, drops it on the floor, and shrugs out of her jacket, which she tosses at the stool. It misses and drops with a hiss of fabric and a tap of buttons. Her pupils are blown, and she's not smiling. She reaches for my jacket, bunching the blue fabric in her fists, and pulls me to her. "I want to order take out, but not until after this."

Then she's kissing me.

Oh, fuck, she's kissing me. It's a kiss filled with a promise, and that promise is sex.

My heart leaps, slams up against my chest, and I frame her face with my hands, answering her kiss with a promise of my own.

"Yes?" she asks, her mouth still on mine.

"Fuck, yes," I tell her and shrug out of my jacket, tossing it toward the stool—it misses and falls to the floor—and then I grasp her hips, angling my head to kiss her deeper. *Yes. Yes. Yes*, my brain chants, now the only thought in my head, walking her backward through the apartment toward her bedroom.

She angles her head in response, making a sweet sound as her hands slide up under my shirt and push it up over my torso.

We break apart, and my t-shirt falls to the floor.

Her eyes are wild, the blue intense and dark. "I don't want to wait anymore," she says, her hands moving across my chest, down my stomach, which makes my muscles twitch, to the button of my jeans. She yanks the top button open.

"Let's not wait anymore," I say and restore our connection, kissing her again. I wrap my arms around her and lift her, mouth tasting her and lighting a forest fire inside of me that's heat rushing through my bloodstream. Her legs wrap around my waist, and I walk us the rest of the way to her room, using my foot to shut the door behind us. We are an extension of one another, every uncovered place seeking connection. Mouths, tongues, hands, arms. Together, we help each other out of our clothing: jeans and t-shirts and socks, underthings, until there's nothing left between us.

"I want to look at you," I tell her.

She disconnects and takes a step away, then another as she backs toward the bed. She's fucking beautiful. Her curves. A goddess. The memory of lying between her legs, so close to sex over a week ago, of touching her, of being between her legs and tasting her since then and hearing her orgasm, to her mouth helping me reach my own orgasm, a mutual giving and taking with one another, all reinforcing my fantasies. Her eyes skim my body, get caught on my erection, then jump back up to my face. She sits on the mattress, retrieves a condom from a drawer by her bed, and sets it near her. What undoes me, though, is when she leans back onto her elbows, spreads her legs, and says, "I want you, Seth."

I groan and waste zero time getting to her, climbing up the bed, over her to settling between her thighs. My mouth seeks hers and my hands skim her skin, seeking refuge in the soft places.

I kiss down her neck, kiss her breasts, kiss her stomach, revel in the feel of her hands in my hair when I kiss her between her thighs, her vulnerability offered freely. When she comes—a beautiful sound of her letting go of the wall, of allowing me the opportunity to catch her—I retrace my path, find new places to kiss, new ways to offer her my worship.

"Seth." She breathes my name, then repeats it.

I settle my hips between her legs again, my need pressing against her tender flesh. "What is it, Hannah? Is this still okay?"

She nods. "Yes. Yes. Please." She helps me with the condom, her fingertips skimming my erection and stealing my breath.

I position myself to enter her, braced on my arms, but wait, though every cell in my body is screaming to go. "Hannah?"

Her gaze slides up from looking at where we'll join to my face. "What is it? You still want this?"

I nod. "Yes." I nod again, trying to find words. "I don't want this to end."

She grabs hold of my face. "It won't last forever." She smiles. "Even if we want it to."

"Not the sex, Hannah." I meet her gaze. "You and me."

Her smile fades, and she makes an emotive sound that pushes my pulse a little faster and draws me down to kiss her again. Then she reaches down between my arms, grasps my ass, and pulls me into her, tilting her hips to meet me. Gasping against my mouth, she finds her breath to say, "I want that too. All of you. I want you, Seth."

The sensation of being wrapped up completely in Hannah is perfection. It's as if I've been traveling this one road toward an unseen destination, and suddenly there's a new path. I take it, and there she is, the destination, waiting for me with her hand outstretched. When I reach her and take her hand, we walk the road together, side by side.

She makes this beautiful moaning gasp that tells me she's with me on this journey. That sound is perfect too. I can feel her finding her way, her body wrapping tightly around mine as she mewls out a broken sound with my name, and I join her, losing myself in the moment. I let go just after she does.

When my breathing evens out, I take care of the condom and return to her side, lying on my side to look at her.

Hannah smiles at my movement, eyes still closed, little tears sitting in the corners of her eyes. Her hands move over the skin of my back, a gentle caress. Back and forth.

"Are you okay?" I ask.

"I'm perfect," she says. "Perfect." She turns her head to look at me. Then she does something absolutely devastating. She smiles.

And I'm a goner. Obliterated. Love, yes, but the forever kind.

"What are these?" I run a thumb across the tear that has left a trail over her temple.

"Happiness."

I wrap my arms around her, filled with so much emotion that I can't find words, or rather, they'd never be able to find a way through my throat that has suddenly constricted with feeling.

There's a fleeting thought that perhaps I'm making more of this than I should; Hannah has been on my heart for a long time, but it's a temporary flare in a dark sky. That realization is in and of itself the point. Hannah has been a tattoo on me all that time, a permanent trace stamped into my heart and waiting for the opportunity to reemerge and remind me who I am. The sun in my solar system.

But I am suddenly at odds with myself.

Hannah has seen the ugliest parts of me and still wants me. I'm a fool to allow insecure thoughts any purchase in the beauty of now, so I release them like helium into the atmosphere where they squeak away into nothing.

"Seth?" Hannah's fingertips move back and forth across my back as if she's tracing pictures or writing words.

I hum a response, eyes closed, enjoying the feel of her in my arms, of her fingertips, of her breasts pressed against my naked flesh, of her legs intertwined with mine.

"I love you."

I stop breathing, before oxygen rushes in like I was deprived of it. I remember the first time I caught a wave. I'd spent so much time in the icy cold of the Oregon ocean, trying to catch one in the mess of the whitewash. It's doable, but it takes time and patience to learn it. That first time, I remember the elation, the feeling like I was the first and the only.

That's how Hannah's declaration makes me feel.

I squeeze her tighter, burying my face into the safety of her skin. "I love you, Hannah. So fucking much. I'm never letting you go again."

I have never told a more singular truth.

*My Heart Insists It's Time for Forgiveness*

When we graduated from high school, I remember this moment during the ceremony when our valedictorian told us a story about our kindergarten field trip to a grocery store. While his story focused on the idea of the experience of growing up, I remembered the trip for a different reason. I'd stood there in my red graduation gown, recalling five-year-old me standing in the aisle of that grocery store, the cereal aisle, with Seth beside me, his hand in mine. My crush on him by graduation was a painful weight in my chest, especially now with school ending and no reason to see him each day. That kindergarten trip, we'd chosen to be one another's buddy. I went to kindergarten everyday excited to see my friend Seth. That day, we'd been scolded for talking about the cartoon characters on the colorful cereal boxes instead of listening to the host. I'd teared up, embarrassed for getting into trouble. But Seth had leaned toward me and said, "It's okay, Hannah. They weren't mad at you. It was me." I leaned toward him and pressed a "thank you" kiss to his cheek. He'd looked at me with wide eyes and whispered, "Now we'll have to get married."

Now, naked, limbs entwined with Seth in my bed, I recall that memory and giggle.

"What is it?"

"You remember going to the grocery store in kindergarten?"

"No." His fingertips move back and forth over my shoulder.

"We were field trip buddies."

His touch stills. "You remember that far back?"

I nod and trace a fingertip across his collarbone. "I kissed your cheek, and you told me we were going to have to get married."

He laughs, the rumble of the sound deep in his chest. "What?"

I shift my head, chin to his pectoral so I can meet his eyes. "Yep."

He scooches down in the bed, so his face is even with mine. "I was a smart kid."

"Yes."

His eyes trace my features. "You have a good memory. I remember bothering you in the third grade by poking you with a pencil."

I laugh. "We probably have dozens of those stories," I say. "I don't remember them all. I just get flashes sometimes."

He leans forward and presses a kiss to my cheek. "Why did you kiss me then?"

"We'd gotten in trouble, and you tried to make me feel better about it."

His lips linger on my skin, drifting kisses from my cheek down to my jaw, then my neck. He shifts, and I roll to my back, offering him easier access.

"Just like now," I say and lay my palms against his back.

"I want to spend my life making you feel good, Hannah," he says and uses his mouth to show me.

"It's working."

He looks up from his position and grins before kissing from my boobs down my stomach. "Do you ever wonder," he says between kisses, "if other people feel this happy?"

"Like who?"

"Like our parents?"

"You wonder about your parents having sex?"

He looks up and scrunches up his face. "No." He shudders. "I can't imagine that."

"Well, they had you," I say, my hands in his hair now.

"I was an accident."

I grab ahold of his head and make him stop kissing me. "What?"

"An unplanned pregnancy before they were married. They got married because of me." Seth settles down against me, his cheek on my belly. "I can hear you gurgling. We should go eat."

I'm still thinking about what he's said. "Did you feel like that? An accident?" His attempt in kindergarten to make me feel better—*It wasn't you they were mad at, Hannah. It was me*—makes my heartbeat with a tender rhythm. I weave my fingers through his hair over and over.

He sighs, then says, "It's hard not to when you got beat up by your dad. And when he drunkenly told you that his life would have been better without you. So, yeah."

I notice he's distanced himself from it.

He tries to get up, but I pull him back to me. "Seth?"

"Hannah?" He smiles, dimples.

There's a lot drifting through my mind at this realization, and I'm not sure where to begin, but it feels too important to let it drift away into the shadows. "And now?"

"Now what? It's time to eat." He's deflecting, and sits up, his back to me.

"You're putting up a wall," I tell him.

He freezes on the edge of the bed.

I sit up and crawl so that I'm behind him, then wrap my legs around him. "No dinner until you talk to me."

He looks over his shoulder with a short smile. "Hannah Fleming is always calling me out on my shit."

"I'm yours. You're mine. And this is what we do now, okay?"

He nods. "I don't feel like that anymore, no. My parents and the therapy all of us have done has helped, but the truth is–" He stops and lifts a hand to grab ahold of my arm stretched around his collar bone.

When he doesn't resume his thought, I squeeze his torso with my thighs wrapped around his waist and my arms around his shoulders. "Truth is what?"

He glances at me again over his shoulder, then turns in my arms, pushing me across the bed, to press me into the mattress with his weight. "I haven't forgiven him. I can't find a way to do it. I'm just so angry at him."

I nod and reach up, skimming locks of hair away from his face even though they fall right back to where they were, enjoying the weight of him holding me down. "Can't say I blame you."

"But?"

"No *but*."

"He might be sick," Seth says, pressing his face into the space between my neck and shoulder.

I freeze. "What?"

"He hasn't been feeling well and the doctor ordered some tests."

His words wind up my gears and I start moving again, touching him, his hair, his back, his arms, offering comfort. "Have you heard anything yet?"

He shakes his head and just lays in my arms, taking a deep breath before looking up. "You know the worst part?"

I shake my head, searching his face.

"Is that I feel like he deserves it. Like life is offering a twisted form of justice. What kind of person does that make me? What kind of son?"

"A human one."

He shakes his head and returns to the space against my neck. "Not one that deserves your love."

"There isn't a correlation," I say, then I realize I'd done the same thing. I'd settled for Sebastian because I hadn't believed I deserved love. I hadn't forgiven myself for being a human being. "You know where I was while my dad was dying?" I say quietly, as if I'm in a confessional booth.

He looks up and waits for me.

"I was drunkenly having sex for the first time with a guy named Hunter." My eyes meet his.

Seth's eyebrows arch over his eyes, and he tilts his head. This isn't a look of judgment, but rather, curiosity, awareness, connection.

"Does that make me a horrible daughter?" And I realize as I say it, it doesn't. It never did.

He shakes his head. "Of course not."

"And when I got back to my dorm the next morning only to learn my father had died, all I felt was this horrible guilt."

He skims my hair with his hand. "You couldn't have known."

"I know." I trace a finger over his jaw. "That's rational. But guilt and shame aren't rational, are they? Neither are fear and anger. You know what my mom told me last time I was home?"

"What?"

"That guilt, shame, fear, and anger are prisons. I never told her about Hunter–" I stop and take a breath– "but she knew I carried them for not being there. It's taken me until just now to forgive myself for it." I offer him a smile as tears slips from the corners of my eyes.

Seth dips down and presses a kiss to my cheek.

"You deserve my love. You are wonderful," I tell him. "You are kind and compassionate. You are sweet and thoughtful." I push his hair off his forehead so I can see his face. "You are perfectly and wonderfully made, and exactly where you were designed to be, Seth Peters. And I love you."

His eyes are glassy with his own unshed tears as he uses his thumbs to wipe away mine.

"I don't know what that means about forgiving your dad or not, but it doesn't make you a bad son. It doesn't mean you don't deserve to be happy or to have love. You deserve forgiveness for being human."

Seth kisses me then, shifting so that we're completely pressed together, our puzzle pieces coming together to form a beautifully whole picture.

*My Heart Insists I Will Find a Way to Mess It Up*

Being with Hannah is both joy and torture. The joy is in the reinforcement of what I already suspected. It has always been about Hannah for me. Now that I can see it, I can't see any other possibility. That alone is terrifying. But when I could have messed it up, she wouldn't let me. I've got it in the back of my mind that I'll somehow fuck this up, but I've shared the darkest stuff, and she still loves me. Which contributes to the torture.

Not only realizing there's so much more to lose, but the physical torture of not being with her all the time takes added effort. It's forced me to be more present, which is what I figured would happen, but fuck if it hasn't backfired and made the physical feel more urgent. Sex with Hannah is addicting. Necessary. I need her. But then, who am I kidding. I think it would always feel urgent with Hannah. All that physical awareness wrapped up in an amazing package that I'm always eager to open.

After having dropped her off at her apartment, I park my car in my designated spot outside my apartment building, but I don't go in right away. She's spending some quality time with Jewel, and I figure I'll hang with Trace if he's around. I know that's a good thing for both of us, even if I miss her like crazy when we're apart. She needs friends to process her life with, and I need them too. When I climb from my car, I'm smiling, and take the stairs looking forward to seeing what Trace is up to. I'm just so fucking happy.

My phone rings.

I pull it from my pocket, hoping it's Hannah.

It's Mom.

"Hi," I say, and the words *did he fall off the wagon* ride the tip of my tongue, but I push them away. It's time to let it go.

A strangled sound accosts me.

"What is it? Mom?"

"Bad news," she says through tears.

I turn to sit on the stairs. "What is it?" I know it's about my dad. My heart crash-lands in my belly, burning with dread, though I'm conflicted by the feeling. So much of my identity is wrapped up in the trauma with this man. And sure, I'm in therapy. And sure, I'm working through my shit, but he's still my father. As much as I want to divorce myself from that, it's impossible. The threads that weave us together are mixed up with love and hate, mistrust, and reconciliation, with hope and forgiveness, but anger and struggle too.

I feel sick and take a deep breath, unsure where she's about to take me.

"Cancer," she says, and the sound of a sob catches on the other side of the phone.

"Shit." I breathe the word and close my eyes. "Where is it?"

"The liver."

"Has it spread?"

"They aren't sure. Tests weren't clear–"

"Could that be good?"

"No."

"What? Why? There's a possibility–"

"His liver is a mess with all the–"

"–drinking. Shit."

"There's a lot of unhealthy tissue which makes it more complicated. The doctor said this kind of cancer is tricky."

"Chemo?"

"We haven't talked about it yet. But I don't think he wants to get treatment."

"What does that mean?"

A sob breaks her words. "He says he deserves this–"

I cough—nearly gag—hearing my own words in those of his she's shared. "Mom?"

I hear voices, the muted give and take between varied tones. There's a rustle of the phone.

"Seth?" My dad's voice.

I open my mouth to say something, tears burning my eyes. All that comes out is a strangled, "Yeah."

"Mom can't really talk."

"I get it."

"She's told you?"

"Yes." I look up and out at the parking lot, the buildings beyond, the naked trees scratching the surface of the steel-colored sky.

"Just, well, I don't want you to worry."

I want to yell at him, to rant, but there isn't a rhyme or reason. I want to yell about him spending so much time drinking and fucking up our life. I want to yell that he's still fucking up everything. I want to yell at him for trying to tell me what to do. I just want to yell, but I don't. I press my teeth together and stand instead, I walk down two steps and turn and walk up three, then turn and walk back down to the platform between the stair sets. Dr. B said anger is a secondary emotion. Why am I angry? I'm sad. I'm scared. Even with all the pain associated with his man, he's still my father.

Leaning over the railing, I stare down at the evergreen bushes and melting snow around them. "What's the plan?"

"There are more tests I need to take to decide a course of action. Chemo might be an option, but they aren't sure yet. Maybe they put me on a transplant list, but there might not be enough time for that. We'll know more after the next appointment."

Words I might say lodge in my throat, scrambling up and losing meaning.

"Don't worry," he repeats.

When we were in the thick of his drinking, and I was in the thick of the abuse, I think I wanted him to die. Dr. B and I have talked about this. I remember her asking me one time if it was really the death of him I wanted, or the death of the behavior, and while I wasn't able to make the distinction at the time, I understand what she means, now, facing his possible death. Despite all the shit he put us through, there are still threads of love there, of forgiveness I haven't tied off.

"Well, it's a little late not to," I say. "Will you do the treatment if it's an option? Mom seems to think you won't."

He sighs.

"And don't tell me some fucked up shit about deserving this. That's messed up." I'd said the same thing to Hannah and tell myself this as much as I'm telling him. But I realize it isn't just about him and say, "I think you owe Mom more life, you know. She chose to stay with you. For better or worse."

There are several extra beats of silence before he clears his throat. "Well, that's probably true."

"It isn't a fucking *probably*," I say. "It's a fact. She deserves for you to fight because she's fought for you. You get that, right?"

There's a lengthy pause followed by a sigh. "Yeah."

I imagine he probably wants to tell me to fuck off and know my role, but to his credit, he doesn't. "When's the next appointment?" I ask.

"Next week."

"Need me there?"

"No. No." I hear something beyond him. The click of a door or the sound of a pan on the stove. I have no idea what it is, but there's something comforting about the normalcy of it. "Stay where you are. Mom and I will fill you in, and–" He stops.

"–and?"

"Just come home when you planned to."

"I'll come home when I'm needed."

"Fair enough."

"Mom okay?"

"She's strong," he says.

"We both already knew that. That's not what I asked."

He sniffs. "I'll make sure she's okay. As best as I can. You keep doing your part."

"Yes, sir," I say.

"I'm going to go check on her."

"Talk soon?"

"Yes." He hesitates a moment as if he wants to say something else, but he says, "Talk soon."

We hang up, and I lean against the railing staring out at the landscape, as if maybe the stasis of it will impact the dynamic fluctuation of all the emotions moving through me.

Cancer.

My dad has cancer.

I roll the thought again, tears filling my eyes, and I swipe them away with the back of my hand. I need Hannah, but I don't want to interrupt her with this awful mess.

I google liver cancer.

Fuck.

Then I take the rest of the stairs to my apartment. There are loud, raucous voices drifting from our place before I even make it in through the front door. When I walk in, there are more people than usual in the front room, and a few heads turn.

One of which is Sebastian.

Fuck. Awful timing. I see red.

I take a deep breath instead.

"Seth!" Trace yells. "You're back. How was the date?" Then he presses his lips together as if he realizes who's sitting in the room.

I don't know if this is by design—that he's throwing me under the bus—or if it's an unintentional slip up. Trace has only been supportive of me and what I've got going with Hannah. I choose to believe the latter for now. Rather than comment on it, I change the focus. "Is DeShawn kicking all your asses?" It's all I can do, my mind drifting in a weird space of disbelief, of needing to feel like I can do something.

"You know it," DeShawn says from the couch, without looking away from the TV screen.

"You coming with us to the party?" Marco asks.

"Naw. I'm good," I say, knowing Sebastian is staring without even looking at him. "Got some homework to do before Monday. Have fun though." I slip down the hall and into the bathroom, then lean forward to stare in the mirror at my reflection as I wash my hands. I splash cold water on my face.

My dad has cancer.

I need to talk to Hannah, but it can wait until she calls. I don't want to ruin her night with Jewel.

I take a fortifying breath, though it seems to move through the holes that have formed in my foundation. I feel shaky, as if a strong wind might whip through and break me apart. The breath seeps through me, and I don't know which way is up. But I know that Sebastian is out in the living room. I can avoid him. The prick. Except when I open the door, there he is, waiting.

"Hey," he says. He's got a smile on his face, all ease and friendliness. I don't note any animosity in his countenance, which feels like a massive lie. He reminds me of my father, way back when—unpredictable. I'm wary, and I hate that I revert to feeling small. With a deep breath, I offer him wary acknowledgment, returning to normal size, and continue down the hall to my room.

"A friendly word of advice," he says from behind me.

I turn at the door. "Is that what this is?"

He hasn't moved. "There's just some stuff I think you should know about Hannah."

Anger rears its head. Sebastian might remind me of my father, but I'm always fighting that monster. That rage is innate. I take a deep breath. "Take that shit somewhere else. I don't give a fuck what you're about to say." I start through the doorway to my room again.

"She's not telling you everything. She's still seeing me."

It's as if he knows my immediate weakness—a quick study, or a great researcher. He's pressed two of my buttons with a single line. First, it's about Hannah, who is mine now, not his. Second, he's implied she's lying, or using me, or whatever conclusions I can jump to with his lie. Logically, I know this. And logically I know I can't trust him, but emotional me slips back to seventeen-year-old me who felt insecure, lied to, and used by the girl I'd liked then. Add to it the precariousness of my emotions, I can't seem to talk myself off the ledge. I start down the hall toward Sebastian, intending to fuck him up.

"You need to take her name out of your mouth."

He grins, and I see the snake underneath the charm; I'm playing the tune perfectly.

I freeze.

"Bash," Trace says, appearing between us. "Marco and them are going."

Sebastian gives me a condescending look, and I hate that he made easy work of me. "Thought you were joining?"

Trace glances at me, and it seems like he sees something there, and says, "Nah. I got homework." He waits.

"Catch you later then," Sebastian tells him, glancing at me one more time. "I got somewhere to be–" An insinuation I know he's trying to make about him and Hannah. He disappears down the hallway.

When he's gone, Trace looks at me. "Dude. I'm so sorry. I didn't know he was coming with Marco. Then I fucking slipped."

"It's okay. Bound to cross paths. I thought you were going?"

Trace claps a hand on my shoulder. "You look like you could use a friend, bro. What's up? You look like your dog died."

"If only it were that." And suddenly I want a drink so bad, I look at Trace and say, "Do we have any alcohol in the house?"

*My Heart Insists This Isn't Real*

My smile is so big it hurts. I look away from Abby on the screen of my phone to inspect the new pedicure I did with Jewel and Joy earlier—a concession for ditching me for a date night with Joy's parents, who showed up unexpectedly from out of town. My pink toes are perfectly painted with sparkles. I considered calling Seth to come and hang out with me, but since we've been with one another constantly, I thought he might be looking forward to hanging out with Trace.

"My goodness, Hannah, you're glowing," Abby says.

I finally look at her, my cheeks heating. "I am. I'm so freaking happy." I flop on my bed and wiggle around excitedly.

Abby laughs. "Damn. I'm slightly jealous."

"If I weren't me, I would be too." I laugh. "I didn't think it was possible."

"What?"

"Being this happy."

"It's possible," she says, but her smile fades.

"What is it?" I ask, feeling a touch guilty as I reach for the socks Seth gave me.

"I'm good."

"Really? Because your face says otherwise."

"You know me too well. You are always so freaking perceptive."

I put on the socks. "What's going on?"

"Nothing. I just think I'm at this point where existing in the motions of how we want things to be, and how they are, aren't lining up right."

"Like for school?"

"Sort of. I just find myself wondering about things like being in a relationship again. And seeing you so happy makes me want that for myself. It's been a long time since I felt that."

"When was the last time?"

She's silent a moment. "It isn't like I haven't been happy, but there's something empty about feeling like people don't see you."

"When was the last time you felt seen?"

"Senior year," she says. "I felt completely free to be me, then."

"With Gabe."

She nods. "And you, and Seth, and our friends," she adds. "I miss that. I have great new relationships here–" She stops. "Dating sucks. There are so many fake people."

"Do you miss Gabe?"

"When I see you this happy because of Seth, yes." She laughs. "Truthfully, I miss him every day."

"You don't talk at all?"

"No. Social media shit. That's it."

"Why don't you slide into his DM?" I smile at her and wiggle my eyebrows.

She grins. "It doesn't change the reason we ended things in the first place. He's in LA and I'm here."

"People make it work. You're older. He's older."

"He's seeing someone."

"He's probably seeing lots of someones. Have you stalked his Instagram?"

She laughs. "Of course!" She scrunches her nose up, then says, "I mean, I think there's a new someone. Like maybe a serious someone. She's been in his IG stories a couple time."

My eyebrows arch over my eyes. "Oh, so you've been that attuned to his IG stories huh?"

Her brown skin deepens with a soft blush.

"Is that why you're being reflective about him?"

"Yeah. Probably."

"Why did you break up?"

"It was just tough keeping connected with 2500 miles between us. Seemed like more of a kindness to one another rather than feeling mistrustful and eventually angry and bitter." She pauses, and I can see she's thinking about it. "It isn't that I want to return to what was. I just think maybe there's a part of me that will always wonder, always feel that tinge of jealousy that I wasn't the one."

I make a noise as I ponder that statement. "Based on that logic, aren't I moving backward by being with Seth?"

She shakes her head. "No. I don't think so. You're both older and wiser now."

"And you aren't?"

"Okay. Okay. I see what you did there." She offers a slight grin and plucks at something off screen.

"Seth is forward for me. We have a past, but whatever we're making is looking ahead. I don't think exploring an older relationship means you're going backward, especially if that relationship has unfinished business, you know? And if that's something you want to discover, why not?" I pause, listening to the sound of knocking at the door. "Hold on," I tell her as I climb from my bed. "I think Jewel might have forgotten her house key."

"So, you don't think it would be weird for me to reach out?"

"I don't think so. Would you want to talk to Gabe again?" I ask as I slide through the hall, pondering sock Olympics and deciding I'll tell Seth that I practiced.

"I would always want to talk to Gabe."

"Then talk to him. There's nothing wrong with reaching out. You were always friends," I say as I unlock the door.

As soon as I open it, I realize I forgot to check to see who it is. It isn't Jewel.

"Hey," Sebastian says. He's leaning against the frame with a strange grin on his face.

My stomach curls. "You need to go."

"I just saw that guy you've been fucking around with at a party. Drunk as fuck."

I know it's a lie and move to close the door, but Sebastian catches it with his hand.

"Hannah?" Abby's voice says from the phone.

"Let go of the door, Sebastian."

"Hannah?" Abby repeats. "Are you okay?"

"Not until we talk." He slams the door against the wall, knocking me back, and my phone flies from my hand. It skitters across the floor as I slip and fall, then scramble to my knees. I have to get my phone.

"This isn't okay," I say, the tone of my voice is high and loud. "I want you to leave."

"I said I'm not fucking leaving until we fucking talk." His voice is louder, and he slams the door shut, rattling the picture frame and mirror on the wall.

I scramble on my hands and knees, desperate to reach my phone, but I'm suddenly yanked from the ground by my waist, my phone sliding across from my grasp.

"Let me go!" I yell. "Let me go!" I struggle against his grip.

"You're going to listen and hear me out." He growls the words, his arms shackles securing mine across my chest even as I kick, connecting with his shins. He doesn't release his grip.

"Let me go!" I scream at him. "Let me go!" I've never felt more powerless.

Despite my struggles, he carts me to my room, kicks the door shut, and tosses me on my bed. His torso heaves with his anger, his face dark with it as he leans against the door.

I scurry from my bed to retreat as far from him as I can. "What the hell, Sebastian? What are you doing?" I'm hopeful for a logical explanation, for the means to talk him down, but I can't get my friends' warnings out of my head.

*Don't be a fool, Hannah. This is bad.*

Sebastian runs a hand through his hair, his brow collapsing over his eyes as he points at me. "You don't speak."

"Don't tell me what to do!" I scream, a sob bursting through with the words. "Let me out of here, now. My friend is on the phone. You don't get to do this." My heart beats a terrifying rhythm in my throat.

*You don't know what someone will do. What lengths they will go to.*

"No!" he yells, his hands in his hair, creating a mess of the strands. "Let me think!" He takes a step toward me, and I press my back against the wall. His giant body is between me and the door. His anger is palpable, unruly, irrational.

*This isn't happening. This isn't happening,* I recite in my head.

Sebastian begins pacing, walking back and forth in front of the door. "I don't know what you're thinking. Him?" I know he's ranting about Seth, even if he hasn't said his name.

*Think.*

*Think!*

*Think!*

*I need to get out of here.*

I picture my phone sliding under the couch. No landline. I need to get out the front door.

"And Marco said you stayed over there. What the fuck, Hannah! How could you? Do you realize how stupid it makes me look?"

Sebastian is cataloguing all the ways I've fucked him over with Seth, all conveniently missing the fact that he's the one who broke things off with me. But I don't say anything. I've already said it and he's refused to hear it. I already know it won't matter. I retreat into myself, trying to make myself smaller.

"Look at me!" he yells.

I open my eyes.

His face is horribly dark and filled with rage as he clamps onto the fact that I've been "slutting it up with this prick," that somehow, I've made Sebastian "a cuck". His gaze locks onto me as he stalks the short space across the room. I zero in on the door behind him and dart to the side.

He catches my shoulder and slams me back against the wall.

My breath comes in shallow bursts, making it difficult to catch enough air to draw strong breaths. My thoughts are a jumbled mess. "Stop!" I scream.

He holds me against the wall with his hands on my shoulders, bending down so he can meet my gaze. "I told you, you are mine. Not his. Not anyone else's. I messed up. How many times do I have to fucking tell you? You pushed me to cheat with Chelsey. You made me think I need to look somewhere else, Hannah. Don't you fucking see?"

"No," I say and drive my knee up to connect with his groin.

Only he turns his hips, and I catch him in the thigh. He grunts, then yells. "What the fuck?" His anger explodes. "Fuck!" he yells and throws me across the room. I land with a bounce on my bed, then slide until my shoulder slams against the wall.

I scramble across the mattress, but not quickly enough. Sebastian is there, pushing me down. "Why are you making me do this?" he yells. "If you'd just listened!"

"Get off me," I scream and struggle, terrified that maybe I'm past the point of no return. Tears pierce the back of my eyes. I kick out and catch him in the leg.

He swears and throws an open hand, catching me on the side of the head. "Calm the fuck down."

The sting of the hit ripples across my skin. At one time, I might have rolled into a ball and acquiesced, but I picture that climbing wall, and I picture Seth's smile, and I imagine Seth reminding me that I'm strong. So instead, I rage and swear, kicking, and screaming. "Get off me!"

"I swear to fucking god, Hannah. I'm going to teach you fucking lesson about what happens when you don't listen–" Sebastian throws another hand, this time with a closed fist. It blasts my nose, cheek, and eye, and feels like I've run into a wall. My vision recedes, tunneling toward dull blackness, then blinks back to awareness, tears leaking from my eyes. I can't find my thoughts. My body is sluggish. My stomach revolts with a twist, and I moan. "Leave me alone," I slur, copper coating my tongue. I reach up and touch under my nose, leaving my fingertips glazed with blood.

"Look what you made me do," he says, the shock in his own voice making it sound slow in my ears. "Oh my god. Hannah. I didn't mean–"

I moan again and twist, a sob wracking my body.

He doesn't release me.

I flail about, unfocused and without purpose. Just movement because I need to keep fighting. I won't go in the hole again. I won't be a cracked glass jar. Never again. "No!" I cry and roll, trying to get away from him.

Sebastian yanks me across the bed onto my back, shakes me, then pins my hands to bed above my head. "Stop, Hannah. Stop!" he yells.

And I cry. "Stop, Sebastian. Stop."

*My Heart Insists It Can't Take Bad News*

I'm staring at the shot of tequila on the kitchen counter and wondering why I thought it was a good idea to go there. Dr. B would ask me to consider my choice and its context. So I do. I'm emotional. My dad has a serious form of cancer. I shouldn't have googled it. I miss Hannah and want to talk to her but feel like I need to give her space, and her ex-boyfriend just mind-fucked me. I'm not in a good headspace. I shouldn't take that drink.

Trace tips his first shot back, scrunches up his face, chasing it with a lime. "Fuck," he says. "Tequila isn't my drink of choice, bro."

"Mine either," I say. "Why do you have it then?"

"It's what was left over after the last party we had here." He glances at my still full shot and tilts his head toward it. "You were supposed to do that with me."

I look up from the shot glass and meet Trace's gaze. "I don't think I can."

His brow scrunches together. "What's up with you?"

"My dad's an alcoholic." I don't filter myself. I don't think I can anymore, as if a switch inside me was flipped and all I've got is brutal honesty.

"Oh shit. That's heavy."

"He's sick." I look back at the shot and reach out to turn the glass so that the picture is facing me. "Just found out. It's cancer."

Trace sinks onto a stool. "Bruh. I'm sorry."

"Full disclosure?"

He nods.

"He used to beat me up until I was about seventeen. He's been on the wagon since then. I don't usually talk about him because he's a prick, so I'm not sure how to feel about this"

"That's why you don't party."

I look up at him again and nod.

"You don't drink ever?"

I shake my head. "Used to. But not anymore. Unhealthy cycles. All that–" I wave my hand around, as if that's all the explanation that's necessary.

Trace nods. "I get it. We've all got shit sliding around in our family trees we try to stuff in boxes, you know?"

I turn the shot glass again, the picture facing Trace. "I think I thought having a drink would make me feel… less, but I'm looking at it, and I don't want to feel less."

"What do you want?"

The first thing that comes to my mind is Hannah. I want to talk to Hannah. I want to share with her the ugliness of what's moving through me. She'll put her arms around me and say, *"It's okay. I'm here."* But I don't tell Trace that, unsure how to navigate the complicated way we have to be. But when I think about it and realize Trace has chosen me every time. When I told him about Hannah. Tonight with Sebastian. He's here now.

So I commit to being real with him. "I want to talk to Hannah."

"She doesn't know?"

"She's hanging with her roommate tonight."

"Why's that stopping you?"

"I don't want to intrude on her girls' night, you know?"

"I feel you, but if the shoe was on the other foot, and she found out something important that she was upset about, would you want to know?"

I nod and meet his gaze. "You're right. I would."

"Damn straight, I'm right. Learn it, son." He grins. "How about if I take this?" He grabs the shot glass and slides it toward him.

"Yes. You go."

He throws it back, groans, and scrunches up his face. "Fuck tequila!"

I laugh and stand, patting down my pockets for my phone. But I don't have it. "I have to find my phone."

"Maybe we should go over there?"

"Where?" I ask as I walk down the hall.

"Hannah's."

"Okay. We?"

"Yeah. I'll run interference with the roommate."

"She's not into dudes." I look in my room, through my backpack.

"That's cool, but I'll bet she's into laughing with a bro. I got mad comic timing. Then she won't be mad at us crashing."

The phone isn't in there. I straighten and think back through where I've been. I walk into the bathroom, flipping on the light. The phone is on the counter. I check my notifications as I walk back through the hallway. None. I open my messenger and text Hannah: *Hey. Is it okay if I crash girls' night?* then erase it and sit down at the bar. "I'm not sure what to say. It sounds sketchy."

Trace looks over my shoulder. "No sense trying to sound cool. Tell her the truth."

I glance at him as he carries the bottle of tequila across the kitchen to the pantry, where he stashes it.

I text her: *I need you.*

I hit send and wait. I figure she'll need a bit of time, especially if they're having a good time, but once she reads it, she'll probably call.

"Game while we wait?" Trace asks.

I follow him into the living room. He boots up the console, and we set up our teams, talking stats. I'm glad I know shit about football even if soccer was my sport. I check my phone. When I check my phone, there's no answer. I reread my text again and wonder if she thinks I mean sex. Shit. So I text her again: *I didn't mean to make it sound like I needed sex. Not that I don't want sex with you. Totally do. I mean, I need to talk to you.*

Then I realize it sounds like I need to talk, which has a sketchy sound too. Like maybe I want to break up. Fuck.

"Dude. Your play."

"Sorry." I pick the play and run it. Trace gets an interception and hollers about it. I laugh but dial Hannah. It rings through to voicemail. Would she have turned off her phone? That seems weird. After what happened with her dad and how that haunts her, I can't imagine she would do that. I don't leave a message, but I feel tension starting to creep into my muscles and roll my neck to work it out.

I attempt to stay in tune with the video game, but ten minutes later, I still haven't heard from Hannah, and she always texts me back right back.

*Ten minutes! It's only been 10 minutes,* I tell myself. *Stop acting like a lunatic.*

But something feels off. Hannah always texts me back. I wish I had Jewel's number, but I don't. Maybe that's a good thing. Her roommate would think I'm a lunatic.

"Want to just go over there?"

I glance at Trace. "Sorry. I'm distracted."

"It's okay, dude. You're freaking out about shit. Bad day."

I nod and take a deep breath. That's it. That's why I'm all kinds of insecure. A bad day.

When my phone rings, however, I dive for it, nearly dropping it. "Hello?"

"Bro–"

It's Gabe.

I pull the phone away from my ear to double check. Yes. Gabe. "Wow. You're calling. Everything okay?"

"I don't know."

"Please. I can't take any more bad news today."

"What? Bad news? What's going on?"

"My dad. But you didn't call about that. Or did you?"

"No. Bro. Abby called me."

"Oh, shit. What?!" That makes me happy for him, but I don't know how he feels about it. "That's–"

"No. Listen."

My internal mechanism that's been waving red flags at me for the last twenty minutes sounds the alarm.

"She said she was on the phone with Hannah, and some guy showed up at her apartment. Who's Sebastian?"

I shoot off the couch. "What do you mean? Sebastian is her ex–"

Trace looks at me, eyes wide, the game still running without either of us.

"Abby said she called the police for a wellness check because something was wrong. Hannah answered the door while they were on the phone, thinking it was her roommate, then told that Sebastian guy to leave. Then Abby says the call got cut off. She called me because she was freaking out and didn't have your number anymore, hoping I did."

"I've got to go. I've got to go," I chant.

"Call me, okay?" Gabe says. "Let me know everything's alright."

Trace stands, tossing the remote into his chair. "What's up?"

"Okay. Thanks," I say and end the call. "Sebastian," I tell Trace. "He's at Hannah's."

"I thought he was with Marco and them."

I shake my head.

"Isn't she with her roommates?"

"I thought so, but–" I turn and rush down the hall to collect my wallet and car keys.

When I get back to the living room, shrugging into a sweatshirt, Trace is putting on his jacket. "Let's go."

"I can't fucking take any more bad news today."

*My Heart Insists It's Got a Little More Fight*

"Baby," Sebastian says, his full weight on me, his hands swiping at my tears. "Don't cry. This didn't have to happen."

I can't breathe but draw in a stunted breath through the tears leaking from my eyes. I wonder if Sebastian is going to kill me. I never thought of him that way, but now I'm not so sure, and the thought makes the tears flow faster. I don't think Jewel's aunt thought her boyfriend would kill her either. Do any of the many women killed by someone they thought they loved and who claimed to love them?

My sob catches in my throat.

My life finally felt like it was on the right track. I was derailed for some time, but after a few repairs, I started in the right direction. And now– "I feel like I need to throw up," I mumble, turning my head to the side.

"You're okay, Hannah. It will pass. Baby–"

"Don't call me that. I'm not your baby." My voice sounds distant, hazy, and my thoughts are slow. I want out from under this weight. "Get off."

He hushes me. "Enough. It didn't have to be like this. Stop fighting this. Stop fighting us." He releases one of my pinned arms and uses his hand to smooth my hair, his thumb to wipe the blood under my nose. "See. We'll get you cleaned up. And everything will be good as new."

I move my arm, but I feel dazed and sluggish. With the heel of my hand, I hit him, but it connects.

He grabs it, and with one of his, pins both of my hands above my head again. His heavy body weighs down my legs, all of me, so I can't move. With his free hand, he continues to clean my face with the edge of his t-shirt. "See. I'll take care of you. I'll always take care of you, Hannah. I love you–"

Which makes me cry harder. "This isn't love," I sob. I know what love is. Seth loves me, and I'm afraid. Afraid of what's going to happen next and my absolute inability to fight. No room to move. No strength left.

Except I keep thinking about the wall.

About the bubble gum hand holds. About making it halfway up, and Seth asking, "Just one more? Got one more in you?"

I need my brain back online so I can figure out what to do, only it doesn't want to cooperate.

Sebastian continues to talk to me, his tones lowered and dulcet, as if that's enough to placate me.

I relax, hoping he'll get off me.

But it doesn't stop the tears, however. It makes them flow harder, until I'm sobbing.

"Please, baby. Stop," he says, and I hear his frustrated tone. "Don't make me hurt you."

I try to staunch them to keep his anger from climbing, hiccupping under the duress of trying to find my way through this nightmare. I'm alone. No one knows. Maybe Abby, but who could she call? Jewel should be home soon—I hope—unless she's going to Joy's. But I don't want her hurt by Sebastian. Seth won't know. No one will come for me.

I take a deep breath through the tears.

Sebastian continues his ministrations. "Look at me." He uses his hand to squeeze my cheeks and force me to look at him. "I'm doing this for us. You know that, right? To prove to you how much you mean to me? See what you do to me? You make me crazy."

Then he kisses me, his lips soft on mine. He pulls away and looks at me, taking in my face. "It can be good again, Hannah. If you let it." He brushes my lips with his thumb. "I can forgive you for your indiscretion with that other guy." He presses another kiss to my lips. "We're soulmates. Remember?" This time when he kisses me, he tries to use his tongue, but I refuse to open my mouth. "Let me in, Hannah."

I shake my head, turning my head to end the kiss.

He grabs my face again with his hands, pinching my cheeks harder this time. "I told you. Don't make me punish you, Hannah. You can stop this."

"Let me up."

"I can't."

"You're choosing not to."

He shakes his head. "No, you are. You're overly emotional. I just wanted to talk, and you freaked out. And I didn't mean it. Didn't mean it. It was an accident. I was trying to calm you down. You were freaking out–" He stops talking and turns his head to listen.

I hear it then, a knock at the front door, and a deep voice, though I can't be sure what's being said. "Here!" I start, but Sebastian's hand clamps over my mouth and nose and presses.

"Shhhh," he says vehemently.

*I can't breathe! I can't breathe! I can't breathe!*

I don't have air. I struggle under him.

His head is turned away, listening.

*I can't breathe! I can't breathe!*

My vision crackles, turning both black and alive with brilliant stars.

I'm dying.

Jewel will find me. This makes me feel sad. She's seen too much bad stuff in her life.

My mom and sister will have to bury another family member. I hate that I'll bring them pain this way. Will they celebrate both dad and me on the same day?

Seth. At least he knows I love him.

And then air rushes in because Sebastian has released his hold. "Fuck!" He snaps it like he's hit something.

"Let me go," I say between fresh tears. I want to rant that the police are coming, even if that isn't true. I want to rant about him ruining his life, ruining his football career, but I don't. I'm suddenly so afraid, I can't find it in me to do anything but beg. "Please, Sebastian. Let me go. You don't want this."

"I want you."

I want to contradict him. I want to tell him he doesn't, but I don't. I don't care what he wants. I know what I want, and it's to live, and to see my sister compete as a cheerleader, and see my mom date again, and hear Jewel talk about how much she loves Joy and attend their wedding, and talk to Abby about life, and hear about her life in Hawaii, and kiss Seth again, laugh with him, feel my hand in his.

"Not this way," I say. "Not like this."

"What do I need to know, Hannah?"

I'll tell him anything he wants to hear. "There's only you. It's only you." I feel like gagging on the lie, but I need him to let me go.

"See." He smiles. "That wasn't so hard. Why did you have to play so hard to get?"

"Let me up."

"Kiss me first. Prove it to me."

The idea is repellant, but if it gets me up, I'll do it. I lift my head and place a kiss on his lips, then drop my head back onto the mattress. "Let me up."

He smiles. "I need more than that," he says and shifts over me. I feel him grow hard against me, and I want to scream.

"I can't move, to give you anything better."

"But this is hot," he says with a grin, his eyes maneuvering down my length pinned under him. "You all subdued this way."

I want to fucking punch his nose and break it, but my hands are still pinned over my head. So, I offer him a fake smile he seems incapable of reading.

His free hand moves from my face, down to my breast, where he grabs hold, squeezing too tight. Punishing. "It's been a while, Hannah. I think you deserve some punishment for teasing me. For spreading your legs for another guy."

"Let me go."

"Kiss me," he says and leans down. "Show me how you want me."

I kiss him. I let him put his tongue in my mouth. I make noises to make him think I'm into it. That isn't hard. I've faked it with him before, and he's too selfish to know the difference. I wiggle so he relaxes into his turned-on body, until he releases me. He moves his body, rising onto my pinned hands, his legs framing my body. Leaving him completely exposed. I take the shot.

I draw my knee up and ram it into his balls as hard as I can.

He cries out, and rolls to his side, curling with a groan, coughing, and sucking air.

I don't wait. I run.

*Our Hearts Insists Life's Messy and So Are We*

SETH

When I park my car in the lot of Hannah's apartment complex and park, I see Jewel starting up the stairs. Trace and I get out and I call her name. She notices and stops.

"Sebastian–" she says, pointing at a car near mine.

"Sebastian–" I tell her at the same time, wondering why Hannah was alone. "In the apartment." I run across the lot, Trace right behind me.

"Fuck," Jewel says and starts running up the stairs.

Trace and I follow, taking three steps at a time.

We meet two police officers on their way down, their radios chattering at them. When they see us, they both turn down the volume.

"Everything okay?" one of them—the shorter of the two— asks. His eyes bounce from Jewel to me to Trace.

Jewel and Trace freeze, backing up to let them pass without responding. So I say, "My friend called in a welfare check. We're here to open the apartment."

"Which apartment?" the taller of the two asks.

"445," Jewel says.

"Just coming from there. No answer," the shorter one says. His name is Officer Reagan.

I grip my hair. "Fuck," I mutter and start up the steps. "She's in there."

Officer Reagan blocks my way with a hand. "Calm down, son."

*It's bad. It's bad. It's bad*, I think, unable to reorient my thoughts toward a more rational path. "That's my girlfriend." I start up the stairs again. "He's got her."

"Who's got her?" the second officer asks.

"Her ex."

"That's his car." Jewel points at the black car in the lot.

"Maybe they went somewhere in hers?"

"No." Jewel shakes her head and points out Hannah's car. "She wouldn't have gone anywhere with him. He was bothering her. I think she reported him to our campus security."

"And you are?"

"Her roommate." She rattles her keys. "I live in that apartment. I'll take you in."

The officers follow us back up to the fourth floor.

Jewel inserts the key in the lock.

My heart bangs in my throat. I'm terrified. It can't be a worse day. *Please don't let it be a worse day,* I pray to an entity I've never grown up believing existed. I picture Gabe sitting on a chair in a chapel praying, though I don't know where or when that happened. Not sure why I would have been there, but his plea about needing me to stay. I did. *I need Hannah to stay,* I pray. *I need her to be okay. Please.*

Jewel opens the door.

Chaos ensues as if in slow motion.

Hannah running down the hall toward us, her face smeared with blood.

Jewel screaming her name.

Hannah looking over her shoulder.

Sebastian stumbling after her, slamming into the wall, his hands cupping his crotch. He falls to his knees.

The cops step between Trace and me and the door, moving Jewel out of the way. Their voices are loud, but I don't know what they're saying.

I see Hannah. That's all I see.

She bursts out the door between the officers, right into my arms, sobbing. Her arms are around me, her face pressed into the nook between my neck and my shoulder.

"I'm here," I say, holding her tightly against me, walking away from the alcove of her apartment, away from the police arresting Sebastian.

I lean against the wall, Hannah's head still in the crook of my neck, blood and tears mixing against my skin and shirt. Her thoughts are incoherent as she rambles aloud through her tears. I try to comfort her, my hand rubbing her back as I repeat, "I'm here," and "you're strong," and "they've got him," over and over. I know this isn't over—far from it—but Hannah will never have to face it alone.


# HANNAH


Seth's arms are around me, his heartbeat thumping a comforting cadence in my ear. I squeeze him tighter, and his hold tightens around me. They led Sebastian from the apartment in cuffs a while ago as Seth sheltered me from the view.

"Miss?"

"Hannah?" Seth asks and leans so he can meet my gaze. "The police officer needs a statement. Do you want to do that now or go down to the police station?"

I don't want to go anywhere without Seth. "Now."

"Is there somewhere we can sit?" the officer asks. His name tag reads Louis.

I nod and holding Seth's hand, lead the officer to the counter in the kitchen. Sitting on a stool, I reach up to cover Seth's hands, now on my shoulders as he stands behind me, and swivel to face the policeman on the stool next to me. He's pulled it out and a way so there's a comfortable distance between us, now flipping open a notepad.

"I need to talk with Hannah," he says, looking at Seth.

"I want him with me."

The officer's radio crackles with a voice, and he turns it down. He starts to say something, but Seth says, "I'll be right here." He moves to the living room and sits on the couch where I can see him.

"When you're ready," Officer Louis says. "I'm just going to write down what you tell me."

The recollection of events is strange. I'm somehow removed, as if I've decided to tell him the plot of a terrible book. Every so often, I look at Seth sitting across the room. I'm not sure what he's feeling, and I'm worried for him. I'm disconnected enough to rationalize that if it had been him running through the hall, I'd be a mess. Except I can feel the chaos waiting to erupt. The disarray is under my skin, waiting for me to unzip it and let it out.

Sebastian attacked me.

I suck in a quick breath, and the police officer tilts his head. "Ma'am?"

Tears fill my eyes, blurring the officer. "I'm—"

I start to tell him I'm sorry, but Seth's eyes meet mine, and I recognize the truth. This isn't my fault. I didn't ask for this or invite Sebastian here. I was honest and told Sebastian it was over. Repeatedly. This wasn't something I did. I didn't deserve this, or ask for it, or invite it. I sniff and nod. "I'm okay," I say, then finish telling him the events.

A few moments later, an EMT walks in through the door.

The officer stands. "This is Jen," he says. "She's going to make sure you're okay. See if you need additional medical attention."

I nod.

The EMT and Officer Louis converse. It's clear they know one another; it's a small town.

The EMT checks me. "I'm going to transport you in to get looked at by a doctor," she says, handing me an ice pack for my nose. "They'll be able to give your head a check, and make sure that your nose is set properly." She puts her things in her bag, then stops and adds, "It also creates documentation." She looks at me just a touch longer than necessary, as if to make a point. It's one she doesn't need to push.

I glance at Seth, thinking about him and his mom, how many times they had to go to the hospital because of what his dad had done. I wonder if he's okay. If this is dredging up too many bad memories.

## SETH

The EMT tells us she'll wait by the door.

"My phone is under the couch," Hannah says, drawing my attention back to her. "I was talking to Abby. I better call her."

"I did it," I say. "And Gabe." I get down onto the floor to retrieve her phone that's under the couch.

When I hand it over, Hannah looks at me over the icepack pressed to her nose.

"Abby called Gabe because she didn't have my number. She's the one who called the police and Gabe called me–" I see her eyes curl with a slight smile.

She nods. "She finally called him."

I huff a short laugh through my nose and smile with her. "They both know you're… everything is okay." Even as I say it, I know it's not okay. Hannah has a broken nose. She's jumpy and keeps looking at her room like it might come alive and suck her back into whatever nightmare occurred.

I want to fucking kill Sebastian.

## HANNAH

I step into Seth's embrace again. "Will you come with me? To the hospital?"

"I didn't think I'd be anywhere else."

"And after? I can't stay here–"

"Where do you want to go?"

I like the sound of his voice in his chest. "Anywhere but here."

"My place?"

"You can stay with us as long as you need to," I hear Trace say.

"What about you, Jewels?" I ask.

"I'm going to Joy's tonight," Jewel says, and as if she's conjured her, Joy—looking harried—appears in the open doorway where the police and the EMT are talking.

"What the hell? Jewel? Hannah?" Her dark eyes fly around the room, taking everything in. "I got your text," she says to Jewel. "Hannah?"

"I'm okay," I say, even if it isn't exactly true.

"Sorry, baby. I didn't mean to worry–"

"Of course you worried me. Shit." Joy rushes to Jewel and puts her arms around her.

I'm struck with how perfect they are together. The beauty of Jewel's strength and Joy's vulnerability. How when Jewel needs comfort, Joy is there. I offer Joy a wan smile, leaning a little more into Seth. His arms are strong around me.

# SETH

I can see in Jewel's eyes, shining with tears, she's blaming herself for not being here.

I'm blaming myself for not being here.

"Don't," I tell her over Hannah's head.

"Don't back at you," she says and sniffs. Joy's hands touch, seeking to offer comfort, and Jewel turns into them. She looks at Hannah. "Want me to pack you a bag, after the police say it's okay to go in?"

"Yes, please," Hannah answers.

"We'll take it and Trace to your apartment, so you don't have to wait," Jewel says, looking at me. "That way you can get her to the hospital."

I nod. The cold of the ice pack is seeping through my sweatshirt, but I think it's a small price to pay for being able to hold Hannah again. I kiss her temple, so grateful I get to. So angry. Thankful the cops were there, because if I'd gotten my hands on Sebastian, I would have been arrested.

Once in the emergency room, the harsh light and abrasive scent are a bit overwhelming and make me think about my dad. I've been in similar places because of what he's done, but instead of going there, I think about how he and my mom have been spending time in places like this the last few weeks.

*He has cancer.*

*My dad has cancer.*

I watch a nurse move through the room to a woman waiting against the wall. They talk while the woman picks up her things, then follows the nurse past us and behind the curtain of a different room. I wonder who she's here for? A partner? A sister? A parent?

Hannah squeezes my hand, and I look at her.

"Where did you go?" she asks.

"Just watching. It's easier than thinking."

She nods and leans her head on my shoulder.

"I'm sorry," I whisper and press a kiss to the top of her head. My mind is replaying Hannah running down the hallway toward me, blood on her face, and I blink to reconnect to the present.

"What for?" she asks.

"I wasn't there for you."

"Don't." She sits up to look at me. "Don't. Please. You have only been here for me since walking back into my life."

"I didn't–"

She unlaces our hands and reaches up to hold my face. "You've only reminded me that I'm strong. I didn't believe you, but the more you reminded me, the more I remembered who I once was. And you put me on that wall–" Her voice cracks with a partial laugh and a partial sob, and her hands leave my face to return to her lap.

I don't rush her through whatever she's saying.

She's looking down at her hands, and I can only imagine her thoughts, knowing where mine have gone.

When she's able she says, "I was ready to give up, and I heard you ask me in my head, 'got one more in you?'" She looks up at me and smiles a teary smile. "I knew I did. Knew I was strong enough to keep fighting. See?"

I nod and offer an equally teary smile back, then pull her back into my arms, knowing exactly what she's talking about.

"I'll never stop fighting. Never again," she says, tucking herself back in against me, and we sit that way for a while, waiting.

## HANNAH

I'm relieved when we finally walk into Seth's bedroom at his apartment. I know I need to call my mom. Without a doubt, fighting back is going to mean pressing charges, and I'll need her guidance and support. But I don't want to call her in the middle of the night. Tomorrow is soon enough.

"Are you hungry?" Seth asks.

"No. I just want a shower. Then I just want to get into bed with you and sleep for a week."

He holds out his hand. "I'll help you with that tricky shower."

I follow him into the bathroom, and he helps me undress. He pulls the shirt over my head and folds it, laying it on the counter next to the sink. "Seth?"

"Let me take care of you," he says and kneels to remove the socks he gave me, followed by my sweatpants, and my bra and panties, until I'm naked. There's nothing sexual about the disrobing. It feels reverent somehow. He helps me into the shower, then follows me in, still dressed in his t-shirt and jeans, where he helps me wash my hair, his fingers sliding across my scalp.

"Does that hurt?" he asks.

I shake my head. "It feels wonderful."

Next, he runs the soap over my body, his touch born of a need to serve me, love me, treat me with tenderness.

But I don't want him to think I'm broken. I will never be glass-jar Hannah again.

I turn and face him, reaching for the hem of his t-shirt, peeling it from his body to lift it over his head.

"Hannah?"

"It's my turn." I pop the button on his jeans and push them over his hips and down his legs, followed by his boxer briefs. He steps from them both.

"But–"

"Seth."

"Yeah?"

"Shhh. I know what's okay. For me. Is this okay for you?"

He nods.

I run my hands over his slick skin, "I love you," I tell him. "I want to find comfort in you. In us."

He grabs ahold of me, his beautiful, capable hands framing my face as his gaze trips over my features. "I could have lost you." He gathers me into his arms, and I realize I'm not the one who's the glass jar at the moment.

"You didn't. I'm here."

Our bodies are aligned, perfect puzzle pieces no matter which way we're arranged.

"I could have lost you," he says again.

"I'm here."

Then time stretches and seems to stop. The shower spray, the heat, the feel of Seth in my arms, only he's holding onto me as if I might melt away. I realize he's shaking.

"Seth?" I ask.

"My dad has cancer," he says, the words catching in his throat. He squeezes me tighter.

# SETH

I hadn't intended to tell her. Not just yet, only Hannah's arms around me and the realization I could have lost her hit me like I'd run headfirst into a wall. I could have lost her. And then the only thing I could think about as she told me, "I'm here" was that my dad has cancer and I need her. As much as I want to hate him and not care because he's an asshole for what he did, I do care. Hannah's ordeal has me unsteady and shaken, like marbles in a jar. A few got removed and now what's left is knocking around inside the container, shaking things loose.

"Oh, Seth," Hannah says, leaning back. "When did you find out?"

"Today."

Her eyebrows rise over her eyes.

Today, of all days.

"What can I do?" she asks.

"This," I say, and fold her back into my arms. "I want to take care of you, though. Right now."

"It doesn't work that way." Her fingers skim across my back. She pulls away and squeezes some shampoo into her hand.

"What? Yes, it does."

She shakes her head and reaches up to massage the soap into my hair. "You were right."

"About?" I ask but think about the feel of her hands in my hair. I concentrate on her words.

"Sebastian being between us. Rinse," she says.

I want to growl at the mention of his name, but instead put my head under the water. Then I say, "I think you're going to have to elaborate." I straighten.

She takes a deep breath and runs soap over my body. "Not Sebastian so much as our experiences. Our lives. I wanted to shelter you from the mistakes I made, from my struggles, thinking I had to bring the perfect me into whatever we were starting."

"I just want you–" And I'm beginning to want her in more physical ways, her hands on my skin taking me away from what we're talking about.

"Same." she says, and rinses me, clearly seeing that I'm now aroused. She looks at me, smiles, and grabs a hold of my erection. "I want who you are, all of you. The good stuff, the struggling stuff. The real you. That's how relationships work, I think. The ones worth having."

I groan and grab her bruised face with my hands. "Stop." I smile. "I can't concentrate on this important discussion with you when you're touching me like that."

She smiles, and I'm so, so grateful.

We rinse and get out of the shower, wrap towels around our bodies, and return through the dark hallway into my room, glowing gold in the lamplight. I look for clothes.

"Don't," Hannah says, climbing into my bed. "They're just going to come off anyway. Unless you don't–"

"I do, but I didn't think you would probably feel–"

"Rule one," she says, "never assume how I'll feel. Ask me."

"How do you feel?"

"Lots of ways. Angry about Sebastian. Hurt for you. Turned on by my boyfriend standing naked across the room." She smiles.

I climb into bed with her, smiling and grateful.

Hannah rolls to her back and wraps her legs around me so that I'm cradled between her thighs.

I bend down and kiss her, my hands drifting over her hair, down her face. "I love you."

Hannah replies with a kiss that's filled with love but also longing. "I want this," she says when we break apart. "I want a memory to make today a good day," she breathes, grabbing my hips. "You. Seth. I want you."

I join with Hannah, and together we find a way to right the ills of the day, at least for a little while.

After, as sleep looks for me, Hannah says, "Tell me about your dad."

Dr. B's wisdom about finding the ability to be vulnerable in the right relationship connects. Hannah's fingers caressing my skin, reminding me she's there, help me to share the words. She's safe. She's strong. When she needed my strength, I was there. And now when I need hers, she's here.

I know then, no matter what, we will be okay. Whatever happens. Whether it's standing beside me while my father faces cancer, or whether it's because we're in a fight for a stupid reason like me fearing my anger, or when we're looking at a setback, we'll fight. Together. And that's the way it's supposed to be. I don't have to face the complicated feelings I have for my father alone. I don't have to run from them. She doesn't have to face her fight against Sebastian alone. Not when we have one another.

Love might be messy. Life might be complicated. But being at home with your person means being all in, the good, the bad, the messy, the ugly, the beautiful. All of it.

I tighten my hold around Hannah, the sound of her breathing evening out, and before exhaustion claims us both, I say, "I love you."

Her arms tighten around me.

# HANNAH

*My Heart Insists Everything is Going to Be Just Fine*

He's nervous.

I know this because I've spent the last five months observing him. Usually, I'm the nervous one. His jaw is clenched. He's fiddling with the knobs on the control panel of his car and adjusting himself in his seat, as if he can't find a comfortable spot. The hand wrapped around the steering wheel is white-knuckle tight. He sighs, then swipes the other hand down his thigh before turning down the music.

I lay my hand over his, now resting on the gear shift.

He glances at me and smiles.

No dimples.

It's the first time he's bringing me home to meet his parents, and though Seth and I have a lot of history, I've never met them outside of a brief interaction when he was in the hospital or when I saw them at one of his games. Sure, I've spoken to them over Facetime. It wouldn't be so much to make the trip, but Seth hasn't been ready. So while he's gone home to help his mom or help with his dad, I work the advocacy stuff I'm doing to help teenage girls in abusive relationships and prepare for the impending case against Sebastian. After his arrest and arraignment, he's out. I wish I could say his choices ruined his football career, but he still got drafted in the second round. At least we'll have our day in court.

Seth's parents have just returned home from Portland after his dad underwent an experimental procedure while he's waiting for a transplant candidate. Seth offered to come home and help his mom and asked me to come with him. A milestone, I think. Maybe he's regretting it now.

"Talk to me," I tell him and run my thumb over his knuckles.

We've made it to Benson, and he changes lanes as we take the off-ramp into town.

"You're nervous."

"I've never brought anyone home," he admits, glancing over his shoulder and merging into a lane.

"Never?"

"Abby and Gabe don't count. We were kids. They never actually met my parents. And–"

"–you don't know how he'll be."

Seth glances at me, and I see the worry strain the corner of his eyes. He looks back at the roadway and brings the car to a stop at the red light.

"You asked me to come with you to support you, remember?"

He nods. "And you nagged me about it." He grins, a real one, turning his hand over and threading our fingers.

"If I could have spent more time with my dad–" It's a broken record. I have nagged him. If I've learned anything over the last two years, it's that you can't know what the next day will bring. I've stopped beating myself up over the circumstances surrounding my father's unexpected death—therapy has helped— and I see the futility in mulling over the what ifs and should haves and could haves. I've faced what happened with Sebastian and understand the futility in regretting it. It just is. Like Seth and his dad. I know Seth understands, he's said it in so many ways, but I know he also struggles with his painful memories associated with his dad. "I know he doesn't deserve your forgiveness, but you do."

He lifts my hand to his lips and kisses my knuckles. "Have I told you today that I love you?"

I grin. "I never get tired of hearing it." Leaning across the center console, I press a kiss to his cheek.

I look out the window and enjoy the quaint town, not unlike Cantos. It's high in the Cascades, the peaks of snow-covered mountains—even in June—settling around it like sentries on guard. The buildings are brick, the streetlamps resembling olden-style gas lamps. Antique shops, alleyway restaurants, little boutiques, sporting good mom-and-pop shops, a used bookstore, a quaint coffee shop. There aren't any chain stores on this street. People are layered in colorful light jackets. It's early summer, but there's still a chill in the air as evening arrives.

"It's cute. I like it."

"You do?"

"You don't?" I ask.

"When we first moved, I hated it. Everything about it, especially the snow."

"You missed me." I smile as we pass a woman walking her giant, hairy Newfoundland dog down the sidewalk. I look back at Seth.

He's smiling. "You're right. I couldn't stop thinking about you and dry humping you on the beach."

I laugh.

His smile fades. "What if he's mean again?"

"Why?"

"Because of the pain and the medicine."

"Don't you think your mom would have said?"

He takes an extra beat of time to consider that. "Yeah. Probably. What if he looks like he's dying?"

"He is, Seth."

His head snaps my direction before snapping back. "Yeah."

"And you're a good son."

He takes a deep breath, making another turn. We've entered a neighborhood of Craftsman style homes, the street lined with evergreens and deciduous trees dressed for summer. He drives the car into a driveway of a two-story Craftsman. It's quaint, like the town, and humble, but well-kept.

"This is cute," I say. "So far, I like everything about this place."

He turns off the car, sets the brake, and turns in his seat to look at me. "Really?"

"Especially who I'm with." I grin and lean toward him. "Really."

Seth leans forward and kisses me, slow and deliberate, his hand wrapped around my neck to keep me close. "It's going to be okay," he says against my lips, as if he's giving himself a pep talk.

"Of course, it is."

"Thank you for coming with me."

"There is no place I would rather be than with you."

Seth presses his forehead to mine and sighs. "Okay. Let's do this."

I nod. "Let's."

When I climb from the passenger side of the car, I take a deep breath of the chilled mountain air. I turn to the house. Seth's parents are already standing on the porch, as if they were waiting at the window for him to arrive. His mom grins from ear to ear and hurries down the steps, her arms already open. A noise of joy bursts from her as she moves toward Seth. "It's almost your birthday," she says and hugs him. Then she turns to me. "Hannah. I'm so excited to finally meet you in person."

I smile, hug her, and glance at the man on the porch in a wheelchair, wrapped in a sweater. He's thin, obviously ill, but he's smiling. It's clear, as Seth approaches him and they shake hands, the old growth between them is burning away and making room for the new.

Seth turns and looks at me. "This is Hannah." He smiles and holds out his hand.

I take it.

"You've met my mom. I'd like to introduce you to my dad, Jack."

"You must be very important," Jack says, extending a hand.

I take Jack's offered hand. My heart knows that no matter what, everything is going to be just fine, and give Seth's hand a squeeze,

# AUTHOR'S NOTE

In 2020, the #blackandwhite challenge circulated on social media. Women posted a black and white picture of themselves to highlight empowered women, only I remember learning after the fact that the impetus of the black and white photos got lost, like playing a game of telephone. The origin of that particular "challenge" was rooted in Turkey, when women woke up to yet another black and white photo in the newspaper of yet another murdered woman. This time it was of Pinar Gultekin, a 27-year-old Turkish woman who'd been murdered—strangled, burned, then buried in concrete—by her ex-boyfriend in what was called an "honor killing." Why? Because she told him "no." Because she didn't want to date him. Because she had moved on, he hadn't, and had decided to choose for her. The unfortunate reality is that Gultekin's photo in the newspaper was one of many black and white photos of murdered women in Turkey. Fed up and needing a way to fight back, Turkish women created the black and white photo reminder to increase awareness about the horrifically high femicide rates, specifically in Turkey, at the hands of their intimate partners.

They wanted change.

Pilar Gulekin's story might have appeared in black and white—a photo and words on the page—but her life was lived in color, in a collection of experiences and relationships that made her a real human. Just like the many other stories and statistics we're able to access in black and white but rarely offer the color image.

Consider these black and white statistics from the United Nations and the World Health Organization:

- Of the approximately 3.9 billion women in the world, over 736 million of them have been subjected to physical or sexual violence in their lifetime. It roughly estimates to 1 in 3 women, though this statistic doesn't include sexual harassment.
- Most violence against women is committed by intimate partners or former husbands, and for those women who have been in an intimate relationship, 16% of those women will experience violence perpetrated by their partner against them.
- In 2020, 81,000 women and girls were killed, and over half of those were at the hands of their intimate partner or other family member. (*And that's only the ones we know about.*)
- Less than 40% of women who experience violence at the hands of family or an intimate partner seek help, and less than 10% of those reach out to law enforcement.
- Globally, violence against women disproportionately affects women in lower-middle-income situations.

I'm a fan of Crime Junkies (the true-crime podcast) and watching true crime documentaries. I'm not exactly sure why that is, though due to their popularity, I know I'm not alone. Though many of these stories shared offer context and work to flesh out the truth about the victim, I wonder if they provide the listener with a voyeuristic ability to stand outside of it. As if we're passing by a terrible car accident and need to see the gruesome reality but sigh with relief that it didn't include us. What gets to me about these stories: most of the cases are crimes against women. I wish I was surprised by this, but the unfortunate (and frighteningly pervasive attitude) is that violence against women is the norm, and worse, the undercurrent that somehow it was probably her fault.

No one does black and white voyeurism better than Americans. We're great about looking at a black and white photo of a woman who's been murdered in Turkey and distancing ourselves from it. It isn't in our country, right?

Except there are black and white statistics that say it is. In a study done by Asher and Lyric about women traveling on their own in the world and how they might consider their safety relative to various locations in the world, Asher and Lyric ranked the countries using datapoints that examined things like "walking alone at night," the country's "homicide rates against women," "nonpartner sexual violence," and "partner sexual violence," as well as "attitudes about women and violence against women in general." Out of the 50 countries examined, want to know where the United States lined up? Nineteenth with a C- sandwiched between Tunisia and Ukraine. And get this, the United States ranked 7th highest for intimate partner violence. (Only Brazil, Morocco, India, Thailand, Turkey, and Chile ranked higher in that category.) Turkey was 5th.

Take that in for a moment.

We want to distance ourselves and claim that kind of violence doesn't happen in the United States, but those black and white statistics, those black and white photos in newspapers, and the words written to offer the latest true-crime story offer us surface level truth. When we look closer—and every single one of us should be looking closer—the evidence tells us a deeper truth. Each of those faces, every single one of those names, and every statistic is linked to a full-color story.

Hannah's experience in *The Messy Truth About Love* is meant to showcase the subversive way abuse occurs in an intimate partnership. I'm going to go out on a limb and claim that women don't walk into a relationship thinking it will be or become abusive. But once immersed in that situation, getting out of it isn't a black and white solution of just walking away (even if we'd like it to be). How does one leave without financial stability? What if there are children? Does she have supportive friends and family to help her? And even if a woman leaves, what if their partner doesn't get the message? What if he doesn't adhere to the law? Or what if there aren't any laws to protect her?

Hannah's experience in this story is mild (I needed a positive and hopeful ending, folks). She's a singular perspective. The truth is that the women most adversely affected by these black and white statistics are women of color, women immersed in low socio-economic circumstances, trans women. I can't trivialize their experiences and say that their stories all wind up hopeful and positive like Hannah's. There are too many cold-case files, too many murders, too many statistics, too many young children without mothers, too many stories to say that women's stories aren't happy or hopeful. It's heartbreaking.

I need hope.

And yet, I don't have anything very hopeful to offer with respect to this issue. I don't have that glimmer of light to say: "Look! We can get better." As I write this, our nation's highest court is on the precipice of overturning the landmark Roe versus Wade which will reverse women's bodily autonomy, so my hope meter feels like it's running a little low. Why? While body rights may seem a separate issue from intimate partner violence, they aren't that disparate. Both issues communicate an attitude about women and where her agency lies, both of which say it's outside of her own autonomy and in the hands of someone else. As Americans, we want to distance ourselves and say intimate partner violence isn't an American problem, but it is. It's a national problem. It's a global problem.

Women must stick together. That's what I've got for you.

If you are a woman in trouble, please reach out. Here are some national resources for you:

https://www.thehotline.org/ or 1-800-799-SAFE (7233)
https://www.rainn.org/ or 1-800-656-HOPE (4673)
Please call 9-1-1 if you are in immediate danger

# playlist

| | |
|---|---|
| **Swimming Pools at Night** | Talltale, Laur Elle, Father Bobby Townsend |
| **Snow** | Jome |
| **Lost** | Blake Rose |
| **Lose You to Love Me** | Selena Gomez |
| **Saving Me Still** | Justin Jarvis |
| **Would You Still Want Me?** | Mokita |
| **Lovely** | Fly By Midnight, Betty Who |
| **Love Alone** | Mokita |
| **If You Stay** | The Millennial Club & Tori Romo |
| **this is how you fall in love** | Jeremy Zucker, Chelsea Cutler |
| **Ease** | Joel Ansett |
| **speeding up** | Mokita, slenderbodies |
| **I Don't Want to Let You Go** | Jordan Hart |
| **Biblical** | Calum Scott |
| **Sitting Ducks** | Curtis Walsh |
| **I'll Find My Way To You** | Elderbrook, Emmet Fenn |
| **Fall** | SG Lewis |
| **You and I** | SMYL, Charlotte Lawrence |

For more songs, look for the book title on Spotify

# ACKNOWLEDGEMENTS

If you're still reading. Nice. So… about that dedication…

I am surrounded by amazing women. AMAZING. The truth is, my road to feminism was a roundabout journey. I grew up in a very small, agrarian community within a very conservative, fundamentalist family. My ideas about womanhood were archaic, even though I watched women—raised in that same system—push against it: my mother owned her own business, as did two of her three sisters. Two of my aunts left abusive husbands. Still, a "woman's place" was ingrained in me in a variety of messages. And I was opinionated about it. There was a reason my high school classmates thought it would be hilarious to predict I would be the president of the National Organization for Women.

I love that prediction, even if it started out in jest. It set me on a path to curiosity.

When I went away to college, I garnered friends who offered new ideas about women. I was a resident assistant in my college and gained even more understanding about issues facing women. When I became an educator, and when I started in the workplace, I was surrounded by women who demonstrated empowerment daily helping students facing crises. I heard stories that offered perspective I hadn't had access to before. With an open mind, I read, I listened, and I learned. I sought more. I asked questions and I've found my way.

I may not be the president of NOW, but I sure as hell will do anything I can to advocate for women, women's rights, and continue to tell stories about empowered women who have agency and autonomy.

That said, many wonderful women had a hand in this book. Thank you to Lavinia, Beth, Becky, Stephanie, Misty, Rayna, Willow, Janine, Marissa, Kori, Anuhea, and Marcie. Your reader's eyes helped so much. Thank you to my salon group—all amazing women—who lift me up especially when I'm low. To Kate, my editor, who makes my work shiny. Thank you. And to Mridu—

cover artist extraordinaire—who came in clutch with not one but two covers. You really are the best. And to my friends and family who inspire me and support me: my aunts, Sue, Danice, Judy, Rocky, Leilani, and Charlene; my nieces, Asia, Karlie, Kamalei, Meghan, and Ruth; my sisters, Susan and Connie, and sisters-in-law, Lori, Shandelle and Sandy; my daughter, Anuhea; my mother-in-law, Corina, and my mom, Terry.

To my son, La'anui. We have a lovely symbiotic relationship. I listen to all the basketball stuff, and he listens when I talk about women stuff. And to my husband, Vince. He isn't soft or cuddly, but his actions always showcase his love. Thank you for your support, your love, and your devotion.

Thank you to all of you—the readers—who made the decision to pick up this book. To buy it and gift it. To read it and review it. To subscribe to the newsletter and engage with me on social media. I am so grateful. I'm able to do this because of you. So, thank you.

Finally, to the OG feminist and patriarchy challenger: my Lord and Savior Jesus Christ. You told Martha to leave the work to sit and learn just as her sister Mary was doing; you took water from the Samaritan woman even though she was thought to be "unclean" then trusted her to teach others about you; and you saved the adulteress from being stoned by saying, "Let those of you without sin cast the first stone." I'm grateful and humbled by your blessings in my life.

Enjoyed Hannah and Seth's story
in The Messy Truth About Love?

Go back to where it all began...

## THE CANTOS CHRONICLES

The following excerpt is from book 1,
*Swimming Sideways*

# A DIMPLE AND A WALL

Good Abby has done a thorough job of keeping Bad Abby in place during English class and maintains control when it's time to move on to the last period of the day. When I get to the art room, most of the chairs behind tables arranged into the shape of a giant horseshoe are filled. I sit in one insulated on either side by an empty chair.

Once I'm seated, a boy entering the room catches my attention. He assesses the scene of the space. His countenance is assured and confident; a fist bump with another student near the door confirms he's part of the pack. His gaze connects with mine and a charge buzzes the bottom of my spine, but his look bounces away to talk to the fist-bump guy.

I can't help but watch him, his demeanor enigmatic but magnetic. He's got this enchanting, dimpled smile that lures me. It's the perfect complement to his features. His jaw is strong; his lips are full, but not feminine; and his nose is slightly crooked as though it was broken once, adding character to his otherwise perfect face. He's lean, tall, and lithe. Locks of wavy, light brown hair with sunny highlights fall effortless against his forehead. I'm reminded of the surfers at home, shaped by the water like hands shape their surfboards.

I look away when he starts across the room toward me, chagrined to have been caught staring at him, and convinced that he probably gets stared at a lot. Good Abby isn't happy with my staring, but then, he seems to be a part of the right crowd which reassures her. Bad Abby, on the other hand, is interested and that is dangerous. We know where that leads.

He takes one of the empty seats next to me, and glances my way, offering that easy smile. His eyes—brown with flecks of gold—twinkle, like he's got a secret, and it bothers me that I can feel that look as concretely as if he touched my skin. I also don't like that this practiced art of charm works. I'm reminded of Kanoa and feel shame reach up with gnarled fingers to squeeze my throat.

With a deep breath, I turn my attention to something innocuous, reaching into my backpack for a pencil. I notice that Adorable Dimple leans back against his chair, one leg stretched out, the other knee jutting out to the side. Someone on his left says something. He laughs. Familiarity brushes my consciousness with watercolor strokes. I have the urge to hug him and ask him how he's been, but check the impulse, horrified. My cheeks heat knowing how embarrassing that would be. Switching gears, I adjust my bag, straighten in my chair, dismissing the strange whim.

The second bell rings just as another student steps into the room. The Wall I bumped into earlier! A glance around the room, I realize he'll have to sit next to me since all the other chairs are taken. I feel a rush of unease. I'd been awful the moment someone had shown him disdain and feel ashamed of myself. But what could I do differently? There is so much riding on this new start. I can't go backward.

He walks around the border of the desk arrangement toward the chair next to me. His lips, the bottom just slightly fuller than the top, nears the edge of a frown but seem to want to communicate apathy. His eyes study the floor as he walks. He swipes a hand over his forehead, pushing back his dark hair, the edges of it curling over the dark skin of his hand and pushes the hood of the hoodie off. The dark curls of his hair springs back around his face. When he glances up, his look collides with mine. I'm struck again by the depth of his blue eyes; how startling they are in contrast with the weighted countenance of everything else about him.

I look away, hoping he didn't notice I've been watching him. There's a curious effervescence of movement in my cells. A shiver— not unpleasant—steals across my skin while the chair legs of the seat next to me scrape against the linoleum floor. The Wall sits, crossing his arms over his chest. I sneak another glance. His profile is rigid and emanates the suffering artist. I'm so curious and Good Abby says, *cut that shit out*. Bad Abby says nothing but wants to keep staring at him.

The teacher's voice catches my attention, but barely. I draw my look away from The Wall and focus on the teacher in the middle of the horseshoe.

"Welcome back *arteests*," he says. "Let's take a bit of time this afternoon to continue getting to know one another. Names again. And this time," he pauses for effect, "a little-known fact about you. I'll model. Mr. Mike Andrews. Again, please call me Mr. Mike. Let's see. Ah. I got it. I play the guitar in a garage band, and I don't mean the video game kind."

A few in the class laugh. "Mr. Mike, no one plays that game anymore. It's ancient."

The teacher grins which makes me smile. "Laugh all you want about my ancient wisdom. One day soon you'll join me in the non-video-game-garage-band ranks. Let's start with you, Kara." He holds out a hand toward the petite girl at the edge of the horseshoe.

One by one, the students share their names and a fact. I can feel my palms sweating, anticipating the moment I have to share something about myself. The words others say are incoherent. Are they speaking English? I'm running through possible things to contribute—something safe. There isn't anything that I want to divulge. Whatever it is, the fact must be innocuous, so it isn't memorable. How could I know that one day this "fun fact" wouldn't be used against me?

In the time it has taken my gut to work itself into a writhing coil of sea snakes, the boy to my left is speaking. "I'm still Seth Peters," he says, "and my fun fact is that I surf."

"That isn't 'little known,'" the fist-bump boy says.

"That's 'cause I'm an open book, Ball." Seth smiles. "I've got nothing to hide."

That dimple again.

The Wall makes a noise, a whooshing of air from his mouth as though he were going to say a bad word but stops himself.

I wonder about it but then zero in on Dimple's name: *Seth.* That name adds to the watercolor painting in my mind that his face started. My subconscious analyzes the information for something with which I'm familiar. *Seth. Seth. Seth Peters.* It begins to coalesce into a tangible, recognizable work. I once knew a Seth Peters. I look at him directly. Could he be the same one? I want to ask him about it, but realize the room is silent. All eyes are on me, waiting for me to share.

Mr. Mike gives me a cue, "Next."

"Sorry. Abby Kaiāulu," I pause, embarrassed and flustered and add, "I just moved here from Hawai'i." It seems safe enough.

"Nice to meet you, Abby. Thank you," Mr. Mike says.

I look to my right at the Wall.

"Gabe Daniels."

A random voice blurts, "Freak," just loud enough so that the class collectively stifles laughter.

Mr. Mike clears this throat and telegraphs a disheartened gaze around the class. "Mutual respect is a non-negotiable," he says. "And your fun fact, Gabe?" Mr. Mike encourages him to share.

"I like sports."

"Boxing especially," someone mutters clear enough for the rest of the class to hear. Snickers, eye rolling, and elbow jabbing make a wave around the room.

I glance at Gabe and his jaw tenses. I see the muscle work, bunching up slightly as he presses his teeth together. He removes his hands from the tabletop, shoves them into the front pocket of his sweatshirt, and slips down a bit further into his seat.

"Enough," Mr. Mike says, the ease of his smile and easy-going nature gone. "Any more comments get you sent out of this class and into cleaning the room just through that door," he points to an open doorway beyond his desk, "where all of our dirty paint brushes, old clay buckets, cutters, palettes among other art supplies are waiting for volunteers to clean them. Is this non-negotiable clear?" Mr. Mike pauses, the look on his face drawn by gravity toward the floor.

I wish I'd had a Mr. Mike last year, then think about *Kumu Ike* in whose room I'd often hidden away during free periods. I suppose I had in a different way, but no one had stood up for me like Mr. Mike just did.

Mr. Mike says, "Thank you, Gabe. Next."

I take that moment to look at Gabe again as the name game works its way around the horseshoe. I'm confused as to why he would he cause such a reaction. His handsome looks and imposing stature should have commanded premier social standing. It didn't make sense. What could he have possibly done to be the social outcast? He leans back in his chair, his long legs out in front of him, his arms crossed over his chest, and stares straight ahead. I see that he isn't as indifferent to his classmates' reactions as he wants to appear. Something we have in common.

In the next instant I realize that I'm staring into his disconcerting eyes. One of his eyebrow's arches in question at my perusal. Mortified, I look away at my notebook where I can doodle away my embarrassment. It's then that I see a note has been scrawled in the margin:

*Abby? Really from Hawaii?*

I write back: *Yes.*

Seth, the boy who I think I know, reaches over my left arm to respond. His warm skin brushes against mine as he writes:

*Did you used to come to Cantos during the summertime? Spend time with your Grandma Bev?*

A smile blossom grows on my face and tension in my shoulders dissipates like steam. I write:

*YES! You're Seth? Grandma Bev's next-door neighbor, Seth?*

I look at him, and he smiles with that dimple again. I remember all those summers spent at Grandma Bev's before she'd moved to Arizona. Seth, the little boy who'd lived in the house next door. Seth, my first crush!

I smile at him, a real smile. For the first time all day, it's a smile I don't feel like I have to measure against one of Abby's rules.

"I can't believe it," he says with a shake of his head when Mr. Mike sets us free to look at art books for inspiration.

"I can't remember the last time–" I turn the page of a Van Gogh coffee table book. When I look up, Seth watches me.

"Six summers," he says.

Something peculiar happens in my stomach when he says it. A sense of déjà vu. A moment that seems to hint I'm exactly where I'm supposed to be. A feeling that announces to my heart that of everyone I have interacted with today, this person is safe. But how can I know that? I barely know him, and the last time I did, I was ten. A lot can change in six years. I should know.

"That's right," I say, turning the pages of the tome. "Grandma Bev moved to Arizona six years ago."

Seth looks at an equally large book about Rembrandt. "I was sad when that happened," he says, flipping the page. He keeps his eyes on the book, leaning forward to scrutinize one of the pictures more closely. It's a painting of a man who's holding his son down, an angel grasping the man's arm and a knife falling from the man's hand. I glance at the title, *The Sacrifice of Isaac*, and shiver. "Nana Bev was an awesome lady," Seth says his eyes on the image, then he straightens back up.

I nod and smile, thinking about my Nana traipsing around the world and snow birding in Arizona. "She is. She's the world traveler now." I tell him about what Nana Bev's been up to.

Eventually he asks, "Do you surf?" He looks at me then, his smile a little different this time, not so bright and practiced. It's as if those edges have softened and something less tangible but more real emerges. A slight variation, but I notice it.

"I do; surfing was born in Hawai'i you know." I glance at Gabe who's flipping through a volume about Dali. He looks up at me. His attention darts from me to Seth, then he looks back at his art book. He appears bored.

"I love this one," I say and point at one of the Van Gogh paintings. Seth leans toward me and our shoulders graze. My muscle memory kicks into gear, and my nerve endings spark at our touch.

*Don't get caught up, Abby,* Good Abby warns. *That's how we got into trouble last time.*

Seth leans over his book to mine and follows me on my journey through Van Gogh land. We laugh at a skull smoking a cigarette.

Coming
2024

a

new

novel

by

CL Walters

CL Walters writes in Hawai'i where she lives with her husband, two children and acts as a pet butler to two pampered fur-babies. She's the author of the YA Contemporary series, *The Cantos Chronicles* (*Swimming Sideways*, *The Ugly Truth* and *The Bones of Who We Are*), the NA Contemporary romances *The Stories Stars Tell*, *In the Echo of this Ghost Town,* and *When the Echo Answers*, and the adult romance, *The Letters She Left Behind*. *The Messy Truth About Love* is her eighth contemporary novel. For up-to-date news, sign up for her monthly newsletter on her website at www.clwalters.net as well as follow her writer's journey on Instagram @cl.walters.